Readers Love
Amy Lane

Dex in Blue

"The writing was evocative and descriptive leaving me in constant awe of the author's talent. Amy Lane brings these people to life and, honestly, makes me want to live inside her head where all of her amazing characters reside."

—Rainbow Book Reviews

"If you haven't read Amy Lane or the Johnnies series yet, drop everything and run! It's the perfect combination of sexy and sweet, angst and romance. This is Amy Lane at her best!"

—Under the Covers

Ethan in Gold

"*Ethan in Gold*… is an emotionally tactile story of pain and redemption… a story of forgiveness and absolution and of loving someone so hard, even when he doesn't believe he's loveable, that he can't help but finally understand it's not about how much he is worth but about how much he is worthy of that gift."

—The Novel Approach

"Lane just hits that sweet spot between the angst and intensity and the fabulously rich character development and creates something so wonderful here."

—Joyful Jay

By AMY LANE

NOVELS
Behind the Curtain
Bolt Hole
Clear Water
Gambling Men: The Novel
The Locker Room
Mourning Heaven
Racing for the Sun
Sidecar
A Solid Core of Alpha
The Talker Collection (anthology)
Three Fates (anthology)
Under the Rushes

THE KEEPING PROMISE ROCK SERIES
Keeping Promise Rock • Making Promises
Living Promises • Forever Promised

THE JOHNNIES SERIES
Chase in Shadow • Dex in Blue • Ethan in Gold

NOVELLAS
Bewitched by Bella's Brother
Christmas with Danny Fit
Hammer and Air
If I Must
It's Not Shakespeare
Puppy, Car, and Snow
Truth in the Dark
Turkey in the Snow

THE KNITTING SERIES
How to Raise an Honest Rabbit
Knitter in His Natural Habitat
Super Sock Man
The Winter Courtship Rituals of Fur-Bearing Critters

GREEN'S HILL
Guarding the Vampire's Ghost
I love you, asshole!
Litha's Constant Whim

TALKER SERIES
Talker • Talker's Redemption • Talker's Graduation

Published by DREAMSPINNER PRESS
http://www.dreamspinnerpress.com

BEHIND
THE
CURTAIN

AMY LANE

Dreamspinner Press

Published by
Dreamspinner Press
5032 Capital Circle SW
Suite 2, PMB# 279
Tallahassee, FL 32305-7886
USA
http://www.dreamspinnerpress.com/

Behind the Curtain
© 2014 Amy Lane.

Cover Art
© 2014 Anne Cain.
annecain.art@gmail.com
Cover content is for illustrative purposes only and any person depicted on the cover is a model.

ISBN: 978-1-62798-509-3
Digital ISBN: 978-1-62798-510-9

Printed in the United States of America
First Edition
January 2014

So I let my daughter read this one, and she said, "Geez, Mom, you must have been paying attention when I was working backstage in dance!" I said, "Hon, I was in theater from middle school through my second year of college," and she said, "Huh. The things you don't know." So this is for Chicken and the things she didn't know, and for Mate, because we survived nine months living behind the curtain, and it sorta sucked.

INTROIT

DAWSON LOVED the guy like a brother, but seriously, he was going to kill him for this. "You left it where?"

Benji Gomez grimaced, the little divots at the corner of his apple cheeks growing deeper. "Well, I didn't really *leave* it, but it's up on the catwalk."

"So, like, your five-pound physics book can come catapulting out of the sky onto the stage at any given moment—that's what you're telling me."

"I really don't think it's going to come catapulting from anywhere, Dawson. It's just...."

Dawson looked up above the stage and noticed that the third light, back tier, was *still* crooked. "Benji, you're killing me. I got you this gig so you could get some hours in—you know, join the guild, we could be—"

Benji nodded. "Yeah, I know. Backstage brothers. I hear you. But I want a degree to go with that guild, you know that!"

Dawson knew. Light and sound engineering so he could *design* the stage productions. He'd be good at it too—if anyone on the planet still wanted to work with him when he screwed up like this. "Yeah, but dude! Look at it! What's the degree going to get you when you're the techie who beans the biggest star our stupid theater has ever seen!"

Jared Emory—star of the Los Angeles Ballet, was coming *here* to frickin' *Rocklin*, California, for a four-day gig. Go figure. Dawson hadn't seen him yet, but he'd heard girls squealing about him all week. Dawson had been too busy rewiring the light board—with Benji's help, actually, so maybe Dawson should shut up about his fuckups.

It didn't help that Benji, his best friend since kindergarten, was looking at him with soulful brown eyes and a smirk. God. Dawson was such a sucker for that look. Benji had a plan—Benji's plans were always the best fun.

"Okay, okay," Dawson muttered. "I'll go get your book." Dawson's boss wasn't supposed to know Benji had been working on this design—Benji wasn't in the guild yet. But if Dawson could get his professor to sign off on Benji's volunteer work, he *could* be in the guild, and then Benji could quit waiting tables and Dawson and his buddy could be the joined-at-the-hip twins they'd always been.

Of course, Dawson might be better off finding someone he could be joined at the groin with instead, since Benji's unrequited crush on his fitness instructor had sucked up what little free time he had between work and school. It was pathetic—Benji swore he was making progress with the lovely Darian Ritter but Dawson kept telling him the poor girl probably didn't know Benji's name.

But then, Dawson thought, looking at Benji's boundless enthusiasm as he tried to work the curtain, that unrequited thing sort of followed Benji around, didn't it?

"Here," Dawson snarked. "You call that stagecraft?"

Benji rolled his eyes. "I taught you how to do this, Dawson."

"Yeah, and I passed you up—you're making it jerk like a duck with hiccups."

"Nice metaphor, smartass—oh shit—who's out there?"

"Who's out... oh crap!"

The voice that floated across the stage was a surprising light baritone, a dry sort of voice, with no rough edges. "There's a shadow here. Man, did someone leave something on the catwalk?"

Dawson and Benji exchanged agonized glances. "I'll get it," Dawson mouthed, because in spite of the fact that he tended to knock stuff over with his elbows and bony hips when he walked, he was the one with the guild credentials to actually *be* up on the catwalk when it wasn't a school production.

"No!" Benji got distracted sometimes when he was studying, but that was because schoolwork didn't come easily to him. When it was something *physical*, he moved like a silken dancing god, in spite of broad shoulders and biceps that had been expanding exponentially since high school. If he could deliver a line with any semblance of organic humanity, he would be on the other side of the stage.

And when he was trying to save Dawson's ass—which was how Dawson had survived high school, frankly—he could move with shocking speed.

Which was why he ended up on the catwalk, scampering like some sort of tree animal, to get his book back.

And how Dawson ended up right behind him, because Dawson didn't have the sense God gave a fucking tree animal.

Benji didn't make a sound as he skittered along the walk, grabbed the book, and headed back, because the stairs up the walk only hung from one side. Unfortunately, that was where Dawson was, clinging to the dusty iron with clammy hands. Every muscle in Benji's body tensed as he literally ass-clenched to a halt, sending the catwalk swinging on the iron chains attached to the ceiling, and Dawson startled backward to give him some room.

The catwalk swayed and one of Dawson's hands slipped. Benji dropped his physics book and grabbed his hand, and Dawson's other hand splanged out as he tried to get his balance. The physics book went fluttering and thumping to the stage as Benji grabbed that flailing hand. Except the near hand was under the catwalk rail, so Dawson ended up with the corner post of the catwalk in his chest, and *that* was when his feet lost purchase and when Benji ended up hanging over the catwalk with the post digging in his neck, holding Dawson above the stage.

"Oh fuck," Dawson said, and Benji rolled his eyes, grimacing in an attempt not to let Dawson fall, grime from the catwalk smudging his long-jawed brown face.

Dawson grimaced back at him, squinting at all of the dislodged dust that was falling in his eyes, and then some of it hit his nose and the sneezing fit took care of the rest.

He plummeted the remaining eight feet to the stage, smart enough to let his legs collapse as soon as his feet hit and dumb enough to let his head bonk as his spine unspooled on the wooden stage.

"*Dawson!*" Benji yelled, and it was gratifying, really, how worried he sounded. Fourteen years of friendship really did mean something to the guy, in spite of how much time he spent in the gym trying to get the pretty girl fitness trainer with the limpid brown eyes and adorable tiny nose to pinch his taut round ass.

"Fine," Dawson said automatically. His head ached and he could still see stars. Of course, he was looking up into the blackness of the stage ceiling and all the lights were on, so maybe that was it.

"Fine?"

Dawson swallowed. Okay, there *were* stars in front of his vision, and they were getting in the way of the prettiest *man* Dawson had ever seen.

Ink-black hair, mercury-blue eyes—and they looked real too, not contacts—and perfectly eye shaped. Round in the middle, pointy on the sides, and wide. Dark stubble carelessly covered a square jaw and a perfectly angled chin. There might even have been a hint of a divot under that stubble, but Dawson was too busy looking at the firm, not-too-pillowy, not-too-lean mouth, and the way the perfectly rectangular eyebrows were arched in surprise and concern.

"Hey," Dawson said, blinking up at the perfectly perfect man. "Sorry. Did you want something?"

"Well, I was hoping techies wouldn't be crashing on my head during an actual performance," Too-Pretty replied. Which meant....

"Oh shit. Jared. I'm sorry." Dawson started to push up and then his neck and head both creaked.

Benji thundered up in a minute, rolling his eyes and pushing Dawson down. "Jesus, Dawson—if I'd known you'd wanted to be a trapeze artist, I would have studied something totally different!"

Dawson squinted up at him. "Yeah. 'Cause that's why we go to school. To be acrobats."

"Your sarcasm is functional. Time to get up."

"Wait—he could be hurt!"

Dawson smiled at Jared Too-Pretty. "He's nice," he said, looking at Benji for agreement.

Benji was scowling at the pretty man, though, and didn't respond. "He *could* be hurt," Benji said dryly, "but I'd be more seriously worried if I hadn't seen him do something like this every month for the last fourteen years."

Dawson giggled. "Heh heh heh... the time I fell out of the car when it was moving was the *best*."

"You were in the hospital for three days. Not the best. Not even close. How're the stars?"

Dawson squinted and realized that the swimming baby fish in his vision were receding into darkness except when he looked at Jared. "Mostly setting. *He* seems to be collecting them, though." Dawson smiled at his star-sieve. "You're like the *king* of pretty. Do you collect stars for a reason, or do they just gather around you 'cause you're so bright?"

Jared startled back, looking indignant. "Is he feeding me a *line*?"

"Oh, you wish," Benji snapped protectively. "If he was half that smooth, he'd have gotten laid by now. C'mon, Lothario, let me help you up."

Benji's big hands moved tenderly on his neck and shoulders as Dawson sat up and counted the fish. Benji started rubbing gently with his thumbs and suddenly Jared spoke, that light baritone getting sharp all of a sudden.

"Do you have *any* idea what you're doing?"

"I learned this in football," Benji said. "Sports medicine was going to be my major."

"Your major." Dawson looked up to see Jared Too-Pretty arching one of those oddly rectangular eyebrows, and he wondered if anyone else heard *Your major. Isn't that a laugh given that you're in a teeny-tiny junior college in a Podunk town on the edge of the Northern California Bible Belt, and stop rubbing his neck or you'll give him brain damage* packed into the three little syllables.

"Benji's smart," Dawson said, melting into Benji's touch and the comfort of the guy he'd known forever. "Benji's my brother."

"Brothers." How did he *do* that? He didn't even put a question mark at the end of it. He just let his silence etch in a zillion words. *Brothers, even though neither of you look alike and you're obviously both the same age and he's a Latin god and you're a pale collection of elbows, knees, and ears—I remain skeptical.*

"Yup," Benji said, rubbing a comfortable hand from the base of Dawson's skull down his spine to his lower back. "And brother, you're good to go—I've got a class."

Benji stood, and before he could get into place to offer Dawson a hand up, Jared was there, sending Benji a look from under brooding black brows.

Benji narrowed his eyes. "Be careful with him," he said after a moment. He nodded at Dawson and Dawson took that as a cue to trust the amazing-looking dancer with the mercury-blue eyes. He put his hand in Jared's and felt himself gently and bonelessly pulled upright, and then turned around while Jared felt his back and manipulated the muscles at the base of his skull like a pro.

"How's your vision?" he asked tersely.

Dawson focused on his fish-free feet.

"No longer swimming," he said. "Or is that 'swimmingly,' you know, like Cary Grant would say? 'My vision is doing swimmingly, darling, I can almost walk on two feet now.'"

"I'll take that as 'good,'" Jared said dryly, and Dawson wanted to step on his foot.

"Really? You don't respond at all. I mean, I practically fell on top of your head, you know—a little wonder? A few quips? Some laughter to ease the tension?"

Jared's amazingly firm fingers kneaded into the base of Dawson's skull some more. "If you were any less tense you'd be comatose," he said without inflection. "Now, did your friend really just run to his next class without his book?"

"Oh *fuck*!" Dawson lunged away from those amazing hands to grab the book off the ground and winced as his shoulders threatened to seize up. He tried to turn his head to talk to the dancing mangod, but that hurt his neck, so he ended up turning his whole body and backing up. "Hey, could you tell Professor Weber I'll be back in a sec? I'm getting double duty for this one—money from the tech guild and credit for the class. I don't want him to think I'm shirk—oh fuck!" He ran into a stack of flats and they went slithering down across the floor. "Oh God, I'll fix tha—*ouch*!" And he stumbled down the stairs and off the stage onto his ass. "Oh Jesus. Don't worry. Don't come over. I've got to find Benji or he'll spaz out. Ouch. That's gonna hurt. Fuck." Fumbling with the book, Dawson scrambled to his feet, actually *turned around*, and staged a tactical retreat.

He got to Benji right before he walked into the science building, and gasped out his name.

Benji turned, his almond-shaped brown eyes widening. "You brought me the *book*?" he asked. Dawson grabbed hold of the doorframe, bent double, and tried to get his breath. Benji fished in his pocket for his asthma inhaler and offered it—they'd shared the same prescription since kindergarten, which had been where they'd bonded. In the nurse's office, both of them hyperventilating into paper bags while the nurse double-checked their paperwork.

Dawson nodded and took a hit of albuterol, then handed back the inhaler and struggled to catch his breath.

"Where's yours?" Benji asked sternly. Dawson gestured vaguely back to the stage, where his backpack sat in a dark corner. "Dammit, Dawson—I left you near your backpack, with your inhaler, with a *perfectly nice hottie* rubbing your back, and you kill yourself to give me a *book*?"

Dawson took one more breath and decided he could stand up. "The damned book was what had me falling on the stage in the first place!" he argued.

Benji glared at him. Dawson studied his shoes.

"Okay. Fine. The book was my excuse to leave."

"And why would you want to do that?"

Dawson wiggled his toes inside his tennis shoes and watched the rubber over the Converse canvas ripple. "He was bossy."

Benji sighed and took two steps away from the building, looking down at Dawson's wiggling toes and waiting for Dawson to look him in the eyes. "Dawson, you know I love you, right?"

"Yeah." Of course. No doubts. Benji loved him just like a brother.

"Then I need you to find a guy who loves you like a boyfriend, okay?"

Dawson hated this conversation. "Darian still won't give you the time of day."

Benji held the book, with its newly broken binding and teased and fluffy pages, in one hand. "Possibly not," he said with arched eyebrows, "but I was hoping she'd let me read off her book."

"What the—I didn't even know she *had* this class!" Dawson stood up and glared at him indignantly. Benji grinned back, his eyes lazy and deceptively innocent.

"Oh. *Oh.* Ooooohhhh...."

"Oh." Benji's voice was flat and infused with meaning, and Dawson actually realized that he and Jared had that much in common.

"I have had it up to my eyeballs with guys who communicate with one syllable, do you get me? Done. Finished. Completely." Dawson turned around and started back to the ugly theater with the green copper roof and the big fake owls hanging from each corner to scare the starlings.

"Dawson, I'll see you at home tonight!"

"Your turn to bring dinner, ass hat," Dawson grumbled, and Benji laughed, probably because he knew it was actually Dawson's turn, and Dawson was due for the cleanup too. But Benji would bring it anyway, because he was Dawson's boy and he'd feel bad about the inhaler and the book and Dawson falling from the catwalk.

Benji really was that good of a guy.

Which didn't quite make up for the fact that Jared was gone when Dawson got back to the theater. The flats had been restacked, the curtain returned to its original position, and light 3F had actually been positioned correctly, complete with the half gel Dawson had wanted but Benji hadn't put on it.

And Dawson's serviceable black backpack sat on the corner of the apron, leaning against the proscenium, like somebody had found it and wanted to put it out for when its owner came back.

"Nice job, Dawson." Professor Weber's voice was surprisingly short on irony, and Dawson looked out into the darkness to see his tiny bent form as he hobbled out of the tech room and down the aisle. Professor Weber had spent his life in the theater, doing tech when he got too old to act and teaching when doing tech was too hard on the body. He used to direct a play a year at Sierra College, but in the past five years, he'd turned that over to the local theater guild, supervising the facility use only. He was probably in his eighties, and Dawson— who had been raised by a *very* patient father and appreciated a patriarch who didn't want to kill him after a minute and a half—sort of loved the old geezer.

For one thing, he'd been exceedingly gay in a time when nobody wanted to admit theater majors were often exceedingly gay, and he'd managed to come through that and not hate everybody including himself.

For another, he got Benji and Dawson, and not many people bought the whole "platonic friends since diapers" thing, *especially* teachers, which was why they'd frequently sat at the far corners of any room within the first week of class.

That usually lasted until the second week of class, when the teachers claimed their psychic vibrations were fucking unnerving. (Okay, that was *one* teacher, but most of them conceded that they were actually less disruptive when they could sit next to each other. If nothing else, Dawson helped Benji with his homework and Benji helped Dawson get there on time and remember what day it was. A match made in kindergarten, if not heaven.)

Professor Weber had watched them push-pull each other through their first year at school and had declared them "brothers of the heart"—and had let them be. Occasionally he gave them a little bit of help, like now, when he was going to sign off on Benji's hours for the guild.

"I didn't do it all, Professor," Dawson said now, looking at the stage dubiously. "In fact, I came back to fix the stuff I knocked over and try to reposition that light—I think the bolt is stripped."

They both looked over Dawson's shoulder as the light fell out of position and sort of hung, dangling, facing the floor.

"Can Benji fix it, do you think?" The professor had a faint accent—Dawson wasn't sure where it was from, whether it was Yiddish or Polish, but he loved it. The remnants of his white hair tufted out from behind his ears, and his nose was unapologetically rumpled and large.

"Probably—he's good with that stuff."

"If he can't, I'll get the custodian." Professor Weber nodded earnestly, but Dawson shook his head. The custodian assigned to the theater sort of hated them—or, well, Dawson had maybe said something disparaging about his intelligence level in his hearing, so maybe he had cause—but Benji was better at that physical stuff anyway.

"No, Benji can do it," Dawson told him. He hopped up on the apron and grabbed his backpack, noticing a piece of paper fluttering away from the back. He picked it up curiously.

Take two Motrin and stay away from catwalks. —J

Fish. Fish mouth open, fish mouth closed. Gasp for air. Close mouth. Blink. Stare at professor. Remember to speak.

"Who is it from?"

"Uhm, Jared—you know, Emory? The dancer?"

"He was *here*? What's he like?" Suddenly the gray hair and corrugated bloodshot skin became insignificant, and the rheumy eyes sharpened to angel blue. "I hear he is a handsome boy."

Dawson allowed himself to moon a little. "Prof, he would turn your knees to water—"

"And your other parts to stone, yeah?"

He could almost *feel* those strong fingers kneading into his back. "Yeah," he agreed, nodding emphatically. Carefully he folded the note and tucked it into his pocket. "All parts would be affected."

Professor Weber laughed and then grew very sober. "Good," he said. "Benji can't be your world forever."

Dawson swallowed. "Yeah, so everybody says." Including Benji, who was the only person whose motives Dawson *didn't* question.

Benji loved him. That wasn't going away.

"Look, Prof," he said, pulling out his phone and grimacing. "I've got an English Comp professor who's going to *crucify* me if I don't get my ass in gear. Benji and I will be back tonight after he gets off work, okay?"

"Yeah, sure. You still go swimming in the afternoons?"

"Yeah-huh!" Dawson ran lightly down the apron. Without pausing, he put a hand on the rail for the stairs up to the stage and swung himself down in one heave. "Leave a message on my phone if you need me, okay?"

"Yeah, sure," Professor Weber said, waving his hand. He had a little office along the side hall by the stage, with a comfortable corduroy couch that was known to occupy his afternoons until his son came to pick him up. The theater department could probably be made vital and thriving with a newer, younger professor at the helm, but nobody wanted to displace Weber. He was an institution.

Dawson waved good-bye and went tripping off into the chilly February afternoon.

AT SIX o'clock, the indoor pool in the relatively new gym complex had no aqua aerobics, no recreational swimmers, and, often, nobody but Dawson, doing laps in that happy, mind-numbing splashy echo of one person in a swimming pool. He'd been on the swim team in high school and had won a handful of bronze medals, but nobody had ever accused him of being a superstar. That didn't stop his love of what swimming did for his body.

He was doing his cool-down lap, backstroke, so he could float a little and feel the blessed pull of his arms in the water, and play with the drift to see how quickly and how far one stroke could haul him. And then another. He let his feet bob and stuck his toes through the water and heaved himself back with satisfying double-armed strokes closing his eyes and drifting in for the last few feet. His hand bumped the edge of the pool and he looked up....

And right into the blue-mercury eyes of Jared Emory.

His hands went up and his elbows shot out and his ass sank down and his knees rose up and for an entire nanosecond he was 155 pounds of thrashing limbs and blinking eyes under the blue. A hand of steel latched under his arm and he remembered he had a brain and actually *grabbed hold* of the edge of the pool and caught his breath.

Jared Emory was still there, water dripping from his hair, his gray hoodie, his jeans, and his spectacular eyebrows, which were now raised to his hairline.

"You just did that." Again, that uninflected voice, but Dawson wasn't stupid. *I can't even believe you are this stupid, clumsy, and weird. You disgust me.* Dawson could hear all the things Jared didn't really say, and as usual, he couldn't *fix* them.

"Apparently so," he said, pulling his swim goggles up so he could get a better look at Jared's sardonic black-fringed eyes.

"Do people actually let you *out* by yourself? Do you have to apply for a pass? They don't assign you a keeper?"

"Well, usually there *is* a keeper—but he's on a date." Because against all odds, Benji had convinced the super-adorable Princess Darian to grab a bite to eat before Benji's shift at the little Mexican food place off Taylor.

"That guy doesn't count," Jared snapped, annoyed.

"That guy was born for the job," Dawson declared with dignity. "Now was there something I can do for you, or were you just here to scare the crap out of me?"

Jared stood up and brushed water from his zippered hoodie and smoothed it from his hair too. "I need to rent you."

Dawson swiped water from his eyes and tried to process that. "I'm not that kind of a boy."

"No, idiot—I need a techie for tomorrow. My manager said if you were working the stage you had to be guild, and he set it up with the school. I'm running a free dance workshop tomorrow, and we didn't get the staff set up yet." Jared looked uncomfortable for a minute. "The kids are disabled. They want to dance across a stage with lights and music and think they're superstars, and I need lights and music."

Dawson mentally consigned his two hardest classes to the four winds. "That's really fucking awesome. I'm in. What do you need?"

"You. Out of the pool."

"And presumably in clothes and dried off." Dawson grinned, because that went without saying if he was going to run the light board. Eschewing the ladder, which meant going under the four lane lines to his right, he put his hands on the pegs of the starter's platform and hauled himself up. It was awkward, which was why nobody did it, and as he was scrambling to get his foot on the concrete while he sprawled on the rough platform on his stomach, he felt two impatient hands on his thighs helping him swing around and find his feet. The platform scraped across his abdomen and he let out a startled squawk, pushing himself up and backward and right into Jared Emory's arms.

"Oolf!" Jared staggered back, but, well, he *was* a dancer, and with a little help from his own bare feet on the wet concrete, Dawson found himself pushed back up and steadied.

The echoes of their thrashing died around them, and the pool house fell awkwardly silent.

"Uhm, yeah. Thanks," Dawson grunted, looking at his abnormally long feet and feeling stupid.

"Don't thank me," Jared snapped. "*Clothe* me! God, I'm sopping wet and all my shit's at the hotel!"

Dawson turned around and grimaced, because sure enough, Jared Emory, star of stage, sky, and stratosphere, really was standing across from him sopping wet.

"I, uh, have some extra clothes in my bag," Dawson muttered, and yes, it was true, but it meant he was going to have to put on the clothes he'd worn into the gym, and they still had some of that day's hot dog and chocolate cake, which he'd had for lunch, smeared on the front.

But, well, it wasn't Jared's fault he was a spaz, either.

"Which way to the locker rooms?" Jared asked. His lower lip thrust out sulkily, but he sounded civil, so that was a plus.

"Uhm, follow me!" Dawson chirped, hoping to make up some goodwill.

Jared's gaze swept from Dawson's swimmer's shoulders, down his back, down his *backside,* and to his long and narrow feet.

"No," he said flatly, and although his hair was dark, his skin was fair enough for Dawson to see the dull red wash up his cheekbones.

Dawson reached behind him to make sure his Speedos weren't sagging.

"Don't make them *tighter,*" Jared commanded, and Dawson froze, midwedgie.

"Uhm, okay." Dawson grabbed his towel and wrapped it around his shoulders. "Uhm, lead the way—around the pool, toward the back, look for the little stick guy with two legs instead of a skirt."

"I'll do that." *You're babbling, and because somehow your Speedo has offended me mightily, I'm going to be shitty and snarkastic until we no longer have to interface, so deal with it.*

"You know, *you're* the one who startled *me*." Dawson felt compelled to remind him of this, because right now Jared was going to be wearing pants that were short and a shirt that was too tight, and considering he seemed to be a genuinely awesome guy, this was not the impression Dawson had ever wanted to make.

"I'm sorry."

Dawson waited to hear the subtext, but nothing was forthcoming. "Uhm, you are?"

"I didn't mean to startle you." *And now you're belaboring the point.*

"You move like a cheetah."

Without warning Jared whirled around, shoulders hunched in a classic theater exercise of a stalking cat. Dawson squawked and backpedaled, running right into the wall, and Jared laughed silently and turned back around to the locker room.

"Nice," Dawson said. He was trying to keep the whole "arrogant-nerd" vibe going, but the truth? He could hear his heart doing an entire tap-dance chorus in his ears, and the thrum of his pulse was actually beating in his *wrists.* Jared Emory was *beautiful,* and for an equally beautiful second, Dawson had been afraid (hoped!) the guy would eat him alive.

"Sometimes. When you want me to be."

Dawson listened for the subtext, and for a moment, he thought he heard an entire hallelujah chorus of it being shrieked in Latin. It was loud enough to echo in the silent locker rooms, but then, Dawson didn't speak Latin.

"Uhm. I, uhm. Yeah. Here's my locker." Jared leaned against the adjacent one and Dawson's hands shook as he rotated the tumbler. "Once around right, thirty-one, once around left, seventeen, straight right to twenty, and—" He tugged on the lock and it thunked, securely closed. "Okay, oh shit, once around... crap, missed it. Okay, once around... *fuck!*" His hands kept slipping because his palms were sweaty, which was weird. They were wet and cold in the locker room and—"Once ar—"

Jared's hand closed over his, and for a second Dawson smiled up at him, sort of charmed. Wasn't that sweet? He was calming Dawson down.

"Move."

Oh, yeah. He didn't even need to translate the subtext for that one. He stepped to the side and in short, quick moves, Jared opened the lock and pulled it off the locker, and Dawson's backpack and clothes did to him what they usually did to Dawson.

Attacked like hyenas high on the scent of a fresh corpse.

"Augh!" The backpack came first, and it was heavy, and the clothes came next, and Dawson grabbed those because his underwear were on top, and, well, *dude*, and Jared stepped sideways and let the collection of iPod, wallet, cell phone, and earbuds slither down on top of everything else as it hit the wet concrete ground.

Dawson could not pick his shit up fast enough.

"I'm sorry about that, okay? I, you know, if I'd known you were going to get it open that quick, I would have warned you. It's just that I sort of have a system, right? I open the locker and shove my hand in and generally one or two things fall down." Electronics and wallet shoved *in* the locker, dirty clothes tucked *under* the arm, and backpack with change of clothes bailed *out* of the water. Dawson held it up and smiled ingratiatingly, hoping for peace. "Uhm, my clean clothes are in here, and I don't think the water got to them, but, well, if you could take that and settle it down on a bench, I can, you know, get organized."

"I doubt it." The words were flat, spoken dryly, with only a lift of an eyebrow as Jared set the backpack down. Of course his *meaning* ran rife with subtext, but behind the ironic eyes, Dawson could see the hint of a lip curl and even a few even white teeth. Oh holy Jebus blessed be—a *smile*.

Dawson relaxed fractionally, and he tucked his towel under his pits so he could straighten his clothes. "Yeah, well, uhm, you know. Organized for *me*. I'm sorry about all the trouble, you know? I'm not normally—well, I *am* a spaz-puppy, but I don't usually spread the misery quite so effectively."

Jared's mouth quirked up a little more and he inclined his head. "If it wasn't forty degrees outside, I wouldn't mind being covered in... misery, okay? Let's get changed—I haven't eaten yet, and it would be great if I could tell you what I need before I go."

"Oh, hey!" Dawson said, rifling through his bag. He pulled out a matched set of PowerBars. Like his asthma inhaler, he never left home without them. "Want one?"

"Thank you, yeah—let's get changed first, but yeah."

Dawson handed Jared the roll of fresh jeans, underwear, long-sleeved T-shirt, and hooded sweatshirt, and turned his back so he could put on his old stuff.

"Oh my God," Dawson said quietly, eyeballing his underwear. He was relieved to find that in spite of the rather odd day, he had not once *actually* crapped his pants, and he shucked his Speedos quickly and tucked them in the little plastic bag so he could shove them in the front pocket of his backpack.

"You have the whitest ass I have ever seen on a living human."

Dawson flailed and pulled his towel up around his waist. "I was *saying* 'Oh my God, I'm *finally* comfortable enough not to be a danger to the whole frickin' world' and you've got to say something like that?"

He risked a glare behind him only to find that Jared had changed at faster-than-human speed. He was currently belting Dawson's jeans around his waist, and his waist was narrow enough, but the jeans were tight against his thighs and groin because, well, Jared had serious muscles there like any self-respecting dancer.

"Okay. Those jeans are dangerous," he conceded, and Jared glared at him. "I'm sorry! Seriously! I didn't mean for any of this to happen!"

"That's nice," Jared said when he was done with the button. "Am I circumcised?"

Dawson widened his eyes and stared hard. "Uhm, I'm guessing no."

"Good guess." He gave Dawson's shirt a few stretches with his elbows and then pulled it over his wide chest, where it adhered like a Band-Aid.

"Uhm, nice poky nipples also," Dawson observed, apology dripping from his voice like water down his backside.

"Are you even dressed yet?"

"Are you going to make any more comments about my ass?"

Jared thought about it for a moment. "It's nicely proportioned, almost hairless, and sort of sweetly round. *Now* can you get dressed?"

Dawson turned his back again and proceeded to move silently, mortification etched into every line of his body. "I, uhm, haven't had it described like that before," he offered as he was pulling his stained baseball shirt on over his head.

"Yeah?" Jared sat down creakily, given how tight his clothes were, and tried to lace up his sneakers. "How is it usually described?"

Dawson propped one foot up on the locker room bench. "Virginal."

Jared broke his shoelace. "Goddammit, Dawson!"

"You're going to blame that on me?"

Jared shook his head, staring at the offending lace. "Yes. Yes, I actually *am* going to blame this on—olf—you!"

Dawson finished tying his other shoe for him. "Here, don't stress. I'll tie them. I'm sure somewhere out there is a nice boy or girl or pansexual god who will miss that thing if you self-circumcise on my jeans."

"Currently it's only me," Jared said, and once again his temper evened out as Dawson sank to his haunches and knotted the ends of the lace together so he could tie Jared's tennis shoes. "And my *ex*-boyfriend didn't miss it so much because he spent his time with other 'things' besides mine."

Dawson glanced at Jared's crotch and then grinned up into his amazing eyes. "Well, he was real fucking stupid, 'cause I'm telling you, that thing looks like it's worth waiting for."

Under all that stubble, Jared's mouth pursed, a definite smile in the corners. "Well, thank you. You're sweet. But then, that's sort of West Hollywood, you know?"

Dawson stood up and offered Jared a hand. He took it, leaning heavily as he tried to flex under the constraints of the damned pants. "Nope," Dawson said, taking a step back so they didn't crowd each other. "I've got nothing. I'm like, *terminally* small-town."

Jared's gaze traveled a speaking circle, taking in the surrounding gym and probably the campus of the junior college and the environs of the bedroom suburb that was Rocklin. "Do you want to change that?"

Dawson shrugged. "Yeah. Sometimes. I've been to LA. Sometimes I want to be lead tech at the New York Met or San Francisco ACT. But sometimes I want to be one of the people who changes shit in Sacramento and helps put it on the map. And sometimes I want to be like Professor Weber and just make the world better by teaching boneheaded kids this thing I really love. I'm only twenty— don't I get to decide?"

Jared's formidable eyebrows knit together. He crossed his arms in front of him and gnawed absently on his thumbnail, which was bare almost to the quick in both the cuticle and the nail. "Twenty. Huh. Yeah. Yeah, I guess you do." He sounded like he'd really thought about it.

"You seem surprised."

Jared shook his head and shrugged, shaking his arms out and grabbing the zippered hoodie with resignation. "It's not going to zip," he muttered.

Dawson grunted, still guilty. "Yeah, you have the pecs of a god— rub it in some more. Why would that surprise you?"

"Because," Jared said, pulling the sweater over his arms and wincing when it tightened on his biceps. "Because you're twenty and you've got all your choices ahead of you, and I'm twenty-five and most people think I'm counting the hours until injury ends my career. I just forget, that's all. That twenty is young."

He rolled up his wet clothes into a little bundle and started out of the gym. Dawson followed slowly, making sure all his shit was tucked in his almost-empty backpack and that his Speedos weren't going to drip all over his iPod before he zipped it up.

He caught up when Jared was crossing the almost-deserted quad, and silently handed him the PowerBar.

"Thanks."

"No worries. I'd take you out for a late dinner, but, well, I'm broke, and seriously, all we've got that's open this late is Denny's."

"I know. It's right by my hotel. It'll do."

"You got Adalberto's down in LA?"

"Nope."

"Well, if you ever want to go off your ballerina diet, you need to try one of their carne asada burritos. Their drive-through is open all night."

Jared turned in the foggy moonlight and flashed him a grateful smile. "Nice rec—we'll see how much I gain by the end of this trip, and I might just stop there."

Dawson grinned, happy to help, and, quite frankly, happy to take some of that pensiveness out of their conversation. They got to the stage and Dawson pulled out his keys and turned on the house lights.

"Do you need the stage lights?" he asked, concerned. They'd been off for some time, and they always took about twenty minutes to warm up.

"No, but I do need to see what your light board and sound board look like."

"Yeah—no problem." Dawson opened the tech booth and showed him in. Standard stuff—of course Benji had set it up, so it was better than standard.

Jared nodded. "Okay—I'm going to need a couple of things. First, I've got a CD—the tracks are in order and I'll give you cues from the stage, okay? First, second, third—but we may need to repeat. You can't just doze off, okay?"

"Yeah, no problem. This is a guild gig. I like to be on my toes."

"Good. And as for lights, the setup you have going for my performances should be good, but we're going to need someone to man the spotlight. Can we do that?"

"Yeah. Benji's got tomorrow off and his classes end at eleven—will that be early enough?"

"Yeah. The workshop starts at twelve, that's fine. He needs to pay attention, though." Jared swallowed and looked at Dawson like he meant business—but he also seemed to be almost pleading. "These kids have to think that they're the real thing. Like... Cinderella and Prince Charming and the whole fairy tale, you got it? That spotlight has to follow them, and their music has to be on cue, and all the little stuff that makes a pro performance professional? That has to happen for these kids. They can't ever think, 'Well, it was just a workshop,' okay? They've got to think they're superstars."

Dawson nodded firmly. "I hear you. We'll take it real serious. Benji's a good guy—honest. Hasn't let me down since we were rug rats. I'm...." He looked out at the stage where he'd almost landed on this guy's head only hours before. "I know you didn't see us at our best, but I swear, Jared—this place? This place is where *I* dance."

Jared nodded, and there was a space there, like he'd really listened. "Okay—standard light setup?" He sat down in front of the board.

"Yup."

"Then here's the cues." He reached into the jeans rolled up in his lap and pulled out some sodden Post-it notes, thankfully written on in pencil. "Okay—you got a pen?"

Dawson reached into the front pocket of his backpack and handed one to him, and they spent the next twenty minutes talking about cues and music while Jared wrote down which lights should come up with what number on new Post-its. Dawson watched him, taking notes with half his brain, because this stuff came second nature to him. The other half of his brain was trying to reconcile the slightly arrogant diva to this guy who was putting himself out for a free gig, and what he came up with was sort of heartening.

Jared Emory wasn't a bad guy, really. Now if only Dawson's galloping pulse could admit that he really *was* a guy instead of a *god*, this whole gig would be cake!

"Oh yeah—one more thing," Jared murmured, looking at a sodden notebook that had apparently been in his hoodie pocket.

"Look—I might not need this, but can you or someone else come up on the stage if I need you to?"

"While I'm running light and sound?"

"You could put that stuff on hold and have Benji spotlight you. I just need someone to model."

"So you don't want to ask, like, a *dancer*? Haven't you been practicing with them all day?"

For the first time since Dawson had fallen out of the sky onto his head, Jared looked uncomfortable.

"I need someone *nice*," he said after a moment. "Someone *normal* and not perfect. It'll help if you're... I don't know, *you*. Awkward. I'm going to be correcting your feet and your posture, and they need to see that I'm not just doing it to them. The other dancers can fake it, but trust me—it's better when it's you." He paused. "Or, uhm, someone like you." Another pause. "And I might not need that anyway. It depends on how high functioning the kids are. Sometimes it's all they can do to move across the stage."

"Okay, then." That intensity was a little frightening. "Well, if you need me, give me a holler—I swear I won't be reading my English lit."

"Herman Melville?" Jared asked out of the blue.

"No, because I'm not suicidal. Nathaniel Hawthorne."

Those eyes lightened, and when Jared's just-right mouth relaxed into a smile that showed actual teeth, Dawson's entire groin/abdomen area constricted, waiting for the sucker punch of desire.

"Good—the romantics were hopeful," Jared said, and Dawson couldn't breathe, couldn't *move* for a moment, because there *was* no guarding against that much raw want.

He nodded mutely, knowing his plain brown eyes were wide and probably limpid with *oooolf,* and that Jared couldn't help seeing it.

He did—he must have. He smiled wearily and stretched and said, "Okay, I think that's all we need. Time for me to get some dinner and some yoga pants and crash."

Dawson shook himself. "Do you need a ride?"

Shrug. "My rental is at the hotel. I can walk—it's not far."

"Yeah, but it's, like, dark. And foggy. And people drive like assholes. My car is small, I mean"—oh God—"you may need to unzip my pants to get in, but—"

He stopped because Jared had crossed his arms and was now laughing into his hand.

"Uhm. Yeah. Stupid idea."

"No, no." Jared waved at him to lead the way from the tech booth. "Any activity that needs me to unzip your pants is a good one."

"Guh…." Oh God.

Jared bumped him from behind as he stalled out at the doorway. "Dawson, I haven't slept in twenty-four hours. Tell your hard-on to give it a rest and I'll take that ride, okay?"

And just the mention of his hard-on was humiliating enough for Dawson to be able to walk again.

"Twenty-four hours?" he asked, moving like it was just a normal, everyday thing.

"Yeah. Performance last night, pack, airport, plane, arrive—find a shuttle. I mean, I'm not sure if you know this, but your airport is out in Bumfuck—"

"And this campus is a little north of Yemen, and LAX is the armpit of Satan—yeah, I'm aware." Dawson led the way out of the theater and down the walkway to the crosswalk. It was about a quarter of a mile to his car, but that sort of beat a mile and a half to the Denny's.

"Satan's armpit has more class than LAX," Jared said dryly. "I take it you've been there?"

"Yeah, to visit my mom when I was little." Dawson's pocket buzzed and he pulled out his phone. *Bringing Darian to movie night. Don't hate. She's bringing popcorn flavoring so you'll like her.* He grunted and the crosswalk light turned green. He looked to his right anyway, because not everyone stopped in the fog, but Rocklin Road looked clear. "Dad would send me out, her driver would pick me up, and I'd spend the rest of the summer by the pool. Didn't see much of LA, but I knew that shitty airport."

"They've fixed it up in the last five years," Jared told him.

Dawson shrugged. "Yeah, I saw some of that. Four years ago I told Mom I was gay and she could just put money in my college fund. My little half brother was two by then, she had her hands full 'cause she kept losing nannies, and she took me up on it." Dawson sighed and led the way to his little Honda. "She's been a name on a check ever since."

Jared grunted a little. "So you stay with your dad?"

"He set me and Benji up in our own apartment during our first year of school. I know—we're spoiled rotten. He only lives a few miles away in Lincoln, so we spend weekends there when we don't have a show. Mom's been the name on the guilt check, Dad's been the actual 'Yeah, Dawson, you're gay, I'm not shocked, wear a condom' parent."

Jared's chuckle sort of hit him like hot chocolate in the pit of his stomach. "Did he really say that?"

Dawson smiled at the memory. "Yup. I had Benji come with me to tell him, and we sat down in the kitchen, and Benji said, 'Gee, Mr. Barnes, would you like me to get you some cookies, some milk, a glass of wine, some beer?' and Dad said, 'Thanks, Benji, I can get my own snacks in my own house, but that's really sweet. Why aren't I watching *The Colbert Report* right now?' And I said—well, I said a whole bunch of stuff, and I went back into the history of homosexuality in civilization and the history of theater and the arts and how really, the whole gay thing complemented the career choice, and my dad interrupted me and said—"

"Let me guess," Jared said, unbuttoning his pants and bending down to open the door.

"Yup. 'Dawson, you're gay, I'm not shocked. Wear a condom and let me get back to my show.'" Dawson grinned at him in the darkness as he turned the ignition.

"So what'd you say?" Jared asked, still smiling gently.

"I was sort of like this—" He unhinged his jaw and stared into space. "—but Benji? He was like, 'Does that mean we can go to the movies, Mr. Barnes?' and my dad was like, 'If you stop for ice cream on the way home, I'll pay for your tickets.' And that was it."

Jared laughed that quiet, self-contained laugh again. "That's sweet. How long has Benji known?"

"Since second grade." Dawson pulled slowly out of the parking lot—God, he hated the fog. "He wanted to kiss the little girl in front of us and I wanted to kiss *him*. He said—and I'll never forget this, because Benji's never been super smart, right, but this was really wise. He said, 'If I say no, will you still be my friend?' and I was really hurt, right? But I said, 'Yeah, Benji. I can't make you like me like that,' and then *he* looked really hurt. He said, 'Then I can't make Becca like me like that either. But that's okay, 'cause we're still friends.'"

"Wonderful," Jared said, and suddenly he was talking in subtexts again, but this time Dawson couldn't read between the lines.

"Yeah," he said distractedly, squinting to make sure no one was barreling off the freeway and ignoring the light. Cautiously he stepped on the gas to make the green light, and he let out a breath when they cleared the intersection. God, this little space by the overpass could be a nightmare. "What's wonderful about it?"

"Nothing. Unrequited crushes. Nothing important."

"Right. Just the thing that's gonna squash you flat. How'd you come out?"

"I didn't go home," Jared said just as Dawson was creeping up to the turnoff to Denny's and the Holiday Inn.

"What's that mean?"

"It means that I told my parents I wanted to go to dance school. I was fourteen, and I couldn't think of *anything* better than dancing six hours a day between studies. It... *God*, it was all I could ask of the world."

"Why for?" Dawson asked curiously. He was *always* curious about what drove the front of the house people to go out and figuratively bleed on the stage.

There was a sudden quiet. "It's hard to explain," he answered eventually. "Let's just say... well, it's all I am."

Dawson swallowed. His blithe maybe-plan for the rest of his life seemed reckless all of a sudden, like he was squandering something. "What did your parents say about dance school?" he asked.

Jared's voice gained strength with this answer. "Well, my mom said they'd pay, but if I turned out to be 'one of those *dance* people,' I shouldn't bother to return home. So I graduated from the academy and into the theater and rented a flat with five other theater people who are *also* never home, and I haven't seen my parents since then."

"Names on a check?"

"Yup."

"That sorta sucks. At least my mom tries once a year."

"It just is," Jared said on a yawn. "Here. Drop me off at Denny's—I can walk from here."

Dawson felt sort of bad, but his pocket buzzed again. He pulled to a stop right in front of the Denny's and checked his phone.

Please don't ditch out—I told her if you don't get along this will be the shortest relationship in history.

Dawson sighed and punched in *OMW* and then looked up at Jared. "You know, you could come over to my place. It's movie night, since we're both working the show and the weekend's toast."

Jared rolled his eyes, and suddenly the dick was back. "Yeah. I could be your beard so you could pretend you got over your crush in the second grade. Night, Dawson. Thanks for the help." And with that, he was up and out of the car, closing the door solidly behind him.

"What. An. Asshole." Dawson watched as he walked up to the Denny's—probably to have the world's sorriest salad, no dressing, for dinner—and waited until he got inside. Then he pulled out carefully and made his way down Rocklin Road toward his apartment building on Taylor. He had a death grip on the steering wheel, but at every stop, he rubbed his chest, angry at himself. It wouldn't hurt so much right there if he hadn't started to like the guy to begin with.

ANDANTE

"So, WAS he cute?"

Dawson grinned at Darian Ritter. "Not nearly as cute as you," he said, charmed. Yup. Benji had picked a winner. Round brown eyes, dimples, wavy streaked hair piled on her head—she was five feet three inches of tight-bodied adorability, and she'd *more* than put herself out for this first date.

"You're just saying that because I've got the kettle-corn topping," she said, sticking out her preciously pointed little chin. "Seriously— Benji hated him. It's the first time he's forgotten to try to pick up on me since we met."

Dawson looked to the kitchen, where Benji was sprinkling Darian's kettle-corn topping on the big bowl of microwaved popcorn he was planning to have for dinner. "Is that why you finally agreed to movie night?"

Darian shrugged and lowered her voice. "I was going to cave today anyway," she said quietly. "But when he was so protective over you, it sort of sealed the deal."

"Wonderful. I'm a purse puppy." He said it to be funny, but jeez, he did hate it when it felt like girls were treating him like that. *Omigod, you're gay? Isn't that awesome? Come be my friend, it'll be just like* Glee*!*

Darian smacked him. "No! You could have been a dick—and you are!—but it was just that he needed to make sure you were okay. You know, best friends, babies, dogs, whatever—it means this guy isn't so into himself that he'd throw someone he's supposed to care about under the bus. I mean, think about it—girls are supposed to nurture all the time. It's just nice to think we're not going to be alone in that boat, right?"

Dawson laughed, because she called him a dick, and it was almost like a compliment coming from her, like she trusted him enough to be bitchy to him but she had a sense of humor.

"Yeah," he said with a sigh, suddenly remembering Jared, and how he was a dick *without* the sense of humor. "No, I get it. It's a gauge of whether or not he can treat people right. If it's someone he's not trying to impress and doesn't want to sleep with and he still treats them decent, odds are good he's not going to be a total asshole."

"Or maybe just a little sphincter," Darian said, laughing at her own joke, and Dawson loved that about her too.

But he still had to front for his buddy. "Benji's never an asshole," he said staunchly, and Darian smirked. "Okay. Never a *total* asshole. He can be a partial asshole—like when he tried to leave his book on the catwalk so he could get closer to you."

"But he had his book in class today!" she protested. "I remember—it looked like it had been through a war."

Dawson laughed. "Yeah, well, that was my bad—both the war and the fact he had it. Right, Benji?"

Benji had sodas tucked in his pockets and a giant bowl o' popcorn in his hands. Dawson picked up the remote, and together they sandwiched Darian on the couch.

"Well, it turns out all I had to do was swear about that Jared guy for a while. Boy, he didn't wait to make a move on you, did he?"

"You encouraged that!" Because it was true, he had.

"Yeah, and then he gave off those 'I'm a giant penis' vibes, and I regretted that pretty quick. Darian, do you want the blanket?"

"Yeah, thanks." With a princessy little smile at Benji, she spread the blanket over her lap and then Dawson's.

"Hey!"

"No, if this is a real date, I'll lay on you, and Dawson can snuggle with me."

"You know he's gay."

"I'm counting on it. His whole function is as body pillow."

"She's awfully familiar awfully fast," Dawson told Benji seriously, and Benji smiled at him with such peace, Dawson couldn't say anything else. Oh God. This was it. Benji had been hitting on her for months—first when she'd been training him at the college gym and then when they'd ended up in some of the same classes. Apparently she hadn't been a clueless ice queen—she'd just been cautious.

And now she'd decided. It was like that. Dawson needed to get used to this because Benji wasn't his anymore.

Dawson watched the movie blindly, Darian's arm around his shoulders, Benji's voice rumbling commentary a familiar counterpoint to the action onscreen.

"Really? Are they really supposed to be brothers? The blond guy is at least a foot taller than the dark-haired guy. Seriously."

And Darian seemed to read his mind too. "And what's that guy doing in such a shitty movie anyway, right?"

"He could do so much better."

"Liam Neeson too."

"He's been taking anything since his wife passed away."

"Yeah, so sad."

"Totally."

And so on. As the movie wrapped up, Dawson realized he'd barely noticed another person in the room, the chatter had been so comfortable.

Okay, so maybe not losing a Benji. Maybe gaining a Darian. He could deal with that, right?

"No, he hasn't told me about the boy, Benji. He just met me. You're supposed to ask."

He sat up on the couch and took the empty popcorn bowl. "Do we want more?"

"Naw—you're supposed to tell us about this guy Benji wanted to protect you from. What's he like?"

"I don't know—*shit*!" Dawson hadn't said a word about why he was late. "He actually needs me and Benji tomorrow after our morning classes. He's doing something sort of neat and he wants our help. We'll get paid for it too."

He outlined their duties as they cleaned up their snacks and Benji loaded the next movie, and when he was done, Darian actually cooed.

"Oh my God! See? *See*? That's what I was talking about. When a guy can do something like that, you know he's not a total asshole!"

"Yeah, well, you wouldn't know it by me." As soon as he said it, Dawson felt bad. "But you know, I didn't see him at his best—maybe after some food and some sleep he'll be a human being again."

"Yeah, well, I hope so," Benji muttered. "You pretty much volunteered me for free."

Darian patted his arm. "That's okay. I'll come in and help. I teach dance, and I took ballet as a kid—I'd be happy to volunteer."

Dawson blinked at her. "You're like a Disney princess, piped in from the heavens like sunshine."

Darian batted her eyes. "Just ask him. I want to see you two work."

"Yeah, why are you doing this again?"

"Because I don't get him without you," she said, voice mild. "What do I look like, an idiot?"

"Nope. Still doing the Disney princess thing. Here, let me text."

Benji's girlfriend teaches dance and aerobics. She'd like to help. Let me know if that's okay.

"You know, he's probably asleep. I may have to text you tomorrow, and I'm not sure how much you're at the college—"

"All the time."

Benji has a girlfriend?

"Oh my God!" Dawson frowned at the phone. *Yes, and it's not me!* he texted to Jared.

At the same time, he said, "I'm there 'cause I help run the theater—why are you there?"

Darian smirked like she was fully aware he was having two conversations at once. "'Cause my dad is the dean of math studies," she said, and Benji ran into a wall.

Darian and Dawson turned to gape at him.

Benji backed away from the wall, rubbing his forehead. "Yeah, I did that. I was just thinking about how many times I've barely skated by in that department." He grimaced at Darian, and Dawson's phone buzzed.

Don't be a dick. I just had two more kids sign up. I'll take the help.

You're welcome, by the way.

Good night, Dawson.

Dawson glared at his phone. "He says that's fine," he told Darian sourly. "And I think there was a thank-you somewhere in the subtext, but no guarantees."

"In the subtext?" she asked.

Dawson looked at Benji. "Were you *trying* to impress her father?"

"Well, I'm *trying* to get recommended to engineering school, remember?"

Dawson connected the dots. "Oh. Oh God. Darian—please tell me your dad likes all boys who try to date you!"

Darian looked apologetically at Benji. "Haven't been many since high school—sorry, Benji. I know this was just supposed to be movie night, but that's why I waited so long. I'm thinking you're signed up for Girlfriend 101, pass or fail only."

"Awesome. Can you at least stay for another movie?"

Darian perked up. "Yeah, absolutely. In fact, since it's so foggy, I may have to camp out—*on your couch.*"

Benji nodded, absolutely sober. "Totally understandable. As long as your father agrees."

Dawson laughed a little, because they were adorable—day one, and they were adorable, and he loved her. It was like Benji *picked* her just for him.

And Dawson's pick of the day was holed up in a hotel room, apparently working when he should be sleeping, and practicing being a dick.

Of course he was.

THE NEXT morning, the backup for the shower was unbelievable.

"You let her go first?" Dawson asked, feeling clammy just *thinking* about going to the college still smelling like chlorine, sweat, and popcorn.

Benji was cooking scrambled eggs and whistling. Dawson ducked around the counter from the living room side and grabbed a wooden spoon. Then he poked Benji in the back with it and ducked as scrambled eggs went splatting around the kitchen.

"What in the *hell*!" Benji pulled the earbuds out of his ear and his head out of his ass and set the sauté pan down so he could clean up eggs.

Dawson tried to move his head up off his arms because he was laughing so hard he couldn't breathe. "I was just... I swear, I didn't expect... oh God!"

"How bad does this look?" Darian came out of the bathroom wearing a pair of *Dawson's* sweats and one of Benji's football jerseys.

"You look... uh...."

Dawson's inarticulate friend was covered in eggs and his too-good-for-him insta-girl was looking at him with moony eyes.

"Time to bail," Dawson muttered, still giggling. "I'll try to save you some hot water."

"Oh, hey, *Dawson*!"

But Dawson figured that he got next by simple virtue of Benji being next to get lucky. Or first to get lucky. Either way, someone was splitting the luck—it was the only way to maintain natural balance.

JARED WAS waiting for them in front of the theater, drinking from a thermos with a tea-bag tag dangling from the top. Dawson wondered if that was all he got to eat for breakfast, because the guy looked neither fed nor rested as he, Benji, and Darian trotted up from different directions.

"Jared, you met Benji yesterday, and this is his friend Darian. You ready?"

Jared looked Darian up and down. "Do you have a leotard or anything?" he asked, eyeballing her in her makeshift outfit.

Darian didn't look put out at all. "I grabbed one from my locker," she said, patting her backpack. "I can go change while you guys set up."

Jared nodded. "That would be best."

"Thank you, Darian, for volunteering for an absolute stranger to come do this thing which is close to my heart!" Dawson prompted.

Jared had the grace to look embarrassed. "This is nice—I really can use the help." And then he turned and watched pointedly as Dawson let them all in.

Dawson and Benji turned on all the lights to warm them up, and then Benji set about aligning them on the stage. Dawson gave him a few more practices on the curtain, because there really was a knack to it. By the time they finished, Jared stood up at the door greeting parents and their children as they came in. He wore a pair of tight-fitting black jazz pants, a black ballet shirt, and a red sash of all things, as well as his black slippers.

Dawson had to swallow, and then he had to pull his vitaminwater out of his pocket and swallow some of that, because the hard facts were, with his black hair combed back from his forehead and a pleasant smile on his face, he really *did* look like Prince Charming, and it was tough to remember he had the potential to be a real diva instead.

Dawson disappeared for the light and sound boards as soon as Jared gathered the kids onstage. The mix of ages, abilities, and genders surprised him.

A couple of big girls posed up there, easily five feet tall, their shoulders rounded and heads cocked in classic Down syndrome pose. One girl was very articulate and repeated all of Jared's directions as he spoke, and the other girl didn't speak at all. The younger children were slightly more functional, listening and repeating instructions and doing exactly what Jared asked. He and Darian had brought out the barre, and the first thing he had them do was repeat a series of movements and positions while Dawson played the soft strains of a classical piano riff in the background.

Darian repeated the movements as Jared called them out, and then Jared moved from child to child, fixing their feet gently and having them repeat the move to the best of their ability.

He was, in fact, really wonderful at it. Patient and attentive, and Dawson could see he was putting his full concentration into making sure every child really *did* believe that he or she was a prima ballerina about to bathe in the spotlight.

Four moves—that was all they practiced and all they made perfect. First position, plié, chassé, and third position. They spent twenty minutes doing that, using the barre for balance with the pliés, and when those restless, placid bodies couldn't work on that anymore, Jared had Dawson change the music to something lighter and more contemporary. "Do you all know how to play Simon Says?"

There was a silent chorus of wide-eyed nods.

"Good. Darian here is going to be Simon. She's going to tell you to do a move, and *you're* going to do the move she says as she says it, okay? Does everyone see the tape on the ground? Good. Everyone move there."

And so on. As soon as they were all established, the girls in their pink leotards and pink ballet shoes, the boys in their jazz pants and black shoes, all of them looking as grown-up and as graceful as they could, the game began. Darian started leading Simon Says and Jared got rid of the ballet barre. Benji, because he was a good guy, fixed the spotlight on the dancers and hopped off the spot stool and helped him.

When the stage was clear, Jared told the parents they could come up for five minutes to assist with a bathroom break or a water break, and while they were doing that, he walked up the aisle to talk to Dawson.

"It's going great," he murmured, sticking his head in the sound booth. "But enough of them showed up that I think I'm going to need your help for this next one, okay? When I tell you to, put the next track on loop and come down."

Dawson nodded soberly and then grinned. "They're having a good time, aren't they? You're really great with them."

Something odd happened to Jared's face. It grew softer, more boyish, and sweet. "They really are having a good time. Thank you." The smile he gave Dawson then was a little bit shy and as pure as the ones his students had just given him, and Dawson had to clutch at his heart a little as Jared walked back down to the stage to greet the kids. God, where had that come from? It was like... like he was *human* or something.

Dawson watched him walking, delicate and powerful and beautiful, and wondered at the heart in the guy that he would do something like this, and how hard he worked to hide that.

Darian had been right. The asshole test was all about truth, and apparently this guy had just passed.

Good to his word, after assembling the students and going through the sequence of moves again, Jared called for Dawson to set the track on loop (which, Dawson was sure, was going to get damned irritating after a while) and to run down to help.

First Jared stood on the far side of the stage and asked Darian to repeat the moves on her own. Dawson figured that if she hadn't shown up, he would have done this part himself, and he felt a little cheated because he would have liked to have *Jared* position his feet and touch the small of his back or his shoulders. As it was, he watched Benji's new girlfriend carefully execute each move in rhythm to the Nutcracker piece that was playing. The stage was the same barely sanded, hollow-booming piece of equipment it always was, but the spotlight followed her every move, and in that moment, Dawson got why the light and the sound. Darian was a personal trainer and an aerobics instructor, so that helped, but in the black leotard, she looked like a prima ballerina on an international stage. Dawson got the whole idea, just like Jared had told him.

These kids were going to be *stars*.

When Darian got to the other side of the stage, she ended with her feet in third position, one hand over her head and the other delicately at her waist. Jared stood there and waited for her to arrive, like a prince in a fairy tale, and when she hit her final mark, he tucked one foot behind him and bowed.

There was a half minute of silence at the end of the loop, and the parents in the audience and the kids on the stage clapped, and then they broke the tableau. Jared walked to Dawson and said, "Okay, so Darian and I will be onstage with them, but we need you to take each kid's hand and walk them to the blue tape right there." He pointed to the little strip on the stage. "Just make sure the kid is standing there when the loop starts again, okay?"

Dawson grinned and very gallantly put one hand behind the small of his back and extended the other hand out at chest level and executed a geeky little bow. "My pleasure, Prince Charming. My wish is but to serve."

Jared bit his lip and smiled.

There they were, standing *onstage* in front of a bunch of kids whose entire *world* revolved around being the star of the show for a forty-five-second music riff, and Dawson's heart fell down at his feet and exploded.

Oh, holy God. Jared *bit his lip*, even white teeth sinking into that not-too-plump, not-too-lean mouth and *making* it plump and red and....

"Yeah, do it just like that," Jared was saying while Dawson fixated on his orifice. "They'll love it."

Dawson nodded, feeling dumb, because really, his entire world had sort of collapsed around that tenderly bitten lip.

But he managed to snap out of it when the music loop started again.

Darian was currently escorting the next student, a young man, to his tape, and when the countdown started again, she backed up and let the young man perform. While she was doing that, Dawson turned to the next in line, a short, solid girl who was probably around twelve or thirteen in spite of being under five feet tall, and bowed. The girl smiled delightedly and put her hand into Dawson's. Dawson straightened, threw his shoulders back, and pressed the back of his other hand into the small of his back, escorting the girl to her spot with the pomp and ceremony of the Queen of England. When he got to the place, he said, "Remain here, my lady," and bowed, releasing her hand.

"You're my prince!" she said, her voice cracking loudly over the music and the other student dancing.

Dawson grinned at her and bowed again, winking, and she clapped her hands.

"My prince!" she said and then waved as Dawson turned around and readied the next student.

It was sort of magical. The girl who thought Dawson was her prince was relatively high functioning—she got to her mark and painstakingly performed every ballet move Jared had shown her, and when she finished the final move, Jared bowed and she curtseyed and she turned to the audience and beamed.

In a way, it was like an assembly line of stardom. Darian and Dawson took turns leading the dancers to their solo places, and then either Darian or Jared would assist or simply wait until the soloist had performed and then bowed at the end.

Their smiles when they bowed were usually bigger than the spotlight, bigger than the sun, and Dawson saw Darian wipe under her eyes once or twice and didn't think any the less of her for it.

One of the bigger girls, the one who really didn't speak, ignored all of her cues and turned toward her shadow in the spotlight, and then moved silently, *almost* in time to the music, trying to touch her own shadow. It was haunting, and, in its way, beautiful. When the music cue ended, Jared walked up to her and took her hand and bowed, and her body went slack and limp again, her face falling into the vacant lines she'd had during the exercise. For a moment Dawson was saddened, because it felt as though her soul had flown with the last strains of the music, but then he saw the expression on *Jared's* face and realized that for *this* child, he had somehow given her something wonderful, something that made this entire afternoon worth it.

And for some stupid, irritating reason, that made *Dawson* almost tear up.

After the last dancer moved into place, Jared gave Dawson a sudden, panicked, jerky nod, and Dawson read his mind.

Very quietly he ran down the stage steps and up to the control room, and arrived in time to turn the music off before it looped. Jared looked up at him and gestured him back down again, and Dawson hustled back, rolling his eyes and holding his side, because hey, he was running his ass off here, but when he got back to the front of the stage, it was worth it.

"Ladies and gentlemen, I give you the Sierra Afternoon Dance Troupe!" Jared boomed, and stood to the side, clapping, while all of his students bowed hand in hand.

Dawson was right there with all of their parents, clapping and whistling and whooping and hollering, and Jared was right. Each kid up there was a superstar, and nothing could take that away.

When it was over, Jared handed out DVDs that apparently featured him leading a basic dance workout so the students could dance every day, and the parents wanted pictures of their children with him.

He hugged them closely, not like the hugging was a chore, and he accepted their kisses on the cheek without reservation. When Dawson's little blonde princess took her turn, she turned to Dawson and said "My prince too!" Jared gave that little jerk of the head that Dawson was starting to learn, and Dawson stood up with them, getting his picture taken and hugging her close and accepting her kiss on the cheek like a gift.

He would be the first to admit that if he hadn't watched Jared do it, he wouldn't have known how.

Finally the parents led their dancers out beyond the red-carpeted stairs of the theater and into the blinding foggy daylight. Benji clicked off the spotlight, and the subtle hum of white noise it gave whined sharply and then died, and Jared gave a sigh and flopped into one of the theater seats.

Darian capered like a cheerleader in the aisle next to him. "That was *amazing*! Oh my God! I want to do that *again*! Jared, tell me—how did you set this up? I could do this every day! I could do this for a *living*! That was wonderful—where did you find the kids, the parents, the—"

Jared chuckled weakly and held up his hands. "It's something I do when I travel. My manager sends out fliers to the local dance classes that enroll disabled children, and people sign up. Dolph sets up time on the stage and pays the guild and here we are." He stood and held out his hand. "And I've got to say, I totally owe you, Darian. You were like a gift from the gods, because I didn't expect this many people to show, and I would have had to run Dawson off his *ass* if you hadn't helped me out."

Darian laughed and shook with him. "And God forbid Dawson run any of his ass off—there's not enough of it as it is!"

"No gawking at Dawson's ass," Benji growled. "You're supposed to be gawking at *my* ass."

"Besides," Dawson said with dignity, "you heard the young woman. I'm a prince, and princes don't *get* their asses gawked at."

Jared coughed and it sounded like a word, but Dawson couldn't be sure until Benji and Darian cracked up.

"What?"

"Nothing." Benji smirked. "Are we going to turn out the stage lights or not?"

Dawson groaned. "God—we only have two hours. Such a choice." It took them a half an hour to warm up, but nobody liked to leave them on when there was nobody there. "Leave them on. We'll be back in an hour anyway for setup." He looked around and deliberately included Jared in his next sentence. "You all want to catch some lunch? I'm all for a burger or something."

"Yes," Jared said, looking up unexpectedly. "I'd love to take you out—my treat. You sort of saved my life today."

"Free food? We're there!" Dawson grinned at Benji, glad that some things hadn't changed since second grade.

"Oh great," Darian muttered, shoving Benji's arm. "You're cheap. Just like my dad—there had to be something."

"Not cheap, just broke!" Benji protested, and Dawson nodded.

"Aren't we all. Tell you what, Jared—you come out with us just because we don't have BO today and lunch will be *our* treat. You pretty much let us feel good about ourselves for the rest of the year. We can officially skip recycling once this year on accident, and we'll still be in karmic balance."

Jared smiled that sudden, shy, lip-biting smile, and Dawson once again didn't know what to do with that.

"Yeah. Let me and Darian go put on some street clothes, okay?"

"Oh God yes!" Darian nodded. "Just don't let my dad catch me in Benji and Dawson's clothes or he'll think I didn't sleep on the couch!"

She and Jared took off for the backstage dressing rooms, and Benji turned to Dawson with a quiet frown. "Stop that," he said.

Dawson turned to him with an open mouth, which was how he'd gotten away with stealing cookies from Benji's mom for their entire childhood. "Stop what?"

"Close your mouth and stop crushing on him. He's cute—I was thinking he'd be good for you to flirt with, but no. Not the way you look at him. He's going away in four days, Dawson."

Dawson nodded soberly. "And God forbid he leave a baby in my belly, Pa!"

Benji smacked the back of his head. "Don't be an asshole. I'm saying don't get hurt."

"How do you know he'll hurt me? I've had lube and condoms in my drawer since we moved in."

Benji shuddered delicately. "And other things—I was there when you came back from that store, remember? Scariest bag of novelty items I've ever seen. Anyway, just...." Benji took a deep breath through his nose. "Don't do anything... what's that word?"

"Fun?"

"Asshole?"

"Okay, I won't be an asshole!"

"Irrevocable!"

"I'm irrevocably an asshole?"

Benji took a deep breath, pinned Dawson with his big sloe brown eyes, and said, "I will beat your ass until your brains pop out your nose, because you *are* irrevocably an asshole and I'm trying to be a nice guy here!"

Dawson shrugged and almost clocked Benji in the jaw with his shoulder. "It's lunch, moron. We're all gonna be there. And look at him—he's so clenched he probably keeps his cash in his ass crack. He's not the type who's gonna bone me in the bathroom between snootfuls of blow."

"You watched *American Psycho* again, didn't you?" Benji asked, not batting an eyelash.

Dawson grimaced. Two days ago—Benji had been flirting with Darian and Dawson had been alone. "Well...."

"*Without me?*"

"I'm sorry—it'll never happen again."

"If it was *Fight Club*, I'd be moving out."

"Understood."

"You have no respect, you know that, right?"

Dawson socked him in the arm. "No respect? I *showed* you that movie!"

"Yeah, because you saw it on a *date* with Genie Spencer!"

They both stopped and grimaced. Yeah. That had been an... well, an odd time in Dawson's life. He could still hear Benji's voice in his head. *Dawson, I know you're gay,* you *know you're gay, why are you going out with this girl again?* Dawson couldn't remember what he'd answered then, but now, all grown-up and in college and shit, he knew the answer was that for a brief period of time, he'd wanted badly to be normal.

Of course, since then, he'd figured out that whatever made him and Benji happy, that was normal.

"Well, I made up for it," Dawson said now, because the first thing he'd done when he'd gotten back from Genie's house was order the movie on Amazon to show Benji. And as soon as Benji had seen it, he'd said, *You watched this movie with a girl?*

Yeah, well, I was sort of wishing it was you.

Next time just ask me over to watch the movie and leave the girl out of it.

And the fact that Benji had never qualified that with "and it's not a date or anything" made it official. They *were* brothers, and the gay thing really *wasn't* going to get in the way. And come to think of it, besides family vacations and Dawson's last trip to see his mother, movie night had been their tradition, and the only serious change it had seen was the night before.

When Darian had been there.

Oh, she was sneaky, that one—she had Dawson adoring her before he truly realized how significantly she was going to change his life.

"You did not," Benji was saying, and it took Dawson a minute to realize he was still talking about *American Psycho.*

"I did too!"

"No, you didn't—you've now officially seen it two more times than I have!" Benji shoved at his arm and Dawson shoved back.

"I can't take back the first time—and you and me are pretty even on *Fight Club*—ergh!"

Benji grabbed him in a headlock and proceeded to noogie the crap out of his already rumpled hair.

"Benji!"

"Doesn't count!" Benji panted, because Dawson was fighting back.

"Does too!"

They were still tussling when Jared and Darian walked back, and although Darian smacked Benji on the top of the head and told him to knock that shit off (the appropriate response, as far as Dawson was concerned), Jared pulled back from them.

"Charming. Are you sure you want to go to lunch, or did you want to break out the olive oil and wrestling mats?"

Dawson and Benji managed a four-foot leap backward.

"Ew!"

"Gross!"

"Not since second grade—what's a guy gotta do for you to let that go!"

"Don't be a prick!"

Jared arched his magnificent eyebrows and smoldered at them from underneath. "Just let me know when you're going to grow up, okay? Especially if I have to appear in public with you." He turned on his heel and led the way up the aisle with an attitude that said he fully expected them to follow.

Dawson's mouth dropped in outrage and Benji narrowed his eyes.

And then they both met eyes and grinned—and made hideous faces behind his back as they followed him.

"I can hear that!" he called, and to Dawson's relief, there was a hint of humor in his voice.

"Mno voo canb!" Dawson called because he had his fingers in his mouth to pull his lips back.

Jared whirled and caught him in the act. Dawson grinned around his fingers and Jared just shook his head and turned around—but he was fighting a smile, Dawson saw it.

To his relief, lunch was actually pleasant. Jared managed to battle his sphincter and come out on top (on top, get it? 'Cause he seemed like a top?), and he chatted pleasantly with Dawson and Darian about productions he'd done, and what LA was like, and why five men (gay and straight) living in a two-bedroom apartment was a bad idea.

"It's like we have five of everything—five different deodorants, five different hair gels, five different shampoos, right? And then we buy extra because nobody wants to run out, and then we forget where we put it, so you can't open a door or look into a bag without being assaulted with someone's grooming products, and then, all at the same time, we'll run out of something stupid like razor blades."

Dawson cracked up over his carne asada burrito. He noticed, rather sadly, that Jared had ordered the equivalent of chicken and lettuce with nothing else in between. That was no way to treat Adalberto's, but, well, what could you do?

"Who straightens the apartment?" Benji asked, as hooked on the story as everyone else, but Jared ignored him, taking a bite of his salad and trying not to show his distaste for the lack of flavor. Well, they'd tried to warn him, but he'd insisted on at least *going* someplace they loved.

"No, seriously," Dawson intervened, not even wondering why the two of them couldn't seem to cut each other a break. "Who's supposed to clean?"

"Well, all of us—isn't that what you guys do?"

Dawson and Benji looked at each other and burst into laughter.

"Oh *hell* no!" Benji muttered. "Dawson buys groceries, we both cook and do dishes, and I vacuum, dust, and straighten. And sometimes, when I feel sorry for him, I throw him a bone and fold his clothes, otherwise they just form this… this *strata* on the floor of his room."

Dawson grimaced, thinking that might not be something you wanted to tell the guy you'd been crushing on for the past day. "I clean up," he protested. "When I have company. Or I would. If I ever *got* company. Because besides theater people, nobody ever sees my room. Or, well, the house. But if someone I gave a shit about was coming over, I'd clean it. I swear."

He looked up to see Benji and Darian closing their eyes almost in tandem—it was cute—and Jared regarding him quietly over a bite of crappy no-dressing chicken salad.

"So," he said with a little half smile, "if I was going to come over, would you clean your room?"

"Absolutely," Dawson said without hesitation. "Because you've got this total disdain thing going on, and if you just looked at me like you were going to fry my pubes off with your glare alone, I couldn't deal. I'd go bananas. I'd donate all my clothes to charity and run around in a bathrobe—"

"If you owned one," Benji supplied.

"If I owned one," he agreed, "or my sweats, except Darian's wearing them."

Jared's eyes opened wider, and Dawson would have bet actual money he couldn't have done that without straining something. "So you don't want me to come over?" he said dryly.

"No! No, you know, you get to know us, we don't scare you, you can manage to not be a dick to Benji, then yeah! I'll invite you over. But you gotta give me a minute, or a day, or something. You know."

"To clean your room."

Dawson nodded like they'd decided something and popped the rest of his burrito in his mouth. "To clean my room," he agreed grandly, not sure if he'd actually agreed to do it so that Jared actually *would* come over or if he was just speaking in hypotheticals.

Jared nodded, smiling that other smile, the secret, sort of sad smile that said he knew something Dawson didn't. "If I decide not to be a dick to Benji," he agreed with mock sobriety. Or maybe he really *was* that serious. Dawson realized he didn't always know with this guy—it kept Dawson on his toes.

"Yup. That way we'll *both* be grown-ups," Dawson said, stealing one of Benji's carne asada fries because he wasn't eating them so much as playing with them.

Jared narrowed one eye, like he understood Dawson had gotten a little dig in there about maybe not trying to make a thing between Benji and Dawson when there wasn't one, but he didn't really agree. He took a deep breath and looked sideways at Benji, who was busy showing off to Darian by shoving as many fries as possible in his mouth at once.

"Right," Jared said. "Grown-ups."

And Dawson understood that in whatever obscure game they were playing, Jared had just solidly won a round. "Jesus, Benji, you're killing me here!"

"Wha'?" Benji asked through a full mouth, and Dawson would have slugged his arm, but he probably would have choked to death on all those goddamned fries.

CRESCENDO

DAWSON HAD a hard time watching the light board that night, and he *never* had a hard time watching the light board. The reason it was different *this* time was that, well, he was hard.

He was having a hard time being hard.

Jesus.

Jared Emory was sex on legs, and the *things* he could do with that *amazing* body were just….

Gungh.

"*Dawson!*" Benji hissed into his earpiece, and Dawson jerked himself back to his board for the one hundredth time that night and cued the lights down for the end of the scene. Usually, this was the sort of thing he was good at—that half-a-heartbeat anticipation so that the lights were actually fading before the audience realized the scene was over. It was one of those things that, when you were doing a gentle fade-to-black in a drama, allowed the moment to be more poignant. In a relatively athletic dance like Jared had just performed, one in which he'd seemed to have his partner held over his head for a multi-bajillion dance steps, it kept the audience from seeing that his arms were shaking and sweat was pouring from his forehead and his chest was vibrating like an Olympic sprinter's.

Which were all things that were just making Dawson harder, but that maybe the audience might not want to see, so, well, it was a good thing Benji wasn't thinking with his dick, because Dawson was having trouble in that department.

Still, that was the only cue he actively flubbed, and that one was subtle. For the rest of the night, he watched avidly as Jared did his job and made sure Dawson looked good doing *his.*

God, he'd never been so hung up on the person in front of the stage before.

For one thing, they'd all seemed to be (in Dawson and Benji's experience, anyway) the kind of people who needed to be the funniest at the party and the prettiest at the ball. The timid people didn't get picked to go in front of the world, and the funny-looking people with confidence got all the character roles. It was *great* being a part of the theater crew, but for Dawson and Benji? All of the *real* work of the make-believe went on in the tech booth or backstage.

But watching Jared that afternoon with those kids, and watching him sweat buckets and move with the grace of a god?

Well, Dawson wasn't so lost on self-awareness that he couldn't recognize his first celebrity crush.

Or, as Benji had pointed out with mutton hands, the potential for it to hurt like a sonofabitch when it all went south.

But warnings apparently didn't matter. The final strains of music faded, and Jared Emory was alone in the spotlight, holding one of those poses that looked physically impossible, with one toe planted on the badly sanded stage, one toe pointing almost directly at the sky, and Jared's opposite hand, held over his head, stretching for the farthest point of imaginary light.

Final chord crash—and darkness.

Curtain closed. Thankfully smoothly—Benji had practiced a little before the kids had arrived for their show.

And then that dead thought-bomb of silence that came after a *really* amazing performance that inspired the holy hell out of people, right before the sweet cacophony of applause.

Dawson actually hooted and screamed from inside the booth, pausing long enough to punch the front lights so the dancers on the apron were superstars in the glow, and kill the sound completely, so that the only thing the dancers and tech crew could hear was the ocean roar of a job well done.

Topher, who ran the secondary sound board next to Dawson, glanced up from setting everything up for the next day and grimaced.

"Oh God. Don't tell me you're going to chase him just like all the girls."

Dawson shrugged with his entire body. "I can appreciate the scenery like the next boy. He's got his good points."

Topher rolled his eyes. "*I've* got good points—I don't see you jumping up and down and clapping for *me*."

"Stop whining like a baby and maybe I would," Dawson shot back, annoyed. "That guy from the dorms was chasing you and you turned around and caught you some of that. Don't look at me if I'm unimpressed." The guy had dumped him too, and Dawson was pretty sure it was because Topher was an insufferable pain in the ass.

"Oh God. You mean because I'm not like *Benji*, who caught the pretty girl through the magical persistence of his amazing fucking dimples?"

Dawson grunted in disgust, watching as the dancers all came to join hands and bow. Jared got his own bow, and then the lead girl of the flock, and then Jared showed his inscrutable face, the stoic one that betrayed nothing, the one he showed the world. Jeez, after a show like that, you think he'd smile, right?

"God, he's so serious all the time. I wonder if he'd just shatter apart if anyone made him fuckin' laugh."

"Well, if he's laughing at you," Benji's voice came in over his earpiece, "he's not the right guy."

"Dammit, you're supposed to poke me when I'm doing that."

Benji cracked up into the mike, which was pretty fucking hilarious, actually, because his brain went there before Dawson's.

"You're sick," Dawson said with pride.

"You taught me everything I know."

Dawson grinned and looked out at the crowd. They were still applauding, but it was starting to die down. Jared deserved every nanosecond of the glory, and Dawson felt like he was getting some just because he knew Jared on a first-name basis—and that's when he saw it: Jared, bending at the waist in a full bow, looking out to the tech booth and executing a little roll with his hand.

"I saw that!" Topher snapped, standing up and shooting his rolling chair out behind him. "That was for *you*! Oh my God, Dawson, did you put out for that guy? You won't go down on *any*body!"

Benji's growl over the headset vibrated their earpieces, low and threatening, and Topher threw his hands up. "Okay, okay. I'll lay off. I just can't believe you think that's going anywhere."

Benji's growl didn't stop, a low, muttering, murderous counterpoint on the speaker. "Topher, shut up. Just shut up, or I will beat you against the wall and leave you for dead. No more bullshit. This isn't any of your business."

Dawson kept his mouth shut and let Benji do the job he'd elected himself for back in the second grade. The applause faded to the point where he could lower the stage lights and hit the house lights, and the curtain closed one more time. Dawson sat down in his chair and turned to Topher.

"You might want to get out of here early. You really pissed him off tonight."

Topher stood up and pulled his lip back. "Yeah, you go ahead and find another guild member for the rest of the run. I'm over you, Dawson."

Dawson rolled his eyes. "It's a job, asshole. The guild is *overflowing* with people who want jobs. You bail on this because I wouldn't sleep with you, who do you think is going to hire you again?"

"Bite me." Topher stalked out of the sound booth, slamming the door shut, and Dawson winced. The crowd was still filing out, and he almost pegged a sweet little woman in the face when he did that. Dawson would be sure to put it into his report when he had Professor Weber ask for another tech on the fly.

"What. A. Fucker." Benji's voice echoed moodily in the earpiece, and Dawson grunted.

"I won't tell Professor Weber you threatened to rip his balls out his nose."

"Maybe you should. He likes you. It might put me on his permanent good side."

Dawson laughed a little, took off his headset, and set everything to the point where they could turn off the house lights on their way out the door. Then he grabbed his windbreaker and his backpack and locked the tech booth.

The set was a basic backdrop piece—a starry night sky with icy treetops underneath, so the dancers had essentially flown through the air until the end. It wouldn't need to be taken down for another three nights, and Dawson was relieved. He and Benji had homework.

But that didn't stop Dawson from pulling out his English book and propping it up on his knee so he could read it in the dim house lights until Benji was done. Dancers were leaving out the front doors since the back ones were already locked, and Dawson paused and smiled and waved at some of the girls who recognized him, and then returned to his studies. So there he was, immersed in *The Scarlet Letter*, when an almost-familiar smell, warmth, and presence made itself felt at his back.

He turned and looked over his shoulder and startled back from Jared's face, which was intimately close. Jared smiled—barely—put a hand on his neck, and lowered the other one to the text.

"This part always pisses me off," he said. "I mean, there he is, *talking* to the guy he practically threw his wife at, and every word is like poison."

Dawson shuddered. "He's like one of the freakiest characters I've ever read. And the real freaky part is sometimes you're like, 'Uh-huh, I get it, you're smarter than everyone else, you get something for that,' and then you're like, 'Oh wait—that's *insane!*'"

There was a soft puff of breath at Dawson's ear. "Yeah. I liked that book. Well, not, you know, *liked,* but it was—"

"Fascinating," Dawson mumbled, because he was so close and he smelled so good. Theater sweat—it was one of his favorite things.

"So," Jared said softly, "do you all go out or anything? All the girls left—I guess they've got classes tomorrow. I know most people go home after the Thursday show."

He doesn't want to go back to the hotel.

The thought came out of nowhere, but Dawson knew it was the truth, because hey, who would want to be alone in a hotel?

"We're actually going back to my place to do homework," Dawson said apologetically. "But if you want to watch TV on our couch, I swear ours is comfy. It's still pretty firm, and we put a little top mattress on it. Darian said it didn't fuck up her back at all. I mean, you don't have to. I know you've got a perfectly good hotel room, but, well, if you don't like the quiet—because I wouldn't. I mean, I'm not a fan of quiet on the best of days, but it sort of sucks to go home after a show with no one there, you know?"

"Darian slept on the couch?"

"Well, yeah." Dawson smiled at him, unable to make it a cheeky grin. "We're simple folk here, Jared. None of your fast West Hollywood ways up here, right?"

Jared nodded, and Dawson could tell he was going to say no.

"Don't be a dick. I've got to hire a new sound tech tomorrow because the last guy got all huffy 'cause I wouldn't put out. Here we are, offering our couch and unlimited Xbox time, and the least you can do is say yes."

Jared looked down at his hand as it still burned on Dawson's shoulder. His night-dark eyelashes stood out starkly against skin paler than Dawson's.

"Thank you," he said at last, simply. "If you don't mind, I'll follow you home. Do you want me to stop for food—"

"Naw—we've got ice cream, fruit, frozen pizza—you name the after-show carb fest, we can hook you up."

Jared squeezed his shoulder, and Dawson couldn't hold back a shudder.

"You know, you really do dance like a freakin' angel," he said, because someone had to say it.

"It's all I ever wanted to be," Jared said softly.

Dawson nodded. "I wanted to be a superhero—like, an invisible one, who could clone himself and be four places at once and run faster than light, and maybe fly—"

And then, wonder of wonder, the most amazing sound interrupted his ramble.

Jared's laughter.

He stood up straight, tilted his head back, exposed his brilliant white teeth, and simply allowed the joy to take over his tense dancer's body and obliterate that blank stoicism that was all Dawson had seen so far.

"Okay, I see what's going on here," Jared gasped when he was able. "Your entire body is a superhero in training. It all makes so much more sense."

Dawson grinned at him until his cheeks pushed up into his eyes. "Dude—us superheroes—it's really a full-time gig."

Jared bent down so quickly that Dawson didn't see it coming, but Jared's kiss on his cheek burned on his skin for the rest of the way home.

BENJI DIDN'T hardly raise an eyebrow when Dawson told him Jared would be following them back. "Yeah? He up for our couch?"

"Apparently so," Dawson said, almost gleeful. Then he sobered for a moment. "I think he's lonely."

"Yeah, well, it's gotta suck. New town every week or so, new cast, new crew. And then he goes back to LA and it's all cutthroat competition, right? I mean, doesn't everybody want to *be* Jared Emory?"

"Or do him," Dawson agreed.

"Yeah, well, right now that's only you."

Dawson went quiet then, thinking about Benji, his stalwart companionship, the way he'd stayed friends even though Dawson's crush had been helpless, gentle, and persistent.

"You're always so good about it," Dawson acknowledged suddenly.

"Good about what?"

But Dawson was too busy getting this off his chest to bother with trivia. "You had to have worried, you know? I mean, what if Darian had been the opposite? What if you and me, you'd driven her off? I mean... I've known her two days, and she's your *soul mate.* What if she was, I don't know, a huge antigay freak, or her dad was, or—"

"Then she wouldn't have been my soul mate. You worry too much, Dawson." Benji laughed. "Yeah, this guy's going out of town again, but do you know how my parents met?"

Benji's dad had died when Benji was little. Dawson didn't know if *Benji* knew how his parents met.

"No idea."

"Well, my mom was a nursing student in Colombia, and my dad was a visiting professor. They met on the last day of his visit, and... I don't know. They had a *day*. One day, and my mom swears there was no magic sex or anything. They just talked, which was rough, because at the time my mom didn't know any English and my dad didn't speak a whole lot of Spanish. But they managed, right? And they flirted and played and looked shit up in their little dictionaries. My mom thought it was just that—a day. But two days after he left, my dad sent her an e-mail. She said it was the worst Spanish she'd ever read, but they moved on from there. That was five years before I was born. You and this guy, you at least speak the same language, even if *I* think he's from Mars. Tonight he's crashing on the couch. Maybe tomorrow he'll send you a text. It'll be good."

Dawson looked at his friend in admiration. "You're so lucky. You got the cool mom who told you great stories. I got the idiot father who—"

"Loves you so much it hurts to go eat Sunday brunch with you," Benji said. "It's like I'm ripping his child out of his arms when I want my roommate back."

"Oh God." Because it was true. If Dawson left town to become the greatest light-board engineer in the country and revolutionize stagecraft everywhere, what would become of his dad? "Yeah, okay. We both won in the parent department. I hear you. So, Jared."

"Yeah?"

"Maybe it's just our job to give him a couch to sleep on."

"Maybe."

"You're right. Maybe we should start there."

IT TURNED out to be okay. Benji and Dawson got back and fixed a snack of rice cakes and hummus, and then they both put their books up on the tiny kitchen table, divvying up their space equally. They opened their laptops, and while Dawson's was booting up, he walked through the living room and caught Jared standing in the space between the battered brown couch and the wall, staring at the wall itself. Benji and Dawson decorated with the thing they had plenty of—the fliers of every show they'd ever worked on. They'd been smart about it—they taped the fliers to each other in sheets and did it neatly, then pinned the reinforced corners of the big sheets, so when they moved, they could roll the posters up and use them again. But they'd been doing theater since middle school, and they'd both kept as many fliers as possible. The wall behind the couch was impressive.

"You like?" Dawson said, pride in his voice.

Jared nodded. "Wish I'd thought of it for my own space."

Dawson grinned. "Well, your flier's going up as soon as the show's over. You can have space here."

Jared looked like he was going to smile, and then he turned suddenly thoughtful. Dawson let the moment slip and ran to root through Benji's drawers (because Benji was bigger) so he could find Jared some sweats and a T-shirt.

"Man, go ahead, eat, take a shower, watch TV—we've got some DVDs down on the shelf, some Netflix, some Xbox—it's like home, except now my dad doesn't have this shit anymore, so, you know, my place is better."

He shoved clothes into Jared's arms, looped a companionable arm around his shoulder, and steered him out of Benji's bedroom toward the bathroom.

"See? We clean—or, well, Benji cleaned this time, which is good because his mom taught him, and quite frankly I forget to mop up the floor behind the toilet. Drives him crazy. He's going to strangle me in my sleep—"

"Especially since you're the one who misses, you fucker!" Benji called from the living room, which was Dawson's cue to shut up and get to work.

"Anyway, see, towels on the rack behind the toilet, and, you know. Home, meet Jared. Jared, meet home." Dawson gave him a bright, nervous smile, and Jared nodded. His hair was stiff and soaked through with sweat, and fatigue darkened the skin under his eyes. If nothing else, Dawson hoped he copped a nap on their couch before going back to the hotel. He bobbed his head nervously and turned to leave, and Jared stalled him with a hand on his arm.

"Thank you. It was nice of you to ask."

For a moment God froze the game of life. It was just them, Dawson and Jared, looking at each other, Dawson losing himself in those technicolor eyes, Jared's lips parting softly. The entire little bathroom with the sea-green shower curtain and the bottle of matching bath salts Benji's mom brought them echoed with the sound of their breathing.

Dawson looked up, because Jared was a little taller. He felt like here, in the stupid bathroom, they had common ground.

"Well, you know," Dawson managed when he realized too much time had passed. "I... I uhm...." He blinked slowly.

"Homework," Jared said, and to his credit, he sounded reluctant. "You have homework."

Dawson pulled away from Jared's arm and the moment, and play resumed. "And you have that whole body odor thing you have to resolve. Benji and I use the same soap and shit—knock yourself out."

He wandered out of the bathroom and took a minute to pour himself a soda over ice before he sat down. In the background he could hear the water start, but he'd sat down in front of his computer before he thought of the obvious and spit out his soda.

"What?" Benji asked. Without getting up, he reached over to the counter and grabbed a towel, which he handed off to Dawson.

"I just had that thought," Dawson said, feeling gobsmacked even as he wiped his screen and keyboard down. "You know... *that* thought."

"You just realized he's naked in our bathroom, didn't you?"

"Didn't *you*?"

"Yeah, but it doesn't mean the same thing when I do it."

Dawson pitched the towel over the counter and into the kitchen sink—he hoped, or it was going to be on the floor. "God. God, no. It doesn't mean the same thing at all."

"You've got *The Scarlet Letter*, Dawson. Finish that. *Then* lose your virginity."

"Yeah, okay. That's fine."

"Sure it is. Open your book, open your SparkNotes, one, two, three—"

"Whee!"

Dawson was good to his word about doing his homework, but even when Jared wandered out, his hair limp and wet against his head, weariness etched in every line of his body, and flopped on the couch to commandeer the remote, the vision still remained behind Dawson's eyes: Jared naked to the skin, every muscle shiny and luminous as the water touched him all over.

The Scarlet Letter had never given a boy a harder boner.

AT ONE in the morning, there was not enough soda and coffee in the world.

At around eleven, Benji got up, stretched, and walked to the linen closet. He came out with the same mattress pad, pillow, and comforter Darian had used and set it up on the corner of the couch.

By the time Dawson stood up and stretched and pronounced the paper a load of crap that wouldn't fool anyone but the best he could do, Jared was stretched out on their couch, eyes closed, fast asleep. Benji sighed and shut his laptop, and they fist-bumped over the table.

"You finish?"

Benji shook his head. "I'm setting my alarm for early. I've still got a couple of problems to go."

"God, your classes suck." Dawson stood and rounded up all the soda glasses and coffee cups to put in the sink while Benji turned everything off and locked the door. Benji's pocket buzzed and he looked up shyly—Darian had texted him a couple of times as they'd been working, and he texted back, smiling. Wasn't too hard to guess who it was.

"Tell her hi for me. Tomorrow's Friday—you two going out afterwards?"

Benji grimaced. "I hate to leave you...."

"No." Dawson shook his head. If he hadn't seen this coming, he wasn't as smart as he liked to think he was. "Have a good time. Tell her I think she's a skanky ho who's stealing my friend."

Benji laughed because Dawson didn't mean it even a little, and then turned off into his room.

Dawson paused at the couch in the darkened living room and looked down at their very quiet guest. He was peaceful in sleep, dark lashes fanning his die-cut cheekbones, but not even his messy hair could make him look boyish. It was like he needed a conscious effort to do that, and Dawson was sort of pleased he'd been the one to make it happen.

"Great. You are a perv."

Dawson flailed backward. "And you're *great* at faking sleep!"

"Go to bed, Dawson. If you want, we can go out tomorrow night since your friend's busy."

Dawson smiled shyly, glad Jared couldn't see him over the back of the couch. "Yeah. All right."

"Your enthusiasm is soporific."

"At this hour, so's fireworks. Good night, Jared."

"Night, Dawson."

Dawson slept surprisingly well, but he woke up and remembered he had a date that night after the show, and suddenly his stomach was buzzing cold like Christmas or the first day of school.

AS A replacement for Topher, Professor Weber got Dawson a goth girl with a ring through her lower lip, chipped black fingernail polish, dyed black hair, and monosyllabic conversational skills.

She was *dynamite* at her job. She was so good Dawson actually asked her if she wanted to go out afterward, "but, not, you know, as a date, because I think I've got a date, and he already hates my male friend so I'm not dating you. But, you know, because you rocked and you were last minute and not everybody can do what you did, and—"

"Tomorrow," Amber grunted. "Tonight, gotta gig at a rave. Later."

The crowd was filing out, and she waited for a good time before she disappeared out of the booth. Dawson watched her go and thought that it took all kinds, for one, and that he was damned glad Darian was Benji's because Amber was a tough cookie to figure out.

And then he forgot completely about Amber, and Darian, and Benji, for that matter.

Jared was walking up the aisle toward him, and it hit Dawson—yeah. Yeah, this really was just for him. The brooding mouth, the die-cut cheekbones, the mercury-blue eyes—whatever *actually* happened at the end of the date, for right now? Dawson was the reason that man was walking his way.

Suddenly Dawson wished he dressed better. Wished he wore more fashionable jeans, wished he knew what kind of T-shirt to wear, just, in general, wished he looked like a man on a date. He hadn't been thinking like a man on a date when he'd gotten dressed that morning. Jared had been gone, his bedding folded neatly on a corner of the couch, a little note left on top that said, *Thank you—I needed this more than you know—J.* So Dawson had been thinking like a man with classes and then a job where nobody saw him. But a man with a date would smell a little bit like aftershave, and Dawson and Benji didn't use any, and a man with a date probably didn't spaz out when his date walked toward him, because he'd be confident that his date was actually excited about seeing him, personally, and not just going out with him because it was a small town and there was nothing else to do.

Dawson was to the point where he couldn't imagine why Jared could possibly opt for Dawson over free cable and a beer—but just like money to go to school or his father's love, he was not going to question it because that seemed like bad luck.

He switched off the lights and closed down the booth, and when Jared poked his head in, Dawson already had his jacket in hand.

"Ready?"

"Almost—gotta hit the house lights on the way out. All the girls gone?"

Jared rolled his eyes. "Yes. Can you not hear the silence?" And again with the subtext, but thankfully, this time it wasn't aimed at Dawson.

"Yeah, I don't know why girls make all that noise—although my copilot was sort of the anti-noise-making girl. Man, you should have not heard her. She talks less than *you*. And I guess she's doing this DJ gig tonight, at a *rave*, and I'm like, who is going to pop out of her body and *talk*, right? And I don't want to go to a rave, have no interest in even *being* at a rave, but suddenly I just want to see this chick in action because it would be like seeing, I don't know, your furniture get up and dance the cha-cha, except more unexpected because I think my shit moves."

"Well, I can no longer hear the silence." *But that's okay, because you are mildly amusing and I am enjoying hearing you ramble on like a Led Zeppelin song.*

"Oh my God!"

"What is it this time?"

"Your subtext changed!"

Jared's smiles were always so quiet, but damned if they weren't deadly. "Dawson, I have no idea what that means. Now do you want to go get dinner or not?"

"Denny's?" Dawson said brightly, walking out of the tech booth and into Jared's space. He was not surprised in the least when Jared put the proprietary "I am the top dog in this relationship" hand in the small of Dawson's back. Well, there *was* a slight height difference, but other than that? Dawson very much got it. If there had been anything dominant about Dawson *at all*, he'd sat on it and killed it in his effort to be able to say and do anything he wanted without accountability. Not in a bad way, but he had a hard time making up his mind about breakfast—he frequently ended up eating *all the things*—

"You don't have something classier than, I don't know, *Denny's?*"

"Jared, it's eleven at night in *Rocklin. Northern California.* We're *lucky* Denny's is open, or our date would be a drive-through burger in my car. Roseville is only about ten minutes away, I guess. They've got a Mel's and that place by In-N-Out and the waterslides. And Lincoln isn't far either—but the fog gets worse when you go out that way, and I hate the galleria."

"You're not selling me on this part of the state, you know that, right?"

Dawson shrugged. "It's really not bad. I mean, it's sort of a bedroom community to Sacramento, but there's malls, and if you've got a day, there's Tahoe up east and the ocean to the west. In Sac proper there's some great places—clubs, music, that sort of thing—but that's about forty minutes away, and I don't know it very well."

He hit the house lights from the foyer and grabbed Jared's hand to lead him out of the darkened theater. It was an instinctive thing, like he'd do with anyone, but Jared laced their fingers together, and suddenly it became an act of intimacy. They walked outside hand in hand, and Dawson wondered that Jared's hand seemed cold and his palm was a little damp.

He squeezed it gently. "Are you nervous?"

"Shut up," Jared said without heat.

"Why would you be nervous? It's me. You've seen me spaz out at least a million times, and you've only known me for three days."

Jared shot him an annoyed look and stopped in the quad in front of the theater. Dawson realized he had to give directions or a plan.

"Here—let's take your car, because my car has a student sticker on it. It can stay overnight and no one will give a shit."

"Yeah, okay." Jared took a left instead of a right, which was where Dawson would have gone, and he automatically seemed more comfortable leading the way. Dawson didn't mind so much. He was good with someone setting a plan. Benji could do it—that thing with the textbook had been classic Benji, and Dawson never saw it coming. It didn't bother him in the least that Jared wanted to take him places.

Dawson had too many ideas at the same time to ever pick just one.

"Ooh!" Dawson slid into the rental car and rubbed the seat appreciatively. "Crushed velour instead of Naugahyde. Power windows! Satellite radio! Nice!"

Jared cocked an eyebrow at him, and for a moment Dawson read his subtext as *Provincial much?* And then, ever so subtly, his teeth glinted in the light from the soda lamp.

"You're easily impressed" was what he actually said, but it sounded like a compliment, and Dawson was reassured.

"I'm not, actually," he answered, not wanting to kill that smile but wanting to be honest. "My dad has money—he's sort of a high-profile lawyer guy, defends the really wealthy innocent—or at least he hopes they're innocent, because he's a nice guy. Anyway, he gave me a choice—a really awesome nice car for my eighteenth birthday, or he'd pay mine and Benji's rent through college so we could room together, even when we both move to Sac State after junior college. I took the piece of shit car because, you know—"

"Benji." Jared sounded thoughtful and not judgmental, and that was an improvement.

"Yeah." A pause in the car seemed to sink through the floorboards. "I'm not in love with him, you know. I mean, I probably *could* be, because he's a good guy, but just so you know. I'm not stupid. He told me in the second grade he didn't want to kiss me. But you know, he never, *ever* didn't have my back."

"Yeah," Jared said, so quietly Dawson almost couldn't hear him. "You forget. Family, right?"

Dawson squinted at him. "How do you forget family? I've got three people—my dad, Benji, and Benji's mom. Give her a month, I'll have Darian, 'cause she's pushy and I think Benji is locked and loaded for an entire life with her. So not that many people, but you know."

Jared pulled into the Denny's parking lot and put the nice car into park. "My sister," he said softly. "My little sister. She...." He looked away. "Down syndrome," he said quietly. "She's got her own nurse and everything. But I haven't seen her since I turned eighteen. They let her get my letters, though. She sends me cards back."

"See?" Dawson said, wanting to pet him or something. His voice ached. Dawson's *chest* ached for him. "Family—you can't really turn your back on it."

Jared seemed to withdraw for a moment, that cloak of "far away" so sudden and so complete that Dawson almost told him to knock that shit off. Then he turned off the car and said, "I'm glad you're smart enough not to fall in love with Benji," before getting out.

Dawson slammed the door and trotted after him. "Hey, why? Why are you glad that—"

Jared stood at the door, holding it open for him, and Dawson was taken again by those old-world manners.

And by the subtext of one raised eyebrow.

"Oh," he said, smiling a little and blushing as he walked past Jared. "Yeah. Yeah. Okay. So, you know. I'm not in love with anyone else either."

"Neither am I," Jared said, practically in his ear. He was so close Dawson could feel the heat from his breath and his chest permeate his jacket and sweatshirt.

"That's good to know," Dawson murmured as they waited to be seated, but Jared only smiled.

Sometimes Dawson thought that because it was so intrinsically awful, Denny's made all of the conversation great. You couldn't swoon over the food, because it was basic food. The décor was basic Denny's, and the employees were just trying to earn a living. The fact that they were nice to you was a benefit, and it was like you let them talk to you as much as you could stand because conversation made what had to be sort of a shit job better. If you were really good, you even made them laugh, because they would forgive you if you'd used up all of your allowance and had only a mediocre tip.

So really, you had to find other stuff to talk about.

Important stuff.

...so why theater, Dawson?

"See, my parents split when I was, like, in the first grade, and Benji's dad died before we met in kindergarten, and we were little kids, and we were *lonely*, like little kids get. So it was just the two of us together, bumping along together like two peas in a box. It was a good box, 'cause the two of us were in it, but it was a box made up a lot of 'I miss my mom' and 'I miss my dad.' And Benji's mom would read to us all the time, and my dad has a library like *whoa*, and there were stories there, good stories, about people who didn't have moms and dads, just like us, and we decided we wanted to *make* the stories. So when they had auditions in middle school, we were so there. Except, you know, Benji can't read a line onstage to save his *life*, and, well, you've met me, right? And we were *awful*, but our teacher—this was the young guy who said our psychic fucking vibrations were freaking him the hell out so he sat us together on like the second day instead of waiting a month like the other stupid teachers—anyway, *this* guy puts us both on props and special effects. We were doing *The Tell-Tale Heart*, right, so special effects were like, Benji going 'ba-bump ba-bump ba-bump' into the microphone to be the heart."

Jared spit out his water, and Dawson grinned triumphantly. You didn't just tell that story to anybody. You had to tell that story to someone who'd laugh.

"It didn't matter, though," he said, catching his breath. "Benji and I were hooked. All those stories we read or told each other—there we were. Making them come true. So that's us and the theater—what about you?"

During a moment's pause, Jared toyed absently with a sugar packet. "It's not a good story," he said softly.

Dawson deflated a little. "Which is code for it's too personal to talk about."

Jared shook his head, still looking at his long, graceful hands. "It's personal, but it's sort of pathetic, really. I like your story better. It's bouncy." He smiled at Dawson then, and for the moment, Dawson could forget the little space around Jared and enjoy the fact that Jared enjoyed the space around Dawson instead.

...so your little sister? What's that like? Benji and I just had each other.

"Well," Jared said, sprinkling vinegar, no oil, on his salad. The waitress had smiled hopefully at him when she'd set it down, and Jared had given her this pleasant smile with no soul. Dawson realized how lucky he was never to have gotten that particular smile. "See, my parents—you know the people who plan everything? Well, I think they planned on two children, and so I was born, and six years later, Sophia came imperfect, and they just... stuck with the plan. So she came along, and... well, especially in the first years, you need nurses and stuff, so there was a lot of this little person with support staff, because it's not like my mom was in the nursery a lot for *me*, right? We met for dinner, that was about it—"

"You were *six*! When I was six, my dad and I were like... glued at the hip from the minute he got home!"

"That sounds terrifying," Jared said frankly. "It's easier when you're on your own. Except, you know, for Sophia. Down syndrome kids—their bodies don't have a lot of muscle tone, and when they hug you...." Jared ate his salad quietly for a few minutes, and when he spoke again, it was like Dawson hadn't been holding his breath as well as a piece of Super Bird in his mouth for what felt like a thousand heartbeats.

"It's special," Jared continued into the silence. "It's special. And I miss it."

"You can't visit her without them?"

Jared shook his head. "No. They've left orders at the home. It's spite, mostly. They know lots of gay people—I think they're just mad at me because I wouldn't conform. They had *one* imperfect child, it was my job to be perfect, and if I wasn't going to do my job... well, there you go."

Dawson finally took another mouthful of sandwich.

"I didn't mean to kill the buzz," Jared said after a minute.

"No, no," Dawson said through his food. "I just keep thinking about how my parents' divorce is really just so passé, you know? I mean, like, it happens to everyone. And that's like the worst thing that ever happened to me. Sort of sad, really."

Jared shook his head and looked sideways at him with a little shy smile on his face that Dawson was learning to treasure. It looked real. It wasn't effusive or huge, but it meant something that Jared let that much happy escape. "No, not sad," he said quietly. "Good. I *like* knowing that people live good lives. You know dancers—it's all drama and pain and bad relationships and obsession. I like knowing that your life didn't hurt. It makes me happy."

Dawson's entire body flushed. For a minute, just eating without choking was sort of the maximum functionality he could achieve.

...so how'd you learn about sex?

Dawson giggled, because that was another good story. "See, the thing is, I came out to my dad with Benji across from me, but Benji sort of outed me to his mom before that happened. Nobody talked about gay people in our school—this little corner of the world, it's like the Northern California Bible Belt, it's weird. I mean, Sacramento, yes, sort of, but Rocklin? Anyway. So middle school again, because that's when boys get boners and start to talk and you get all the films about sex anyway, and Benji and I start talking about condoms and pregnancy, and I say something stupid like, 'Yeah, that's one thing I don't have to worry about!' Now, I *meant* pregnancy, but Benji—I mean you have to remember, his dad *died*. So anything that could result in *death*, that's just something you don't fuck with, right? Anyway, he *literally* grabbed me by the ear and hauled me into his kitchen, where his mom was baking cookies, and said, 'Mom, tell Dawson why gay guys need condoms too!' And I was like, 'Benji, you asshole!' and he whispers, 'She doesn't have to know you're gay!' and she probably heard him, because you've met the guy, secrets are not things with him, but she pretended she didn't and sat me down and fed me cookies and told me about STDs. And after that, I always assumed she knew, and she did, but when I 'came out' came out, it was to my dad."

Jared laughed quietly. He'd ordered a diet soda after his salad, and he sipped it delicately. "I just got the standard state-issue health warnings, Dawson. How could you not know about STDs?"

Dawson sniffed. "Well, I did. But you know kids—you need someone to make it personal so all the other shit sinks in. Right? I mean, when did it become personal to you?"

Jared made a "hmph" sound. "When I was sixteen and my school went cross-country for a performance. We were at a hotel, but the nearest place for breakfast was down the street, so I was in a Starbucks in Chicago when one of the other dancers—he was a little older but not much, and he'd been sort of eyeballing me for the past month—waved, because we were there at the same time. I waved back, thinking I wouldn't have to drink my coffee alone, and he walked by me on the way to the bathroom. He bent over and whispered, 'I've got a lubed condom—meet me in the first stall.'"

Dawson had eaten the Super Bird and a small fudge sundae, and now he thought he might throw them both up. "That's *it*? That's how you lost your virginity?"

"I… I hadn't been home in two years, and I was starting to realize I didn't have one. The boy I'd been crushing on had just graduated and moved in with his boyfriend, and it was just so hard to get to know anybody else. It… it was just—I wanted something to happen."

"So that happened in a bathroom?" Yup. Still felt like throwing up.

"He's married now—he never really looked me in the eye after we did it, and I never said a word to him about it."

Dawson shuddered. "God. Yeah. See, I need it to mean something. I mean, yeah, I know it's old-fashioned, but if I was...." Dawson looked at him, suddenly realizing that this conversation meant something, and it meant something important, and that they were on a date and that sex was where dates often headed. "When I sleep with someone, I need it to mean something. I need to know someone would look me in the eye and be there the next day, and the next week, and the next month. I'm not stupid—I know it doesn't always mean forever, but you have to at least think it *could* be forever. There's a *possibility* of forever before you even touch, or you're just touching to hurt yourself. I can't be just a quick fuck in the bathroom."

Suddenly they weren't looking at their food or their hands or their sodas or the sugar packets. Suddenly they were looking each other in the eye and waiting for the actual words, no subtext needed, or the night would end right there.

"I wouldn't do that to you, Dawson."

"I wasn't saying you... well, I'd hope you wouldn't. But how would this work? You live in West Hollywood. I live here."

Jared looked away. "Texting, I guess. Phone calls. Skype. I visit you when I can. I...."

They had gravitated closer on the cheap vinyl seats, until their asses and thighs were mushed together, and when Jared turned away, Dawson really couldn't see his face. He leaned his head on Jared's shoulder instead, and he could feel when Jared turned back toward him, feel his breath in Dawson's rumpled hair, feel the ghosting of firm lips on his temple.

"I swear," he whispered quietly. "I swear it wouldn't be a one-and-done over a toilet, Dawson. I swear I'll make it sweet."

Dawson struggled to sit up next to him. "Me too," he said, nodding. "You can stay the night and everything."

Jared's lips quirked up. "Are you sure Benji won't greet me in the morning with a shotgun?"

"Not if you make him french toast. He'll totally sell me out for someone who cooks."

"Both mornings?" Jared asked quietly, and Dawson had that cold feeling in his bowels, his thighs, his stomach. *This is going to happen,* he thought. *This man wants to touch me. A lot.*

"Well, you know. On the second morning you can make pancakes."

"Deal," Jared said softly. "Let me go get my stuff from the hotel."

Dawson waited in the car when he did that, thinking about Jared all alone in the hotel room and how awful that felt. Jared came out with a small duffel bag, and for the first time since Dawson had almost fallen on top of him on the stage, Dawson got a sense of how alone he had been—not just on this trip, but for maybe most of his life.

They drove quietly back to the apartment and climbed the stairs in the cold-concrete silence of the complex. Benji and Darian were on the couch when they walked in, watching *Nick and Nora's Infinite Playlist.*

"Oh no!" Darian whined when Jared walked in. "Which one of us gets the couch?"

Dawson winked at her but couldn't summon a grin. "You do. Jared'll sleep in my room."

Benji's eyes widened, but when he turned toward Jared, they were narrowed. Narrowed and flinty. "I know where his dad keeps his gun," he said, his voice perfectly serious. "Ouch! Darian!"

"Leave them alone," she said, softly. "I want Dawson to like me when it's my turn to sleep in your bed."

Benji smiled slackly, sort of stupid. "Is, uhm, that gonna happen?"

"Maybe."

"Soon?"

"Maybe."

"How come now that Dawson's gonna—*ouch!*"

"'Cause that's Dawson's business. Now shut up. You're missing the movie."

Benji wasn't done yet. He disentangled himself from Darian and stood up, grabbed Dawson's shirt, and hauled him into the hallway. "You're ready for this?" he asked seriously.

Dawson tried not to whine. "You lost your virginity in high school!"

"I was ready! I dated that girl for a year!"

"Well, if I was gonna throw it away for the sake of an orgasm, I would have slept with six guys before now," Dawson told him. "I've had offers!"

"Topher doesn't count."

Dawson grimaced and rubbed under his nose with the edge of his forefinger. "Three guys."

"Name them." Benji's forehead wrinkled in a way Dawson *swore* he'd learned from his dad.

"Leon Minton in senior year, Greg White last year, and Alex Jeffries—"

"He's gay?"

"Claims he's bi—he wanted me to be his experiment."

Benji's forehead wrinkle evened out. "He's cute. I mean, I could see the appeal."

Something in Dawson relaxed. "It's not just because he's asking."

"Or because he's lonely."

"Or because he's lonely."

Benji shrugged. "You got your—"

"If you ask me if I've got condoms, I won't get it up for a week."

"Bullshit. You whack off twice a day as it is."

Dawson's mouth opened and he sucked in a great lungful of dry air. "How did you—"

"You're loud, Dawson. We're gonna turn the TV up in about fifteen minutes—let that be your cue."

"Jesus."

But Benji was walking back to the living room. He looked at Darian and made little "C'mon, you know you want this!" gestures until she straightened on the couch and let him slide in behind her. He wrapped his arms around her and pulled the afghan on the back of the couch down so they could snuggle. Jared was sitting on the opposite arm of the couch, and he looked up from the screen to meet Dawson's eyes across the room.

"I've got a TV in here," Dawson said, and it was totally true—a small-screen television his dad had gotten for him when he was fourteen. But that wasn't what he really meant, because what he *really* meant was making his mouth dry and his throat shrivel and his nuts freeze and contract and swell and ache all at the same time.

"Yeah," Jared said, and he deliberately grabbed his duffel bag and walked across the living room and into Dawson's bedroom.

Dawson shut the door behind him, and when he turned around, all ready to find Conan on cable and sit in awkward silence, Jared grabbed his chin, suddenly so close Dawson's breath trammeled up in his chest because he was afraid there wasn't room for both of them to take oxygen at once.

"Dawson?"

"Yeah?"

"I promised." And Dawson closed his eyes, so when Jared's lips touched him, that was the only thing in the world, the sweet glide of tender skin on tender skin.

Dawson gasped and Jared let himself in, sliding his tongue between Dawson's lips like that happened all the time. Dawson let him, and sucked on it a little, just because it was there. He felt Jared smile and pull his tongue back.

"Was that bad?" He sounded anxious. It was pathetic, but although he'd kissed before, he just wasn't—

"Okay," Jared said. "Ground rules."

"Great. I suck at rules."

"I figured. But first rule. If it's bad, I'll tell you. If it would hurt you, don't do it. If you'd like it, give it a try. And if all we do is make out and fall asleep...." Jared's smile, shy, devastating, peeked out from under those rectangular eyebrows.

"Yeah?"

"That'll be good too."

Dawson smiled moonily. "Awesome."

Jared's palms felt dry against his cheeks, rasping faintly on the stubble, and his mouth on Dawson's pressed firm again, in charge. Dawson let out a breathy moan.

And Jared growled, pinning Dawson against the door and diving into the kiss like a tiger into an infinity pool. Dawson opened for him, content, breathless, pushing his skin through his clothes to be the body Jared swam in.

Jared reached behind him, cupped his ass, pulled him forward. Dawson could only cling to his sweatshirt, shaking, as Jared slid his hands, palms down, under Dawson's T-shirt, smoothing across the plains of his back, the slight softness of his stomach, the gentle flex of his pecs.

Suddenly Dawson realized that Jared—*Jared*—was going to be looking at *his* scrawny, underdeveloped, nonmuscular body.

He grabbed at Jared's hands, trying to bat them away.

Jared pulled them out of his shirt voluntarily, leaned his forehead against Dawson's, and caught his breath. "What?" he asked, placing a little microkiss on the corner of Dawson's mouth.

"You're going to see me," Dawson breathed, not sure if he could put voice to the horror that entailed.

"I've seen you already," Jared muttered, full lips quirking. "You have the whitest ass I've ever seen." He kissed the side of Dawson's neck. "And the slenderest back." And a kiss at Dawson's jaw. "And these hollows under your clavicles." Dawson turned his head for the kisses behind his ear. "And your nipples are dark, dark pink."

Dawson pulled back, shocked. "You *saw*?"

Jared nodded urgently and then took his mouth again, and Dawson took greedily to the wet, meaty smacking of lips, teeth, and tongue. He wanted it… *craved* it. *Needed* Jared's taste in his mouth, his touch… oh God. His touch.

"You can touch me more," he panted into Jared's neck. Then he slid his hands up along Jared's ribs and shuddered, because the feeling of that skin under his palms, the corrugated muscle—that was enough to send cold sizzles up his spine.

Jared slid his hands down the back of Dawson's jeans and cupped his ass again, and Dawson whined and thrust his groin forward because the pressure on his ass felt so good.

"God, you're easy," Jared muttered, but since his next kiss was deeper and more urgent than the one before it, Dawson hoped that was a compliment. Something must have been going right, because he was being maneuvered, turned, walked backward, until he ended up against his bed, pushed down until he was lying flat with Jared on top of him, holding most of his weight on his knees between Dawson's spread thighs.

Jared scooted lower and shoved his sweatshirt up until Dawson's nipples puckered in the air, and then Jared bent his head and kissed the soft skin above Dawson's navel.

"Oh!"

"Sh...."

He kissed more of Dawson's concave stomach, up to his ribs, and oh God weren't they sensitive! For a moment (a horrifying moment) Dawson squirmed, afraid he'd start giggling, that it would tickle him instead of arouse him, but Jared wasn't stupid. One wiggle and Jared popped up and locked his mouth over Dawson's nipple and suckled hard.

"Oh... oh God!"

"Mmff?"

"I'm gonna... I might come, God, just from that—"

Jared slid his hand down Dawson's pants and grabbed his—oh man, grabbed his *dick* under his underwear and squeezed, and stroked, and squeezed and stroked and pulled some more on his nipple and—

Dawson clapped his hand over his mouth to muffle his scream of climax in what must have been the most humiliatingly short distance from making out to orgasm of all time.

Jared's hand grew hot and slick against his cock, and Dawson let out a whimper as the squeezing started to hurt. Jared pulled out of Dawson's pants and rested his palm, slimy and sticky, on Dawson's stomach as he leaned a sweaty forehead against Dawson's shoulder.

Dawson covered his eyes with one hand and held the back of Jared's head gently with the other.

"I'm so sorry," he muttered.

"Damn."

"I didn't think—"

"You must be the horniest man on the planet."

"I'm saying."

"Wow."

"I'm embarrassed, can you not see that?"

Jared surprised him then with both a warm, dirty chuckle and a quick suckle on Dawson's nipple. "Don't be embarrassed," he said gruffly. "And look at me."

Dawson lowered the hand over his eyes. He couldn't help it. Jared's pupils were blown, leaving a thin ring of technicolor turquoise around the center.

Dawson caught his breath. "You still wanna...?" Oh boy!

"I wonder how many times we can make *that* happen before the end of the night!" Jared breathed, and Dawson grinned at him.

"Wanna see?"

"Oh yeah!"

Dawson reached under his pillow and pulled out a towel, and the dry arching of Jared's eyebrows indicated he knew what that towel was for. He took it and wiped off his hand, and instead of jumping right back into the tonsil hockey, he just started kissing Dawson gently again.

Dawson closed his eyes and relaxed back into the kiss. When Jared started unfastening his jeans (no belt today—go Dawson, you aced Sex Readiness 101!), Dawson didn't protest. Mostly what he did was wrap his long, bony fingers around Jared's extraordinary biceps and hang on for the ride.

Kiss after kiss, each one from a slightly different angle, each one going deep and long until Dawson felt fused to him, attached at the mouth, penetrated, invaded, skin-to-skin a part of this boy... man.

The shock of air as it hit Dawson's groin made him pull back, lose that attachment, and he missed it. There was rough wiping around his cock and his abdomen and then Jared saying urgently in his ear, "Kick off your shoes and take off your shirt, okay?"

"Yeah, okay," Dawson mumbled. He stood up and kicked off his clothes and noticed Jared was doing the same. Oh God.

Naked.

He dove under the covers and pulled them up to his chin and buried his nose in the pillow.

"Yeah," Jared muttered, almost to himself. "That's going to work."

Dawson risked a look at him: he'd stripped down to his boxer briefs and was neatly folding his jeans, his T-shirt, and his sweatshirt into a little pile that he set down on Dawson's gaming chair.

He was going to say something sarcastic. Something like *Should I clean up my puddle-of-come boxers, or can we just assume I'll be stepping on those in the morning?* But then he got a real look at Jared's body.

The waxed, the ripped, the perfect V from shoulders to hips—that he understood.

That his cock was large and uncircumcised, well, he'd already guessed that.

But the whole package... oh God. All together, tanned smooth skin, muscles, right down to the chiseled granite of his crack-a-walnut ass, and that—oh my God, that was a naked cock!

Oh Jesus.

Dawson pulled the covers over his head, hid his face in his pillow, and didn't listen to what Jared had to say after that.

The light changed in his little cocoon under the covers, grew darker, and he felt a rustling at his side as the mattress sank. Warm hands slid across his shoulder. Jared's breath fanned his skin along with a soft kiss. He relaxed a little and sighed, and then Jared moved to the back of his neck.

Dawson groaned softly, shivers coursing his spine, and Jared whispered in his ear. "Is it the body or the shy?"

"Do I have to pick?"

"No. But if you keep your eyes closed the whole time, you'll never get used to the body." Jared punctuated this with a little nibble of Dawson's earlobe, and Dawson couldn't help it. His entire body stretched out because he *had* to move, and he *had* to take Jared's mouth. Oh jeez, he tasted like the other half of Dawson's soul. Dawson wanted more, pushed the kiss, stroked inside Jared's mouth, and Jared groaned like Dawson was doing it right.

Dawson kept kissing him, ran his hands up the smooth planes of his back, down his (oh God, so tight!) ass, down his flank. When Jared wrapped his leg around Dawson's hip and started thrusting against Dawson's groin, just the fact that their cocks were touching, being squeezed by their bodies, was enough to make Dawson hard and aching and needy all over again.

Jared broke away long enough to whisper, "Touch me!" and Dawson wanted to so badly, he didn't even think about being nervous. He stuck his hand between them and seized Jared in his fist, stroking softly at first. Jared let out a greedy whine. "Harder... harder, rougher, faster... please, Dawson—*yes*!"

He was thick and fat, and stroking him was amazing, almost like Dawson could feel it in his own cock, because Jared reacted immediately, frenzied and joyful. He groaned softly and sucked on Dawson's collarbone hard enough to hurt, but the sharpness was *glorious*, and Dawson whimpered.

"Touch *me*!" he commanded, and Jared's arm was harder to fit but *so* worth it. His hand around Dawson's cock was... oh God... *wow*!

This time it was slower, stronger. First his *entire body* washed cold, and then his balls jerked hard under his ass and that pressure around his base increase, the stroking on his crown, and it all... all *exploded* and....

Their mouths met, and they groaned into each other, both of them shuddering and spasming, the light behind Dawson's eyes so bright it blinded him to everything but the gorgeous, toe-curling orgasm that was the end-all and the be-all and the now.

Coming down was hard. For one thing, he didn't want to let go of Jared's cock because the mess of both of them was *fantastic*.

For a moment their breath echoed harshly in their ears, and then Jared released his grip on Dawson's cock and said apologetically, "Uhm... Dawson?"

"Yeah?"

"Let go."

"Oh yeah, sorry."

It was hard to do. Jared's softening erection slid silken and sweet in his hand—he wanted to stroke it more and kiss it and taste it and—

"Dawson!"

"Sorry! Sorry!" He let go. "Uhm, can I touch it more later?"

Jared laughed softly into the space between his chin and his chest. "That would be wonderful. But maybe wait a little, you think?"

Dawson nodded, breathing hard into Jared's hair. "Yeah. What do you think we should do between that, you think?"

Jared's laugh puffed warm and fluttery against the hollow of his neck. "This is good. Here, where's the towel?"

They cleaned off and tucked the towel back under the pillows and then resumed that position, with Jared huddled against Dawson's chest and Dawson's arm thrown over his waist. It was odd—Dawson felt protective and strong that way, and he was reminded harshly of how vulnerable Jared truly was. He tightened his arm and clutched Jared closer to his chest. Jared didn't object, although it was probably hard to breathe.

"Is it always like this?" Dawson whispered. "This buzz in my stomach and my chest—how happy I am to hold you? Does it always feel like this?"

Jared lifted his face in the dark, his lower lip full and swollen from kisses, his eyes shiny. "No," he said soberly. "No. This is special."

Dawson grinned at him, delighted. "Yeah, I thought so."

Jared returned the grin, only his version looked a little quieter, a little more bemused. He studied Dawson's face in the faint light that came under the door from the hallway. The television had gotten louder for a while, but now Dawson couldn't hear it at all, so he thought maybe Darian had gone home or gone into Benji's room. He found the thought did nothing but make him happy for his friend.

Dawson's grin faded. "What?" he asked, suddenly caught by the mood of quiet in the darkened house. "What's that look?"

"It *is* special." His voice throbbed like the thought made him sad, and Dawson felt the urge to comfort him. This time Dawson led the kiss, and Jared opened for him. Dawson kissed down his neck, tasted the salt of his sweat, licked his collarbone, licked cautiously at his nipple. Jared's breath caught, and he arched his shoulders, urging Dawson to take more. That pop of flesh in Dawson's mouth, the tickle of the nipple against his tongue—it was wondrous and amazing and addictive.

Dawson suckled harder.

Jared let out a gasp and tangled his fingers in Dawson's hair, simultaneously pushing Dawson down and tugging him away.

Dawson split the difference and went for the other nipple, and this time it wasn't a gasp, it was a *groan.* Dawson covered Jared's body with his own, being very careful to put his knees on the mattress and not on Jared's sensitive places. Jared arched up into him urgently. *He's hungry to touch me.*

It was an *amazing* thought. Dawson made sure his chest and stomach made full-body contact as much as possible, and when Jared's noises got frenzied to the point of pain, Dawson pulled away. He kissed pecs and ribs and a washboard stomach, being sure to suckle the flesh gently and tease with his teeth. Jared let out a whine when Dawson got to the point where he could feel Jared's erection pushing near his throat, and Dawson looked up over all those rippling muscles and clenching sinews. *C'mon, Jared, look at me. Tell me I get to do this.*

And this time Jared read *his* subtext.

"No man in the history of ever has turned down a blowjob," he gritted.

Dawson grinned at him, and when Jared lowered his hand, Dawson fully expected it to get all bossy and directive in his hair.

Jared rested it on his cheek instead. "Firm but not painful," he said, his voice gentle. "Teeth are bad, tongue is good."

Dawson's grin blew up salaciously, and he opened his mouth wide, said, "*Nom!*" and dove right in.

The whole thing in his mouth, all at once. He kept his teeth shielded and sucked on it hard, recognizing the tang of Jared's earlier climax and the salt of sweat. Jared made a muffled sound, and Dawson looked up to see he was muffling his moan in his palm.

The idea that it felt *that* good made Dawson want to try harder.

He pulled back to let the head cool in the air and wrapped his fist around the base—his finger and thumb could touch, but only because his own fingers were the sort of long ones with big knuckles that came with the long gangly body.

Other than that, Jared's cock was pale and straight and *not* nine inches long, but plenty long enough to be a little intimidating. Dawson stroked up with his fist and watched the extra skin lap over the crown, and thought that must feel *amazing*, so he did it again. Jared made a little grunt—the good kind—and Dawson didn't even look up at him before he covered his teeth again, made his mouth slick with spit, and sucked in the crown while pumping down to the base.

That got another soft grunt, and Dawson was suddenly *greedy* for it, for the taste and the feel and the sounds—*all* the things about this experience were awesome, and Dawson wanted them *all* in his mouth, in his hand, against his skin.

What followed was a loud, slurpy, noisy suckfest that echoed in his ears and tangled with his breathing as he tried to suck and squeeze and mouth and lick *all the cock*. Jared's noises heightened, grew more muffled, and when his legs twitched too much he did Dawson a solid by bracing his feet on the mattress, which was *great* because it spread his thighs and gave Dawson better access. *Whoo boy!* Dawson licked his balls, ignoring the surprisingly soft fur, and then, delicately, took one of them in his mouth. Jared arched off the bed, and Dawson felt something hot and liquid spurting over the fist stroking the cock.

Yes!

Dawson lunged up and over, opening his mouth, tightening his lips, sucking Jared into his throat with reckless abandon for taste or gag reflexes or Jared's whispered, "But Dawson, I'm... *oh hell*!"

And Jared was spurting down his throat, hot and thick—not as salty as Dawson expected, and it slid down his throat sort of slimily, but not bad. Dawson kept squeezing and sucking until Jared said, "Getting tender," and then it was hard to back off.

Dawson grinned up at him, expecting praise, because *hello*, orgasm down Dawson's throat, but instead Jared looked troubled, almost like he was going to cry.

"What? What'd I do?"

"Dawson, you weren't supposed to swallow."

Dawson grimaced. "Well, yeah, but statistically there's less than a percentage of a chance any sort of disease could be carried by—"

"I don't *care.* It's too big a chance—I need to be tested and it's a stupid risk and what if it wasn't me? I use condoms, what if—"

Dawson grunted in annoyance and hauled himself up to flop next to him so they could have this naked conversation civilized. "Jared?"

"Yeah?"

"Do you *always* use condoms?"

"Yes. Yes, I do."

"Then maybe—just maybe—you go get tested, because you should anyway, right? And if something pops, *then* you come unglued. Me? I just gave my first blowjob. It was a success. I'm gonna lie here and bask." Dawson stretched languorously, flush with pride in his new accomplishment, and the weight of Jared's head on his shoulder was a welcome response to his invitation.

"You're very wise for a virgin," Jared admitted. His voice sounded sour, but his head on Dawson's shoulder? That was so, so sweet.

"Ex-virgin," Dawson hummed. "Penetration is unnecessary."

Jared's laugh sounded at his side, sleepy and confused. "Well, when we get to that, maybe you'll change your mind."

Dawson was getting sleepy himself. It was now two in the morning, and he figured they could call the night done and good. "You mean it?" he mumbled. "There'll be more?"

Jared turned his head just enough to kiss Dawson's shoulder and barely, subversively, lick a little sweat from it. "Yeah," Jared whispered. "You were very clear, Dawson. This didn't come as a one-time thing."

"Excellent." Dawson covered a yawn with his free hand, cocked his hips so he was angled toward Jared, and smacked his lips, because, well, he was making a conscious decision to fall asleep with come in his mouth. He decided it was something he could live with and smiled to himself as Jared's soft breathing filled his bedroom.

Time for good little ex-virgins to fall asleep.

JARED WAS there when he woke up in the morning, curled up on his side in a tight little ball.

Benji was knocking on the door quietly. "Dawson! Dawson, you awake?"

"Not so much, no."

Dawson stumbled out of bed and realized, oh hell, he was naked. He looked around the room wildly, found a towel on the floor, and wrapped it around his waist, thinking, *No!* on the boxer shorts next to the bed.

He cracked the door and peeked out at Benji, who looked tired and casual in jeans and a sweatshirt. "Okay, so I'm a little awake. What's up?"

"I'm taking Darian home—"

Dawson looked past Benji and saw that there were no covers on the couch. He raised his eyebrows, and Benji rolled his eyes. "What— I've known her for *months*, you've known this guy for *hours*. Don't judge."

"I'm not judging," Dawson said mildly. "I'm just wondering when the black hole is going to open up and swallow the earth. We *both* got lucky—do you realize the *odds* of that?"

Benji's eyes got wide, and he shuddered. "Yeah, I'm gonna go throw some salt over my shoulder. Anyway, I'm going to take her home and, uhm—"

"Dodge her father's guns?"

"Yeah. You got bail money?"

"My dad's a lawyer."

"Aces."

Dawson quirked up one side of his mouth in sympathy, thinking maybe he got off easy in this department. Nobody was going to accuse him of debauching their little boy. "So this needed a newsflash why?"

"'Cause I need to know if you want me to bring donuts back or if you'd rather I spend a long time at the grocery store?"

Dawson turned around and watched Jared's chest rise and fall for a few moments. "I think he needs family," he said, so quietly Benji had to duck his head to hear.

"Donuts it is," Benji murmured, and Dawson smiled a quick thanks before closing the door, ditching the towel, and crawling back in bed to plaster himself along Jared's back.

"Whatwuzat?" Jared mumbled, and Dawson nuzzled his neck. His hair was a little long, and with the product sweated out of it, it ran sort of wild. Dawson wondered how soft it would be when it was clean.

"Call for donuts. I said yes."

"I can't eat donuts. I'm a *dancer*. Ask him for fruit."

"We've got cottage cheese and applesauce."

"Deal. Thanks."

Dawson refrained from telling him that the only reason they had cottage cheese was because Benji had been on a high-protein low-carb diet right up until he started losing muscle mass as well. It seemed like extraneous information.

"Why do you have cottage cheese?" Jared asked, rolling over to his back.

Dawson smiled at him, so goofy-happy his cheeks hurt. "For Benji's six-pack diet."

"How'd that work?" Jared was blinking hard, trying to wake up in the pleasant darkness of the room, and Dawson ducked in for a quick peck on his cheek.

"Outstanding. He lost twenty pounds, his stomach muscles popped like corn, and he snarled at anyone who looked at him funny. I told him to gain back the weight and become a human being again. He compromised. He does more crunchies and eats more pizza. Works for me."

Jared's sleepy smile felt warm and open. "What about the applesauce?" he asked lazily as he reached a languid hand back to tangle in Dawson's hair and pull him forward for a kiss.

Dawson kept his mouth pressed tightly closed and said, "It helps us poop," through his teeth.

Jared's laugh tickled, but Dawson still didn't want to open his mouth.

"I don't care about morning breath," Jared said softly, and finally Dawson smiled against Jared's lips before he opened up for the kiss.

This time Jared gave the blowjob. It was amazing. Dawson took notes. He wanted to practice these things with Jared as much as possible before he had to go.

THEY SHOWERED together, and that was new too—slick skin and soap, the awkward intimacy of Jared's hands on his body when he wasn't expecting them, the feeling of being completely, irrevocably naked with someone in the daylight.

It was worth it to see the way Jared's smile lit his face, took the grave watchfulness from his eyes, made him a little younger.

By the time Benji got there with the donuts, they were sitting on opposite ends of the couch, twining their legs, watching *Phineas and Ferb* on basic cable.

Benji flopped on the floor in front of Dawson and held up the box—Dawson took the sprinkles, looked at Jared one more time and took his refusal for what it was, then handed the box back down to Benji.

Besides a break for milk, they spent three hours doing that, flopping around on the couch in various places. When Jared fell asleep on top of Dawson, head on his chest, body tucked between Dawson's and the couch, Dawson met his friend's eyes.

"You were right," Benji said quietly. "About the family. If he comes back? I think you should take him to meet your dad."

If he comes back.

Dawson wrapped his arm more securely around Jared's shoulder and tried not to doubt. He shouldn't doubt. Jared had shown him so much faith, hanging at Dawson's apartment like this, eating his cottage cheese, taking him for his heart and not his awkward limbs and infodump speech patterns.

He'd come back. Dawson could have faith too. In fact, the world had never *really* let Dawson down. Maybe it was Dawson's job to keep the faith, even when Jared couldn't.

THAT NIGHT, Jared danced.

He was so lovely, so gorgeous, Dawson couldn't put a name to how beautiful he was—not divinely, not spectacularly, not beautifully. He just *danced.*

He looked like a soul clothed in muscle.

In his final bows, he made one of those little rolling gestures with his hands again, and Dawson *knew* it was for him. To his right, he heard a suspicious sound. He looked and there it was again, and Amber, with black hair and black polish and black lipstick, wiped a hand under her eyes.

Dawson jerked his gaze back to the stage, and next to him Amber said, "Something that pretty—is that really *yours*?"

"For the rest of the night," Dawson said, and it wasn't until he spoke that he felt the tightness in his throat, the thickness in his voice, and he thanked God for testosterone or he'd be in as bad a place as Amber.

"You enjoy the fuckin' night," she grunted. "And don't worry about asking me out—I'll do takedown instead."

Dawson looked at her, surprised. "That's nice of you—you don't have to—"

She glared at him. "My whole life, you ever think I'll get to touch something like that?"

Dawson shrugged. "I don't see why not. You seem like a perfectly decent human being to me."

Amber cast him a sideways look crusted in eyeliner and mascara, much of which was still freely running down her face. "Yeah?"

They stopped for a moment while Dawson brought up the house lights and Amber killed the sound.

"Yeah," Dawson said. "In fact, you know—here." He pulled out the card he'd had made when he'd become a guild member and had started looking for gigs. "You know. Call me. Benji and me, we've got an apartment, we hang—give me a call, we can do movie night."

Amber smiled at him—a real smile. "You're a good guy. No wonder you get angel-man down there." She wiped her face on her shoulder then, and fortunately she was wearing a black The Clash T-shirt, because you couldn't see a thing.

Dawson compromised with her and *helped* with the takedown, and Jared sat with Darian and watched them. They chatted quietly, and every now and then Dawson looked over and saw that she was laughing. So Jared *could* be social with his friends—good to know.

Benji ran along the catwalk like the athlete he was and Dawson held the ropes, and they took down the backdrop. Amber helped him roll the giant canvas up for storage while Benji lowered the light bank to the catwalk so they could pull the gels off to go in the same place. They didn't use any actual set or props this go round, so it took them about an hour, but when they were done, they were done.

"So," Darian said brightly, "Denny's?"

For a moment Dawson thought of protesting. They'd *done* Denny's. But then he thought of that bevy of ballet dancers running out of the theater giggling and hyper, and of Jared not joining them because they were local and he was getting on a plane the next day.

"Yeah, for a few—Jared, you okay with that?"

Jared rolled his eyes, but he smiled at the same time. "Next time I show up, I'd *better* see something besides the damned Denny's!"

Benji grimaced. "Yeah—sorry about that. The fog's a bitch this time of year. The only reason you had an audience is because, well, you're *you*. You come back in a month and it's really nice—we'll take you out to the lake or the river. There's parks and shit. It's worth it to come back, honest."

Jared's smile grew thoughtful, and he nodded. "I'll take you up on that." He looked directly at Dawson. "I promise."

There was something addictive about talking in Denny's—everybody had new stories to tell, and even Amber opened up a little. They all got jittery from too much coffee and giggly enough to make little sand sculptures in emptied packets of sweetener.

They talked about camping trips with family or the time Benji's mom spotted the mouse running through the kitchen and Benji and Dawson spent two hours crawling around the floor on their hands and knees while she sat up next to the sink and ate carrot sticks and told them where she *thought* it might have run. Amber told them about the rave where the bad X had gone around and everyone had gone on a really bad trip while she was playing "Ziggy Stardust," and Darian told about the client who loved exercising but couldn't lose any weight because she snuck chocolates in the pocket of her sweat suit.

They broke up around one and invited Amber to come sleep on the couch. By then, the fog was so damned thick Dawson couldn't have found the apartment if he hadn't recognized the color of the lights around the entrance (they were yellow as opposed to the standard city pink), and Amber agreed just because she lived in Lincoln and the fog only got worse on the drive out.

They were all tired—everyone pretty much split to their rooms after Amber was set up on the couch. Dawson and Jared undressed down to their boxers and dove under the covers in the coldish apartment, and Dawson laughed as Jared buried his cold nose in Dawson's neck.

More snuggling, more giggling, more chilly hands moving over skin. It wasn't so much of a turn-on as it was getting to know each other, and Dawson loved that. Finally they were situated, Jared's head at Dawson's chest, Dawson's leg thrown over Jared's thighs. They were as close as they could get without penetration, and Dawson was pretty sure that wasn't going to happen.

"So," Dawson asked uncertainly, "it was okay? Amber, Denny's, talking."

"You have nice friends," Jared murmured in a stunning lack of commitment.

"But...."

"I thought you liked sex."

Dawson laughed softly, feeling like the older, wiser one. "I do," he said. "I love it. I want more of it. But I want you to come back. You can get more, better sex with anyone. But you can only get the whole Dawson experience when you're here."

Jared pulled back, and Dawson could see his eyes narrow in the darkness. "You manipulative little shit!"

Dawson grinned. "You liked it, right? The Dawson experience? You want more of it, right?"

Jared sighed, his breath warm against Dawson's neck. "I get what you're offering me," he said after a moment. "You're saying you want me to come back. And that this will be here. You, your friends, this weird little corner of the world—"

"It's actually really boring," Dawson told him in the interest of full disclosure.

"So it's only you that makes it weird?" But he was kidding— Dawson could tell.

"Pretty much. What time does your flight take off tomorrow?"

Jared grunted, probably because the change of subject left him dizzy. "Twelve thirty."

"Too bad. If it left later, we'd take you to lunch with my dad—"

"With your *dad*!" Jared sat up in bed, the comforter sliding down his magnificent chest. His nipples darkened and popped in the cold, and Dawson reached out to touch one, because he knew now it would spring back under his thumb.

Jared batted his hand away and Dawson glared at him, annoyed.

"Yes, with my dad. We wouldn't have to tell him we were having sex—we'd just tell him you're a friend, and he'd be happy to see you. He'd probably light up, because he's always trying new recipes for Sundays—sometimes they're really tasty and sometimes they're just… ick. Last month Benji and I ordered out for pizza, 'cause damn, I don't know what it was supposed to be, but edible ain't it. Anyway, Benji's gonna bring Darian if they're still together, and you know…." Dawson stopped for a minute and looked up as Jared eased his way back down onto the bed, giving Dawson furtive, cagey looks as he went. "Yes. I want you to come back. I'll be a whole new world—" He started to warble, badly. "I can show you a life, shining, shivering, *splen-did*—"

Jared pounced on him, clapping a hand over his mouth and convulsing with laughter. "Jesus, God, no singing! I'm coming back! I promised! I'll even visit"—his shudder was obviously unforced and unfaked for drama—"God, your father—just don't launch into song!"

Dawson grinned under his hand and stuck out a tongue to lick the center of his palm. Jared just glared at him, so Dawson began to move his tongue sensuously, dragging it across the roughened skin and around the soft webbing of his thumb and forefinger. Jared caught his breath, and his hold across Dawson's mouth slackened. Dawson pulled back and sucked his entire thumb into his mouth, and then *really* went to town, suckling, nibbling, laving, until Jared ground up against his thigh, panting quietly in the dark.

He pulled his thumb out with a little pop and took his mouth hard and relentlessly, and Dawson kissed back. And again, and again, and again, until they were both sweaty and tingly and aching. When they arched into each other's hands for a slow, seamless climax, Dawson could swear he felt Jared's heartbeat in the throb of his cock, and he couldn't tell which whimpers were his.

They panted together, come-sticky and huddling for warmth in the aftermath, and Jared spoke harshly. "Dawson?"

"Yeah?"

"Since I'm coming back, could you promise me something?"

"My heart? My soul? My kidney? A limb?"

"Your *ass*? God, I want to… just *everything* with you. Time alone? For a plane ticket from LA—is that too much to ask?"

"Yeah, no." Dawson nodded, thinking Benji would give him this. "Not too much to ask. I want that too."

"Good. Good." Jared tucked his face against Dawson's neck then, and Dawson thought sadly that he wanted to get used to falling asleep like this. It wouldn't take long at all.

HE WOKE up the next morning to the sound of Jared in the shower. By the time he'd thrown on some clean boxers and some sweats, Jared was out and Dawson had started coffee and scrambled eggs. Benji stumbled out of bed and started moving around the kitchen, taking on toast and fruit, and by the time Jared came out of the bedroom, the girls were yawning and sitting at the table nursing coffee.

Jared's bemused look as he came out, duffel packed, shoes on, jacket over one arm, would have been funny if it hadn't broken Dawson's heart a little.

"You got time," Dawson said, looking at the microwave. "You don't need to leave until ten."

Jared looked too, seemed to shrug, and folded himself like a cat in the seat next to Darian. Dawson grabbed the mug that said *Fruits, nuts, and flakes—what every growing boy needs for breakfast!* with an assortment of pretty young men baring their asses with technicolor glee, and filled it with coffee. He set it down in front of Jared with a kiss on the cheek and watched, relieved, as Jared picked it up and nursed it lovingly, as though Dawson had given him the elixir of life.

"That's revolting," Amber muttered. "But it gives me hope."

"I didn't get a kiss with *my* coffee," Darian pouted, and Benji was *right there* with her plate of eggs and a full-court press on the kisser.

Jared's eyes went dinner-plate wide, and if he'd been a little asleep before, he was wide-awake now. "Oh my God. I'm trapped in an eighties sitcom."

Dawson grimaced. "No, no—don't say that. It means some character we don't know has to die to give the show depth."

Jared spit out his coffee, and Dawson stared at him. "What are you so upset about? We've *slept* together—not only are *you* safe from the minor-character curse, but I'm pretty sure I don't have to worry about dragons anymore. It's win/win."

Jared blinked, one of those quiet smiles reaching the corner of his mouth. "Was there a dragon problem *before* I spent the night?"

Dawson shrugged and brought over two plates of eggs, then set one down in front of Jared and the other in front of Amber. "Not so's you notice, but you never want to tempt that sort of thing."

"Dragons can be very sneaky," Amber muttered through a forkful of eggs. "Righteous chow, Dawson. I'm moving in."

"All we ask is that you do the dishes," Benji said, and Darian grabbed his hand.

"Deal."

"I'll have to do them next time," Jared apologized, looking at the clock and nibbling daintily on a piece of dry wheat toast. He'd eaten his fruit but not his eggs, and Dawson wondered what it would take to get him to eat a full plate of protein. He felt sort of sad, thinking of all those people looking at him adoringly and all the sacrifices he had to make to be just that beautiful. Jared finished his toast and chugged the last bit of his coffee and then stood up. Dawson went to go with him, but Jared stopped him.

"Don't," he muttered. "Just… don't. I checked my schedule. I get four days off in six weeks. I'll be on the first plane out. Wait for me?"

It was raw and pleading, in front of everyone at the breakfast table, and Dawson wondered why he hadn't said the words in private, at the door.

"No worries," he said, thinking that he'd waited this long to lose his virginity, he could certainly wait for the guy who found it to return. "Text us—we'll pick you up at the airport."

Jared nodded tensely. "I'll hold you to that." He stood up and dove in for a kiss then, fierce and demanding and fucking serious, and then tore himself away and grabbed his stuff and practically ran out the door while he was still putting on his jacket. It was a lot of frantic activity, but it did not disguise that his eyes were shiny and wet and his jaw was set so hard it looked like his teeth would crack. Not from Dawson.

Dawson looked down at his eggs and felt his lower lip wobble. And then his eyes got bleary. And then Darian was over his back hugging him like she was someone he'd known his entire life, and he let her, because the worst part about being comforted was that Jared had literally run out his door in tears, and he didn't have a soul to comfort him, not for six lousy weeks.

INTERMISSION

THE NIGHT before Jared was supposed to arrive, Amber showed up at Dawson's door with two haphazard suitcases of stuff and a pleading look on her face.

Dawson was *very* relieved. Amber had been hanging out at the apartment a lot and had let drop some *very* unnerving things about her ultra-conservative family and a stepfather from Dawson's worst nightmares.

"I'm so lucky," Dawson told her sincerely the week before. "I barely know my stepfather, and he was pretty happy to let it stay that way."

"Mine keeps asking to see my piercings so he can tell me they're ways for Satan to get into my body," Amber said, grimacing, and Benji and Dawson both did the oogie dance for her, because it made her laugh, and something should.

So to have her show up now meant Benji and Dawson could take care of her, and they *liked* her. She said funny things at funny times and either did the dishes or did the cooking, and she cleared off the coffee table *every night* she spent on their couch.

Which now would be every night.

"You couldn't stand it anymore?" Dawson asked, and Amber did the best oogie dance he'd ever seen.

"He came in when I was showering, Dawson. *Showering.* I got out of the shower and he was there, eyeballing my belly-button piercing and my boobs. I told him that I'd rather live with the two guys in the crappy apartment, because *they* don't want to sleep with me while hating me at the same time."

Dawson hugged her hard and figured Jared would have to adjust to one more roommate on the couch.

And one completely drunk roommate for the entire weekend.

"I'm gonna need your help anyway," Dawson said. "Darian broke up with him about an hour ago. He's on his first case of cheap beer, but he's gonna need us."

Amber grunted. "Awesome. Something real. Bring on the ice cream and the barf bags, I'm here for you."

And that, in a nutshell, became their mantra.

"Benji, man, you can't drink anymore."

"I'm not that drunk," Benji slurred about an hour later.

"Yeah, but you're going to have to help me pick Jared up tomorrow morning, and you can't do it hungover, and I don't know the way to the frickin' airport."

Benji slouched low on the couch, his legs sprawled out in front of him, his long, asymmetrical face slack with an entire six-pack of cheap beer. His head lolled sideways, and he looked mournfully at Dawson. "I'm so glad you've got someone, man. I am. I love you. I'm so glad you're happy."

Dawson sighed and ruffled Benji's hair. "And that's why I love you back."

Benji shook his head loosely. "No, man. See, I'm glad, but I'm worried. He's quiet. I mean, he's ice, I mean nice, but he's quiet. And he lives a long away away."

"Away away," Dawson had to agree, although the past six weeks hadn't seemed that long. They'd seemed *long*, and Dawson looked forward to Jared's texts and his e-mails every day, but really, it had been like Christmas. Christmas was *coming*, and the texts and the e-mails and the phone calls were like the decorations and the carols and the animated specials—they all *pointed to Christmas*!

So the fact was, he *missed* Jared, but Jared had only been a really spectacular weekend, and now he was going to get *another* really spectacular weekend. In a way, it was like the visits he'd had with his mom before she'd decided he was better off not coming. He liked the two weeks by the pool and being chauffeured to the mall and having food cooked by someone who knew what they were doing. (*Not* his mom. Invisible Stepdad had a staff.) So it was exciting and very, very awesome, but not intrinsic to his breathing.

But that didn't mean he wasn't looking forward to seeing Jared some more.

The night before, Jared had texted him with *Sunsets—the sappiest things make me happy.*

And Dawson was suddenly struck with how much he wanted to see Jared *at* sunset. And how much those daily texts meant to him. He texted back, *With me it's Phineas and Ferb*, and Jared had replied, *I know what we're going to do TOMORROW.*

Jared could definitely fit into his and Benji's lives. He could.

But he had to *be there*.

So Dawson was perfectly sincere when he reassured Benji. "Yeah, that's okay. He's *going* to be here. He *wants* to be here. That's important!"

"No, man," Benji wept. Oh boy! The weepy drunk part was here. "No. 'Cause Darian wants to be here too. Didn't stop her from walking out."

Dawson grimaced. "Darian's got it complicated," he said after a minute. Darian *did* have it complicated. It had finally occurred to Darian's father that his little girl was not staying on the couch, and that would have been fine—Darian could have moved in with Benji. There wouldn't have been a problem there. But Darian's father was threatening to kick Benji out of school.

It was probably just hot air—people didn't really *do* that, did they? Like comic-book bad guys? But Darian hadn't wanted to wreck anybody's life (her words), so she'd told Benji they were off until her dad cooled down.

Amber came out of the kitchen with a big glass of water and two Motrin. "Here," she muttered. "Nobody works tonight, Dawson's boyfriend is showing up tomorrow—it's time to get sober so we can see a movie."

Benji took the water and began to drink. "What movie?" he asked pathetically.

Dawson and Amber met eyes.

"Something with explosions," Amber said decidedly. "And lots and lots of dead bodies. And death. And adrenaline. And no plot whatsoever."

"And hotties," Dawson said, not putting a gender to the hottie.

"Word."

They made it so.

THE NEXT morning, they *all* went to go get Jared, which was good, because Benji was *still* hungover, and Amber had to drive Dawson's POS with the several primered spots and several nameless divots and the engine that purred like a kitten.

She was so short they got one of those O pillows to go under her bottom so she could see over the steering wheel.

"Why aren't I driving again?" Dawson asked from the backseat. Benji was navigating, and Dawson got the backseat of his own car because… well, because why?

"Because we want to live," Amber growled. "Remember the trip to the ocean two weeks ago?"

Well, yeah. Dawson didn't take directions well when he was en route. "That McDonald's trash can *will* recover," he said staunchly. But his car had a new set of bright-red scratches to match the top of the can, so maybe his car was a little more damaged than he wanted to admit.

"Yeah. I'm driving because you don't know where you're going. Look—see? This is me getting off for I-5 and going north. Next time *you* can do this, and you won't need us."

Benji, who had leaned his head against the window and done his best imitation of a dead fish the whole time, actually managed to engage. "You're good with him," he said to Amber. "That's a relief. I need a backup since Jared is sort of an out-of-town amusement and not a real boyfriend."

"He is *too* a real boyfriend!" Dawson defended. He *felt* real. Maybe not integral, not *yet*, but his texts on Dawson's phone had been real.

All three thousand exchanges.

Going jogging. Come with me.

At this hour? Are you insane?

Chicken.

Fine. Let me tell Benji it's your idea so he doesn't have me committed.

Or, just in time for Dawson's class break:

How are the Romantics?

Has it ever occurred to anyone that they were like the singers in the 60's? Without condoms or the cool drugs?

Yes, Dawson, you are not the only person to make that leap.

Well, it felt new to me!

Okay, so there you go. Your semester paper, and you can start collecting ideas.

God, make me feel prepared!

You're the smartest person I know. Finals should not come as a surprise to you.

Do you really think I'm smart?

I'm only so stupid, Dawson—I have no choice.

Complimenting my brains WILL get you laid.

At last, a magic formula—I'm so relieved.

They could go back and forth forever. They *did* go back and forth forever, only it didn't feel like forever. It felt like breathing.

Okay. So maybe Dawson missed Jared a little more than he missed his mom. He'd certainly never felt like his mom was part of breathing.

"Dawson, did you see which way I came? Jared probably takes Southwest all the time, so you need to come to this terminal."

"Geez, Amber, you didn't *look* this bossy when you moved in yesterday."

"You weren't paying attention. Now do we have to do this again?"

Dawson sighed. "Yeah, probably. Me and directions—not so much."

"Yeah," Benji drawled from the front seat. "That's only gonna happen if we don't scare him away this weekend."

"Are you going to need alcohol again?" Amber asked as she pulled up alongside the curb.

"Absolutely," Benji said mournfully, and Dawson squeezed his shoulder.

"Well, on the plus side, Dawson, enjoy seeing him now—Benji drunk again may send him screaming."

"Yeah, okay, that's nice," Dawson said absently, because the truth was, he didn't really hear her.

Jared was *there*, and all of that insouciance Dawson had been proud of evaporated. This was the guy who had *touched him naked*, and who had kept him company and lived in his head for the past six weeks, and he was *right there*.

Dawson had the door open before Amber even stopped the car completely. She jerked on the brake and he went clattering across the sidewalk. Jared, who had been standing there with his duffel, scanning the cars coming and going in front of him, turned his head, dropped his duffel, and opened his arms.

Dawson did his best not to climb him like a tree, because Dawson was bigger than the standard ballerina.

It didn't matter. Jared grabbed under Dawson's ass, and Dawson wrapped one leg up around his hips and used the rest of his brain to *eat* his boyfriend, lips first. Jared tried to eat him back, tongue, mouth, lips, all points engaged. Jared held Dawson's face still, which was good because Dawson just wanted to *flail*, elbows, knees, everything. Kissing. Kissing was *great*. Jared tasted *nummy*, and Dawson could take his tongue and his mouth again and again.

Jared pulled back and they rested foreheads against each other, and Dawson had a moment of panic. Oh God. This really *was* like breathing. He'd thought he was okay without this, but he'd really been *holding his breath*, and after a month and a half of thinking he could do a long-distance relationship, it turned out he was really only alive when he was touching Jared.

"I needed that," Jared panted, and Dawson felt a reluctant smile.

"You think? God, I'm so happy to see you."

"So, you hard yet?"

Dawson's whole south area was swollen and aching. "*Yes*," he wailed.

Jared stepped back and turned his head. "Why is that a bad thing?"

Crap. He hoped Amber was wrong. "Benji and Darian broke up, like, *five minutes* ago, and Amber just moved onto our couch. We're sort of in roommate crisis mode—"

"So we don't get sex?" Jared's eyes opened really wide, and Dawson remembered Jared was *twenty-six*, and he could get sex anywhere he wanted, and he'd just flown a long way to see *Dawson* in order to get him some.

"Well, yeah!" Dawson conceded. "Absolutely. But we can't just, you know, run into my room and not come out for four days. Even though I don't work this weekend and I'd sort of love to run into my room and not come out for four days."

Jared put his hand on the back of Dawson's neck and squeezed. "I'm just so damned glad to see you," he confessed, and Dawson picked up his duffel and leaned into him.

"God, me too," he said, and the thought overwhelmed him. For half of the way home, it was all he could do to sit in the backseat and clutch Jared's hand.

That was unfortunate, because it meant Jared, Amber, and Benji had to carry the conversation. For a moment, Dawson thought that might be a disaster.

"Hello, young sir," Amber said as Jared slid in. "I'll be your chariot master today—is the sky clear of all dragons?"

"Dragons clear." Jared played along. "Is the course clear for the chariot? Have all the horses taken their obligatory crap?"

Benji chuckled because, well, poop humor. "Yes sir, but I warn you, there are hungover individuals present, and we may need to stop for carb loading and caffeine."

Jared nodded. "Carry on, charioteers. Carb loading and caffeine understood." He leaned back and caught Dawson's eyes, and Dawson leaned over and kissed his cheek.

"Have I mentioned the awesomeness?" he asked, and Jared shrugged.

"I need the caffeine myself."

But he didn't need to play with Dawson's friends, and that was what he spent the entire weekend doing.

He let Benji pick out another action/adventure movie to see in the theater, and he let Amber sprawl on him when they went back to the apartment to play video games. When Benji started getting maudlin, he took directions from Amber and drove Dawson's car into Roseville to get bourbon and Coke while Dawson took Benji on a long walk around the block just to calm him down. He didn't slip into Dawson's room that night until Benji was drunk and asleep and Amber was safely tucked in on the couch. Dawson came out of Benji's room (he'd brought a barf bucket and showed Benji where it was, just in case) and watched as Jared bent down and kissed Amber's forehead and got a good-night hug. Dawson stopped to do the same.

When they got into Dawson's room, Dawson was half-afraid Jared was going to let go of the perfect façade of perfect boyfriend and let Dawson know exactly how shitty his entire first day of vacation had been.

Instead, he stripped down to his boxers, pulled back the covers, and said, "God, Dawson, are you still dressed? C'mere, I'm *dying* to touch you!"

Dawson stripped to *his* boxers too and turned off the light. "Man, I'm sorry about sending you to Roseville for alcohol. We've probably got closer liquor stores, and we usually go to Safeway, but—"

"But they don't have it cheap enough for Benji's first heartbreak—I figured that out when you and Amber were counting the pennies in the couch. Don't worry. *We* bought enough to keep him buzzed for a couple of days. By the time he clears his hangover on Sunday, he'll be happy to be sober again."

Dawson launched himself into Jared's arms with no reservation. He wanted to fret, because he knew they'd asked a lot of Jared, but all Jared wanted to do was *touch* him, and geez, Dawson could use that.

Kisses, long, slow, and languorous; hands on naked skin; the first orgasm came in each other's fists, and it wasn't breathless or hurried— it just crested upon their heads like a sneaky wave at the ocean. They were left still itchy with desire but replete for a moment, panting in each other's arms.

They talked quietly as they cleaned up, and then Dawson rested his head on Jared's chest and told him the actual *reason* for the breakup.

"Would he really do that? Darian's dad, I mean," Dawson wondered out loud, glad to have someone to ask. "I mean, Amber's parents are twisted, but, I mean, you know I haven't met them, but Benji and me, we sort of got good ones. Is the whole evil-parent thing—does that happen a lot?"

Jared's sigh dusted Dawson's ear. "I am the wrong person to ask, Dawson. I haven't spoken to my parents for years."

"Yeah, but…." Dawson turned over so he was on his stomach and resting his chin on his hand on Jared's pec. "You're *Jared Emory*. Don't they even send you fan letters? I mean, who *are* they that they're too good for their own kid?"

"Dad owns a bunch of businesses," Jared said. "They're sort of king and queen of the chamber of commerce in Orange County. I mean, West Hollywood? Very liberal. Orange County? Very conservative. It's sort of like having nitro and glycerin really close to each other. Anyway, they just… just don't get the dancing, don't get the gay, don't get *me*. And, I don't know." Jared sounded like he was thinking about something he didn't usually think about. "I'm just not the kid they wanted," he said, and his shoulders tried to move like he needed to shrug but Dawson's body wouldn't let him.

"Well, you're the guy *I* want," Dawson said, feeling lame, but it seemed to work because Jared kissed him, and the whole sexy-sexy thing started again. Even though Dawson appreciated the sexy thing for what it was, he was also thrilled that his roommate problems didn't seem to have put Jared off in the slightest. In fact, Jared really seemed to be happy to be there.

Jared, in particular, was happy coming in his mouth as he practiced the whole blowjob thing.

Dawson just swallowed—well, mostly—and when the entire mess, uhm, thing, uhm, orgasm was done, he wiped his mouth on the corner of the sheet and grinned up Jared's hairless body. "So, getting better, right?"

Jared squeezed his eyes shut. "I hope that was mental rehearsal and not practice."

Dawson only half laughed. "No!" he said, pulling himself up. Jared extended his arm with a little bit of authority, and Dawson took his cue and rested his head on Jared's chest. "I wouldn't do that to you! Besides, we're still waiting for your window to close, right? I mean, I've got to be honest—I *have* condoms, but I bought them two years ago in a fit of optimism."

Jared shot him a look of pure outrage. "*Dawson*, Jesus! Don't screw around with that! I mean—"

"Well, you said you got tested—who else am I going to do this with?"

The outrage settled, tamed down, turned into that shy smile. "Only me," he said smugly, and Dawson nodded and licked right near his armpit to see if it tasted sweaty. It did, but he still had come breath, so it didn't bother him.

"Ew!" Jared flicked his forehead.

Dawson grinned at him unrepentantly. "Hey—I understand rim jobs are part of sex too. You gonna flick my head if I give you one of those?"

Jared threw his head back against the pillow and made a noise like "gungh!" while Dawson cackled. "That's really mean, baiting me like that!"

Dawson stopped laughing. "Not baiting you—we're doing the boyfriend thing. There *will* be experiments in salad tossing, tea bagging, cream pie, making the banana cry, and other non-food-related food-named activities."

"That's a promise?" Sudden seriousness there.

"Well, it was supposed to be a joke, but yeah. It's a promise. I mean, you're sort of seeing us at our worst here—"

Jared cut him off with a shrug. "I've seen bad breakups before. Lived through a few. Benji's sad, but he'll get better."

Suddenly Dawson's attention focused in a totally different place. "Lived through a few? You gonna tell me?"

And the warm sweaty man under his cheek turned into an ice block in his arms. "No," Jared said, and that was that.

Or it would have been if Dawson hadn't been the one on top of him. Dawson was just a naturally warm force of nature—sort of like a tropical storm. "No, seriously—bad breakups. Am I not the kind of boyfriend who gets to hear about the other boyfriends?"

Jared closed his eyes and thawed a little. "Maybe not this time around," he said, his voice dropping. "Maybe this time around we just... I don't know." Jared swallowed and put on what Dawson recognized as his stage face. "Today, I am a hero," he said, eyes crinkling, voice embellishing the word with curlicues and banners and everything. "Let me be a hero for the weekend. I need it. We learn a new show next week—when I get to feel stupid, lame, inept, and clumsy. I want to ride the hero high."

Dawson laughed and smacked his arm gently. "'Stupid, lame, inept, and clumsy'—really? I've seen you move, I'm not getting the connection."

Jared shook his head. "God, you know that year, your freshman year, when you grow six inches and four shoe sizes?"

"Ten inches," Dawson confirmed. "I was five one at the beginning of my freshman year. I'm almost six feet now, and I did it all that year."

"Yeah—well, when you're dancing all the time, you don't know where your center of gravity is. So for two years, I broke *everything*. Both wrists, my ankle, I popped my ACL. It was heinous—"

"God, the knee thing—that's *bad*—I've heard dancers. That'll end your career!"

Jared nodded soberly. "Yeah, but I was young. It healed a lot more quickly than I think I had a right to. And I have to baby it. Anyway, you don't ever recover from that time. It doesn't matter how much you try to fix from when you felt clumsy, lame, and whatever—"

"Inept and stupid," Dawson filled in for him.

"Yes, clumsy, lame, inept, and stupid, well, it's still there, right in your head. And every time I learn a new show, I'm right there at fifteen again."

"The horror!" Dawson was all sympathy.

"Fifteen was bad for you?" Jared said, and his smile suggested he knew it had been.

"Me? Elbows, knees, ears, and mouth? If it hadn't been for Benji, I would have spent the whole year in a trash can, having my meals thrown in and tossing my homework out to passing teachers. Dire, I tell you, *dire!*"

Jared laughed, but he sounded kind. "So did Benji mean that thing he said in a drunken stupor tonight?"

"Which thing would that be?" Because Benji had been talking a *lot*.

"The thing that went 'You a goo' guy, gwea' guy, but you hur' my boy, I keel you!'"

Dawson snickered. "Yeah, I think he meant that. That's not just alcohol-fueled bullshit—Benji'll take care of me."

Jared "hmmed."

"What?"

"I just—I don't want to hurt you. I… I was so happy to see you, I just forgot about the other end of the relationship thing. I'm… I mean, *I* think I'm a good boyfriend, but, you know." Jared's gaze went suddenly sober. "I want to be worth the waits between the visits," he said sincerely, and Dawson smiled so hard his cheeks hurt.

"You *are*. Oh my God, you're already there! I mean, just *look* at you—you're in my bed and *naked*! I could wait for you for*ever*—"

Jared laughed and kissed him again to shut him up, and that was the end of the conversation.

Saying good-bye to him sucked. He spent the entire weekend hanging with Dawson's friends. They took a trip to the zoo (for random reasons nobody was ever able to explain later) and ate at Chili's (because it was better than Denny's, and Jared was treating) and saw more movies than should be allowed by law or optometrists. Jared got up every morning to run and jollied Dawson out of bed with him, and Dawson sort of loved that quiet, chilly time in the thin March sunshine. Every night they had sex and talked and had sex some more. Jared actually made Benji french toast on the last morning, like he'd promised the last time he'd been there.

The first time they'd had to say good-bye.

The second time was worse. When Dawson stood with him at the curb and opened his mouth to let him in, he couldn't pretend the long-distance thing was an adventure or a convenience. It was painful. It was painful, and watching Jared walk away hurt.

And it wasn't until he walked away that Dawson realized how much he didn't know about the life Jared was walking back to.

It was something that would haunt him later. Something that would wrench out his soul.

Until that moment, he hadn't even asked.

SECOND ACT

TOPHER WAS *literally* begging for Dawson's forgiveness, and Dawson wanted to dump coffee on his head. Annoying douchemonkey—did he think Dawson was just going to forget that he left the production high and dry last time?

"Seriously, Dawson—I'm not getting any love from the guild. I'm not going to be able to pay my dues or my rent or anything!"

Dawson narrowed his eyes. "Well then, maybe next time you have a job, you see it through." He looked around the coffee shop, wondering how, if Topher was so broke, he was going to be able to afford the promised cup of coffee. His question was answered after Topher placed his order and then looked apologetically at Dawson. Not once, in their entire friendship, had Benji ever assumed Dawson would foot the bill because his dad had the money. Not *once.* Dawson wanted to smack this guy. He paid the bill and retreated to a table and glowered.

"Yeah, but how am I going to prove that if I don't get another chance?"

"You're going to buy me a goddamned cup of coffee or meet me somewhere else," he snapped.

"Jesus, Dawson, I'm just looking for a frickin' break!" and only the buzzing in Dawson's pocket saved Topher from a royal ass-reaming.

What're you doing?

Trying not to kill Topher, why?

Is that the douche who bailed on you?

Yup.

Why are you even talking to him?

Because depending on when your next flight up is, I could get the night off.

Don't do it. It's your reputation on the line.

Might be worth it. When's your next flight?

Two weeks—Th-Mon.

And that's right in the middle of show. Hold on a sec.

His pocket buzzed angrily and he glared sourly at Topher. The barista had called out their coffees while he'd been texting, and Topher had the grace to go fetch like he belonged there.

"I've got a show in Sacramento," he said sourly. "It's four days— I only want to work two. You wouldn't be lead, you'd be Amber's monkey."

"Amber the goth dyke who looks like she eats babies?"

"Amber my roommate who sleeps on our couch, pays rent, and cooks dinner, which as far as I can see makes her a whole other *life-form* above you, you fucking ape."

"So let me get this straight—in one weekend you meet your boyfriend and adopt your second chair as a pet. What the fuck was in the water?"

Dawson wanted to know that too. He'd asked his dad that Sunday after he'd said good-bye to Jared the second time, and Stan Barnes had smiled a little. "That's sort of what college is all about," he said. "It's why parents save so hard for it—so you can go and meet your best friends for life over coffee and weird shit happening at Denny's."

"How'd you know it was Denny's?" Dawson was impressed. He hadn't mentioned it and it was like his dad was clairvoyant or something.

"It's always Denny's," his father said. "It's like some sort of rule."

And that was what made his dad great, actually. He understood the rule of Denny's.

And right now, looking at Topher, who was apparently regarding the whole thing with unbridled contempt, Dawson realized he couldn't expose their fragile, happy little household to this interloper who was still bitter because Dawson wouldn't blow him.

I'm sorry, baby. You're right. I can't let this asshole work my shift.

I get it. We'll have time.

Don't you want to have sex?

Darian's little sister had turned up pregnant. In high school. *Surprise!* The upshot was that Darian showed up on their doorstep the week after Jared's visit, with flowers, chocolate, and vodka. Benji had left the vodka outside and taken the flowers and the chocolate—and Darian—into his bedroom and not come out for two days. So if Jared was coming over and Benji was no longer heartbroken? Dammit— Benji *owed* him!

Don't worry. We'll have sex. I'll get a hotel room for one night.

That sounds really sleazy.

Well, it IS for sex!

Crap. Can we just, I don't know. Wait for a place?

Where's your play?

Downtown.

I'll get us something nice for Friday night. And since I'll be here Sunday....

You'll meet my dad????????

Dawson practically pee-pee danced in his seat. He hadn't exactly kept Jared a secret, but it was hard to convince your father you weren't fantasizing a boyfriend when he was never there.

Promise.

Hotel room it is! I'm a kept man!

Dawson looked up at Topher at this point, aware that the guy was glaring at Dawson while he arranged his life by text.

"No," Dawson said, standing up smartly.

"No?"

"Yeah. Changed my mind. No. I'm not putting my reputation in your lame hands, and no, I don't think it's weird that my whole life changed in a weekend, and no, you don't get a secret pass to the clubhouse, because you're mean and mean people can't stay. So basically—"

"No," Topher snarled at him. "Thanks for fucking *nothing*, Dawson."

"Yeah, thanks for trying to get in my pants, ass hat."

Dawson grabbed his coffee, glad he'd bought it because otherwise he would have had to leave it in the store. His phone buzzed some more and it was Jared, asking him about Amber, asking him about Benji and Darian, asking him if he should bring anything to lunch with Dawson's father.

God, even on the phone, the guy was better company. Dawson congratulated himself on his taste and walked to his next class.

BENJI DROVE so Dawson could memorize the way, because he was pretty sure last time with Amber hadn't helped. He could also hop out and help Jared with his bags. As they pulled up, there Jared stood, unconsciously beautiful in designer jeans, a slick microfiber T-shirt, and aviator glasses.

"God, look at him," Dawson breathed. "He looks like some sort of movie star!"

"He looks damned hot," Benji said critically. It was late May— and around ninety-five degrees. The front of Jared's gray shirt was soaked through with sweat. "Remind him to wear cargo shorts when he comes in the summer."

Dawson chuckled wickedly. "I'll remind him to wear nothing if he wants to come at all."

"Oh, God, *Dawson*!"

But it was slowing down and stopping time, so Dawson got to hop out of the car (wait for it to stop completely first!) and throw himself at his impossibly glamorous boyfriend, who was making the sere, flat brownness of Sacramento look *cool* just by standing there.

Jared's million-dollar dance-diva smile flashed just as Dawson jumped in his arms.

Their mouths connecting was like a hot, wet time machine—the melding of their tongues cut through the past six weeks, made them nonexistent, as though the two of them were still sharing the last desperate good-bye kiss before Jared had left for the second time.

Dawson slid his hands up the back of Jared's shirt, and even the sweat pouring off his back didn't distract Dawson from his goal of splaying his hands across as much skin as he could stand.

And then, as he skated his hand along Jared's spine, he felt it. Jared's heat seemed to strike him the same blow that coming out of an air-conditioned building into the swelter of the valley's punishing sunshine did. That's when he realized this wasn't the healthy I-want-to-fuck-you-blind sort of heat he'd been hoping for.

He took a step back and yanked Jared's sunglasses off.

And saw for the first time the pallor and the bags under the eyes and the exhaustion.

"You're sick," he said, and he'd meant to say it gruffly with anger and irritation, but he couldn't.

"I'm… well, yeah," Jared mumbled, backing away. "I'm sorry. It's just… I hadn't seen you and we had all these plans, and I just kept hoping I'd get better."

He crossed his arms in front of him and Dawson saw his hands were shaking. Dawson was going to put an arm around his shoulders, but right then, he realized how very badly Jared probably *didn't* want to be touched, here in the sweltering heat. He wanted to take the kiss back, really, but he didn't, because it had felt good and Jared seemed to like it, and Jared needed *something*.

"Here, let me get your stuff," he muttered, reaching for the suitcase. Jared's eyebrows said something really heinous about Dawson's upper-body tone, and Jared grunted, picked up the suitcase—

And dropped it.

"Jesus!" Dawson picked it up unhappily. "Jared, how'd you even perform last night?"

Jared grunted and looked away, and Dawson struggled with the wheeled carry-on until he could throw it in the trunk of Benji's car.

"What? How'd you perform? It was rhetorical—what do you know that I don't?"

Jared's shrug was meant to be casual, but what it became was apologetic. "Uhm, vitamin C and a bump of coke?"

Dawson dropped the suitcase in the trunk, tripped, and then whirled around to face him.

Oh God. He looked like hell. But Dawson couldn't—he just couldn't!

"You don't have any of that shit *here*, do you?" he asked in an outraged stage whisper, and Jared was not too sick to roll his eyes.

"It's in the stage manager's first-aid kit," he said patiently. "No, I don't buy that shit myself. I...." He shrugged and looked away. "I just... I wasn't going to make it without something, Dawson. I don't know what to tell you."

Dawson sighed and suddenly felt very grown-up. "Okay. You've got to promise—Jared, this is my home, I've got friends, we don't do that—"

Jared held out hands that shook. "I promise," he said quietly. "I'm sorry—I shouldn't have told you."

"No... I mean, *yes*. You *should* have told me—because now I can totally fucking stress over you. *Jesus*, Jared—what were you thinking?"

Jared's gaze wandered for a moment, and a shudder sort of took over, and Dawson sighed. "You were thinking perform or die. I get it. Okay, Scarface, get in the car."

Jared nodded meekly and Dawson let him sit in the front.

Benji looked at Jared sideways and then cast an alarmed look at Dawson. "We're going where?" he asked.

Dawson grimaced. "The nearest drugstore—we need flu meds, a cold pad, and a crapload of Gatorade."

Jared made a little whine, and Benji and Dawson both looked at him.

"What?"

"Something for my stomach too," he humbly confessed.

Dawson hid his face in his hands. "Babe... you're killing me."

"I'm sorry."

"Don't be sorry—just... just don't be. C'mon, Benji—he's gonna pour through the seam in the door if we don't get him back to the air-conditioning."

TWO HOURS later, Dawson helped Jared out of a cool shower and into clean sheets, with a stop on the way for boxer shorts and nothing else.

Jared huddled under the covers, looking at him miserably, and Dawson sat quietly, smoothing his hair back from his face.

"You could have told me you were sick," he said, thinking that the disappointment would have been easier to deal with.

"I don't get sick," Jared mumbled. "I really don't get sick when I travel across the damned state to get laid."

Dawson couldn't even laugh. "I would have come down," he said. "I would have asked my dad for the money, and he would have whined, but I would have come down."

"Why? So you could fight with my roommates for space to sit by my bed?" Jared half laughed, and Dawson swallowed.

"Is the competition fierce?" Over the past months, Dawson had heard about Jared's fellow dancers, and about the stage crew, and sometimes about his agent and manager, but not really about his roommates.

"Only for space," Jared muttered. "We've got, like, a linen closet with a bed in it. If the guys want to get laid, they take turns using that 'room.'"

"Gross."

"Yeah—what's really gross is that they're not all gay. *Girls* consent to go in there. I really thought they were supposed to have better taste."

Dawson snickered, and then saw Jared's sly smile and realized he'd done that on purpose. "You're trying to distract me."

"You're trying to be mad at me."

Sigh. "Yeah. I'm mad at *someone.* Drugs—which were stupid, but I think you know that—"

"They made me worse," Jared confessed into the pillow.

"Yeah, shocker. But…." Dawson swallowed against a tightness in his jaw. He remembered how cool and arrogant Jared had first seemed when he'd practically broken Dawson's fall. Yeah, sure, a lot of that aloofness was just a quiet nature, but some of it was just… loneliness. There was something so intensely lonely about Jared snorting his bump of coke so he could get onstage, because he knew no one was going to hold his hand if he didn't. "But I'm mostly mad because… because this. Because you needed to be here, and cared for, and loved, and you weren't."

Jared's shadowed, mercury-blue gaze sought Dawson's out. "I am now."

Dawson leaned over and smoothed his lips over Jared's temple. "Someday, you and me are going to have a real talk about what dance means to you. But not now."

Jared struggled to sit up. "You're not breaking up with me, are you?"

Dawson put his big hand in the middle of Jared's muscular chest and gave a little shove. "No, but it's gratifying to watch you panic about it." That really *was* a good sign, wasn't it? "Nope. What I'm going to do is *much worse*."

Jared whimpered and huddled under the blankets some more. "Do I want to know?"

Dawson felt a little guilty, actually. "Well, you don't leave me much of a choice! I completely alienated the only guy who could take my place at work because, well, he was a douche, but I don't have anyone who can take my job, hotel sex is obviously out, and I'm not leaving you alone while I'm gone!"

"Wait... if you're not leaving me alone and I'm not going anywhere...." He looked *so* confused, and Dawson sort of shrunk in on himself.

"Well, it's not like you could meet him on Sunday anyway!"

Jared's bloodshot eyes widened. "No," he begged. He tried to sit up again, but if Dawson could push him down once, he wasn't going to be able to fight him again now.

"Don't go anywhere," he snapped. "He's not going to get here for another couple of hours."

"But Dawson—"

Dawson grinned. Übercool boyfriend had just totally disappeared. What was left whined like a five-year-old, and that was really freaking endearing. "No. Don't 'but Dawson' me. You got sick, you didn't take care of yourself, and you ended up in bed without me naked next to you. This is your punishment. You're going to go to sleep, wake up, eat soup, take your medication, and sit on the couch while Dad comes over to watch the game."

"What game?" Jared asked blearily, and Dawson grimaced.

"Basketball. I'm sorry."

"Hasn't been the same since they didn't let Karcek play," Jared muttered into his pillow, and Dawson had to agree with him. Yeah, everything was cool with Jason Collins *now*, but two years ago Xander Karcek had been screwed out of the finals when he'd come out with his former teammate. Everyone's heart had broken then.

"Well, you know. We can always dream." Jared was almost asleep, so Dawson slowly lifted his bottom to make his escape.

"Not gonna dream about Karcek," Jared muttered. "Gonna dream about you."

Dawson grunted and sat back down. Well, fine. Make him not mad anymore. Jared's eyes closed and his labored, even breaths sounded against his pillow. Dawson stroked his hair back from his slightly cooler forehead and sighed.

He hadn't anticipated this.

Long-distance relationships—he'd already failed the one with his mom, right? He'd expected almost anything when Jared had run out the door the first time with the promise to return. He'd expected to get bored and forget he had a boyfriend—because Dawson wasn't always so pro with the consistency. That hadn't happened. He lived for Jared's texts, for the weekly phone calls, for the IMs when he was on the computer. Turned out that long distance in the technological age really *did* have some hope, right?

He'd expected to worry that *Jared* had gotten bored, and was cheating, or his eyes were wandering, or that he'd figured out that he was (trying to) sleep with a helpless nerd who got off on the power he wielded in the tech booth like a petty tyrant got off on invading small countries. *That* didn't seem to have happened. The need in Jared's voice, to see Dawson, to spend his hours of peace in the little apartment, even to know how Benji and Darian were doing and if Amber's horrible stepfather had called lately—that didn't dim or lessen or fade. In fact, it seemed to get worse and more intense.

In fact, a little desperate.

Dawson wasn't proud—he'd looked up Jared's bio on just about every media he could find. He'd seen praise for Jared's workshops with the disabled in the cities he visited, and he'd seen vague references to an "estrangement" with his parents, but the two things Dawson *hadn't* seen were the most telling. He hadn't seen any references to Jared's little sister, and he hadn't seen any references to a companion or a friend or someone of importance.

That memory, the image of the single prince on the winter stage, seemed more and more significant. That was the life that Jared lived. The stage was the most real thing he had.

Until here he was, sick and sad and so desperate for contact with someone who cared about him that he'd catch a plane across the state when he could barely walk.

Dawson's hand started to shake as he brushed the hair back from Jared's clammy forehead. He bent at the waist and kissed Jared's temple. "Jared?"

"Hm?"

"You're pretty fucking sick, right?" The thermometer said 103 degrees.

"Naw. Need sleep."

"Good, so you're at death's door, and you can't run away when I tell you something."

"What?"

"I think we're in love."

"Yup. I'm out of here." Not a muscle twitched.

"Good. I love you. I'm pissed at you. If you ever do blow again, I *will* break up with you, but I love you."

"Love you too."

"No more drugs."

"'Kay."

"Promise."

"Promise."

"How do you feel?"

"There's an elephant sitting on my head and torso."

"Awesome. I'll let you get teabagged by an imaginary elephant, and I'm going to go call my dad."

Jared's body shook painfully, and Dawson figured he'd done his job.

"I'll suck elephant balls," Jared muttered into the pillow. "But a rim job's right out."

It wasn't until he felt the smile tilting at the corners of his mouth that Dawson realized how truly worried he was. He bent down and kissed Jared's cheek. "Well, I'm glad to know you've got standards."

And with that he crept soundlessly out of the room.

DAWSON HAD dark-brown hair, pale skin, dark-brown eyes, and a little turned-up nose with pitcher ears. His father had the same nose and ears, but he'd been ginger in childhood and his hair was graying blond now. Apparently Dawson's mother's genes were enough to affect his coloring and his build but not his personality, which he figured he had his dad to thank for.

His dad could be just as odd as Dawson when he let his guard down.

"I'm here to babysit your boyfriend. Seriously—did you do this on purpose just to hear me say that?"

This was Thursday night—Dad had come straight from work in his third-best brown suit with his tie loose around his neck and his graying blond hair pushed around his head.

"Did you bring beer?"

"Are you twenty-one yet?"

"I've only got two months!" he whined.

His dad shrugged. "Then I'll bring it in two months. And you're deflecting. Why the hell am I here?" Dawson's dad knew how to make himself at home. He wandered in, hung his suit jacket up on the peg by the door, untucked his shirt, kicked off his shoes, and went to the refrigerator for the lemonade Benji loved to make from the big honkin' container with the powder.

"Because he's sicker than hell," Benji said, coming into the living room from the bedroom. His bedroom was starting to look more like Darian's bedroom, actually—her quilt on the bed, her scarves hanging over light fixtures—it was like Benjarian's cave of heterosexual lurve, and on the one hand Dawson thought it was adorable, and on the other, it was sort of revolting. He couldn't decide which one, most days.

Today, in front of his dad, it was adorable, because it made Benjarian look married, and that made Dawson's helpless attachment to the phlegm-and-fever-infested mangod seem slightly more mature and less pathetic.

"You made that assessment, Benji?" Dad grinned crookedly, because he liked to give Benji his ration of shit. "You and your engineering degree in the making, you decided he was 'sicker than hell.' What if he's not *quite* as sick as hell? What if he's *exactly* as sick as hell? What if hell is not an accurate measure of sickness?"

Benji grinned back. "You're being a real asshole today, Mr. Barnes. Well done—you been practicing?"

Dad smiled, obviously relaxed. "Yeah, you know, kid, a few minutes a day, you can work that muscle with the best of them."

They shook hands, but Dawson wasn't fooled. Stan Barnes wouldn't trade Dawson in for any other kid in the world, but part of that was because Dawson came with the kid that *nobody* would trade in for any other kid in the world. Benji's mother was just as crazy about Dawson—the fact that the boys hadn't ended up as a couple was really a miracle of gay chromosomes and straight, because by all rights they should have been married by now.

Dawson let his dad and Benji chat for a minute while he started a kettle for tea. He pulled out the special rosehip chamomile blend Benji had made him buy when he was buying four other kinds of fever and flu medications at the drug store.

He came back into the living room with a soda for his dad, who was already sprawled out on the couch, surfing with the remote.

"I'm making tea," he said, and his dad's sardonic eyebrow said volumes about being Captain Obvious. Dawson blew out a breath. "And there's tinned chicken soup. And orange juice. And...." He swallowed and looked over his shoulder to his bedroom. "And he's asleep now, but he's going to wake up and this isn't his place, so if he's out of it, try not to shoot him or anything. He might not like basketball, but he knows you're gonna be watching it, so don't worry."

"I know how to babysit, Dawson. Do you want me to go home and get out Candy Land and Monopoly?"

Dawson bounced on his toes and tried not to say the stupid, sappy thing. "Dad…." Whine, whine, whine. "Dad… see, he's… he likes us to think he's all cool and self-contained, right? I mean, I didn't even know he was sick. I think he was going to try to fake it and he could barely stand. So he's not. All cool and self-contained, I mean. I think he could be, but… you know, for some reason he *trusts* us here. And you're new, and you need to be trustworthy, okay?"

Dad's eyebrows shot up and he turned to Benji. "Your assessment?" He smiled slightly, and Dawson knew that was his dad's shorthand for *My idiot son is making no sense. Maybe you could interpret for me?*

"Don't intrude on his space. He thinks Dawson walks on water—"

"The hell—"

"No, Dawson, I'm serious. He thinks Dawson walks on water for some reason—just, you know. Let him dream. And, uhm." Benji darted a guilty glance at Dawson for this one. "Uhm, be… circumspect, Mr. B. He's… he's like—like… like, *fragile*."

"Fragile?" Dad looked Dawson square in the eye. "Three months you've been raving about this guy and 'fragile' doesn't enter into it?"

Dawson fidgeted for a minute. "Well, to be fair, it's more Benji's word than mine," he apologized, and whoops! There went those red eyebrows.

"And your word for the guy you're nuts about and see every six weeks is…?"

Dawson wasn't going respond. Nope, nope, nope, nope, nope… he wasn't going to finish his dad's sentence for him. It was his *dad's* sentence, and dammit, Stan was a grown-up and didn't need Dawson's interference to finish a perfectly good construction of subject, verb, complement—

"Fucking alone," Dawson blurted, and then he looked over his shoulder and thanked *God* that just this once, Jared stayed put, probably unconscious in Dawson's room.

And then Benji started humming Green Day's "Long View," and Dawson *literally* smacked his forehead with the palm of his hand.

"I will beat you!" he threatened.

Benji put his hands up. "I'm sorry—you started it! Why didn't you just pick my word?"

Dawson wrinkled his nose and shifted uncomfortably. "Because," he said, thinking of Jared shivering under his comforter, closing his eyes in trust. "Because I only see him every so often and I don't like to think of him alone," he finished miserably. He looked at his dad with sort of a plea in his eyes. "Dad, please. This conversation never happened, okay?"

Stan Barnes pursed his lips and sighed. "I get it. He's adamantium, you're the soul of discretion, and I'm the schmuck giving him tea and chicken broth."

Dawson nodded, his expression completely sober. "You're the best dad ever."

"I am. Now go. I understand you're gainfully employed. I *like* this trend! Keep it up!"

Dawson rolled his eyes, because it was a patent ploy. Fact was, Dawson and Benji were reliable enough to actually make most of their rent and food. They still needed help with gas and school expenses, but in an industry known for its divas and excessive personalities, the two of them were damned close to making a living simply by being dependable and talented.

"Yes, Father. I will continue, and I'll study and ace all my classes—just, you know...." He made vague gestures in the air.

"Don't sabotage your love life."

Dawson nodded gratefully, and he and Benji grabbed their keys, their wallets, the girls, and then hopped into Benji's POS (different from Dawson's only by make and model—the dings, primer spots, and bald tires came standard) and left, rolling down the windows to spare the AC until they got to the freeway.

Once the AC kicked in—and the windows were up—Benji was the brave one who said something first. "You didn't tell your dad about the drugs?"

Dawson sighed. "I didn't tell my dad about the *desperation*," he murmured, because he was pretty sure the drugs weren't the real problem. "I didn't tell my dad about the kid in the man."

"He's twenty-six," Amber muttered from the back of the car, and Dawson threw himself back in his seat.

"It's hard to explain." He held his fingers up against the AC, which never seemed to blow hard enough. "It's like... I mean, he's all the cool stuff I saw that first time, and all of that awesome thing we saw onstage, but at the same time, he's...."

"Human," Amber growled from the backseat. "We see it all the time, Daw—the pretty people on the stage have the most fucked-up lives. You know that. They get together for six weeks, sleep together, break up, drink too much, smoke too much, tweak to lose weight, get the audition—whatever. Everybody gets sucked into it at least once— why would you and Jared be any different?"

Dawson grunted and crossed his arms. "You guys aren't hearing me." He thought of the last time Jared had visited, and he'd taken Dawson's car and wandered unfamiliar streets to come back with a DVD of his favorite movie and a fifth of bourbon with soda so they could get Benji drunk and his mind off Darian. He thought of the texts every morning at seven, saying, *I'm running. Join me.* Dawson ran with him not because he needed the exercise but because he didn't want to think of Jared on the streets alone.

He thought of the actual handwritten postcards he'd gotten from the places Jared saw daily in LA, or the places he'd gone to perform. He had postcards from Disneyland, Malibu, the Chinese Theater, and New York. He had actual letters, on stationery even, saying quiet things like *The worst thing about being on the plane is that the engine noise plays in your head for the next twelve hours. I bet you'd talk the whole time.* That *I could hear.*

"Then use your words like a grown-up," Darian said into the silence. She hadn't been here last time. She hadn't *seen* Jared come back with an armload of action-adventure films and alcohol and then sit down and try to think of funny things to say when he wasn't great at it. She *really* hadn't seen him running for a cool cloth and ice water when Benji was hungover the next morning. She hadn't *seen* him be nice to Amber, or pull a vintage Ramones T-shirt out of his duffel for her because his roommate was going to throw it out and he knew she'd like it.

Darian would get to know him, Dawson had no doubts about that, but right now, it was Dawson's job to make sure Jared was as important to her as he was to Amber and Benji.

Dawson clasped his long fingers, reassured by their warmth against the chill. "He's even better as a person than he is on the stage," he said after a minute. "On the stage, he's… untouchable. And I know that he fucked up, and I know it scares us all that he could be one of the people we see fuck up on a regular basis, but it's, like, *worth* it, to know that he can fuck up. He can be one of us."

There was silence in the car then, and Benji grunted. "Dawson, maybe he's always been one of us. Maybe the fucking up is just a sign that he needs you more than every now and then, you think?"

"Yeah," Dawson sighed. "I just don't know what to do about that. 'Hey, Jared, I know you've got a place on the top of the food chain and we're all muddling along on the bottom, but, you know, the bottom's not gonna get you hooked on drugs or dying in a hotel room alone, so, how 'bout it?'"

The peanut gallery didn't reply. Amber reached from the backseat to squeeze his shoulder, and Benji turned up the music, and that was how they drove into Sacramento.

THE SHOW was one of those experimental things—plot optional—and not even Benji's brilliant light plan and sound engineering could keep the entire audience from going, "Huh?" at the end.

"Thanks, Benj," Darian said as they got in the car. "I gave up a Thursday night with Dawson's dad to watch that."

Benji sighed. "Yeah, well, tomorrow night *you* can stay home and babysit Dawson's boyfriend. Sorry, baby—just not lots of good options with this one."

"Sleep," Amber grunted. She'd done another show the night before, and she had classes too. "Sleep would be an excellent option. Dawson, you're not gonna have to work to kick your dad off the couch, are you?"

"Hold on, let me text him and tell him we're on our way."

"Right." Amber yawned and curled up in a little ball in the corner of the car, and Darian folded her arms and pouted in the backseat. She could pout beautifully—in fact, Dawson was pretty sure this pout meant Benji was going to get some tonight, and good for Benji. Dawson was going to get nothing but worry, *that* was what *he* was going to get.

All done. On way home.

I'm torturing him with pins and hot pokers.

I'm sure he's enjoying that.

Text him yourself. He looks lonely.

Oh. Okay—big lesson. Relationship 101: talk to your boyfriend. That was a revelation.

Hey—you conscious?

I must not be. The Lakers are losing. It's like a dream.

And I missed it? Who are they playing?

Who cares? LOSING. I'm so happy.

I had no idea you were this passionate.

I hate LA.

This was news to Dawson.

You're the idiot who lives there. Come live here. I understand we have a booming experimental theater program.

Long pause, and Dawson's dad texted right as they were approaching Roseville.

He fell asleep, D.

Oh. Almost home.

Dawson's dad knew Amber lived on their couch—it was hard to miss the dresser they'd moved into the living room so she had someplace to keep her stuff. One of the things they had to do every day was clean up the various water glasses and soda cans that accrued on the top of it, which she did when she cleaned off the coffee table. It was sort of her thing. So Dawson's dad was up and grabbing his suit jacket and putting on his shoes almost as soon as the key turned in the lock, because he was just that good of a person.

"Good show?" he asked, taking in their rather irritated looks.

"That depends on your point of view," Benji muttered. "The technical department was *fantastic*!"

"And the play?"

Dawson shrugged. "Dad, there was a live goat onstage. He took a dump. It was the only part of the play the audience understood."

Amber shook her head. "And that fucker missed his cue."

Benji's eyes got wide like he suddenly understood something. "Oh! Was *that* why the spotlight was on the guy in the corner doing airplane signals?"

Darian rolled her eyes. "Yeah, honey—he was trying to talk to the goat!"

"Oh!" Benji scrubbed his face with his hands. "It all makes so much more sense now!"

Dawson looked at him. "You're a total freak, because it's still bullshit to me."

"I was being sarcastic, Dawson." Benji scowled and then looked at Dawson's dad in supplication. "*I'm* twenty-one, Mr. Barnes—is there any way you could bring *me* beer if you come tomorrow?"

Dawson's dad squeezed his eyes shut and pinched the bridge of his nose. "Oh my God. *I* need beer just knowing there's a stage production with a live goat!"

"Better than that Edward Albee play with the dead one!" Darian chirped hopefully, swinging toward the refrigerator. "But yes, Dawson's dad, I would throw over my own family for you and you alone if you brought us some alcohol to cope with that tomorrow."

"You know I'd be sent to jail *and* parental hell if I listened to you whiners, don't you? And was there *really* a play that featured a goat?"

"I'm outta here," Amber muttered. "I'm sleeping on Dawson's floor, next to the dying guy. I *worked* that show—I don't need to discuss it."

"He's not dying, and omigod—I thought *nobody* worked that show. I thought that show died when it debuted." Dawson grunted.

"It won a Tony," Jared said from the doorway. "Amber, you're welcome to sleep on the floor. Dawson, the floor is wobbling."

Dawson turned to where a *very* shaky Jared was standing in the doorway, and he rushed to Jared's side and put his hand on his forehead very much like his dad had done when he was younger. "Oh Jesus—when was the last time you took drugs?"

"Legal ones?" Jared said woozily. "'Cause that was right before you left, remember?"

"Yeah, well, let's get you some more. And you're soaking wet! God, are the sheets that bad?"

Dawson's dad caught his eyes and nodded. Without breaking his gaze, he said, "Amber, hon, if you'll take me at my word not to bother you, would you like to sleep in my guest bedroom for a few? I can bring you to school in the morning. I think it's gonna be a rough night here."

Amber, growly Amber with the half-opened eyes and the perpetual scowl, actually launched herself at him in a hug that looked half-hilarious because she barely cleared his ribcage. "You're the best, Mr. Dawson's Dad. Let me get my stuff."

There was chaos then, and Benji got a towel so Jared could sit on the couch while Dawson changed the sheets. His dad walked into his room while he was tucking corners and said, "If he doesn't get better by tomorrow, you may want to think about taking him to the doc's. He's going to need fluids if nothing else."

Dawson looked up, swallowing hard. "Was he this bad—"

"No—he fell asleep a half an hour ago, as you guys were driving home. He was fine. His meds wore off, that's all—but buddy, I think he was really sick before he got here."

He would *not* tell about the vitamin C and bump of coke. Because it was private, that was all. Instead, all he could think about was the *I'm running* texts, and the *Good house tonight, but I'm a little wiped out* texts, and the *I keep thinking about the stupid stuff I do in my day and wondering how you'd make it not stupid and not boring* texts. He thought of running through the streets with his asthma inhaler, feeling put out and like he was being all brave for his demanding boyfriend.

And the whole time, there had not been a single *I feel like hell and I'm all alone* text. Not one.

Long-distance relationships—maybe not so awesome, even *with* the technology.

IT WAS a good thing Amber went over to his dad's house, because the night was *rough*. Around four in the morning, Jared's fever spiked again, and this time it took revenge on all of the fluids Dawson had been trying to pump down Jared's throat, and the results were... unpleasant.

After an hour falling in and out of sleep sitting on the side of the bathtub while Jared dry heaved into the commode, Dawson had to concede defeat.

"Jared?"

"What's left of him."

"You ready to go to the doctor's yet?"

"It couldn't be more embarrassing than this."

Dawson's puff of breath woke him up a little. "Embarrassment? That's what you're worried about? 'Cause Benji and I once had the runs in this bathroom. At the same time. Trust me. I'm good."

"Awesome." Jared coughed. "I'll remember that visual when I'm hiding in shame."

Dawson rubbed his back, the fever burning through his sweat-soaked shirt. "Please tell me it wasn't this bad for the last week."

"No," Jared muttered. "I saved up all the fun stuff for you."

Dawson couldn't smile, but he appreciated the effort. "Baby—baby, you're done. Let's get you to the doc, and get some fluids in you, and when you can actually stand up, I'm going to yell at you, because...." He swallowed. He couldn't say it. Not now. Not when Jared had just tried to make him laugh.

"I'm sorry," Jared whispered, resting his cheek against the seat. "I'm sorry. I should have stayed home."

"So you could be like this in front of guys whose names you don't know? Fuck that. If you've got to fly to Sacramento to have someone take care of you, do that, okay?"

"God," Jared mumbled, his voice echoing into the bowl. "I'd just rather die."

Something sproinged like a broken piano string, and it snapped across Dawson's chest so brutally he gasped and looked at his shirt, surprised he wasn't bleeding through.

"That's a shitty thing to say," he muttered, his voice full and thick. "And I'm gonna go get Benji so we can get you into the car."

It took two of them to haul Jared—who was stripped down to his boxers—into Dawson's POS. Jared had Kaiser, which was a blessing because they didn't have to hunt for a hospital. There was an ER in Roseville, and Dawson pretty much floored it, partly out of fear that Jared would lose his stomach lining and God knew what else in his front seat, but mostly from worry.

Jared was drifty but conscious when he they admitted him, which was good because he knew all sorts of things that Dawson didn't, like if he was allergic to penicillin and when his last tetanus shot had been, and if he was HIV positive (no, apparently he'd just cleared his window), and when his exact birthday was (about two months later than Dawson's—he'd be twenty-seven). In general, he had to provide the tiny details that made up a person's medical history that you only got to know if you were so intimate with someone you memorized their Social Security number to help them fill out paperwork.

The hospital staff wheeled him down the hall and got him set up in a bed, and Dawson tried to follow.

"I'm sorry, are you family?" the nurse asked, and Dawson felt his chin wobble. She seemed like a nice woman, older with wide gray eyes and a kindly smile. Maybe he didn't have anything to be afraid of.

"I'm his boyfriend," he said roughly. "He... he flew all the way to Sacramento so I could take care of him because he's got nobody else."

The nurse's eyes widened, and she gestured him down the hall.

When Jared got to his room, the nurses took his vitals and attached monitors, then administered an IV for fluids. The staff left after telling them the doctor would be there soon, and Dawson pulled up a chair. Jared was lying, eyes closed, body shaking, and he seemed too miserable to talk to. Dawson himself was exhausted. He put his head on the mattress next to Jared and closed his eyes, waiting for the doctor to come so he had a course of action, something to do.

Two hours—apparently that was the standard wait for a doctor these days—and when the guy walked in, he looked as young as Jared and as exhausted as Dawson. "So," he said, raising his eyebrows. "The flu?"

"Yeah," Jared said, his eyes still closed. "Sucks."

"I guess. How long have you had it?"

"Mm…." Jared seemed to think. "What day is it?"

"Friday morning."

"Since Saturday night."

"*Jared*!" Dawson was suddenly wide-awake. "Jared, that's *horrible*. You've been performing like this for a *week*?"

"My agent kept telling me I needed the exposure," Jared mumbled, and Dawson narrowed his eyes. Agent. He'd heard vague references—his agent was the one who set up the charity work and who made sure his venues were big enough to be worth his time.

"Your agent's a douche," he said without mercy. "He couldn't see you were this fucking sick?"

"I'm sorry," said the doctor. "Who are you?"

"I'm his boyfriend," Dawson said, feeling raw. Boyfriend—geez, that seemed to mean a whole lot more than what Dawson had been to Jared so far, didn't it?

"This is Dawson," Jared said, his eyes still closed and his mouth quirking at the corners. "He grows on you. His dad is a nice guy, and his best friend really doesn't want to get into his pants."

The doctor laughed, opening his sleepy eyes a little wider, his stubbled face seeming alert for the first time since he walked through the door. "Well, Dawson, that seems to qualify you as someone to talk to. Seriously, he's pretty dehydrated, and I want to get his fever down through the IV for at least a day before we let him go. I'm saying he stays off his feet for at least a week before he goes back to—it says here you're a dancer?"

"For the LA Ballet," Dawson muttered. "So he's going to have to get on a plane before he goes back to work."

More big eyes. Dawson figured if he wasn't currently freaking out over his boyfriend, the doctor's bony face and perpetual surprise might have made him crushworthy, but not right now. "Okay, then. I'm making it an order. No dancing until next Friday."

"Thursday," Jared begged quietly. "Please? I can give the understudy the job until Friday night, but I need a day to rehearse."

Dawson grunted, unhappy with that but thinking he'd have Jared to watch over at least until Wednesday afternoon. The doctor nodded in concession, wrote out the order, and left, telling them it would be another twelve hours at least before Jared was discharged.

Fuck. Dawson pulled out his phone and tapped in an alarm.

"What are you doing?" Jared asked, his voice raspy.

"Reminding myself to call Topher. That douche bag is going to have to sub for me after all."

"No—"

"Look," Dawson snapped, so at the end of his emotional reserves he had nowhere else to lash but out. "We only have room for one of us to be the workaholic, okay? And right now, you're the one in the hospital, so guess who gets the red-carpet treatment, jerk-off!"

"I'm sorry," Jared whispered, his voice breaking, and the hell of it was, Dawson *knew* he was.

Dawson grunted and laid his head next to the Jared's again, tracing the dark stubble line between his cheeks and his cheekbone. "I... baby, are we good enough, solid enough, that maybe, when you can talk, you can tell me *why*? Why dance? Why kill yourself with it? Just... something real, okay? I haven't been this scared for someone pretty much in my entire life. I just need to know why."

Jared nodded almost imperceptibly, and Dawson took that as agreement.

Good. Good. Okay. So Jared would tell him, and he would feel better about the world, and everything would be happy-fine.

A NEW SHOW

MAYBE.

Maybe it would be happy-fine, once Jared got the tube out of his arm and Dawson could have him back in his little college apartment, where all his friends were waiting to make sure happy-fine was at least on the menu.

TOPHER WAS, of course, a complete asshole about taking over for Dawson right up until Dawson told him he'd get his professor to do it and Topher didn't have to bother, and suddenly Topher was all sweetness and fucking light.

Dawson told him that if he said one wrong word to Amber as first chair, he'd give Amber permission to castrate him. Topher laughed at first, but Dawson wasn't kidding, even a little bit. Nobody fucked with Amber.

And then Dawson went down to the cafeteria, bought himself some breakfast and a cup of coffee, and went back to sleep in the room with Jared for a little while.

Jared was sort of drifty. The meds were making him sleep, and he obviously didn't feel as completely shitty as he had, but he wasn't all aloof and Jared-like anymore. Dawson sort of wanted to take advantage of that.

Jared's guard was so hard to slide down it might as well have been a wet suit in a cold ocean. Maybe Dawson could take advantage of better living through chemistry.

He brought Jared some orange juice, since the nurses had already brought him some and he'd downed it. He set the OJ down on the little table, then tucked himself back into his chair, curling his feet under his bottom and leaning forward so he could lean his chin on his hand and trace delicate patterns on Jared's skin. His skin tone was darker than Dawson's, which Dawson liked, and the hair on his arms was surprisingly black. After a day without shaving, he had a pretty decent beard going, and Dawson wondered how often he had to wax.

"You should go home," Jared said softly, and Dawson looked up to see that Jared was studying his face as intensely as Dawson was studying his forearm. Way to prioritize.

"They're bringing me a cot," Dawson told him. "I've got a sub for the night—"

"That asshole who—"

"Doesn't matter, Jared," Dawson said bleakly, reaching up to touch his cheek. He wasn't sweating anymore, but his skin felt papery, and Dawson figured his body had about reached its limit. "Why dance? I mean, I know you love it. I'm around actors enough—everybody's got a reason. Why dance?"

Jared looked away and closed his eyes. "It's private," he said softly.

"It's a deal breaker." Dawson heard his voice and wasn't even sure he said it until Jared jerked his head around and stared at him, betrayed.

"Dawson—"

"I'll forgive it all, Jared. The being sick and hiding it, the using coke to wreck yourself, the flying into my arms to collapse—all of it, totally worth it. But, I mean, I don't know your Social Security number or your parents' names or your little sister's name or your roommate's name or your fucking agent's name—but I have to know why dance?"

"Sophia," Jared murmured. "Her name is Sophia. I already told you this, Dawson. She doesn't live with my parents anymore—they put her in a home. You know this. You know I'm not allowed to visit."

That did it. The burning in Dawson's eyes spilled over into tears. "Awesome," he said thickly. "You're right, you already told me this, but it adds to the crapfest of the last two days. Why dance?"

Jared grunted. "She's six years younger than I am," he said, and Dawson wanted to snap at him, but he was making an effort to concentrate, so he backed off. "And my parents... they hired nannies and physical therapists and stuff, but really, I was the only one there for her. And one of the nannies had a cousin who danced. And he was beautiful, you know?"

Dawson thought of Jared sweating and alone in the spotlight, and of the way the skin of his chest felt under Dawson's palms, and the way Dawson could look at those high cheekbones and square chin forever, just to see the way they were put together that made them so appealing. "I know," he said dryly, but he wasn't sure if Jared heard.

"And he was patient with Sophia, and, and...." Jared closed his eyes. "And I just sat and watched him, you know?" He took a minute to breathe, and Dawson thought, *I know where this is going*, but he didn't say anything. He kissed the back of Jared's hand, but this once, he kept quiet.

"I was...." Jared's voice wandered to that place where people counted age. "Nine," he said in surprise. "About all he could do with Sophia was whirl her around in his arms, but it was a job for him. And I just... watched." Deep breath. "And he noticed me. Told me to come and be in the spotlight. Showed me the positions, with my legs." Breathe. Dawson actually *heard* the excitement, the pride, the shame in his voice. "Gave me my first kiss. Told me it was okay if I got hard, but he was too old for me. Told me to not be alone in a corner. Made me feel special."

Dawson's throat tightened, and Jared wasn't looking at him, so he let some of the exhaustion and the worry spill over, and then he wiped it away. "Jared," he said when he'd gotten himself under control, "Jared, I need you to look at me."

Jared did, and Dawson thought, *God, he's pale*, and then he said what he needed to. "What was his name?"

"Mario," Jared said, smiling a little, and Dawson just bet the guy had been beautiful and graceful and perfect and not Dawson.

"Jared, my name is Dawson, and I'm more important to you than that guy, okay?"

Jared blinked and trailed his hand over Dawson's cheek. "Yeah, I know that."

"No, no, you don't. He gave you dance, and that's fine, 'cause dance gave me you, but... but I'm the one you came to when you felt like hell, and I'm the one who took care of you. So I need to be more important than the dance, you understand?"

"Dance is more than Mario," Jared said, seeming to focus for a moment.

"Yeah, well, tell me."

Jared took a fortifying breath—and then coughed, which did not make Dawson any more receptive to what he had to say next. "I dream sometimes," he said through a raspy chest. "I dream I can't move. My body is frozen, and I'm invisible, and I wake up sweating, checking my bones, checking my knees and my feet. I'm *terrified* I'll never fly again. I'll be trapped flat on the ground like a rock. Like I'm already dead. *That's* dance. I need it to breathe."

Dawson's whole body ran cold. "Baby—baby, do you need to be onstage in front of people to do that?"

And he thought about it. That pause, right there, that was the thing that gave Dawson faith.

"No," he answered. "No. Just dancing… being inside the music. That's all I need."

The ice in Dawson's bowels thawed a little, and he realized his hand had gone clammy in Jared's. This whole shitty weekend, and it could have disintegrated if Jared had been more addicted to the stage than to the art.

He caught his breath and was able to finish the conversation. "Well, listen to me. You won't be able to dance unless you heal. You need to stay here till Friday and *not dance* until Saturday like the doctor said. You need to take time off—not just for me, although that would be great, but for you, because you're exhausted and you have no life, and *you're mine*, and I want you healthier than that, okay?"

Oh, hell, not okay. Jared's gaze wandered, and this was a shitty thing to do to someone who could barely hold his head up.

"I need to call Dolph," Jared said after a minute.

"Who in the fuck is *Dolph*?" God, non sequiturs and subtext, they were gonna kill him.

"My agent," Jared said, and he yawned. "Dolph will tell me if I can."

Dawson nodded, thinking that he knew where Jared's phone was, and if anyone was going to talk to Jared's agent, it was going to be Dawson.

"Get some sleep," Dawson mumbled, feeling the completely shitty night in his bones. "I'll be here when you wake up. You'll be able to smell me from Mars—that's how you'll know."

Jared nodded, and his dark lashes fanned his pale cheeks for a moment. "Don't leave."

Dawson's eyes spilled over. "Swear."

The nurse brought in the cot in a few minutes, with a little pillow and a blanket, and Dawson crawled in and closed his eyes and wished he could be a grown-up when he woke up.

NO DICE. The magic grown-up fairy did not just appear, sprinkle some dust, and tell Dawson how to put Sacramento next to Los Angeles without crashing the rest of the state into the ocean. But *Benji* showed up with some better food and a change of clothes and a pillow and the fuzzy blanket from the foot of Dawson's bed, the one in bright orange that was cuddly forever.

Dawson looked at the collection of stuff in the bag and smiled. "You love me."

Benji lifted one shoulder. "Eh. Are you really going to put Topher in the booth tonight?"

Dawson looked up to the bed, where Jared was still sleeping. The light from the window made the skin of his cheeks translucent and highlighted the remains of what had probably been freckles from his childhood, and Dawson fought the urge to go stroke them with his thumb.

"Yeah," he said quietly. "I was gonna call Professor Weber to sub if he couldn't. That pissed him off—I think the douchebucket might behave."

Benji sighed and sat down next to him, then wrapped an arm around Dawson's shoulder. Dawson leaned his head against him.

"He's going to be okay, right?" Benji asked reassuringly.

"Yeah," Dawson tried to sound happy too—but he couldn't. "This time."

"What—how many times does a guy get a killer attack of the flu?"

Dawson looked up at Benji—self-assured, I've-got-your-back Benji—and tried to imagine a time when Benji had ever needed to stand in the spotlight and be the prettiest one.

"He drove himself to it," Dawson said quietly.

"I figured," Benji replied heavily. "God, Dawson. What are you going to—"

"I mean, we watch them all the time. We sort of make fun of them, right? The guys in the front of the house. I mean, *we* want to make the stories real, and that's why we do what we do. But we don't want to be *in* the stories, because the stories *hurt*. It's *hard* to survive those stories. And you and me, we've got it okay, right? We don't want to see if we've got it in us to live through that. But Jared—he's been alone since… since ever. And he's survived. But if him and me, we're going to make it work, I've got to be that strong, don't I? I've got to be in his story, and not just the guy behind the scenes."

Benji sighed. "Yeah."

Dawson leaned on him some more. "You get a good secondary role, you know."

"I brought you a fuzzy blanket. Does that count?"

"And food. That's better than sleeping with the director."

"Booyah. Go shower. I'll stay here in case he wakes up."

Dawson kissed his cheek because he felt like it, and Benji didn't even roll his eyes or *anything*. "Thanks. He's coming home tomorrow, and he's not going back until Friday."

"Awesome. I'll buy cottage cheese and orange juice." Benji slid his eyes sideways then, and a corner of his mobile, laughing mouth quirked up. Dawson suddenly loved him, all in a rush.

"I'll give you our firstborn," Dawson said solemnly.

Benji rolled his eyes. "I'll give him back. I'm not even playing! Now go shower!"

ALONG WITH the food and the fuzzy blanket, Benji had also brought Dawson's laptop and his backpack. After the shower and the chow, Dawson sat quietly, his back against Jared's bed, his feet propped up on the wall with the window, and wrote his final paper on American romanticism, which was due that Monday. He was in the middle of talking about how American romanticism was the equivalent of the American sixties, only with hard alcohol instead of LSD, when he had a sudden thought.

"Hey, Jared," he said, out of the blue—he wasn't even sure Jared was awake just then.

"Huh, what?"

Apparently not.

Dawson glanced over his shoulder sheepishly. "Sorry, man. I was just wondering—you said you went from dance school to the theater—how do you know about *The Scarlet Letter*?"

"BA in Liberal Studies, night school."

Dawson turned the chair around fully and narrowed his eyes. "God, Jared. You're really fuckin' driven."

Jared turned his head and regarded Dawson sleepily. "Yes," he said, as though it just occurred to him.

"I mean, dance, yeah—I get it now. Dance is a drive. For you it's like food, except more, because you *literally* give up food to dance. But why a BA in Liberalosity? What in the hell?"

Jared smiled and closed his eyes. "It's all about stories, Dawson. Dance tells a story, writers tell a story. Isn't that what you said to Benji? The assholes in the front of the house want to be in the story."

"You were supposed to be asleep." Dawson tried to remember the conversation. Had he said anything untoward? Mentioned any moles or the fact that Jared had a foreskin? Nope. Nope. The most offensive thing about that convo had already been—

"You said you wanted to be part of the story," Jared murmured. "How was I supposed to sleep through that?"

Dawson's face heated, and he saved his work and shut his laptop so he could go rest his head next to Jared's bed.

"I do," he said, and then he thought that needed qualifications. "I mean, no public appearances or, you know, that sort of thing. But Jared, you're gonna make me your emergency contact, right? I get your agent's number, and your home phone and home address and all that shit, right? Because right now, I think about you getting back on that plane, and it's like… like the first time my dad put me on a plane and sent me to LA. He said it *sucked*. He went to work and stared at his screen until he saw my plane had landed and I texted him from the runway. I'm gonna be *just like that* only worse, because *nobody* is going to greet you when you get there. So I'm basically gonna be an electronic bug in your ass. I'm going to want your itinerary, and if I don't bodybug you and link it to my computer to read your vitals, it's because if you so much as choke on a swallow of water, I'm going to be on a plane to LA."

Jared lifted his hand to ruffle Dawson's hair. "You're adorable," he said dreamily.

"Ado—adora… Jesus fuckin' *Christ*—!" Dawson was still sputtering when Jared brushed his lower lip with a languid thumb.

"You're right," he said. "It's love."

Dawson froze midrant and glared. "You say that now. Say that by Friday—"

"Thursday?" Jared frowned and made an effort to focus, but the fact that he had to *try* to look Dawson in the eyes only proved Dawson's point.

"*Friday*. I'll call this Dolph person and tell him—"

"You wouldn't!" Jared forced his eyes open, and for a moment, he was the controlling dick Dawson had first met and loathed. "Dawson, that's my own business connection and—"

"And if he's a business connection, he needs to know you can't perform Friday night," Dawson said implacably. "And if you're going to come to my home and throw up for *hours*, then my opinion needs to be more important than his."

Jared looked like he was going to argue about it—he had the glare down and he was trying to use it to cow Dawson into conceding that he was being an intrusive little shit—but then he yawned and closed his eyes, and Dawson didn't even try to contain his grin of triumph.

"Gloating is horribly unattractive," Jared muttered.

"Well, since I'm probably not getting laid today, I'll file that for later."

"God," Jared groaned, turning his head away. "Dolph is gonna kill me!"

"Yeah, well, he can save that for when you can fend off my bunny slippers. In the meantime, get some sleep. I've got an asshole to call and a paper to finish. And you're going to be here until tomorrow."

"*Fuuuckkk....*"

Dawson patted his hand and turned back to his paper. For the first time since they checked into the hospital, Dawson felt a little better about being there in the first place.

THE NEXT day Jared went pee-pee all by his little lonesome. He took a shower, he ate some pudding, and his fever stayed down with the fever meds but not without it. The doctor cleared him to go home—or the closest thing to it—but *not* to work until Saturday.

"You look like hell, you're twenty pounds underweight, and if I was a rich celebrity type doctor, I'd check you into a clinic for exhaustion and mean it. Go sleep and see if you can't function like a human being after that."

Dawson grinned at the guy as he was writing out the order. "You're a *peach*!" he crowed. "An absolute peach! If I wasn't already taken, I'd blow ya!"

The guy blinked and then raised his eyebrows. "And wouldn't my wife be surprised. But yeah, take him home, take care of him, and get out of my hospital. Deal?"

Dawson nodded enthusiastically and grabbed the bag with Jared's sweaty clothes. Benji brought scrubs for Jared to wear in the car, because Benji was a good guy, but he wasn't going through Jared's suitcase, and that was fine with Dawson.

"Saturday," Jared said fretfully. He looked at the wheelchair the orderly had brought for him and grimaced. "Is that necessary?"

"Hell yeah!" Dawson insisted. "Haven't you seen the medical dramas? You *have* to ride in that thing. It's a liability issue." He nodded sincerely, and Jared glared at him.

Benji and Darian had taken Dawson's car home the day before, and Dawson's dad got pickup duty. Jared got to ride in the front *again*, and Dawson got to ride in the back with—

"Holy hell, Dad, did you buy enough Gatorade?"

"No. Look at him. He sweated out five pounds."

"The doctor says twenty," Dawson said, irritated.

Jared grunted. "The doctor's off by ten," he said. "I'm usually ten pounds light."

Dawson's general irritation was not made any better by that little bit of news. "No more cottage cheese and fruit for you," he muttered. "We're gonna live *large*. You're gonna have yourself some broiled chicken and some goddamned nuts on *your* salad, oh yes you are."

Jared grunted. "Yeah, Dawson. That'll fix everything. Nuts on the salad."

"I called Dolph, goddammit. You're not going back until Friday and not performing until Saturday, and that's that. So see? Baby steps. Today I call Dolph, tomorrow you have nuts on the salad, give it a year, you'll be a real fuckin' boy."

"Great bedside manner, son. I approve. Are you going to wake him up with bright lights and sound tomorrow? Can I help?"

Dawson kicked the back of his dad's seat and yearned for his own bed, with or without a sweaty, sick Jared. He had *not* slept well in the hospital.

He'd actually *dreamed* of tracking Jared's manager down to his office in LA and strangling the guy with a phone cord. *God*, what an asshole.

The conversation hadn't started well.

"Jared, babe, are you ready to take me up on my offer of a week in Bali?"

"Bali isn't particularly gay friendly and Jared's boyfriend might have to kick the whole world in the balls if you did that."

"Who in the fuck is this?"

"This is Jared's boyfriend, Dawson, the one who just spent three days in hell trying to keep him alive."

"What's wrong? Was there an accident? Did he hurt himself? Oh God, please not a knee or an Achilles—that shit takes years to heal. Let me talk to him!"

Dawson experienced rage on a whole new level. "He's unconscious. The doctor sedated him so he could let the fever drugs do their work. You can't talk to him because he's too sick to talk. He's too sick to talk because you let him work until he dropped. Well, this is it. He dropped. He was supposed to be back Monday, but he'll be back Friday and maybe able to dance on Saturday—*with* doc approval. He'll have a note and everything, but until then, you want to talk to Jared, you have to go through me. Here's my cell."

Dolph sputtered, but Dawson was beyond hearing. He shot out his cell number like he was spitting out watermelon seeds and hung up Jared's phone.

Then he turned it off.

He figured when Jared was well enough to ask for it, Dawson would charge it up and he could talk, but until then, nope. It was all sleep and sunshine for his boy. That was just the way it would be.

But that didn't mean Dawson was going to be a happy camper until he got some sleep in his own bed, some food that didn't taste like hospital smell, and some sexy-happy time touching his boyfriend.

Fortunately for the whole damned world, he had the weekend off.

Jared's fever broke the next day. He sweated like a champion for a couple of hours and then took a shower while Dawson changed the sheets. And then he slept—for fourteen hours.

Dawson worked on his finals in the meantime and as support crew for everyone working that night. This included cooking dinner, and he'd had enough sleep to actually smile when Benji gave him shit about wearing an apron. So it was domestic—claustrophobic, because he and Jared were stuck inside on a gorgeously hot May weekend that should have been used for swimming and playing Frisbee in the quad— but domestic, and by Sunday, when Jared was actually ready to be awake and communicative, Dawson's irritated funk had worn off.

They actually made it through a movie, Jared leaning on Dawson in the living room while waiting for everyone else to get back from the show.

Jared grabbed the remote control during a commercial and paused the screen.

"Can I tell you I'm sorry again?" he said quietly.

Dawson looked down at his profile and kissed his temple. "Can I tell you it's okay and I hope I wasn't too much of an asshole?" he responded.

"Yeah," Jared murmured and leaned into the kiss. "Can I have my phone back tomorrow?"

It was the first time he'd asked for it. Dawson had to think for a minute. "That depends. What are you going to do with it?"

"Make my plane reservations."

Alert, alert, alert! "Mm, book plane tickets first, talk to Dolph the douche next."

Jared grunted. "You didn't like Dolph?"

"He started out the conversation asking you if you would run away with him to Bali."

A quiet laugh then, and Jared snuggled into Dawson's arms. "He says that to everybody. I hope you didn't give him too hard a time."

Dawson thought about it. "I may not be his favorite person ever," he said and decided he could live with that.

"Oh God," Jared murmured, like that was going to be the end-all, be-all of his career.

Dawson was beyond caring. "Seriously, I really only care if I'm still *your* favorite person. Am I?"

Jared's voice rumbled low. "You're even more my favorite person now than you were when I got here. How's that?"

Dawson's body hummed lazily. "Think you'll be up for sex before Friday?"

Jared yawned and snuggled even deeper into his chest. "I guarantee it."

"Yeah, well, then being your favorite person just *might* begin to pay off."

They woke up when the group got back from Sacramento, and they stumbled into Dawson's room, stripped to their boxers, and fell asleep.

Dawson's last thought before he went was that he may, just maybe, get some sex this week.

It was like all that other stuff didn't even happen, he was so excited!

THEY LEFT Jared alone to go to school on Monday, all four of them—Dawson, Benji, Darian, and Amber—and when they got back, Jared was up at Dawson's computer, booking a plane ticket home.

Dawson walked behind him, double-checked the date, and growled. "That's Thursday." He grabbed Jared's hand before Jared could press Enter.

Jared squeezed his fingers and sighed, and Dawson's stomach sank.

"I'll lose my place," Jared said softly.

Dawson hovered for a second, a part of him roaringly angry and a part of him suddenly in tears. "I was so happy," he said after a moment. "You and me, we were going to spend some time together—"

"We can still do that." Jared turned and mouthed Dawson's jaw softly. "I just... I can't lose my place. The kid coming up, he's really good. He's better than I ever was—everyone says so—"

Dawson closed his eyes and thought about moving the cursor to Tuesday and booking the ticket then, and then this relationship, this painful, wonderful relationship, could end.

"Everyone says that," he said, his throat dry. "They all say the next big thing is better. Then the guy turns out to be human and they realize that the last big thing was really the best big thing."

"I'm only a big thing for a little more time, Dawson." Jared dipped his head and Dawson watched in horror as he clicked Tuesday on the time calendar and got ready to press Enter. "I'm sorry. It's too much to ask."

And he realized that Tuesday for Jared meant the same thing that it meant for Dawson.

He's going to break up with me.

"Stop!" Dawson snapped the laptop shut so fast Jared barely got his fingers out of the way. He looked up and realized that the entire household was looking at them with way too much sympathy in their eyes.

"My room," he growled. "Now."

Jared got that defensive look in his eyes, and his chin thrust out defiantly, and Dawson had a moment to realize, *Oh no! He's just like me when he's being told what to do!*

"Look, I know you saw me helpless, but—"

"But you don't like to be told what to do. Fine. How about we have a civilized discussion in my room instead of—"

"I'm going for yoghurt!" Benji announced. "Who's with me! Amber, Darian, great, let's go. Dawson, I'll get you some. Jared, you're getting some too, lots of fruit. Back in half an hour, bye!"

Dawson watched, surprised, as his entire household sprinted outside like hell was snapping at their heels. The door slammed and he and Jared took in the backpacks just dumped on the floor, complete with binders and papers sitting next to the crumpled forms, and Dawson managed a laugh in spite of himself.

"I haven't seen a room clear that quick since my dad cooked nutmeg egg tofu casserole."

Jared's look of awe was actually sort of welcome. "That's horrible."

"Actually wasn't bad. The *gas* it left us with made Benji and I the loneliest guys on earth for a week."

Jared cracked a reluctant laugh. "That's funny. I love that about you, that you're funny. That you can take a moment here that's going to break my heart and make it funny."

Dawson closed his eyes. "You love that about me?"

"Yeah."

"So you love me?"

"Yeah."

"So this thing we have, this means something to you."

Dawson still had his hand on Jared's shoulder, and Jared's whole body shook under his palm for a moment. Sweat saturated his T-shirt, and Dawson had to fight not throw his arms around his shoulders, to stop the panic he could *feel* from Jared's body.

"Yeah."

"Do you even have a plan? An *idea* of what you want to do when this is over? Are you planning to just drop dead onstage and let the rest of us bear you off like... like the fucking end of *Hamlet* or something?"

Jared didn't say anything—just looked up at him, his face held so still, Dawson had to swallow.

"Oh no. Oh no." He started pacing, the better to wave his hands in the air and pretend he could do that. "No. No. No. You don't get to think that way. Kill yourself for dance—have you not *seen Sense and Sensibility*? No? Because it's not a good idea. You don't kill yourself for love. You don't kill yourself for dance—"

"I don't have anything else!" He was still sitting—still sitting because he was probably too weak to stand and pace, and that pissed Dawson off like nothing else.

"*You have me!*" In his entire life, Dawson had never shouted at another human being. But that scream—it ripped out of his throat, out of his chest, and he knew he spit when he yelled and he just didn't give a shit.

Jared shook his head, put one hand behind him on the chair, and pushed himself up. "No, no, I don't! Because you need to come first—"

"You're goddamned right I do!" Dawson could see him shaking. *Join the club!*

"And I'm going to leave. I'm going to leave earlier than you want and dance because that's who I *am*, and you're not going to want me back!"

"*Stop* putting words in my mouth!" Wow. His *throat* was getting sore. His throat was getting sore and his eyes burned and he wanted to hit something, but Jared could hardly stand. Dawson strode to the wall, the one covered with fliers from all the shows he and Benji had ever worked, and hit it, the pain radiating out from his knuckles and up his wrist. He shook it out for a moment, his vision darkening with pain, and then kicked the sideboard because it was that or throw up. "Jesus! Would you look at what I'm doing to myself! Jared!"

He whirled and they locked eyes, and then he cursed himself, because the look on Jared's face, the stark acceptance of self-hatred, was going to be his undoing.

"I'll call a cab," Jared said rawly. "I was stupid. I thought… your family, it was just so nice. And you—you made me laugh. But you didn't sign on for this. You—I mean, I could do this to someone who'd cheat on me, or bail on me or, you know…. But you're right. You don't deserve this." He picked his phone up from the table and started dialing.

Dawson got there in two steps and yanked it out of his hand.

And threw it against the wall.

"*Dawson!*"

They stood chest to chest, both of them shaking, breathing hard and, if Jared's shiny eyes meant anything, damned close to tears.

"I'm not going to cheat on you," Dawson said, and his voice was cracking all over the place, and he just didn't fucking care. "Or bail on you. And I don't even know what else—it scares me that there's something else. I want to come first. Someday I will. But you gotta promise me you won't bail on me, either. Yeah, I'm gonna throw a tantrum. I'm *worried*. Jesus, look at you! But don't treat me like a stupid kid and leave to save me from myself. I'm *not* a stupid kid. I was a stand-up guy—"

"You were," Jared affirmed, nodding. "How many times you want to do that, Dawson? How many times before you realize I'm not worth it anymore? Let me know, okay? Because this… this place, this is like… like I never dreamed of something this good. Happy families. Your dad sitting with me to watch a game because you asked him to, just suddenly out of the blue. I just need to know when I'm going to lose it, okay? Just… don't just pull it out from under me. I need to know. Just promise me, okay? You'll warn me. I need to know what line I'm going to cross. You can't keep changing the line. You put the tape on the floor and you stand there and you do the steps and the show ends—I need to know when the show ends."

Dawson wiped his eyes with the back of his hand. "It ends when I say it does. And I'm not calling it quits now. You treat me like a fucking grown-up. Man, that's all I'm asking. You tell me. You say, 'Dawson, I love you, but I cannot do this, not even for you.' You talk about tape on the floor—well, you tell me where the tape on the floor is too. You may be used to being with douche bags, but I'm not used to being with *anyone*. If I'm not a good enough boyfriend, it's your job to teach me!"

Jared made one of those horrible strangled sounds, the kind where you laugh and cry at the same time. "You're a great boyfriend," he said, looking at Dawson and nodding earnestly. He sounded lost and tired, like he wasn't sure how they'd gotten here, and Dawson, who'd gotten *lots* of sleep over the weekend and didn't feel sick at all, suddenly felt the same way.

"Then don't try to leave me," Dawson said simply. He sniffled and felt like a giant kid, with his heart on his sleeve.

Jared's hand on the back of his head reassured him, even as he hauled Dawson up against a hard chest.

Tears. Horrible thing to do to a boyfriend. It must have been in the Boyfriend's Handbook a million times. Don't cry, because you're not a weenie and you're trying not to act like one. But Jared held him tight and Dawson came unglued on him, shaking with sobs while Jared shushed in his ear. Worry? He'd had it. He'd been the grown-up. He'd tried to be the one making the grown-up decisions, but he was barely grown, and Jared wasn't just going to do what he said. That wasn't the way life worked.

Jared clutched at him, and Dawson held him, even though they were getting sweaty through their clothes and Jared's cheek against his was stubbly and sticky and chafed. Jared was trembling, and after a moment, Dawson found he was supporting some of his weight. Easy, so it didn't look like he was being a dick, Dawson steered them both for the couch, and they sank down on it gratefully.

Jared pulled Dawson in again, and Dawson rested his head on his lover's shoulder and stared sightlessly into the apartment, the home, he'd made with his friends. They were quiet then, and for a moment, Dawson thought that was that. He'd lost the argument but won the war, and the thought made his chest tight.

Then: "Friday." Jared's voice floated like a leaf in the silence.

Dawson closed his gritty, bleary eyes.

"Thank you. But you know I'm going to ask—" Because dammit, somewhere in there, Dawson had heard something about the past that made his stomach churn.

"Not now."

"No. Not now."

Jared reached for the remote control, and they both sat in silence and watched *Castle* blindly for half an hour, because it was on TNT. Benji and the girls got back with frozen yoghurt, and they ate it happily, chatting about their classes and their finals and what else they had to do before the week was out.

Dawson acted like a normal human being, like the fight was over. He didn't gloat, didn't crow, because he was a grown-up now. He didn't even make a comment when Jared moved to his laptop after the fro-yo and booked his ticket—for Friday.

Dawson and Benji cooked dinner, and Jared watched TV quietly while the rest of them sat at the table and did homework. At twelve, Dawson's paper was done and even if it hadn't been, he would have set his alarm early, because he needed to have a conversation before he went to bed.

THIS TIME, Dawson lay on his back and pulled Jared to rest his head on his chest. He moved his hand in a lazy line up and down Jared's bare bicep and shoulder, a caress, but not really a sensual one. More like an attempt to make the contact deeper.

"You gonna tell me?" he asked quietly.

"No," Jared responded, his voice weighted with sleep. "Please no."

"When?"

"When we break up and you hate me so much it won't matter."

"Jared, please?"

His sigh gusted across Dawson's chest, disturbing his three chest hairs. "Please what?"

"Have a little faith in us, okay?"

"Friday, Dawson. I did that for you. I'm going to have to fight to keep my lead, you have to know—"

Dawson sighed too. "You have *no* idea how much I get that. None. You think you do, that it's like a chess piece or a trophy or something, so I can say I won, but it's not. It's bigger. It means you think maybe I'll be here if the dance goes away, and I'm not shitting all over that. But this... Jared—cheating, bailing, that's bad. How much worse could it get?"

Jared's regular breathing sounded for a moment, but no answer, and Dawson sighed. Well, he had his last finals tomorrow, and then? They got together time, then. Wednesday and Thursday were theirs, even if they wouldn't be doing all the things Dawson had planned.

"I haven't taken a sick day in almost five years," Jared said out of the blue.

Dawson actually had to *fight* not to splay his limbs all over the bed and stay perfectly still, because he'd almost been asleep. "Yeah? What happened then? Did Ebola hit LA?"

Jared didn't even respond to his physical jerk. "My boyfriend broke my wrist," he said, and by the time Dawson had caught his breath and reassembled the universe as he knew it, Jared had fallen asleep.

MORNINGS WERE always a flurry of five-minute showers (because hey, four people, no hot water) and trying to get your favorite thing for breakfast with those other people vying for space at the refrigerator. No sit-down breakfasts on a weekday; it was all, "If you take the last granola bar, I'm going to put ants in your underwear drawer!" and "Dawson, you got the last milk *last* time!"

Dawson knew his place in the melee, knew to keep his elbows and shoulders as contained as possible because the girls weren't big and Benji could knock him on the floor if he accidentally, say, shoved his shoulder in Benji's groin when he was getting off the ground from rooting around in the bottom cupboard for his hoarded box of Fiber One brownies. Which had only needed to happen once.

Anyway, Dawson left Jared sleeping. He barely stirred with a kiss on the temple and a "Don't go too far, we'll be back by one," because Dawson knew he was probably itching to go running or climb mountains or something, and then Dawson ran out the door and into the car with his fellow escapees.

"What gives?" Benji said, not even making a move to start the car.

"What in the hell?" Dawson sat in the passenger seat, and he looked behind him and realized the girls were both staring at him levelly. "Benji, it's an oven in here, why isn't the air-conditioning on?"

"The fight, Dawson. You two were... just *scary* fucking quiet last night. And you didn't even fight over the orange juice. Spill."

Dawson glanced over his shoulder and then at his watch. Great. They had plenty of time. "Why did we leave this early? Darian doesn't even have class right now." Darian's early-morning fitness was the reason they usually left at eight, but she didn't have a final in that one, so it was suddenly hitting him that this was a setup.

"Because you worry about him, we worry about you, and the world has symmetry." Amber's growl came from right behind him, and Dawson tried to crane his neck to see if she was smiling even a little.

"Stop looking at her and look at me. What's going on?" Benji growled.

Dawson snapped his head back around and fidgeted. "Well, he's staying until Friday, so, you know, go me."

"And?" Benji's mom used to do that thing too, whenever he and Dawson were getting into trouble—she'd just let the sentence hang. It was irritating, that was what it was. In fact, it was just like that thing Dawson's dad did, and Dawson never had a shot when his dad did that—

"Okay, so his last relationships were crap. I think it was like... you know. A test. To see if I'd bail. It was like I was *so* good with the being there when he was sick, he figured he'd make me break up with him so he didn't have to live up to that."

Benji squinted and counted on his fingers like he was trying to connect the dots. He couldn't do it. He shook his head like he was shaking off sleep or an attack of the heebie-jeebies, and made the "wha-wha-wha-wha-wha" sound before he turned on the car. "That is way too complicated for me," he admitted finally. "Darian, you're smarter than I am, what do you say to that?"

Darian was quiet for a moment, and when Dawson looked behind him, he realized she was twisting her fingers. "How bad?" she asked, her voice so soft Dawson almost didn't hear her over the engine noise.

"I'm sorry?" Dawson asked, not sure he'd heard right.

"How bad, Dawson? What's bad? Cheating? That sucks but it's, you know, it happens. How bad?"

Dawson looked out the window for a moment. He didn't really know the answer to that. He hadn't had a chance to talk to Jared yet, had he? But he thought of Jared's answer, quiet in the night, and the assumption that Jared could only have bad people in his life—he wasn't good enough for the good ones.

"I think one of them beat him up," Dawson said, keeping his eyes on the lack of scenery. Rocklin was just beginning to dry up completely. By June, there wouldn't be any green in the foliage, nor in the long grass by the side of the road. But he kept his eyes out there, because that thing he just said seemed to have sucked all the air and light out of the car.

"I think... I think I need to talk to him before I talk about this anymore." Dawson heard his voice and couldn't hardly believe it was his.

"I think you need to tie him to the bed so he can't leave," Amber recommended.

Dawson smiled a little. "That too," he said, relieved. He was just so glad someone else thought like he did, even if it wasn't Jared.

FINALS WERE over—*whew*. Was there *anything* more stressful—or stressfully pointless—than filling in the bubbles on a sheet of paper in order to achieve your life's hope? Benji had successfully made it into the guild, and he and Dawson pretty much had back-to-back shows lined up all the way through the summer. No more waiting tables for Benji, which meant no more free food, but it also meant that their summer stretched out in front of them like a glowing beacon of day trips to the lake and sweaty nights spent in the tech booth, creating dreams in the big black box.

Trotting into their apartment to ditch their backpacks and put on swim trunks felt like being a kid again. It wasn't the lake—not with Jared being too sick to be out in the sun for long—but there was a pool in the center of the apartment complex, with lots of shade to rest in, and that was plenty good enough to mark the start of the summer.

Jared was asleep on the couch, looking like a prince in a story, the kind in a snow globe, suspended between moments. Dawson shook him gently while the girls went to Benji's room to change.

"Jared? C'mon, wanna wake up?"

He squinted a minute, dizzy and disoriented, and Dawson felt a wave of protectiveness for him. God. Look at him. Human and fragile. How could anyone take this much helplessness and just step on it? It would be like squashing a kitten with an SUV.

"Tried to run," Jared mumbled. "Didn't go well. This is one fucking hot hellhole you live in."

Dawson shuddered. "God, here, let me get you some Gatorade." His dad really had brought them a lifetime supply.

Jared cracked a twenty-ouncer open and killed it in about three gulps. Dawson fetched him another one while he was still gulping. He got back to the couch and handed it over, and Jared thanked him before killing that one too. He looked a little less pale when he was done, and he sighed in thanks.

"Yeah," he muttered. "I had like three when I got back. How do people *live* here—it's not even June!"

"Well, we've got these things called pools, Jared. You want to try one of those out?"

"I didn't bring trunks," Jared said, squinting again like he was trying to remember.

"That's okay, you can wear a pair of Benji's."

"Not yours?"

"I think we've already determined my clothes try to trim parts of you I particularly like."

Jared's smile—unfettered and sweet—suddenly eased the darkness that had dimmed the sun all day. "Well, then, Benji's swim trunks. But I refuse to wear Darian's tops. I think that's oversharing, don't you?"

Dawson grinned and ran to make it so.

The water was a little too chlorinated, but other than that it felt cool and refreshing, and the pool was pretty big as far as apartment setups went. Benji and Dawson raced, the girls batted around a squishy sponge ball, and Jared did laps along the three lanes roped off for that reason.

After Benji beat Dawson soundly several times—and Dawson realized Jared had beaten them both just by freestyling rhythmically on his own time—they started playing monkey-in-the-middle. Dawson starred as the monkey and Benji refused to let him be anywhere *other* than in the middle.

He was being a total asshole too, taunting Dawson unmercifully and using his superior height, speed, and strength to pitch the ball to the girls over Dawson's head, under his arms, and around his shoulders. And then… *then*, just when Dawson thought he had it covered, a giant wave washed behind him and Benji pitched the ball straight up—

Right into Jared's hands.

Jared grinned, holding the ball up like Benji had. "You want it? You want it? C'mon, monkey, come get the ball!"

Dawson was delighted. "You asshole! Okay, that's it—you're gonna totally get it!" He splashed awkwardly toward Jared, but, well, Jared was a dancer. He dodged fluidly and pitched the ball to Amber, who pitched it back to Benji, who taunted him again.

"Whatsamatter, Dawson—monkey not getting any? You want the ball? You want the ball? C'mon, monkey, come get the ba—*oh shit!*"

Dawson had one trick in the water. Benji knew about it but conveniently forgot it until Dawson *powerleaped* straight up and over, spreading his arms like Batman and descending on his best friend like the wrath of *Planet of the* fucking *Apes*.

They wrestled for the ball fiercely for a minute, and Dawson managed to rip it right out of Benji's hands. He held it up over his head, crowing, "Who's the monkey *now*, mother*fucker*!" and then Benji erupted out of the water and crashed down on his head.

Benji hauled him up for air with an arm around his neck and then tried to noogie him to death. "Give!"

"No!" Dawson gasped, holding the ball out from his body. Basic physics dictated Benji couldn't both give Dawson a noogie *and* steal the ball.

"Give!" Benji shouted.

Dawson flailed for the back of Benji's shorts, because the guy who got pantsed automatically lost, that was the *rule*. He saw his opening—there, right between Amber and Darian. "Help me, Jared, you're my only hope!"

He skip bounced the ball to Jared, who caught it.

"No!" Benji wailed. "No! Dammit, Jared, I thought you were on our side!"

"Woohoo!" Dawson danced in the water with his hands over his head. "My boyfriend rules and we are the champions!"

"Wait a minute." Jared looked at the ball and then at the two of them. "How did we even win?"

Benji was still throwing his well-earned loser's tantrum, and Dawson continued to celebrate, and the whole time Jared kept asking, "How is that a win?"

"It's a win because Benji didn't get the ball," Dawson said, dropping his arms and sloshing over to Jared, grinning. "Didn't you ever play monkey in the middle?"

"The only game I ever played in the water was how to get a blowjob from the pool boy," Jared told him, and Dawson smirked.

"Way to go, Jared." Amber nodded in approval. "Dawson, get your boyfriend out of the pool before he drops. He's looking a little blue."

Dawson stopped his cheering for a minute and took stock. "Yup. You've officially overdone it." Jared's lips were blue and his skin was pale, and the hand holding the ball shook. "C'mon, baby. Couch time for you!"

Jared fell asleep in his swim trunks on the couch after a bowl of soup—*while* they were waiting for pizza. Dawson walked him to the bedroom and stripped him naked so he could hang Benji's trunks up to dry. The rest of them waited for pizza, then stayed up late playing beer Yahtzee! in celebration of another year survived. Dawson and Benji didn't mention the fact that they only had one more year to go before they would either have to start commuting or shift apartments. That was just depressing, there. That was too close to real life.

Dawson slid into bed around two, a little boozy, a little buzzed, and shivering with the feeling of another body next to his. Jared was lying with his back toward the middle of the bed, and Dawson couldn't resist touching. The feeling of Jared's flesh under his hands—smooth, muscled, sexy—made him want to keep touching.

He did, rubbing Jared's back and his shoulders, along the tautness of his bottom and the cut iron of his thighs. Jared mumbled and undulated, so Dawson kept touching, kissing along his shoulder blades and down his spine. It was lovely, dreamy, and the faint taste of salt and chorine only made it a little bit real.

But still, Jared didn't wake up, and Dawson was just drunk enough to fall asleep, his lips at the small of Jared's back.

He woke up in the darkness with Jared's mouth on his nipple. He was confused at first, his hands flailing for purchase, until his fingers sank into Jared's thick dark hair. He clutched then and tried to focus, and Jared lifted his head enough to murmur, "Sh. It's okay. Just… just feel, okay?"

He felt. Jared laved his nipple some more and then moved to the other one. The slide of Jared's chest across his stomach disoriented him at first. He wanted more. Jared's hand on his cock made him gasp and make a sound he wasn't even sure was human. Jared buried his face in Dawson's soft tummy and laughed, which vibrated straight to Dawson's balls, which made Dawson groan some again.

Jared shifted on the bed and grabbed a pillow, his muffled chuckles still quieter than Dawson's noises. Dawson took the pillow and pressed it against his mouth as Jared shoved his boxer shorts down around his ankles. That way, when Jared's mouth—hot, wet, and firm—closed over his cock, he could muffle his groan with impunity. That worked pretty well too, as Jared's mouth and hand worked him expertly, stroking, squeezing, suckling on the head. He teased Dawson's ridge with his teeth, and Dawson's new sound went something like "gunhghn!"

Jared paused, and a sort of vibration sounded around his bell, and he pulled the pillow away and realized—

"Are you laughing at me?"

Jared kept his grip, but he rested his head against Dawson's stomach to stifle his giggles.

"What?" Dawson asked indignantly. He was waking up now, and his erection was fading, and he'd just registered he had one.

"Jesus, Dawson, you're just so goddamned loud!"

Dawson was going to do it—he was going to beat his boyfriend to death with a pillow—when a sudden loud "*Meep!*" rang through the apartment.

"Oh no," Dawson mumbled, and he wrapped the pillow over his head.

"What?" Jared abandoned Dawson's south side and moved up next to him. "What was that?"

"Oh God." This didn't happen every time. But sometimes, when Darian was drunk or *really* horny....

"*Meeeep!*"

"Oh no. Not tonight."

Jared scooted up so he could rest his head on Dawson's shoulder and kept laughing. "What the hell is that—"

"*Oh, God, Darian!*"

And there was Benji.

"No, wait a sec," Dawson told Jared. He held up his hand like he was conducting an orchestra and mouthed Benji's next line.

"*Oh, oh, oh my God, oh my fucking God, I'm gonna fuckin' coo—*" Dawson paused with his hand in midair. "—*ommmme....*"

"*Meep.*" And with a final flourish, their sex ended and the whole household could go back to sleep.

A moment of complete silence fell over the little apartment, and Dawson held his breath, waiting for the finale.

"*Zzzzzzzzzz—*"

"Wait?" Jared murmured. "Was that *Amber*?"

"Yeah," Dawson said, chuckling to himself. "She discovered the secret to life in the first week."

"Oh God. Let me guess."

"Earplugs!" Dawson said happily. He turned to Jared in the darkness, and Jared's teeth gleamed whitely.

"That's hysterical."

"Yeah, well, I've got my own pair."

Suddenly Jared's grin faded, and the now-quiet moment charged with the lost intimacy. "I want to make love to you," he said into the hush. "I want to make love to you so badly. In a bed, in the daylight. I want to see *all* of you, and touch it all too. I want to hear *all* of your noises, loud and soft. Someday, Dawson, we are going to have a place where it's just the both of us, and we can run around in our underwear all day, and nobody will need earplugs when you want to make noise."

Dawson took in a breath, and then another, and his skin puckered up all over his body as he got the shivers. "I will never let anything hurt you. Not me, not even you," he swore. He heard what Jared was promising. Jared was promising a Dawson and a Jared alone, without his brother, without his college friends, just a them.

Dawson could believe in that.

Jared nodded somberly. "I believe you," he said softly.

"C'mere."

Jared's mouth on his was haven, sanctuary and promise. They kissed in the dark, and then Jared moved his head back down to ground zero. But before Dawson lost his mind again, he managed words.

"Let me suck on you—I swear I won't be so loud."

They moved side by side, and Dawson got to taste him, pull him into the back of his mouth, touch his balls and the skin of his inner thighs. He was awake now, which was good, because otherwise he would have been too scattered, too outside himself to separate the pressure and the pleasure on his own cock from the fullness of Jared's in his mouth. Jared's noises, soft and discreet, were worth listening to—Dawson strained to hear them while he clutched Jared's backside and kneaded and stroked and sucked.

Backside—ooh, Dawson liked that under his hands. He squished the muscles and pulled apart the cheeks, and Jared's next sound was neither soft *nor* discreet. Dawson parted his bottom again and stroked gently down the crease, working hard to remember to be careful of that thing in his mouth. He dipped a questing finger into the significant little pucker, and Jared made a harsh noise. He let Dawson's cock flop out of his mouth, and Dawson tasted a spurt of precome on his tongue.

Oh boy!

Dawson pulled back and awkwardly slid his fingers into his mouth along with Jared's cock. Jared gasped and garbled out something that sounded like "Dawson, what are you doing!" Dawson repositioned his hand so *this* time he could probe a little, rub a little, spread the wetness around and push just *so* while stroking and licking and—

"Mmf...." Jared sank his teeth into Dawson's thigh, and it felt good, like Jared's grip on his cock and the air blowing past the head. But Dawson could feel Jared's balls tightening like his ass cheeks tightening against Dawson's hand even as Jared pushed against his fingers and *bloop*! He popped in.

Jared's soft grunt vibrating against Dawson's skin was the only warning he had after that, and Jared was coming, coming down Dawson's throat and into his mouth. The come spilled over because the taste was still strong and Dawson couldn't swallow it all, so he just left his mouth open, and it dribbled down his cheek and onto the pillow under his head.

Jared stopped arching, his body going lax and his breath panting against Dawson's balls. Dawson had just enough time to wipe his chin on his shoulder and swallow what was left in his mouth before Jared took Dawson's cock all the way to the back of his throat and squeezed his balls, and yup! That was all she wrote. Dawson groaned from his toes, buried his head against Jared's groin, come-y pubic hair and all, and his entire world washed black and white and red as he came.

For a moment their harsh breathing filled the room, and then Jared made an effort to scoot up. While he was doing that, Dawson turned his pillow over so he didn't have to rest his cheek on the wet spot. When they had finally situated, he found he couldn't stop smiling.

Jared rolled his eyes, but he was smiling too. "You're insufferable," he said fondly.

"What?" Dawson cockily rolled his neck against the pillow and everything.

"Just say it!"

Oh God! He was smiling so brightly his eyes crinkled, and Dawson couldn't help it. He lifted a mostly-cleaned-off hand and traced the strong line of Jared's jaw. "You want to be a *bottom*!" Dawson gasped.

Jared shook his head—not like he was disagreeing, but like Dawson got it wrong. "It's not top or bottom," he corrected, and his eyebrows fought for control, like he was trying to be all sober and didactic but couldn't do it—not about sex. "It's, uhm, you know... just...." Yup! Domineering eyebrows lost and the smirk took over his face. "Sensitive!" he managed before he tucked his head in the pillow.

Dawson loved him like this so much. He leaned over until his lips touched Jared's ear. "So's mine," he whispered, figuring it would put Jared out of some of his misery.

Jared turned, and his eyebrows were suddenly back in position— not domineering position, though, just evil-wicked-sexy position. "I can't wait."

It was Dawson's turn to bury his face in the pillow and giggle, and while he was there, Jared started kissing his back. He moved his way over to Dawson's spine, down past his ribs, and then to the divot right where back met buttcheeks. He paused for a minute, licking and nibbling while running his hands all along Dawson's skin. Dawson groaned into the pillow and, knowing what this indicated and not caring, pulled his knees up to his chest to give Jared better access.

Jared got behind him and teased for a moment. He suckled a hickey on Dawson's left hind yab until Dawson wiggled and grunted and giggled and finally pleaded in a breathy whisper. "You're killing me, here, Jared, I'm not sure whether to laugh or to cooo—" Because at that moment, Jared stopped fooling around and licked a solid stripe down Dawson's crease. "—oome!" Dawson squeaked.

Jared pulled back and blew a soft puff of air against Dawson's damp skin. "Come," he said matter-of-factly.

"It's going to take more than just thaa... oh God."

Jared had stopped teasing and settled down to business. He licked and probed with a sneaky tongue and then teased below and drilled inside. He grasped Dawson's thickening cock and began a hard, slow stroke, and Dawson had no choice but to bury his face in the pillow and enjoy the ride.

When Jared pulled back and massaged Dawson's rim with his thumb, Dawson threw himself backward, pushing against the thumb and taking it inside. He heard Jared's chuckle above him and clenched, hoping he'd send the appropriate message. He must have, because Jared whispered, "Reach into your drawer and grab the lube."

Dawson was usually so clumsy, but *this* move he had down—he probably practiced five times a week. He fumbled with Jared's hand for a moment for the handoff, but then, oh blessed, blessed lube, and Jared's fingers, stretching, penetrating, *fucking*, and Dawson wasn't sure there were enough pillows in the world.

Suddenly everything stopped. Jared kept his fingers where they were, absolutely still, and his hand on Dawson's cock too, but he bent down and kissed Dawson's backside. "You want?" he asked soberly.

Dawson pulled his face out of the pillow to peek over his shoulder.

"Yeah?"

Jared's mouth quirked. "You could not possibly be making any more noise than you are right now."

Dawson started to shake *hard*, close to orgasm but needing needing *needing*. "God... yes... yes, please... yes. Please fuck me, please fuck me, please fuck me, pleeease...."

He expected Jared to just ram it in then, because he was begging for it, but that wasn't what happened. Jared's fingers disappeared, surreptitiously wiped on the sheets, and suddenly Jared's strong body draped over Dawson's back. Jared tangled his fingers in Dawson's rumpled hair and tugged, and Dawson looked up.

"Hey," Jared said, keeping his voice low. "I love you."

Dawson worked hard to still the shaking all over his body. "Me too," he rasped. He expected more, bigger, poetry or something, and dreaded it, because his body needed *sex* and his heart was too sore to talk, but Jared's hands were shaking too.

It went so quick. Jared positioned himself right *there*, at Dawson's stretched, oiled backside, and thrust slowly, carefully in.

Once his crown popped in, Dawson could not be held responsible for the sounds that issued out of his throat.

"*Gawwwwd....*"

"Sh!" Jared whispered harshly, but he slid all the way home, his cock impossibly big and stretchy and—*oh yes*—filling, and Dawson needed him more.

"Little… faster," he begged. Jared pulled out and thrust in again, and that was almost perfect. "Yesss! Oh yes, oh yes, oh yes, so good, more, more, more—"

Jared did it again, and again, and a little faster, and a little harder. He kept his hands massaging Dawson's backside, his motions firm but not brutal, and Dawson's entire *body* blossomed. Oh damn, this was better than fingers or plugs or just *anything* he could do by himself, and Jared's every thrust, every drag, accidental or on purpose, across his sensitive spot, every *touch* ramped him higher and higher and—

He screamed into the pillow until his vision went red, and he still felt like he was exploding in awesome.

"*Jared…* God, more, more, *more*—"

"Grab yourself," Jared muttered, and Dawson *never* needed to hear that twice. Oh, his cock in his hand, sweaty, drooling in precome, it felt like the ultimate in dirty, self-decadence with a friend, and Jared wasn't just *fucking* him, he was *touching* him. Hands over his shoulders, his back, his ribs, spanning his waist, caressing his flanks, and Dawson sobbed for breath in the race to his peak.

And abruptly, just that quickly, he hit the finish line, a whine-squawk bursting out of him as his skin unfurled and his flesh sang like starlight to the heavens.

"Dawson!" Jared didn't *sound* like he was going to come—in fact, he sounded exasperated and horrified. But then—"Oh my God, *Dawson!*"—and then he was *coming*, pumping *inside Dawson's body*, and Dawson was so surprised by the feel, by Jared's frantically rutting body, that he jerked on himself one more time and went over again.

And abruptly collapsed into the bed, on top of the wet spot, pulling Jared out of his body and leaking come all points south.

Jared fell on top of him. Dawson wanted him *right there* for as long as humanly possible.

"Am I crushing you?" Jared asked after a minute.

Dawson made a negative noise. "But you *are* drowning me," he murmured, because it felt like he was literally squelching in come.

"Yeah, God. Sheets. Do you have any?"

Dawson nodded, not that Jared could do more than feel him jerk.

"Yeah, but, uhm, we need to put on shorts. And move quietly."

Jared started laughing, muffling the sound in Dawson's shoulder, and Dawson caught his breath enough to glare at him. "What?"

"God, Dawson, do you think there's a person in this complex who *didn't* hear that sound you just made?"

Dawson blinked at him. "Earplugs," he said, nodding like he could make it so.

Jared lifted himself, then fell to the side and shook his head, making sure Dawson could see him. "Babe, there's not enough insulation in the world. People in the next *town* probably just woke up and said, 'Hey! I know that kid! He's getting laid!'"

Dawson snorted. "Exaggerate much?"

Jared shook his head again and then collapsed gracefully, eyes closed. "You get the sheets. I'll lay here for a minute," he yawned.

Dawson looked at him, belatedly concerned. "I didn't just... I don't know, make you sick again, did I? Because if we have to explain that to the doctor—"

"The one you offered to blow?"

"That's not how I remember it. But I don't want to tell him we sexed you into a relapse."

Jared chuckled weakly. "No. Just tired. Need another day of sleep, and some swimming, and some more sleeping."

"Wow. I just got you to admit you needed to relax. Sex really *is* magic!"

Jared opened his eyes shyly. "Only with you," he said, keeping his mouth turned up so it didn't sound quite so hammy.

Dawson decided to take it in the spirit in which it was intended. "Aw, you *do* love me!" He grinned. His entire *body* tingled with well-being.

"Never doubt it," Jared said, eyes closing. Dawson hustled then, got them both boxers, and tiptoed to the hallway linen closet. He paused for a moment and listened, looking around the apartment in the dark. Amber's snores echoed softly, and he slunk back into his room, reassured. Jared was exaggerating. It was okay.

Five minutes later, after spraying some air freshener and opening a window, the two of them slid into clean sheets. The sweat had cooled off their bodies, and Jared was limp with sleep, so it was easy to just pull him, unresisting, until he rested his head on Dawson's shoulder.

Their breathing evened out, and Dawson should have been dead to the world, but he couldn't close his eyes.

He knew—Jared knew too—that the conversation still needed to happen.

"Regrets?" Jared asked, which was spooky because it was like he was reading Dawson's mind.

"No," Dawson answered. "Not any. You know why?"

Jared grunted against his bare chest. "Because now I can't escape you?"

Dawson was going to flick his forehead, but he stroked his sweaty hair back instead. "Because now you *won't* escape me. You're going to tell me everything, and you're going to make me a part of this, and that's going to be okay."

A sigh shuddered out of Jared and blew across Dawson. "Remember when we first met?"

"It was three months ago—I'm not senile."

"No, but you are a sarcastic little shit. I thought that then, haven't changed my mind."

Dawson chuckled and stroked his hair some more. "That's 'cause you're a smart guy. Observant too. But yeah, I remember. You were…." Dawson remembered him on the stage, looking bemused as Dawson regained consciousness, or in the pool house, wet and irritated. "Untouchable," he said after a few beats. "Reaching for you was like reaching for the stars."

Jared grunted and tried to roll over. Dawson didn't let him.

"I like you better now," Dawson said, just to feel that trust in him again.

"Yeah. I'm sure being this needy is extremely sexy," Jared responded. The bitterness in his voice made Dawson flinch.

"Hey! That's not fair. I'm here, dammit. I could have bailed, but I didn't—I *care* for you."

Jared relaxed again on his chest, and Dawson thought for a minute that he was going to just fall asleep.

He kissed Dawson's nipple instead, and then his cheek. "Let me go to sleep like this," he said after a pause. "It's all good. You love me. It's dark and quiet. It's been a really good day."

Dawson was feeling the weight of sleep himself. "Yeah," he murmured. "Yeah. It's been a *really* good day. I love you, Jared."

"Love you too."

Tomorrow, though—tomorrow was Wednesday, and Dawson wanted it out tomorrow. Because Friday was coming too soon, and Dawson wanted it out in the open, and he wanted Jared better, and he wanted some balance before Jared got back on the plane.

It was occurring to him that this long-distance thing, it was living from pocket of time to pocket of time, and he wasn't sure he liked it. Dawson could hardly fit his own *hands* in his pockets, much less big chunks of his life.

JARED WAS still sleeping when Dawson got out of bed and went into the kitchen for provisions.

All of his roommates were there, fully dressed, nursing coffees. Dawson felt the weight of their glares as he opened the cupboard and grabbed a couple of bagels.

"What?" he asked, rifling through the fridge for hummus and tomatoes. "Where's everybody going?"

"Out," Benji said shortly. "Probably to my mom's, 'cause she's got a pool too, and we can sleep."

Dawson squinted at them. "Why can't you sleep here?"

Amber dropped her head into her arms and started to squeak, her shoulders shaking independently of the sounds she was letting out of the little cradle. "*What?*" he asked, a little alarmed. Was she *crying?*

"Dawson," Benji said, and Dawson turned to see pleading in his eyes.

"Yeah?"

"We need you to do something for us."

"What?"

"If we promise to leave you guys alone in the mornings, you need to promise to get all of your sex done then, okay?"

Dawson squinted at him. "What in the hell are you—"

"The noise!" Amber mumbled, and Darian clapped her hand over her mouth and made a strangled noise that sounded *nothing* like "Meep!"

Heat surged up Dawson's body from his thighs, up his groin, around his chest, and he *knew* it was blotching on his neck and his face. "Oh," he said, feeling dumb. "Oh. I thought… I mean, I guess you didn't sleep through it after all."

Benji shook his head deliberately. "I'm pretty sure it woke your father and set off church bells, buddy. We just… I mean, you know. We can't do that again, okay?"

Dawson closed his eyes and turned around before he opened them. Bagels. Must. Make. Bagels. "Yeah," he muttered. "Yeah. Sure. No problem. Uhm, wanna do dinner, you know—"

"We'll be back at four," Darian chirped, her voice breaking in what was probably an attempt to make this less awkward.

"Four," Dawson echoed, unable to look any of them in the eyes.

"With groceries," Amber said, and it sounded like she'd actually taken her head out of her arms.

"That's awesome," he said, spreading hummus on the bagels. "Uhm, bring cilantro and garlic and olive oil and chicken—I'll make fresh pesto and make, you know, food." It was one of his best dishes, and they all usually begged him to make it. He figured it would be a peace offering.

Benji's over-the-back man-hug told him he'd guessed right. "It's a plan," Benji said, and they all filed sedately out.

The door slammed, and Dawson let some of that pent-up tension and embarrassment ease out of his shoulders. He turned back to the bagels, but he really wasn't surprised when Jared's footsteps pattered behind him and he felt the warmth at his back.

"I told you—you were loud!" Jared murmured into his ear.

Dawson relaxed into his arms. "That's embarrassing," he confessed, knowing his entire body was on fire. "I mean, we can *all* hear each other, but—*dude*. I'm louder than Darian?"

Jared kissed the back of his neck. "Yes. You were louder than airplane noise, baby—I don't know what to tell you. Want to hear something extremely embarrassing?"

Dawson shrugged and managed to finish the bagel sandwiches. "Yeah, give it a shot. If you didn't drive your entire household away with your sex noises, I still win."

Jared's chuckle echoed warmly in his ear. "It turned me on like you wouldn't believe."

Dawson put the lid on the hummus and then stood completely still. "Yeah?"

"Yeah," Jared confirmed, flickering his tongue along the shell of Dawson's ear. "After breakfast—"

"And your medicine—"

"*And* my medicine," Jared confirmed. "So, uhm, maybe, you want to make some more noise?"

Dawson sighed and turned around in his arms, smiling. "We have until four," he said. "And you should have a T-shirt on!"

Jared kissed the corner of his mouth, and Dawson gorged his hands on the smooth skin of his arms and back.

"You worry about me," he said, that faint smile on his perfectly shaped mouth.

"I do," Dawson told him. "Not enough people worry about you."

"I love that you do."

Dawson tasted toothpaste in the kiss, and Jared's morning beard prickled his mouth. Dawson remembered this from his last visit, but somehow it was more vivid this time, every detail more dear. He held Jared's stubbled cheeks in his hands and deepened the kiss, suddenly afraid and needing more, and more.

The kiss turned raw, painful, and although they were both aroused, it felt like more than that. Jared pulled away, breathing hard and leaning his forehead against Dawson's.

"Talk first or sex first?" he asked, and Dawson loved that he was completely serious about that.

"Breakfast first," Dawson told him. "Sit down, I'll serve you."

Jared sat, and Dawson actually managed one of their Corelle plates under his bagel, a glass of orange juice instead of a plastic cup, and a napkin and everything.

They sat next to each other at the table, and Dawson started to tell him about the shows he and Benji would be working.

"So mostly Music Circus," he said seriously. "We're excited. We had to have Prof Weber recommend us and the whole nine yards, but it's exciting."

"When do you start?" Jared asked.

"Next week," Dawson said, still bouncing in his chair. "It's like *epic* timing, because we take over for the crew that's been working for the last four weeks—they're going to New York, and the Circus needed replacements, so we start learning the show Thursday, Friday, Saturday, and Sunday matinee, and then we work the Monday show ourselves. We switch over from *Priscilla, Queen of the Desert* to *Flashdance* in two weeks, so Benji and I get to be in on the ground floor, learning the new show in the day and working the old one at night. It's an eight-week gig, which is perfect, because, you know, school starts, but we get this week off after finals—I mean, who gets their dream job, right?"

Jared's unaccustomed quiet stopped Dawson midramble.

"Well, I guess you do," he said, suddenly embarrassed.

Jared shook his head and took a sip of his orange juice. "No. It's just, uhm, you had whatshisname replace you this weekend—"

"Well, yeah, but it's, like, the first time I've ever not shown, so—"

"Yeah. But you did it anyway."

Dawson shifted uncomfortably. "Yeah."

"So that could have put your dream job at risk."

Dawson grunted and looked sideways at Jared's plate. "So I make you a bagel and you eat the tomato and the salmon, and that's it? It's like you didn't even listen to the doctor at *all*."

A crescent of red appeared above Jared's cheekbone, and Dawson was a whisker short of checking his forehead again before he realized Jared was blushing. Very deliberately, he picked the bagel up as a sandwich and took a bite.

"Good hummus," he said through a full mouth, and Dawson humphed, only slightly mollified. He waited for Jared to swallow before firing the cannon shot that was going to end the truce.

"You going to talk about it?"

Jared put the bagel sandwich down, and Dawson could have kicked himself for not letting him take another bite first.

"Not much to talk about," he said, standing up. He grabbed his plate with the rest of the bagel and Dawson's plate, which was down to the crumbs, and took them to the sink.

"Bring me the unopened orange juice when you come back," Dawson said, crossing his arms and glaring. Oh no he *didn't* try to get out of a conversation by leaving the table. His father hadn't let *him* do it in high school, Jared didn't get to do it now.

Jared's hooded look as he set the orange juice down on the table told Dawson he was highly aware of being manipulated by his manners, and that he didn't approve. Well, tough.

Dawson poured a second glass of OJ for each of them and took a sip. And just looked at him, and waited.

Jared raised an eyebrow and took his own sip, and Dawson huffed out an exasperated sigh.

"C'mon, Jared—you can't just let that hang like that. You tell me something that makes me want to beat the shit out of a total stranger, and then pretend it's not out there, in the ether, needing an explanation?"

Jared set his orange juice down and sighed. "It was my fault," he said, almost apologetically. "I mean, not that he broke my wrist, but... I mean, I'd just been injured, and they'd been giving me steroids to help me heal. And Archie—well, he was using a lot of different stuff, and I didn't know it, and he got into my prescription, and I got in his face, and—"

Dawson put a hand on his arm because he was babbling, and he was apologizing, and Dawson just needed him to stop. "So that's your fault how? Get to that part. I'm dyin' here."

Dawson could see the bobble of Jared's Adam's apple and knew suddenly that this was harder for him than being sick. This, admitting to weakness, confessing he'd been less than prepared for what life had thrown at him. *This* right here was hurting him.

"I just... I mean, he was older than me, and I should have known he was using me for drugs, for whatever, but, you know, you get out of school and you're on your own, and having a boyfriend—it's so exciting." Jared shot him a glance so saturated in irony that Dawson felt sick to his stomach. No, no, no, no, he did *not* get to make that comparison.

"Yeah, it's really exciting, not gonna lie," Dawson said, narrowing his eyes. "But, you know, if you tried to, I don't know, beat the fuck out of me, I'd fight back!"

Jared looked away. "Well, I *did* fight back, and that's when he broke my wrist."

"How old were you?" Dawson asked. He'd never wanted to hurt someone so badly in his life.

"Eighteen—"

"Jesus *Christ*, Jared—you can't blame yourself for that!"

"I was stupid, okay? I was stupid, and it happens. Sometimes you're just stupid, and I was just stupid. Dolph wasn't my agent then, but I had a guy who helped. I got out of the hospital and Archie was packed up and moved, and the restraining order was in place, and it was a while before my next boyfriend. So, end of story."

"It's an awful story." Jared's hands sat in his lap as he hunched over the table, and Dawson reached over and grabbed the nearest one and laced their fingers together. Jared's were clammy, freezing, and Dawson leaned into him to give him some body heat.

"I could have had this entire relationship and not had you ever know that," Jared mumbled, looking away.

Dawson wrapped an arm around his shoulders. "Yeah, well, it wouldn't have been much of a relationship if I hadn't known," he said softly. "You remember that night at Denny's?"

Jared still couldn't meet his eyes. "Yeah. Yeah, I remember. It's like this town has a magic Denny's."

Dawson smiled a little. "See, my dad says that's some sort of rule. I'm inviting him for dinner, by the way, so we need to get to that sex thing soon if we're going to be all sexed out by four o'clock."

Jared laughed like he thought Dawson was kidding, but Dawson had no intention of letting the sex slide—not at this juncture. If anyone needed proof that sex was healing and good, it was definitely this guy here in his arms. "Yeah, okay. I'll put it back on the agenda just as soon as my boner comes back," Jared said dryly.

Dawson squeezed his shoulders. "You have *no* idea how much I'm dying to repeat that thing we did last night, okay? I want to scare fish at Folsom Lake right now, that's how bad I want to come."

Jared's rectangular eyebrows shot to the edge of his hairline, and Dawson was proud of that.

"Okay, fine. We'll make that a priority. Am I done baring my soul?" He tried to pull away, but Dawson didn't let him.

"No. No you're not done baring your soul, dammit."

Jared shrugged and thumped his chair over so he was too far away to hug. Dawson frowned and thumped his chair closer, because that was childish bullshit and Dawson could play childish bullshit games better than anyone he knew besides Benji.

"Look," Jared snapped, "this is over and done with, so what's the point? You know I was stupid, and you know my relationships were a disaster, and you just know. And I'm the guy you slept with last night, so, you know, that was your mistake for not asking sooner—"

"Just shut up!" Dawson figured he'd let Jared win this particular childish bullshit game, and he stood up and took a couple steps away from the table and then a couple of more steps back. He stopped right behind Jared's chair and rested his hands on Jared's shoulders.

"You didn't deserve that," he said, and now *he* was finding it hard to swallow, so maybe now he knew how Jared felt. "You didn't deserve to be smacked around by some asshole who was taking advantage of you, but even more than that, you didn't deserve to be on your own when you were eighteen. If I'd hooked up with a guy who was really bad for me, Benji would have beat the shit out of him, and *then* he would have told my dad, and my dad would have had him shipped to a foreign country and dropped off without a passport."

Jared's laugh was painful, but it was a good try. That was important, that he'd try to laugh right now. "Yeah," he said after a moment. "You're probably right."

"Well, *you* should have had a Benji or a Stan Barnes in your life. You should have. You don't talk about your parents or missing them, but they're stupid for not being there for you, and that wasn't your fault either."

"Thanks, Dawson. I could have had years of therapy, but you just cleared that up for me."

Dawson smacked the back of his head—not hard, but he caught more than hair. "Don't be an asshole." He bent and kissed the spot he'd smacked. Jared leaned into him, and Dawson put his hand up against Jared's cheek. "See," he hummed. "You *do* know how this whole thing works. I'm nice to you, you're nice to me, there's happy happy sexy sexy, and someday, cohabitation and shared goals. See? Was that so hard?"

He pulled the chair next to Jared's again and sat on it sideways so he could rest his chin on Jared's shoulder.

Jared grunted. "Dawson, you make it sound so easy, but you're—"

"Young. And inexperienced. And sheltered. Yeah, yeah, I know. I'm, like, the opposite of someone who should know what I'm doing, but Benji'll tell you, that's pretty much the story of my entire life."

Jared turned and raked gentle eyes over his face then. "Yeah? What stories will Benji tell me?"

Dawson grinned. This was a good one. "See? That's a place to start. That shit we talked about at Denny's? That was good shit, but that wasn't even *close* to scratching the surface."

Jared leaned forward and rested his head on his arms, turning his eyes so he could maybe see what Dawson was doing. Dawson draped himself over Jared's back, feeling his body heat seep into his skin.

"See," he said quietly. "We've got so much to find out. You don't get to run in, almost die, and then run away. You came here when you were *sick*. You pretty much sealed your fate. I'm not letting you go now. See, what is it now? Nine in the morning? I say we take showers and then climb into bed naked, and then we talk and you sleep, and I'll clean and maybe get dressed, and then we have sex again, and then we talk some more, and—"

"I get it," Jared said, smiling. "But I don't think we have to do that in order."

Dawson shrugged. "Well, you know, as long as we do most of it twice."

"Most of it?"

"Yeah. If we're going swimming after everyone gets here, we probably only have to shower once."

Jared laughed softly, but he kept up his steady regard of Dawson's face with those black-rimmed mercury eyes. "Dawson?"

"Yeah?"

"I see so much promise in you. So many things you can do with your life. If I'm the reason you don't do those things, I'm a bad part of your life."

Dawson sighed and rested his chin in his hands, looking sideways at Jared with as much seriousness as Jared was looking at him with. "See, the thing you're missing here is that I don't *know* what I want to do with my life. But I'd be really, really happy if I could figure that out while I'm with you."

"But I'm not even *here*—"

"But you want to be. So, you see? We'll make it happen. It will happen in some way."

Jared lifted his fingers and traced a gentle line down the side of Dawson's bony jaw. "What makes you so sure?"

"You know, Benji and I knew nothing about theater in the sixth grade. Not a thing. But we knew we wanted to be a part of it. We auditioned at it and sucked, but our teacher was sort of awesome, and he gave us both tech parts, and that was it. Benji's an athlete, but he never wanted to play football or run track—he just wanted to make that magic thing happen onstage. Both of us. And we had pretty happy childhoods, but it had always been the two of us. We just *knew* that you could make something magic happen if a bunch of people put their minds to it. We wanted to be a part of that. We wanted to be the wizards behind the booths. And then everyone told us you couldn't do that for a living, but we figured out how, and it's how both of us are living, mostly, with some help from my dad, but he would have paid it anyway. Anyway, so hard work, attitude, a willingness to work together, a love of what you're doing—these things count, Jared. These things get you what you want most in the world."

"I thought it was magic," Jared said seriously, and Dawson sank his hand into that coarse, soft hair and stroked.

"Magic is falling in love during an all-night conversation at Denny's."

Jared's crooked smile surfaced, the one that let Dawson know things were going to be okay for now. "That's what it was for me," he confessed, and Dawson grinned his widest, most unfettered grin, just for Jared, because Jared could tell him about being young and vulnerable and hurt and still believe in magic and Denny's and Dawson.

"Well, see? You can't doubt magic, then. And you shouldn't doubt us. Not yet. Not when magic and hard work still have a chance." A heavy silence fell then, and Dawson thought wistfully of the night before, which had felt magical too. Which reminded him—

"Besides," he said indignantly, "you *promised.* You *promised* a you and a me and a place together."

Jared grimaced. "It was an easy promise to make," he said soberly. "A hard promise to keep."

"Well, *try.* For me, okay? I'm holding you to that fucking promise. It's like doing your algebra. Sure, you can fail the test and Dad'll forgive you—as long as you show him the homework."

Jared blinked slowly. "You didn't fail algebra in my house," he said softly.

"Yeah, but apparently your parents failed humanity. Tell me I'll get to meet them someday, okay? I want to embarrass the fuck out of them in public."

Jared smiled a little and thought about it. "They... you know, I used to want my dad's company in the worst way. Before dance, I'd ask for suits and go to the office with him and think about sitting at a desk, telling people what to do."

"Yeah?" Dawson cocked his head, trying to look at him from a new angle. "I can see that. You'd be a real prick."

Jared rolled his eyes. "I *am* a real prick. You just don't care."

"That's not true!" Dawson was wounded. "I *do* care, and you're *not* a prick! The entire point is that you're a nice guy and that you don't let everyone see it, but *I* see it, and that's what makes us special, and—"

Jared kissed him. One minute he was protesting vehemently. The next Jared had captured his chin and was kissing him, taking over, and all of the "I'm too fucked-up for a relationship" bullshit was forgotten.

So was breakfast cleanup and so was the shower.

And the kiss went on and on and on. It migrated to the bedroom, where it turned into them naked, kissing, grinding against each other desperately. Dawson wanted to do all the fancy things—take Jared's cock into his mouth until he gagged on it or pull his knees up to his ears and beg—but first he had to stop kissing, stop feeling Jared's shoulders, stop burying his hands in the silky black hair.

Impossible. Jared made a few good tries to move down—he kissed Dawson's jaw, his neck, his collarbone, but then Dawson would need his mouth again and pull him up, and their mouths would meet, and the kiss would go on. In the end it was both of them held in Dawson's long-fingered hand, rutting inside his tightened fist.

It wasn't enough, and Dawson unleashed a scream of frustration, hanging on the edge of orgasm, needing—precipitously needing—but needing Jared's chest against him, his tongue, his lips, the warmth and haven of him even more.

Jared grunted and slid to the side, forcing Dawson to let go, and then Jared grasped Dawson's cock and Dawson grabbed Jared's, and that was enough. The kiss kept going and Dawson managed to wrap his leg around Jared's hips just for the sheer stinking closeness of it, but that was all.

Dawson grunted into Jared's mouth, frantic, sweaty, desperate, and Jared pulled back to gasp, to roar, and then to bury his face in Dawson's shoulder and bite down hard. Light cascaded through Dawson's vision—white, red, gold, black—and his skin sang hot and cold. Orgasm blew through him like a percussion grenade, and he wasn't sure who spattered come first, him or Jared. It didn't matter—

for a moment, they were immersed in each other's peak, and in each other, and words were too much and touch wasn't enough, but they were human, only human, and it would have to do.

When words were words instead of colors and sounds, Jared kissed his neck. "I can't give this up," he said.

"Then don't," Dawson told him. "Ever."

The sound Jared made wasn't agreement, but it wasn't dissent either, and Dawson called it hope for pretty much the rest of the visit.

FRIDAY CAME way too quickly.

This time Dawson drove, and as he parked the car in front of Terminal A and ran to the back to get Jared's carry-on, he was doing a verbal checklist of all the stuff Jared needed to have in his duffel.

"You got your toothbrush, right?"

"Yeah, Dawson."

"And your new underwear?" They'd gone to the mall the day before. After two days spent either sleeping or doing light exercise in the pool, Jared had needed to get out—and Dawson felt a powerful need to prove to him that there was *something* in the area besides his and Benji's apartment.

"And the clothes you bought for—"

"The shirts I left were yours," Jared said seriously, his still-pale face picking up color.

"You didn't have to do that."

Jared looked sideways. "I... well, it was small and stupid compared to what I wanted to do."

Dawson grinned. "Yeah. Nope. There *is* no appropriate gift for 'My boyfriend nursed me back to health.' You've got no choice—you owe me at least three more visits before you try to break up with me again."

Jared lifted a hand and pushed Dawson's hair back from his face. "I promise," he said soberly.

Dawson nodded, because he hadn't really doubted. That thing that happened between them when they were naked together—it wasn't just isolated or reserved for when they were skin on skin. It was in little things—like that hand in his hair right there, or the way he looked at Dawson shyly, like he was afraid Dawson wouldn't look back with the same sort of love.

Dawson was damned deep in the same sort of love.

"Do you have little Dawson?" Dawson asked, lowering his brows and trying to maintain a straight face.

Jared smirked. "I did yesterday morning!" Because, well, they'd had to keep to the agreement. Everyone else had taken off and let them have all the sex they wanted in the morning, but in the evenings, they had to settle for cuddling. Unorthodox, yes, but anything to keep the household running smoothly, right?

Dawson shook his head, not even sure he was kidding. "Little Dawson, Jared—he's your talisman, okay?"

"Big word," Jared said dryly.

Dawson rolled his eyes. "I know 'em. I got an A in English 30 A, right? Anyway—do you have him?"

Reluctantly, like he was embarrassed, Jared reached inside his backpack and pulled out the little teddy bear wearing the black jazz pants, tank top, and dancing shoes Dawson had bought for him when they'd been at the mall.

"You do realize I'm going to have to hide this from pretty much everyone I know down south, right? Otherwise I might not make it back up alive."

Dawson shrugged. "I don't care. If you don't want me to buy you silly gifts with great emotional import, don't disappear in the middle of the mall."

Jared looked at him crossly. "Hey, I was just trying to find a place to replace my favorite store, which, you might recall, you all told me to boycott!"

Again, Dawson was not impressed. "It's not my fault you live in a cultural desert. Who didn't know those people sucked? Any place that says mean things about my friends—"

"They carry Amber's size," Jared said, and Dawson could tell he still didn't get it.

"That's not the point. The point is, they have a public thing against the overweight and the underbeautiful. Those are my people there, Jared. Those are the people who pull the curtain and write the plays and make the costumes—those are the people who make the dream but who don't live it on the front of the stage. Anyone who knocks those people is not going to get my business. Or yours, because you're better than that."

Jared's smile turned shy, that sweet little under-the-brows smile that Dawson had seen so much of since he'd come back to Dawson's apartment after the hospital. "You're a really good person, Dawson. I won't lose your teddy bear, okay? I'll make sure he's always in my room."

"'Cause you don't have me there to watch over you," Dawson said earnestly. Jared had fallen asleep quickly the night before, and Dawson had lain awake, watching him breathe quietly in the dark, and thinking, *Nobody will do this for him when he goes back. Nobody will take care of him. Only me.*

"I'll be fine," Jared said, his voice infused with patience.

Dawson shook his head. "No. No, you won't. But the next time you're thinking about doing blow and vitamin C to keep you on your feet, maybe you'll think about the teddy bear and feel guilty. The next time you're sick and trying to run in the morning, maybe you'll get some sleep instead, because the damned teddy bear will be there, and you'll know what he's thinking, because it's what I'd be thinking."

"That you wish I was with you," Jared said, and for a moment it was like he grew paler and his cheekbones stood out in even starker relief.

"That I want you to be well," Dawson said, resting his forehead against Jared's. "Be well, baby. Remember we love you. Remember that this is home. Can this be home?"

Jared's eyes grew over-bright, and he closed them. "Yeah. This is home. It's the enema of the state, you know that, don't you?"

Dawson shrugged. "Well, you know. You live in the armpit—either way, it stinks."

Jared pulled back and Dawson threw his arms around those strong shoulders and thought that they weren't wide enough, *he* wasn't wide enough, to walk away from Dawson alone.

"Love you," Dawson mumbled.

"Love you too. Let go, okay, baby?"

"Yeah, sure." But Dawson didn't move. It was sweltering, even at eleven in the morning, but Dawson didn't move. They clung together, their shirts sweating to their bodies, their breath harsh in each other's ears, and Jared didn't say the words.

Finally he kissed Dawson's cheek and Dawson's arms dropped, all by themselves without Dawson's help.

"Eight weeks," Jared said firmly. "Then we both have vacation. Can you wait that long?"

Dawson nodded and wiped his stinging eyes with the back of his hand. "If you can, I can."

They stepped back and Jared grabbed his stuff and turned around, just that easy, hauling his carry-on and his backpack like the professional traveler he was. Dawson watched him go and then got in the front seat of his car and turned the ignition.

And fell completely apart, sobbing with great gulping breaths, at the same time he cursed himself for being a weenie who wasn't strong enough to keep someone like Jared Emory.

CHASSÉ

POCKETS OF time—that was one way to think about a long-distance relationship.

Chassé—that was another way. Everyday footsteps chasing across the stage, waiting for the big movement, the meeting of the two bodies, the carries, the spectacular leaps in faith and logic—a perfect moment in time, the dance.

And then the separation and the chassé.

Everyday footsteps chasing across the stage, and the occasional real, pertinent thing that happened that needed to be shared when your partner arrived on a plane from LA and you could engage in the dance once again.

Dawson became adept at living in two planes at once. There was the stage of the real, with the endless chassé of things that interested him but didn't dominate his attention, and there was the stage of the remembered and the anticipated—the place where he and Jared met, and they danced.

The chassé stage was not, in truth, a bad place to be.

The Music Circus job was on that place, and for Dawson and Benji, it *stayed* on that place, because they got picked up to work after the summer. It meant they had to rework their school schedule—all morning classes—and learn to live with a little less sleep, but hey! They got to be third-tier interns with steady jobs, huddling in the dark of the back of the house, creating magic for the world to see.

The night they were told they could stay on, they went out and bought beer (because Dawson was legal now, thank you very much) and stayed up until the early hours, saluting their childhood and their impending adulthood and congratulating themselves on a job well done. Halfway through their celebration (no girls invited to this one, because they both worked, for one thing), Dawson got a text.

How'd the show go?

They always asked each other that. It was like waking up and saying, "Hi, I love you!" but instead they said, "How'd the show go?"

Great. Benji and I have a job throughout the year.

Wonderful. Celebrating?

One six pack to the wind, one more to go.

I'm sorry I'm missing it.

Even in text, Dawson could hear the sarcasm.

We're thinking about moving. Next year work AND school will be downtown.

All of you?

And Dawson could hear it. The hurt. The speculation.

You have to be here to have a say.

Don't count me out just yet.

Never. How'd your show go?

Fucking awesome. We should have more shows where I fly.

How bad's your wedgie?

You'll see the next time you kiss me. The harness is still wedged up my ass so far it's in my throat.

Dawson had to crack up a little. That line sounded like pure Dawson, which meant he was rubbing off.

That's attractive. Seriously, I'll let you know before we decide—you can get in your two cents.

I don't have any right. I'm sorry I said something.

You've got plenty of rights, buddy. You just need to claim them.

Just don't go running off with any other boyfriends, okay?

That is a fucking deal.

Although what Dawson *didn't* tell him was that something about seeing the great Jared Emory seemed to be making Dawson *especially* attractive to every loser in the theater department for a thirty-mile radius. He could swear some kid actually came in from Folsom Lake College and one came in from Sac City just to meet the guy who'd managed to capture Jared Emory.

If they were all as douchey as Topher, that wouldn't be a problem, but some of them were just dancers who wanted to meet Jared—and who seemed to like Dawson all on his lonesome.

But Dawson didn't tell him about them, because he figured if Jared thought that geeky, earnest, my-elbows-can-take-birds-out-of-the-sky Dawson wasn't attracting other pretty theater people, that was one less reason for Jared to think they were doomed.

It was hard enough sustaining momentum when Dawson missed him like crazy as it was.

Don't meet anyone else while I get my shit together, okay?

Oh wait—maybe Jared *did* know other people found Dawson attractive.

You're the only other person on the planet who'd want me.

A lie. He hated telling them.

Please don't. If you think I don't know what I left behind, you're not paying attention.

Well, I don't notice anyone who's not you.

And that at least was the truth. But, well, not all of the truth, because that blond kid from Folsom Lake College had been sweet, and earnest, and he'd had crooked teeth and a sweet smile. But Jared wasn't stupid. His next text was a picture—he must have had someone else take it, because it was of him standing in a dance studio streaming with straw-colored light from the gleaming boards and mirrors. He stood doing pliés in front of a mirror, wearing a black T-shirt and black jazz pants. Dawson could see his face in the mirror's reflection, and he was concentrating hard for this most basic of dance moves—the faint bar between his eyes showed how very far away his mind was.

He was beautiful and strong and driven—and lonely.

Dawson's heart gave a constricted *thump*, and he almost couldn't read the next text.

I love you. Enjoy your celebration. Two weeks.

Dawson sent back a little heart and turned to Benji with his hand extended. They were sitting out by the pool, the only two people out there, and the swim had invigorated them just enough to get well and truly toasted.

Benji did what best friends did and smacked another beer in his palm.

"What did he say?" Benji asked quietly.

"That he knows I'm getting hit on." Dawson showed him the picture. "And that he knows I need to see him."

Benji took a swig of his beer. "That's impressive. How's he know that?"

Dawson thought about it and smiled a little. "He just thinks I'm good enough for everyone to want."

Benji held out his beer bottle for a toast, and Dawson clinked their bottles gently together. The first time they'd ever gotten drunk, they'd been fourteen and Dawson's dad had a bottle of vodka in his cabinet that was probably worth a hundred bucks. Once he realized neither of them were going to die from alcohol poisoning, he tormented them with a list of what that money could have bought them instead. With the exception of the "lost Darian weekend," Dawson and Benji didn't get drunk very often, but when they did, it was the good stuff, because when they'd been throwing up that bottle of vodka, they'd known the price of every heave.

"You know, if your boyfriend didn't live in LA, he'd be almost good enough for you," Benji said woozily, and Dawson sighed.

"If you and Darian move to Sacramento, you may have to go without me," he said, because Benji was already melancholy.

"Why? Dawson, Jared can spend as much time in the place as he can stand—"

"Yeah, but...." Dawson couldn't find words, so his hands started working overtime. "He—this is his home. *This* is his home. He'll love wherever I am, but if I move from here, he's got to have a say. So, you know, either he's here when you're looking, or—"

Or Benji and Darian got to move out and be on their own.

Benji sighed. "Well, it had to happen sometime," he said philosophically, and Dawson clinked bottles again.

"But it doesn't have to happen tomorrow."

And it didn't.

But it *would* have to happen eventually, and the moment was a sober reminder of the other things that would have to happen. Dawson and Benji would have taken about every class they could at Sierra College by the end of their third year. They'd *have* to transfer to Sac State, and yes, a move would be prudent, because right now they were going through a porn star's buttload of gas between work and school, and that wasn't healthy for anyone.

And beyond that, there was graduation from college and a decision as to whether Dawson wanted to be a part of something larger, or if he wanted to stay here in Sacramento and be quietly happy instead of the Next Big Thing.

This life here, this was chassé—this was the quiet moment between the big moments when everything happened. Dawson knew it—and when the big moments happened, he wanted Jared to be there, to be in on the decisions, to have a say, so it would be *their* future and not just Dawson's.

Because as much as Dawson wanted to believe in *magic + hard work = True Love Always*, there had to be someone next to him to work with, and another body to make the magic.

JARED CAME the week before school started, and stayed for six days. He limped getting off the plane, and that never went away, but it didn't poison their time together.

Dawson took three vacation days, and they drove to Tahoe in his piece-of-shit car, rented a hotel room, and had more sex than should be allowed by law. The hotel room was crap—a tiny little semicivilized hotel at the end of a construction site, across the street from a giant casino. The best thing about it besides the bed was that it sat a quarter of a mile from the lake.

Not that they saw much of the lake.

But the walk along the shore at sunset the second night, when the sky was so blue it hurt the eyes and the wind was as cold as the ocean—that was one of the most gorgeous moments of Dawson's life. He got out his camera phone and took pictures of Jared with that orange light illuminating his face as he squinted into the mountains. Dawson sent the best one to himself, and to Benji, and vowed he'd have an honest-to-God print made out of it, because it was just so goddamned beautiful. Jared looked at the picture, blushed, and grabbed the camera, then wrapped his arm around Dawson's shoulder and took a selfie of the two of them.

There they were, squinting into the sun with the mountains at their back and the soul-aching expanse of blue water stretched out behind them, frothing from the wind.

It was Dawson's turn to blush.

"You're so beautiful," he said, looking for the Delete function. "And me—" Long bony jaw, pitcher ears, quirky asymmetrical eyebrows above brown eyes—Dawson knew what he looked like, but it had never seemed so inadequate next to Jared as it did in this picture.

Jared snatched the phone out of his hands and hurriedly sent the picture to his own e-mail account while Dawson fretted over his shoulder.

"Jared…." He gave the phone back and Dawson turned it off and sighed, shifting it fretfully from one hand to the other.

"You think I don't find you beautiful too?" Jared asked, sounding hurt.

Dawson shrugged, looking away. "I just feel better looking when I can't see myself."

Jared nodded, raising his eyebrows and looking all older and wise and shit. "And I just feel better-looking when you're the one looking at me."

Oh God. It was just so corny! Dawson set his jaw mutinously and resolved not to sniffle. He wasn't a little kid, he was—holy shit—twenty-one, and a grown man. Jared took the phone from him and slid it easily into the pocket of Dawson's jeans and kissed his cheek. There were families out there at the lake, but none of them seemed overly invested in the two men standing by the lakeside out by the old defunct dock.

"You want to go up the mountain tomorrow?" Dawson asked. They'd talked about it when they'd first arrived, before the sex-a-thon had begun. It was a good thing they'd brought fruit, bagels, and hummus, because besides a trip to McDonald's made that evening before the walk, it was all they'd eaten.

"Can we go out to eat somewhere that doesn't wrap the food in a carton?" Jared asked.

Dawson grinned. "I don't know. Am I civilized enough to take to a restaurant?"

Jared grinned back. "We could probably clean you up," he said playfully, and even that made Dawson blush.

"Yeah, well, they don't have a Denny's around here—I don't know what to do with myself," he muttered, trying to stay in the spirit of play.

"Don't underestimate Denny's," Jared said soberly. "There's magic at Denny's."

Dawson shook his head and turned away, suddenly reminded that after this they would go back to the apartment to a barbecue in the afternoon and have breakfast with his dad the next morning and play with all the roommates, and then, Tuesday morning, Jared would be back on the plane and on his way home.

But Jared caught up with him, grabbed his hand, kissed the knuckles, and that, well, that seemed to be enough. Chassé led to the dance, the dance led to the lift, and only after the lift came the separation. You didn't struggle during the lift or it all came tumbling down. Dawson clasped his hand and feathered a thumb over his knuckles, and together they walked back over the sand. Jared limped slightly like he had been doing since he'd gotten off the plane, and by the time they'd reached the pavement, he let out a little grunt of appreciation.

"How bad is it?" Dawson asked.

Jared grunted again and then covered up the sound of pain with real words.

"A few Advil, it'll be better."

"Yeah, but how long has it been acting up?" Dawson asked insistently, and Jared rolled his eyes.

"Since high school—I told you that. It's a weak spot, don't worry about it."

Dawson sighed, and they got back to the hotel without him saying anything about it—or even anything much at all. Jared was too immersed in his own pain to notice, but after they drove to Jack in the Box and got a banana milkshake (for Dawson, of course—Jared was going to finish off the fruit and call *that* dessert), Jared drove up to the shore of the lake and turned off the ignition of Dawson's little car.

"Are we breaking up?" he asked quietly.

Dawson almost choked on his shake. "No!" he protested. Too strongly. "I mean, certainly not this weekend. Not now."

"Then when?"

"Wait—didn't we just protest our undying love for each other by the light of a westering sun?" Dawson asked to buy time. He wasn't thinking of breaking it off—God, no. But he was trying to phrase this question so Jared would know where they stood.

"Yeah, but, you know, this could just be tragic sex weekend," Jared said seriously. "This could be the last wonderful thing we do before we say good-bye."

Dawson scowled. "God. God, that's awful. Have you *done* that with someone?"

"Not every breakup is horrible," Jared said simply.

"Oh God—do I even want to—"

"It's not important," Jared said seriously. "His name was Austen, and he's married in Beverly Hills, and, well, he was when we dated, and I couldn't do it anymore. So I get it. I get it if you can't do this anymore, okay, because I've done that to someone, and—"

"Stop!" Dawson grabbed his hand as they sat, and squeezed. "God, just stop. Jared, man, I don't even... your dating past is *so bad* it would scare the holy fuck out of any single boy on the planet. Gay *or* straight."

"I said it wasn't horrible," Jared said, pulling his hand back and resting his chin on the steering wheel. "It wasn't. He was... kind."

After all the douche bags who weren't. Yeah, still speaking in subtexts.

"Well," Dawson said on an exhale, "I'm really glad someone was, because I think you've needed some of that in your life. But I'm not breaking up, and I'm not thinking about breaking up. I'm just... trying to plan the rest of my life, you know? I mean, Benji's transferring to Sac State next year, and I was going to do that too, but—"

"God forbid we break up the dynamic duo." Jared smirked.

Dawson had to put a lid on his temper. "Yeah, well, that's *exactly* what I'm proposing, dickhead. Do you want me to move down there? We could find a smaller apartment, someplace maybe not so nice but less crowded, and, you know, I could transfer to Northridge, which has a music program and probably a theater program, and I've made a name for myself up here, and—"

"No," Jared said quietly. Dawson risked a look away from his shake and realized Jared was staring at him like he was glowing with the light of holy sex and orgasmic redemption.

"No—you're looking at me like that's a big fat yes. I'm confused. I may need another milkshake to help me deal with the mixed signals." For emphasis he slurped a big noisy mouthful.

Jared looked away to the lake, which was burning gold with the end of the sun. "Can you just wait a little longer for me?" he asked, his voice distant and humble. "I—my knee isn't going to last forever. I've got another year, maybe two, maybe less, and then it's going to go."

"Well, what are you going to do when you're done?" Dawson asked. Plan B was important. If you didn't pass your algebra class, there was summer school—that was the rule.

Jared reached over and *grabbed Dawson's milkshake* and took a big drink, the last of the sugar/cream/ice making a loud splat-splat-splat sound. "I… see, I have money for a dance studio—"

"Wait." Dawson frowned. He heard the dancers talk—he knew this trap. "Isn't this like a step down? I mean, you're where everybody *wants* to be, right?"

Jared sighed and made like he was going to give the milkshake back. And then didn't. "Yeah, well if Suzanne Farrel can do it, I can."

Dawson made a face, because it was a flip answer and they both knew it. Jared was quiet for a minute, and then ponied up. "Yeah. It's going to take some getting used to. But I've already thought for it—I want to teach dance to disabled children, and I think I can get money from the state and parent tuition—I mean, I *think* I can do it, but—"

"That's wonderful! That'll work, I mean—"

"No—not wonderful," Jared snapped, really going for the milkshake and the dregs at the bottom. "Don't you see? That's *all* I've got. See, before Dolph I had this other agent, and he was sort of crooked, and there went three years' pay."

"*Jared*!"

Jared rubbed his eyes. "Do you have *any* idea how much I'd give—how much I'd dance, how far I'd run, for you to not know *any bad thing* about me?" he snarled. He turned and glared at Dawson like it was all his fault. "*Do* you?"

Dawson didn't know what to say. "You... my life's an open book," he said.

Jared nodded. "Yeah. I pray every day it can still be an open book. I go down to LA and I think, 'God, if I'm the *worst* thing to happen to Dawson's life, then he's going to be okay.' But I have to *tell* you these things, and I think, 'Oh God. I *am* the worst thing to happen to Dawson's life, and I *suck*.'"

"You don't suck!" Dawson told him, suddenly feeling young and small. "You don't. But... God, you don't have a crazy wife in the attic, do you?"

Jared laughed, and it sounded strangled and unhinged. "Romantic writers again?"

"Yeah. I read over the summer."

"Nice choice. God, I need to get you some Terry Pratchett."

"I could live with that. Now tell me about the end, the light at the end of the tunnel, when you can come up here and live, since you just told me not to follow you down."

Jared sighed. "Look, I want to quit on a good note. I want to go out on top. I want to quit with enough money in my bank account to not have to worry about food while I'm setting up my business. I've given my *life* to this art—I need some... some reassurances it's not going to just leave me lying dead on the stage when the curtain closes."

And that image, of Jared crumpled in a heap, used up, as the stage went dark made Dawson shiver.

"So, maybe next summer?" Dawson asked, thinking about when he'd need to move from Rocklin to Sacramento.

Jared nodded. "I can do next summer. Let me look at my calendar to see a last show date. I can tell Dolph, tell the company, and I can take a final bow."

Dawson felt a slow smile blossom. "Yeah?" he asked, thinking about how fast his first two years of college had gone.

Jared nodded. "Yeah," he said with decision. "Can you live with that?"

"Damned straight I can live with that. Can I see you dance?"

And in the middle of this… this *life-changing* conversation, there went that shy smile. The one that punched Dawson straight in the gut and made him think being with Jared was like winning the lottery, and Dawson was never this lucky.

"Well, yeah. I'll get you tickets. You can come down and help me move back. But…." Jared shook himself. "I mean, we have a few taped dates on PBS that we're doing around Christmas. I'm going to be performing live. You can see me dance anytime."

Dawson rolled his eyes. "Yeah," he said, and felt his own attack of the shies come upon him. "But, you know, when I'm there, you, you know, dance for *me*."

Jared just smiled and looked out over the lake, nodding like, *Of course. You're the only person in the world I've ever wanted to dance for*, and Dawson had to think that if nothing else, his subtext had improved.

They stopped for two more banana shakes on the way back to the crappy hotel. Jared only had a little of his, but that meant Dawson got nearly three of them, and that was *awesome*—he was *raring* for sex by the time they got back. They walked up the rickety stairs to the porch covered in Astroturf, opened the door, and saw that the bedclothes, which they'd pulled back to air out, were *exactly* like they'd left them that afternoon.

Which was fine, because it meant they didn't have to feel bad about getting them all messy again, to the extent that they had to pull out scratchy towels to lay over their wet spots when they were *finally* ready to go to sleep.

And the in-between part? The part that was hushed voices, whimpers, groans, and the silhouette of Jared looking intently at

Dawson in the moonlight? Dawson would keep that for frame-by-frame playback in his wet-drive, hopefully for the rest of his life.

The next morning, he lay crosswise on the bed, resting his head on Jared's chest and running his fingers along the corrugation of muscles on Jared's stomach. Jared's bad knee was propped up, and Dawson could see the scar from his long-ago surgery and the KT tape on his long, ugly, battered toes that he never took off.

"What are you thinking?" Jared asked, rifling his hair with invading touches of his own.

"I'm thinking that there's a stork mark on the back of your thigh, and that I *know* that about you." Dawson smiled at him, feeling smug. Learning Jared's body—that brown patch on the back of his thigh, the way one nipple was a little more oval than the other, the way you could see where the hair *would* grow if he wasn't waxed, thighs, ass, chest, underarms and all—had to be some sort of reward for reaching adulthood alive and in one piece.

"What's a stork mark?" Jared let his thumb coast along Dawson's ear, playing with a mole that made a bump on the back of it. Dawson preened, because Jared knew that about him now too.

"It's one of those stretchy brown birthmarks. It's where the stork carried you when you were delivered."

Jared wrinkled his nose. "The stork carried *you* by the back of your arm?"

Dawson drew his eyebrows together and lifted his arm, trying to look at the back of it. Jared laughed and rubbed his thumb right on Dawson's blind spot, and Dawson scowled.

"Okay. I'll take your word for it. *You* lucked out, by the way. If the stork had carried you any further up, you would have been wearing pink toe shoes instead of black."

Jared raised his eyebrows. "Oh, no—no *wonder* I've never seen it!"

And this, too, pleased Dawson absurdly.

"We're going to have dinner with my dad tomorrow," he said at random. His dad had actually *liked* Jared by the time Jared left last time. Considering he'd had to babysit the guy when he was at probably the lowest point of his life, that was saying something.

"Yeah, well, basketball season starts up in a month. I'll bet he's looking for another victim."

Dawson was going to protest, but then he realized Jared was probably right. "You don't mind, do you? Being his victim?"

Jared thought about it seriously, which was yet another thing to love. He did that. He took Dawson seriously, even when what Dawson was saying sounded crazy even to Dawson.

"No," he said quietly after a few moments. "I *like* your dad. He... he wants to take care of *all* of you, but, you know, he gives you your space."

Dawson smiled, pleased. "And in return, we give him our presence at least once a week. Yeah. I'm glad we're not moving too far away. We can be family."

Jared closed his eyes and rumpled Dawson's hair. "You guys are great," he said, completely sober, and Dawson decided he'd *touched* Jared's stomach enough, and *really* needed to kiss it. Jared grunted softly and arched his hips, and Dawson kept kissing down his stomach, down his happy trail, and just down, to where Jared's cock was starting to peep out of its sexy pink foreskin.

Dawson had learned to *love* that little cuff of flesh in the last three days. Jared was *incredibly* sensitive underneath it, but that wasn't the only reason Dawson loved it.

It was *play*able. Dawson could pull it up and then pull it down, and then lick around the head and pull it up, and then pull it down and lick some more—it was like ADHD's answer to the perfect blowjob. Give a partner something to *play with* and he could extend foreplay until, well, until *now*, when Jared was thrusting into his mouth and making sexy, incoherent noises, and Dawson was bound and determined, just this once, to swallow everything Jared poured down his throat.

Then Jared pulled him back by the hair and sort of blew his mind.

"Your face," he gasped. "Make me come on your face."

Ooh.... It sounded so *sexy*, so decadent, and Dawson's hard-on grew tighter and harder just hearing it. He pushed himself up on his knees, swinging his hips around so his happy parts were hanging right near Jared's shoulder. He wasn't disappointed when Jared reached underneath him and started stroking too.

Oh God, oh *boy*, it wasn't fancy or perfect or even the e-ticket ride, but Dawson was starting to realize that with Jared, *every* touch was the e-ticket ride. Jared groaned softly and stroked Dawson harder, and Dawson took him down, down, deeper into his mouth, then pulled back to stroke Jared hard and fast until that precome spatter of hot-wet hit his fist. Then he closed his eyes, stuck out his tongue, and kept right on stroking.

The first shot splashed across his cheek, and the second pattered across his forehead and his closed eyes. The third one actually landed on his tongue, and it was perfect, because he got to taste it but not too much of it. (He still hadn't gotten the hang of swallowing, which was, frankly, one of the reasons the sheets were so rank.)

Jared grunted and shuddered under Dawson's hands and then groaned, "C'mere." He grabbed Dawson's hips and hauled them over so Dawson's cock was hanging right into his mouth, and then... *oh man!* Jared's mouth was so *good.* Hot, just *hot*, and he grabbed Dawson's ass and *pushed* and Dawson thrust forward, taking Jared's softening cock into his own mouth for cleanup.

Jared's moan around Dawson's crown felt *amazing.* When he opened his throat and shoved on Dawson's ass again, Dawson was just lost down his throat. His vision went black and his hips thrust forward on their own, jerking hard, but Jared took him, swallowed him, worked Dawson's base with his lips. And then, oh *yes*, the spit-grope of two wet fingers thrusting between his cheeks and into his softened, slack, slick rim. *Omigod omigod omigod!* Dawson let Jared slip out of his mouth, buried his come-wet face into Jared's thigh, and screamed. He didn't care who heard him, there was *nothing to do but scream.*

His hips were still jerking when Jared shoved at him and he flopped over to his side, his wet cock leaving a slippery trail down the side of Jared's cheek as he went.

He nuzzled Jared's thigh and just giggled for a moment, so replete, so *pleased* with the both of them, that he wasn't sure he'd ever find words. Jared's hand rumpled in his hair, and he sounded smug when he spoke. "Dawson?"

"Hm?"

"Someday, we're going to live in a house. We're going to have lots of property all around us, and a duck pond. And at least once a day, you're going to make that sound, and the ducks are going to scatter. Hunters will crouch around our house, waiting for us to have sex so we can scatter the damned ducks."

Dawson couldn't stop laughing, but he was too drained to do more than just lie there and study Jared's ugly dancer's toes, and make limp sounds. He fell into a short doze with Jared stroking the hairs on the back of his calf.

THE TRIP home was delirious with laughter, with conversation, with plans. They made tentative, almost furtive attempts to paint the backdrop of their future with brushes of suggestion.

"So, seriously, you want a duck pond? 'Cause if we want that much property, we should plan to move somewhere else. Oregon, maybe. Property here costs a shitload, and Portland has a good theater scene." Dawson looked at him assessingly, because call him a weenie, but he really didn't want to leave his dad.

"How expensive can it be?" Jared asked, looking around. Of course they were coming down from Truckee, and Dawson had no idea how much *that* property cost. It was the dry season—lots of trees, still some golden grass, because hey, it was August in California.

"Well, maybe not here—honestly, I have no idea how much it costs here, but since what we both want to do is down around more people, maybe think about something smaller. I know Ophir and Auburn *look* like firetraps this time of year, but seriously. They're not cheap."

Jared let out some hope, and Dawson felt bad. But when he spoke next, Dawson suddenly recognized that grown-up thing people called compromise and why it wasn't always so horrible.

"Okay," Jared said, thinking. "I concede—duck pond optional, but I want a *really big* yard, with flower beds and shade and a really big dog!"

Dawson was completely in love with him by then, but if he hadn't been, that would have sealed the deal. "Several," he said emphatically.

"A big one and a medium and a small one. And we can name one of them—"

"Killer," Jared said, nodding.

"You are making me swoon. Honest to frickin' God here. I'm going to swoon."

And even the conversation that turned melancholy was hopeful.

"But, Jared," Dawson prodded as they neared Auburn, "how can you say you'll just give dance up?"

Jared shook his head. "No—no. Not giving it up. Just... I'll be teaching it and performing with the students, and that will be really awesome."

"But we've *got* theater in Sacramento. There are places here that would take you—"

"I don't act, Dawson. I don't sing. I dance. And in a couple of years, my knee is going to be bad enough that I won't be able to do that anymore, not full-time."

"But the *spotlight*, Jared!" Dawson remembered that story of the little boy who wanted to be seen. "The whole world will see you—"

Jared shrugged and stayed silent, and Dawson could tell the idea hurt.

"Look, we don't have to figure it all out today," Dawson said after an awkward pause. "I mean, we're just dreaming here, right? We don't have to—"

"Don't take it back," Jared said fiercely, negotiating traffic coming down the long stretch from Newcastle to Penryn. "Don't take it back. We have *plans*—"

"But you're sacrificing your dreams—"

"I'm *living* my dream!" Jared returned, his voice ripping. "It's *lonely*. Maybe someone else could do it. But I'm not strong enough. I can't do it alone. And I *don't* want you in Hollywood."

"What's the matter?" Dawson cracked, wounded. "Afraid I won't make it?"

Jared shook his head. "*You*? You probably could. You could do anything—believe me, I'm a convert of the Dawson mystique by now."

Dawson had to stop himself from preening at the dreamy truth in Jared's voice. "So what?"

Jared shook his head. "Man, I don't care how good you are, how high you are—that town has a way of making even the most successful people feel small. If you ever felt that way because of *me*? Please. Just don't."

Dawson took a deep breath. "Okay, so, well, we sort of have a plan. We stick to it. We plan to be together and for me to get my degree and for you to start a dance studio specializing in children with disabilities. Are you going to train for that?"

Jared nodded. "I'm already looking into classes." Penryn disappeared behind them, and Loomis came next. A meditative silence fell, and Dawson vowed not to blink and miss Loomis.

And there went Loomis into the rearview. And there they were, in Rocklin, turning off and ready to start the entire rest of their lives.

"It's a plan," Dawson said as they neared the apartment complex. "It's weird. It's like we left three days ago to get laid and we came back married."

Jared pulled into the driveway and found Dawson's usual parking space. He put the car in park and pulled the emergency brake before he turned to Dawson and replied. "I meant everything we said today. I swear."

Dawson looked at him, his jaw clenched earnestly, and remembered when he thought Jared was the leader of the two of them. He *should* have been the leader—he was the older one, the more experienced one. But moment by moment, text by text, touch by touch, it had finally dawned on Dawson that Dawson would survive if their relationship detonated and dissipated in smoke and flames.

Jared would be in the heart of the blast. Scientists with microscopes and DNA detectors wouldn't be able to find him again.

"Jared, I won't let you be lonely," Dawson said, thinking about the rest of their lives. It was a long scary time, but the idea of Jared disappearing when his heart was broken? That was even scarier. "I won't let you down."

Jared nodded, and Dawson could see the muscle in his jaw pulsing. He held his hand up and cupped Jared's cheek, hoping to feel it relax. Jared closed his eyes and leaned against Dawson's palm. "I've never had a promise like this before," he confessed, and Dawson's heart thudded painfully in his throat. "I'm terrified."

"I'm not," Dawson lied. "Magic plus hard work. Remember that."

Jared nodded against his hand, and Dawson sealed it with a kiss. When he got out of the car, he felt more grown-up than he ever had in his life.

HE AND Jared pulled out their party smiles for his roommates, and they fit so good, Dawson forgot that anything but awesomeness happened during the entire trip. Benji was grilling hamburgers on the barbecue his dad had given them as a housewarming gift the year before. Darian and Amber were cutting up vegetables, and Darian was doing something funky with tofu, so Jared could maybe eat a burger or something. After Jared had left the last time, she'd sort of started mothering him, sending him recipes on the Internet and vitamin C supplements and teas in real life. Jared had secretly told Dawson that his roommates were filching her tea, but that was okay, he preferred coffee. Dawson had just kept all that to himself.

But Dawson did not plan to eat tofu on a barbecue day, and he was making that layer cake thing with the pistachio pudding and the piecrust that Jared refused to even *look* at because he said it made his ass bigger.

Jared kept Dawson's father well supplied with beer. That was his job. That and setting the table. Apparently it wasn't enough, or the job was too tough, because Dawson had just finished putting the four-layer dessert in the refrigerator to chill when his dad surprised him over the refrigerator door.

"Bwah!" Oh goddammit—the whole Pyrex dish with the dessert *almost* hit the floor. "Jesus, Dad, you almost started a riot!"

"Mr. B, that shit's nonnegotiable!" Amber said, dropping the pickles she'd been slicing and hurrying over to help Dawson settle the dish. "I've been living for that stuff since Dawson texted the menu to Benji!"

"Sorry," Stan apologized shortly. "Dawson, we're out of beer."

Dawson left dessert to Amber and looked over his shoulder. "The hell we are!" Because nope—the bottles were sticking out of the ice chests on the tiny patio.

"Okay, then I need a lame excuse to talk to you outside."

Dawson raised his eyebrows and hollered to Darian and Amber. "Do you guys need anything from the store?"

"Potato chips!" Darian begged, and Amber flipped her the bird. Amber was on a diet as much as Jared was, but her figure stayed sort of ripely curvy anyway.

"Okay, then. Dad and I are going to get potato chips—"

"With onion dip!" Darian said, and Dawson rolled his eyes, because who'd forget that?

"And the chicken-and-waffle kind, if they have them!" Amber spoke up, apparently losing her ability to diet in all of the contagious excitement. Dawson couldn't blame her. *Chicken-and-waffle potato chips.* There were geniuses in product development, he knew that for a *fact.*

"Gotcha!" Dawson called. Jared was outside with Benji and some guy Amber had dragged over, talking excitedly about acoustics and theaters with really amazing setups, which was pretty much Benji's favorite thing ever. Dawson waved on his way out the door. Jared lifted his beer in salute, and Dawson remembered when he would have thought that move was too reserved for any *real* emotion. He had a better handle on what was real now—or at least he hoped he did.

They got outside and Dawson held out his hands for his dad's keys. Dad flipped them over without even asking—the truth was he'd had at least three beers already, and it really was Dawson's turn to drive.

"So what gives?" Dawson asked when he'd backed up and left the driveway. Safeway was less than a mile away—this was going to be the shortest father/son talk in history.

"You and Jared," his dad said, suddenly sounding completely sober. "You're not acting like two guys who ran off to get laid."

Dawson swallowed. "Yeah. Can I tell you how much it bothers me that you actually think about me getting laid? It's like… unnatural. You're supposed to hold your hands over your ears and deny that I'm that old. I'm supposed to be your four-year-old running down the hall with the towel stuck between my ass crack for pretty much the rest of my life."

Dawson's dad muttered in disgust. "You post one video to YouTube and your kid never forgives you for it—"

"Well, Dad, I was in *high school!*"

His father's chuckle was so evil, Dawson was surprised his car engine didn't smoke and the doors didn't fall off. "Yeah. That was awesome. Teach *you* to sneak out of the house to see *Rocky Horror Picture Show* with Benji."

Dawson shifted uncomfortably. This was *not* how you started a conversation with your father about impending adulthood.

"In my defense, I didn't know you'd gotten me tickets for the next day," he muttered. God, you just could not apologize for that enough.

"Yup. Benji's mom and I had a *wonderful* time that night."

Dawson glared at him. He'd always wondered why that night hadn't turned into more than a night, because his dad couldn't stop talking about what a wonderful woman she was. "You should do that again," Dawson said with meaning, and he was pleased to see his dad's eyebrows go up consideringly.

And then his eyes narrowed just as Dawson hit the parking lot at Safeway. "This isn't about my celibacy, junior—it's about your love life. Tell me about you and Jared!"

Dawson got out of the car and into the gold-colored heat of late August. He leaned against the top of the car, disregarding the dust, and waited until Stan got out and leaned against it too. "Dad?"

"Yeah?"

"How old were you when you met Mom?"

His dad raised those ginger eyebrows and blinked. "Twenty."

Dawson nodded. "So, there you go."

His dad jerked back and Dawson turned toward the store and started walking. It was frickin' hot and he wanted the air-conditioning like, immediately.

"There you *don't* go!" his dad protested. "What the hell does that even mean?"

Dawson got to the front of the store and grabbed a cart. "It means that right now, I'm pretty sure this is the person I want to spend the rest of my life with," he said, making sure his dad could see his face. "And that we're making plans in that direction."

Dad nodded. "Okay. Do I have to say it? Are you going to make me argue against this?"

Dawson pushed the cart through the doors and waited for his dad to catch up with him. "I wish you wouldn't."

"Yeah, but son—I mean, I sort of have to, don't I?"

Dawson knew *exactly* where the chips were. They were one aisle over from the beer. He pushed the cart to the aisle and stopped, letting out a sigh.

"No," he said, suddenly tired. Well, he and Jared really hadn't slept for three days—it would make sense. "You don't. You don't have to say anything. Just listen. See, I know. I met him when I was twenty, and it's a long-distance relationship, and he's sort of light-years above me on the cosmic scale of career and fame and importance—how am I ever going to compete?"

Dad grimaced. "Yeah, well, except for the importance, but the career and fame thing, you nailed that."

God, Dawson loved his dad. "Thanks, Dad," he said, smiling crookedly. "Anyway, so I know all that. You want to hear the thing you don't know?"

With a sigh, Dad started grabbing chips off the shelf, and some crackers, and some chocolate too. "Do you have room for ice cream?" he asked, and Dawson nodded.

"Yeah, the freezer aisle is one over. Chips first."

"Great. So enlighten me."

Dawson saw the chicken-and-waffle-flavored chips and got three bags. Suddenly he wanted to just tear into one of them and eat the whole thing—there would be something ferociously satisfying in just downing an entire bag of something forbidden and fattening where Jared couldn't see him and practice that aching constraint. He reached to the shelf and grabbed another bag. They never lasted. "Okay, so the thing that you're not factoring in here is this. Jared *loves* me. I mean, I love him—you all know that, not a secret, Dawson hanging on to the guy like a puppy, you all see that. We're good. But what you don't see, because he just sort of hangs back and smiles and looks all secret and Jared-y, is that he loves me back."

His dad sighed and went for the onion dip, getting two jars. "Look, I think it's obvious that he cares for you—I mean, flying all the way up here on his week off—"

"And when he was sick," Dawson said doggedly. "Don't forget the sick thing. Why do you think he'd do that if he felt like crap?"

"Okay, fine. That's another thing. So he loves you. He's got no one else. Is that really how you want to base a relationship? Because the other person is desperate for contact?"

"No—don't you see? He could *have* anybody! Who he *wants* is me. And you know the *really* cool thing? He thinks I'm the same way. He's pretty sure I could get anybody I wanted. And I'm going to let him think that, because the way he looks at me is like I'm the last best and only good thing to ever happen to him. Do you think I'd do anything to betray that? I mean, he wants to move here—*here*! Because he thinks I'm worth moving here. And the thing he wants to do with his life—Dad. It just doesn't get any cooler than that. So you know, that thing Benji and I have been avoiding in a big way, that 'what are you going to do with the rest of your life' thing. I think I found it. I want to be with him. Whatever form our lives take, that's the heart and core of it. I want to be with him."

Dawson paused for a second and looked at his father, hoping that the conversation could be over now. Behind his dad, he saw someone look down the aisle curiously and then push his cart *past* the chip aisle toward beer. Dawson didn't blame him. He'd like to skip this aisle and have a fucking beer himself.

Dawson's dad looked inside the cart and sighed. "I need some fucking ice cream," he muttered, then looked up at his only child. "Do you want some fucking ice cream?"

"In the worst goddamned way," Dawson agreed.

They bought four half gallons. With sprinkles, chocolate syrup, and whipped cream. It wasn't until they were loading $150 worth of shitacular food choices into Dawson's trunk that his dad spoke up again.

"I want you to be happy," he said after Dawson slammed the trunk. "I want you to be happy, because I love you and I want you to stay in the area because I'm selfish, and I like Jared, I do, but God. Dawson. You're young and he's broken. You think you can do that?"

Dawson shook his head and got in the car, turning on the ignition before he shut the door so the cold air could start pumping. "Dad? You ever talk to Mom?" he asked.

Dawson's dad shook his head. "You know I don't."

"Neither do I. Why is that, you think?"

His dad grunted. They both knew her complete lack of interest in her oldest son had deepened considerably when he'd come out in high school.

"Because she's a shallow stupid bitch who doesn't know what God gave her," his dad said with feeling.

Dawson grinned. That was his dad. It was the one place in his life where he didn't look at both sides and didn't even try to sound like a grown-up.

"Dad, he loves Benji. And Darian. And Amber. And you. All the people who make me *me*, he loves them, and he gets them. And he wants to be a part of them. See, Mom couldn't do that. She couldn't love Sacramento and she couldn't love you for wanting to stay here and she couldn't love me for me. All those things that broke you guys— those are the important things. And Jared and I have the *opposite* of all those things. I think maybe we can make this work."

His dad sighed. "I hope so, Dawson. It's a pretty thin bridge from four hundred miles away."

Dawson rubbed his face with his hands and realized he actually had stubble. That was new. It used to take him a week to get stubble. He'd shaved the morning before.

"It's farther for him than for me," he said honestly, thinking about Jared not wanting Dawson hurt, about that painful bargain to say good-bye to the one thing that had sustained him since he was a kid. Dawson could probably talk Benji and Darian and even Amber into going down to LA to make a go of it. They'd hate it, and maybe him, but he could go down and have his people. But thanks to Jared, they didn't have to do that. He just had to wait for Jared to say good-bye to everything he'd known.

Yeah.

Further for Jared than for Dawson. That was the truth.

Dad's hand on his head, mauling him into a quick, sideways, sweaty car hug was not unwelcome. In fact, it gave him unexpected strength. He needed the strength too, because explaining what the hell they were going to do with all of that ice cream when they already had dessert took some damned fancy word dancing.

LEAP, LIFT, AND SEPARATE

OH, YEAH—it was easy to be oh so cool when you were convincing your dad you could do it for nine more months, but when you were saying good-bye to your boyfriend at six in the morning on a muggy Friday, well, that was harder to do.

"You could date other people when I'm gone," Jared said while they were negotiating the shitty traffic and construction at the I-5 interchange.

Dawson remembered that lonely picture of Jared at the barre and had to laugh at the incredible reluctance in his voice.

"No," he said, grabbing Jared's hand and squeezing. "No. It's going to be hard enough missing you without wondering if you could deal with that too."

Jared pulled his hand back. "Well, could you deal with *me* see—"

"No," Dawson snapped. "I'd kill him. I'd buy a ticket to LA, get a cab to your apartment, and fucking kill him."

The silence next to him was unnerving. As their lane of cars slowed to a halt, Dawson looked over to see his face. That shy Jared smile was showing, and his eyes were shiny.

"God, Jared—just… of course I give a shit." Suddenly Dawson's throat felt tight and his eyes didn't just stay shiny, they overflowed. "I give a shit. I miss the hell out of you, but I don't want anyone else. I don't want you to find anyone else. I just want… I want *us*. But I can wait for it, so don't worry about me."

"I don't," Jared said, his voice a little thick but sound. "I don't. I should, but I don't."

Dawson grinned, even though he was pretty sure he was going to totally break down and ugly cry again when Jared got out of the car. "And that is one of the many reasons I love you, baby. You can't buy that kind of faith."

"But you worry about me," Jared said dryly.

Dawson hoped he could hold on to his ugly cry until Jared actually left.

"You had a long time for the world to beat you up before I came along," Dawson said with dignity. "I want to go back in time and retroactively kick the ass of everyone who ever hurt you before they even thought to do it."

"I can fight my own battles," Jared said, and Dawson heard the prickle of pride there, and thought, well, yeah. All men had it, right?

"Yeah, but I hate that you fought them all alone."

Jared made a dry sound in his throat. "Don't worry about me," he said again, and Dawson recognized that he was trying to make himself sound like the grown-up. Well, good, yeah. Dawson did that all the time. He liked to think he'd grow out of it by twenty-six, but watching Jared, he got the feeling that *that* wasn't going to happen. Well, his penis hadn't grown a whopping three inches when he turned twenty-one either, so he could maybe live with the dissolution of cherished childhood delusions. In fact, not being a magical grown-up when he reached twenty-six was one more thing that put them on even ground.

They got to the airport. Dawson was starting to hate the place. He thought maybe it was a good thing he was staying in Sacramento, because if he had to say good-bye to Benji and Darian and his dad from this airport for frickin' ever, he'd probably wreck his car on I-80 just to not have to *be* there ever again.

He parked the car in front of the Southwest terminal and helped Jared get his luggage, and just looking at the battered, duct-taped black suitcase, he felt his throat close. Oh hell. Oh please. Let him save the ugly cry for the car and the way home. Let him not—

"I'll be back for two weeks around Halloween," Jared said, his voice rough. He cupped Dawson's face between his palms and wiped underneath his eyes with careful thumbs. "Don't drive and cry, baby. It's dangerous."

Dawson nodded wordlessly, because he didn't think he could say anything that wasn't a sob or a wail, and fuck it, Jared wasn't the only one who had pride.

He threw his arms around Jared's shoulders and found he could whisper. "We meant it, right? It was real?"

"Best, most real thing in my life," Jared whispered back. "I love you."

"Love you too. Safe travels."

And then both of them together said, "Think of me."

And Jared made a suspicious sound before pulling away and wiping his face and grabbing his luggage, so quickly Dawson couldn't even go after him. Besides, Dawson could barely see well enough to get in the car. He ugly cried against his steering wheel until the security guard came and tapped on his window, because he'd been there quite long enough.

Dawson didn't even have words to tell him that he hadn't been there long enough at all. Long enough was when he'd been there in time to see Jared arriving and not leaving.

It sounded stupid when he said it in his head anyway, but he just kept thinking about pockets of time and leaping and chassé. He wanted to leap from pocket to pocket, but he had to make his way in slow, painful footsteps across the stage.

Who the hell wrote this score, anyway?

HE AND Benji were working on *Chicago* before Halloween, which was great, because it meant he had tickets for Jared and his dad to see a show they might both enjoy when Jared arrived. Dawson was pretty proud of their theater in the round and the way the choreographer and director used the entire stage, and the house aisles, and the lighting. Benji had been taking notes for every show, and Dawson thought he was going to be one of the best light and sound engineers in the business—not that Dawson was biased or anything.

Both of them were very junior assistant stage managers, which meant they made sure the props were right where the actors needed to grab them, right on cue, and they were both pretty practiced at moving quietly, wearing all black, to get things like chairs and prop bags where they needed to be.

So Dawson couldn't figure out why Eduardo, one of the chorus members, kept running into him.

Until the fourth time, when he felt a groping hand *right* on his crotch.

He grew hard almost immediately, but that didn't stop him from smacking the encroaching hand. He glared at Eduardo, handed him his chair, and gestured him in no uncertain terms back to the stage.

He and Benji hustled out of door one to run around the back corridor to door eight, where they'd be needed to hand out feathered fans.

"What the hell was that about?" hissed Benji.

Dawson grunted. "He was copping a feel. God, you'd think he'd have better things to do."

Benji grunted in return. "I think he's done this show too goddamned many times and when we move on to *Priscilla, Queen of the Desert* and he has a speaking part, he'll leave your dick alone."

Dawson shook his head. "I mean seriously. He thinks I'm going to give it up to just a grope in the dark? God, even if I was single I'd need a cup of coffee and some fucking conversation!"

Benji clapped him on the shoulder and they made it around in time to duck into the darkened theater and do their jobs, which was always such a surprise. You just didn't *leave* the theater in the middle of a show, but when everyone was focused on the stage in the middle of a round room, you had to do most of your backstage work on the outer hub of that wheel. But it was exhilarating, and they both enjoyed the hell out of it. Darian envied them both—she'd auditioned for Music Circus before, and although she'd won minor bits in some of the larger ensemble casts, her competition consisted of seasoned Broadway veterans with more muscles in their backs than Dawson had in his entire body. Dawson figured he and Benji had been, like, a perfect storm of serendipity, and there wasn't much he wouldn't do to keep his job.

But letting Eduardo grope his privates when he was holding a prop chair made the short list. He wasn't going to do it, wasn't going to put up with it, and he only wished his boner would go away because moral outrage was so much easier when a six-week sexual backup wasn't rearing its ugly cockhead.

The good news, he thought, gritting his teeth, was that he only had two weeks to go, and then Jared and Dawson got to play house for *two whole weeks*. The idea was heady. Two weeks. Could they stand each other for two weeks at a time? Would Dawson start rubbing a raw spot on Jared's nerves? Would Jared start rubbing a raw spot on

Dawson's *cock*? These were questions Dawson desperately wanted answered, and he could hardly wait for the homework to begin!

But he and Benji were nothing if not professional—and they *believed* in the magic of theater. They *believed* every performance was brand-new, and that cast and crew, working in perfect synchronicity, created magic. It was everything Dawson knew about the world right there, in him and Benji getting to position in time to hand out giant pink feather fans.

And this Monday night it worked perfectly.

When the final curtain call finished and Benji and Dawson had catalogued all the props and returned them to their exact place in the prop room so that they could be found by *any* crew member at *any* given time, they both walked out into the fountain courtyard together, close enough to bump arms. The vendors were closed, the audience had dispersed, and the only people left were the cast and crew, talking happily about a particularly amazing show.

Dawson was not even ready for Eduardo bounding from behind into his personal space, draping muscular arms over his shoulders, and hip-checking Benji practically to the other side of the moon.

"Hey, Dawson—a few of us are going out to Gatsby's Nick tonight. You game?"

Dawson heard Benji grunt, and he took a few steps out of Eduardo's octopus space so he could make sure Benji hadn't ended up in the bushes.

"Benji doesn't like Gatsby's Nick without his girl," Dawson said dryly, and watched as Benji rolled his eyes. He'd let his dark hair grow a little longer so those puppy dog eyes looked broodingly out at the world from the hair falling off his brow—and the rolled eyes looked even more sarcastic. Which was probably fitting—Benji, in fact, was the most popular belle at the ball when they went to Nick's to hear music, which was why he usually brought Darian as proof that, yes, straight but not narrow, just wanting to dance with his friends.

"Well, Benji doesn't have to come," Eduardo said, smiling coyly and batting insanely brown lashes over big limpid brown eyes.

"Yeah," Dawson said, nodding like he was talking to a second grader. "Yes, Eduardo, Benji *would* have to come, because *then* I'd have someone to dance with who wouldn't want to get in my pants!"

Eduardo pouted. Dawson was man enough to admit it looked charming. "But Dawson, how do you know you don't want me in your pants if you won't even let me have a grope?"

Dawson stopped at the fountain and turned to make sure Benji was keeping up. God, he felt like a weenie needing Benji to protect his virtue, but Eduardo was just scary fucking persistent. "I've never had the clap, but I'm pretty sure I don't want it either—oh my God!"

Benji had seen him first, but to be fair, he was on Benji's side of the courtyard, and Eduardo had been in his way.

He shoved Eduardo hard enough that he almost went into the fountain and then just forgot about him.

"*Jared*!" And omigod! Dawson just wanted to run up to him and jump into his arms and maul the holy crap out of him. He was stopped by three things.

One under each arm.

And the big brace on Jared's knee.

Jared shoved himself up with one crutch and held out an arm, and Dawson stepped into his space and just held him. He smelled like travel—sweat and worry—and the lines at his eyes were deeper than they had been when he'd left.

"You got hurt," Dawson said softly, rubbing their cheeks together. "You weren't supposed to get hurt."

"Three weeks," Jared said, doing the same thing. "The doc put the brace on, told me to stay off for three weeks. Can I spend them here?"

Dawson pulled back and made a face. "Seriously. You gotta ask?"

Jared glared pointedly past his shoulder. "Yeah, well, I thought maybe someone would be taking you dancing."

Dawson rolled his eyes. "Is he still there? Because dude, I gave him an exit line."

"Jared Emory? Holy shit, Dawson—we thought you were making him up!" Eduardo was right over Dawson's shoulder, trying to have a face-to-face with Jared while *Dawson was still there*.

Jared honest to God growled. "No means no, asshole," he snapped.

Eduardo held out his hands. "Sorry, man. I mean, you've got to admit, he's got a pretty sweet ass, right?"

Jared struggled with his crutches, and Dawson held him around the waist so that he couldn't just reach out and whap Eduardo one using the crutch as an appendage.

"Benji!" Jared snapped after they glared at each other in standoff. "Man, hit him for us!"

Benji was pushing up his sleeves and squaring his jaw, and for a minute Dawson was sure he was going to do it too. "No, dinkus!" He looked over his shoulder and shoved at Eduardo with more meaning than actual force. "Man, could you just go the fuck away! I haven't seen him in a month and a half!" He turned to Jared. "Did you take a cab here?" he asked, still puzzled.

Jared pointed to the suitcase down by his feet. "Yup. Right off the p—"

And Dawson didn't care about the rest of the sentence. He was done with travel details and Eduardo and his grabby hands and lost in Jared's kiss and the solidness of his chest and the fact that he had not one week but three, and Jared was going to be his, all his, and nobody was going to take that way.

THERE IS a rhythm to people living together. You know when the one person takes the shower and the other person takes the dump. You know what to do in the evenings when nobody feels like talking, and you make sure that you *always* talk at least at some point during the day. You learn how to go to bed without making love or feeling like you *have* to make love or feeling like you're a failure in the romance department because you couldn't sprout wood if you woke up as fertile soil and the other guy's dick was bamboo. You learn how to fit making love in between roommates and comings and goings and classes and jobs because that touching, that *connection*, was what you waded through some of the other stuff *for*. To feel like you weren't alone in the universe, and the person inside or outside your body was joined with you somehow, and he wasn't going away.

For three weeks Jared and Dawson negotiated the ins and outs of finding that rhythm, and it was as much like dancing as the rest of the year, but closer, more connected, more intense.

Jared swam in the pool every day while Dawson and the others were at school, but by twelve o'clock, when they got home for lunch, he'd usually cooked something, even if it was just spaghetti with sauce from a jar. (That was their standby when no one had gone shopping. The night after he served them that, Amber took him shopping while Benji and Dawson went to work, and the menu improved dramatically.)

At night, the girls spent time with him when Dawson and Benji were doing homework. They watched television or shared music or books. Darian kept giving him "I'm okay, you're okay" books, but Amber knew her porn, and *she* kept sending him really raunchy romances, both M/F and M/M. Jared finally told them both he preferred murder mysteries, but he appreciated the efforts. The next day, he was eyeballs deep in used Sandra Brown and Lee Childs, and he read every one.

They had brunch with Dawson's dad every week, and Jared watched basketball with him on the nights Dawson was gone.

And Dawson got to answer that question, that scary question, that people ask about themselves when they're a couple. "We *think* we do okay together, but could we really *live* like a family?"

Yes. Yes, they could.

The night before Jared's plane took off, they lay side by side and talked until dawn. Dawson skipped class the next day after he dropped Jared off at the airport. He came home to take a nap so he could function at work, but it was worth it.

For one thing, he got every fractured detail about the state of Jared's health, and it was a good thing he waited until Jared was ready to talk, or Dawson could have spoiled the entire time with nagging, and that would have been a shame.

"Well, it's been bothering me since my last trip," Jared said, adjusting the ice pack Dawson had brought him because he'd gone without crutches that day and his knee was bothering him. "It's just... well, we flew to Atlanta to perform for a week, and I got off the plane and it had swollen double, and by the time I was done with that first performance, I couldn't walk away."

Dawson frowned, trying to remember what Jared had told him about his schedule. "Wait—but you got into Atlanta about three days before you showed up here."

Jared let out a sigh. "Yeah, well, I performed one more night and—"

"Auugh!" Dawson put his hands over his eyes and rolled onto his back. "You *suck*! Why would you do that?"

"Because they had to fly my understudy in, Dawson, and in the meantime it wasn't just me, it was the entire company, the theater, presale tickets, and the techies, and... you know how it goes! The whole ensemble counts on the front of the house—it's not fair, because a great stage play is everybody, but we're the people that people see. I had to."

Dawson closed his eyes, remembered the giant bottles of ibuprofen and Vicodin Jared had gone through, and the limping, and the way he'd gritted his teeth, and the hours in the pool, keeping his body honed even if he couldn't put any weight on it.

"I want the fucking papers" was what came out of his mouth, and no one was more surprised than he was.

"What?" Jared blinked slowly, those impossible lashes fanning the air.

"The papers that say I have some control over this. You told me you'd have Dolph write them up for me."

Sudden realization dawned on Jared's face. "Oh right—I *did* tell him. I even signed them. He has them in his safe."

Dawson frowned and wrinkled his nose. "Don't *I* have to sign them?"

"Oh hell—"

"My God—you're bad at this stuff!" Dawson laughed, because the alternative was getting pissed. Jesus, what did it take to get the guy used to thinking about the future?

"Well—" Jared made a helpless gesture with his one free arm. "I don't know what to say, Dawson. I was in no way prepared for you, or any version of you, or any version of anybody who was going to want to step up and pick me up off the floor when I fell. I'll bring the papers next time I come."

Dawson made a wounded sound, the peace of the past three weeks suddenly punctured by all the things that had happened or could happen or were happening four hundred miles away in the place he could not see.

"You're saving something for me, right?" he asked, swallowing hard. "It's not like... I don't know, any movie about anyone famous *ever*, where you don't save anything for the trip back. You're saving a piece of you for *me*, right?"

Jared was lying on his back, his eyes closed, his hands stretched over his head, his chest just stretched out, every muscle group distinct and ridged, like a breathing work of art. Dawson resisted the urge to pet him, to fondle every part, just to know that the flesh under his fingers was his, because hearing Jared talk about his responsibilities and how he was killing himself for them was a painful reminder: Jared wasn't his *yet*. The past weeks had been lovely, and they'd given Dawson hope, but they weren't *real* yet. Jared was still swimming out as far as he could go, until he couldn't swim anymore.

"I'm trying." Jared sounded thoughtful and tired, and Dawson wasn't sure if Jared was adding the sadness, the resignation there, or if Dawson's imagination just added it because. "I mean, I hadn't planned to, okay?" He made an effort that Dawson could *hear*, and hauled his knee and ice pack around so they were facing each other. "There wasn't a lot left of me in February," he confessed quietly, like this was something Dawson hadn't guessed, painfully, on his own. "I... I mean, if you and me hadn't hooked up, I probably would have found someone, anyone, just for a night, because it had been that long since my breakup, but it wouldn't have been... a thing. It wouldn't have been you. And that's just... just all I ever thought I had."

Dawson closed his eyes. "June, right?" he said, thinking about Jared alone, with no one to bring him ice packs or nag him about eating *something* with all of that medicine. He'd asked, right when Jared had gotten there, if Jared wanted him to top during sex because it was easier on his knee, for one, and because Dawson was sort of excited about doing it, for another. And then Jared had explained what all of those pain meds did to the stomach and digestive tract when you were living off coffee and water and Red Bull, and Dawson hadn't asked again. He didn't touch Jared's distended stomach in bed anymore either, unless it was to cup his hand over the slight mound of it and wish it felt better. Which was what he did now.

"Just a little piece," he begged, aware his pride had utterly deserted him. He felt like a coward, stunned and frightened by how little of Jared might be left by the time their plans came to be.

Jared laced his fingers with Dawson's and moved their hands to his chest. "I'll save you everything I can," he said, and Dawson was proud of himself for not getting angry. Three weeks, and Jared had worked so hard at being the perfect boyfriend. He'd fit himself into the household so easily, the thought of excising him out of everybody's life hurt, like he was a piece of flesh nearest Dawson's heart.

"Aren't I worth more?" he asked, and he was trying to be reasonable, but God. Dawson had seen his knee without the brace—twice its normal size, red, swollen, angry, and Jared said that knee surgery would put him out of commission for longer than it would take to heal naturally. But Dawson knew—*knew*—that delaying the surgery meant the chances of permanent injury got worse with every performance.

The medication and the pain made Jared tired, and the eyes he turned toward Dawson were shadowed and haunted with weariness. "You're the only reason I'm trying, Dawson," he said, sounding patient. "I never thought I'd have a reason to keep anything in reserve. Sorry—if I'd had a Dawson four years ago, I might be in better shape. You were in high school then. Ick."

Dawson grimaced and kissed their twined hands. "Okay, okay. I hear you. Be grateful for the shape you're in."

Jared smiled slightly. "I mean, my shape thus far has given you some amazing moments."

Couldn't argue with that. "*You* have given me some amazing moments," Dawson said, feeling sad. Maybe it was the hour or the fact that Jared would be leaving tomorrow, but something… *something* was aching like an old wound. "I want more. I want… I don't know. My dad couldn't play basketball in school—he was horrible. I've seen tapes. He had my coordination. It was—" Dawson wiggled his shoulders since he didn't have a free arm to flail.

"Lives were at stake," Jared said dryly.

"*Thank* you—you understand! Anyway, so he sucked at it, but he watches it all the time, and he goes to the games he can, and whenever he has to travel for business, he takes in the nearest basketball game. He doesn't discriminate, either. College ball, WNBA—it's what he lives for. He coached my team when I was a kid—like, hours and hours of unpaid work, and he did it just to spend time with me and the game. And he loves it. And it makes him happy. Don't you have anything besides dancing that will make you happy? I mean, I want to see you do this thing with the kids—I think that's going to be amazing. But...."

He didn't know what he was aiming for. *He* was obsessed with his job—*he* watched plays and movies in his spare time, *he* couldn't imagine anything else. Except he could. He could imagine racing laps with Benji when they had time to work out together. He could imagine *Words By Post* with Darian, who was kicking his ass in six different games. He could imagine helping Amber DJ, because she was teaching him, and learning tai chi so maybe he didn't bash himself on so much stuff, and learning to play the guitar and maybe someday learning to spin yarn out of roving because he read a story about it and thought that would be *cool*.

He had so much inside him that he could do *anything with*.

How much did Jared have? Had it all been carved out of him, hollowed out by that need for dance to be his one golden thing?

"Poetry," Jared said out of the blue. "Literature. I got my degree already, but I want to go back and take all the literature courses. *All* of them. Even the weird ones like postmodernism that sound really pretentious."

Dawson smiled at him, and suddenly, just like that, Jared was *his* one golden thing. "That's awesome. I'll take them with you."

"And I want a duck pond," Jared said seriously.

Dawson grimaced. "Man, we talked about—"

Jared shook his head adamantly and looked dead serious. "No—it's nonnegotiable. We *will* have a duck pond someday. Even if it's not our first house or our second, I want a duck pond. I'll *buy* ducks and let them waddle around, and clean up their poop like you would with dogs—"

"We're getting the dogs too, right?"

"Fine. You clean up the dog poop, I'll get the duck poop, and we're doing it." Jared jutted that square chin out like a challenge, and his mercury-blue eyes under the black rectangular eyebrows were alight with sober intention and a little bit of quiet mischief. *This* was the Jared Dawson had fallen in love with.

He was here. All of him. He hadn't been destroyed or hollowed out or any of those terrible things Dawson was afraid of. He was hurt, but he wasn't broken. Well, that was Dawson's car, right? He'd dinged the bumper, broken the light, put a big dent in the door, picked up two nails and had the tires replaced, backed into a concrete post and bent the trunk, and run under one of those metal gates so his hood rippled—but by God, that piece of crap still ran.

Jared was probably in better shape than Dawson's car.

"My dog is going to kick your ducks' collective ass. He's gonna eat ducks for dinner. He's gonna sleep on duck-feather pillows. He's—"

Jared kissed him, and he opened, and the next few moments consisted of the collection of things that meant making love—all of the sensitive parts stroked and licked until nerve endings lit up like a Christmas tree, but even more. There was Jared's throaty voice urging him to swing his hips over, asking him if he could do this one more time. There was Jared's touch, the way his hands shook on Dawson's thighs, the way he had to close his eyes when it was too intense, the way he grappled and pulled on Dawson's neck so there could be a kiss, awkward but necessary, right when Dawson thought he might explode the hardest.

Their breath echoed harsh in their ears, and the sweat cooled on their skin in the early-morning chill. When the last bit of orgasm sang through their skin, Dawson bit Jared's neck, hard, but he still flowed over and cried.

"Did you ever have this?" he panted. "Did it ever hurt to touch someone because you loved them so much?"

"No." Jared's voice rumbled under Dawson's palms. "No. Not until now. Not until you."

"Don't let go of this when you're gone," Dawson told him, closing his eyes. It didn't matter. His face was wet and he couldn't seem to stop.

Jared's hands on either side of his face didn't calm him down. "You're beautiful," Jared said. "Like dance. That perfect moment when it's movement and music and body—that's you. I'll never let go of that. I swear."

Dawson opened his mouth when Jared pressed their lips together, and the taste of salt mingled on their tongues.

CRASHING STARS

DAWSON'S DAD hosted Thanksgiving that year, and he did a good job of it. For once he followed a recipe, and the turkey wasn't too dry and the stuffing was just right. Benji's mom, who had done Thanksgiving the year before, brought side dishes, and she did German cabbage and this sweet-potato thing with cornflakes on top that Dawson swore could be its very own food group.

Jared managed a three-day visit.

Without the damned papers giving Dawson some sort of legal rights.

Dawson tried not to seethe and fuck up Thanksgiving, because seriously. They had three days.

Jared showed up Wednesday morning—when he helped make pies—and left Saturday morning at 4:00 a.m. so he could perform that night. This meant he was there Thursday, when he charmed the socks off of Benji's mom by speaking Castilian Spanish.

"Omigod, *Jared*!" Benji whispered in awe. Darian sat right next to him, in her best, most grown-up dress, nodding in agreement. She looked adorable with her hair piled up and her little white collar like a Pilgrim. Amber had even dressed up in black slacks and a white shirt. She'd scraped her hair back from her face in a neat ponytail, and Dawson wondered if any men ever looked past the scowl and the hair that hung to her eyebrows and saw the really pretty brown eyes and full lips behind all that.

Probably not, which was okay. If Amber ever had to deal with an Eduardo in her life, Dawson would need to hold Benji's coat while Benji kicked the crap out of him.

But back to Dawson's friends fawning all over Jared because he could not only speak *Spanish*, but speak the kind of Spanish Benji's mother had despaired of ever teaching her son.

"I went to college," Jared said, blushing.

"And...." Dawson knew when he was keeping something back now.

"My parents took me to Spain for a year before I went to dance school," Jared said, shrugging.

Dawson filed that away for future reference. It was the only thing *good* he'd heard about them.

Dawson's dad's house was the quintessential mancave. He used no colors besides navy, cream, and brown, and only hung framed prints of sports teams—most notably the Sacramento Kings—all over the walls. He bought soft, comfortable leather couches that allowed the big screen to dominate the room, and still used the massive, stained, and inde-frickin'-structable coffee table he'd had when Dawson was so young they had to worry about furniture with corners. His kitchen was white and gleaming chrome, and after Dawson and his friends provided the pies, they wisely ran to hang out in the living room, where they were less likely to knock over something dear to Stan Barnes but absolutely impractical in any other context. After Jared's fancy trick with the "How are you, Mrs. Gomez, your son is a very good friend of mine," but *not* in English, the rest of them really had no chance of charming the socks off of the grown-ups.

Benji and Amber wanted to watch football anyway, and Darian was making tentative forays back into the kitchen because she was trying to impress Benji's mom, mostly. Dawson didn't understand why she'd be so freaked out over being the perfect daughter-in-law for this one holiday—Mrs. G seemed to love her most of the rest of the year—but, well, maybe that was the cost of growing up. Bringing the SO for Thanksgiving was suddenly a big hairy (or hairless, given Darian and Jared and their waxing habits) deal.

Jared went to stand under Dawson's favorite picture in his dad's living room, the two-by-three, full-color *autographed* picture of Xander Karcek right about to make a three-point shot.

"You know," Dawson said, looking up at that brooding Slavic face, "he's not the *only* player out in the NBA anymore."

"That's not why I like him," Jared said softly.

Dawson moved in closer so they could bump shoulders. "Enlighten me."

"He's just always seemed really alone." Jared cocked his head like there was a special angle for reading men's souls. "And he gave up *everything* to not be alone. And I used to think that was a really horrible sacrifice—I didn't know how he could do it. It seemed really brave, you know?"

Dawson thought of the tape he'd watched ad infinitum during his first year of college, of Karcek coming out after a playoff game. And of the subsequent tape of him getting suspended from play for sleeping with his teammate, Chris Edwards. There were some rumors of him training up to play the rest of what had been an admittedly stunning career, but his impression had been the same as Jared's.

"Yeah," he said softly. "But you know, I saw that whole special—his entire life was pretty brave."

Jared turned to him, searching his face for something Dawson hoped was there. "Did you see? I mean, he was really uncomfortable, but his whole attention—that was on Chris, right?"

Dawson remembered. It was one of the few times he hadn't resented his dad making him watch something about basketball. "Yeah."

"Remember that when I'm gone. That's *me*, thinking about you."

Dawson nodded and leaned into Jared's body. There hadn't been much time for talking or even making love this trip. Mostly, there'd been time for Dawson to nag him about the damned papers, which hadn't felt good at all. "I'll remember that," he promised. "Now are you going to come make football palatable to me or not?"

Jared tried. Benji helped. Both of them explained about tackles and offense and defense, their voices rising in excitement as San Francisco got the ball to the end zone. Dawson tried—Lord knew this was his brother and his lover, and they were totally invested—but at the end, he was as lost as he always was with sports. All he remembered was how the warmth from Jared's body made Dawson sweat through his navy V-necked sweater and his skinny jeans, but that Jared didn't say a word about Dawson's embarrassing clamminess.

Thanksgiving after that was traditional. They set the table and put on the pretty centerpiece with the tiger lilies and marigolds Dawson *knew* his father had picked out just for the occasion, and the adults drank too much wine and the kids drank not quite enough. They told stories of their jobs, their school, their classes, and the people they worked with, and they all saw each other enough that there were no awkward pauses or unforeseen events. Benji's mother, a slightly formal, still-beautiful woman with porcelain skin and dark hair and eyes, smiled shyly at Dawson's father and asked if their sons hadn't grown up beautifully.

Dawson's dad looked them both over and winked at her. "I can't claim credit there, Francesca—those manners are all yours."

"Someone taught you manners?" Jared asked, nibbling at his white turkey breast and salad without dressing.

"Benji's mother thinks so," Dawson said with dignity, and then he winked at Mrs. Gomez, who smiled graciously back. He had to admit, when his own mother had decided to fade off the page, having someone to remind him to set the table and tuck in his shirt had been a blessing.

They all fell asleep in random patterns across the living room floor in front of the Disney movie that came on after football, and Dawson's dad let them nap while he cleaned up with Mrs. Gomez. They must have come out at some point when Dawson was drooling on Jared's lap, because he didn't hear how they'd gotten on the subject.

"Do you think they'll be happy?" she asked.

Dawson's father sounded uncertain. "Benji and Darian? Absolutely. They were married when they met."

"She's a good girl. She needs to stand up for herself, though. She's lucky I'm so shy and retiring."

If Dawson hadn't been mostly asleep, he would have snorted.

"But what about your son?" Francesca asked. "He's obviously in love with the nice boy with the smooth tongue."

Stan made a sort of sad sound. "Yeah. And I think Jared cares for him. But it's a long way 'til June."

Jared's hand tightened in Dawson's hair, and Dawson wanted to wake up and tell them that it wasn't long. It was just around the corner.

It wasn't until the next morning that Dawson realized Jared was still taking pain pills for his knee, and that it was still swollen. And that he remembered he still didn't have the damned papers.

When Dawson dropped him off at the airport, he was limping so badly he could barely walk. "After Christmas?" Dawson asked one more time.

Jared grunted—not because he was blowing Dawson off but because he was in pain. "Yeah. I'll be on the plane on the twenty-seventh. My last performance of the year is the twenty-sixth—they're taping it. You'll watch me on PBS?"

Like he had to ask! "Duh! Whose boyfriend have *you* been sleeping with?"

Jared gave that shy smile. "I'm pretty sure it's mine, but you're going to have to kiss me one more time to be sure."

Dawson helped him with his bags in the black morning and then stood next to the idling car, his arms around the man he loved. "You're saving something for the way back," he asked, because it had been such a short visit and he had to make sure.

"Yeah," Jared said. "I promise."

They sealed it with a kiss, and Jared became a daily text, a voice on the weekend, a nightly IM session, an ache in Dawson's heart, one more time.

CHRISTMAS EVE happened at Dawson and Benji's place. They figured since Benji and Darian were thinking about moving out in February, they would make it a blowout, so they decorated the place in all the tinsel they could manage and got a tree *way* too big for the living room. They invited the parents and some of their friends for Christmas, and they played cards and got a little drunk. The parents stayed, sleeping on the couch and the love seat, and they all opened presents in the morning. The biggest present—a comforter/sheet set from Dawson and a gift certificate from Dawson's dad for a bigger bed—stayed under the tree, waiting for Jared.

They spent the twenty-sixth in a post-holiday torpor Benji and Dawson barely broke to make it to work. When he got home, Dawson sank into the couch gratefully, beer in hand, Benji and Darian by his side, Amber leaning against his knees, to watch the DVR of Jared's performance.

Before they even got to PBS, they saw the footage.

The promising young dancer performing the famous Cavalier's ménage in the Nutcracker Suite collapsing to the stage in agony on the last leap.

TWO DAYS later Dawson was losing his mind.

"No, Dawson," Amber barked at him for the thousandth time that morning, "*nobody has called*. Nobody has called *your* phone, nobody has called *our* phone, and Benji and Darian aren't taking secret texts from your tragic fucking boyfriend that we *all* love and *all* are worried about, and if you ask me again I'm going to rip your spleen out your nose!"

"*Augh!*" Dawson pounded the wall with the side of his fist, stopping abruptly when he crashed through the drywall. "Fuck," he said, looking at it curiously. "I'm going to have to learn how to spackle. Jesus. Fucking Jesus. I can't get hold of Jared and I have to learn how to spackle. *Why won't somebody call?*"

Benji—big, solid, dependable Benji, who had pretty much pinned Dawson's body to the couch two nights ago when they'd seen the tape, again and again and again, of Jared's leg popping at an impossible angle as his knee just disintegrated under what must have been a whopping big amount of pressure—was suddenly just *there* over his back, wrapping those Popeye-the-sailor arms around Dawson's shoulders, pinning him to the wall in the mass of comfort Benji had *always* been.

"I'm sorry about the wall," Dawson whispered.

"Fuck the wall. I'll put another hole in it. We lost the deposit when we set fire to the rug last year."

Dawson looked at the singed spot from Benji's first attempt at barbecue. It sat sideways to his line of sight, right where the rug turned to tile before the sliding glass door opened to the little patio. The melted brown in the middle of the standard apartment-issue tan helped center him. Small catastrophes, big catastrophes—Dawson was resourceful. He could *make things happen.*

"He hasn't called," Dawson said, because stating the obvious just felt better.

"I know."

"Nobody called me." His chest was tightening, and he fumbled in his pocket for his asthma inhaler. He'd been using it nonstop for two days, because just thinking about Jared made him breathe badly.

"I know."

"I was supposed to be his emergency contact. I was going to sign shit," he said after his hit. Albuterol was not a great drug for easing pain.

"I know."

"If nobody's calling me, it's happening on purpose."

"I know. But probably not Jared's purpose."

The last of Dawson's fighting tension bled out of his spine and he melted into Benji's embrace. "I didn't think of that," he confessed, leaning his head shamelessly on Benji's shoulder. This was why Jared had started to love his friends. Because they were awesome, and because they loved Dawson, and they could take care of him when Jared wasn't there.

Who was taking care of Jared?

"I called his agent," Dawson muttered. "The fucker's been blowing off my calls."

"See?" Benji squeezed him extra hard, and Dawson tried to breathe and think at the same time. He'd gone to work the night before—and had missed three cues. He'd endured a verbal ass-reaming from four actors and an incredibly pissed-off assistant director with a sort of dazed indifference. Jared had fallen *spectacularly*, in front of a million viewers, not to mention news footage and YouTube playbacks, and Dawson, the one person on the planet who knew he wanted to keep ducks, had heard nothing.

"I need to get down there," he said, the voice of reason seeming to float out of nowhere. "I was waiting for information, for a call, but if Dolph is there and he's drugged and in surgery, I just need to be there." Oh good, Dawson—way to be a grown-up. "I should have left two days ago."

"You tried," Benji reminded him gently. "No flights for a week, remember? Christmas."

"God...." Dawson tried to bang his head against the wall, but Benji's arms were still around his shoulders.

"Don't worry about it, Dawson," Benji said, leaning his head against Dawson's temple. "Who needs an airplane when you've got your piece-of-crap car? You pack for us, I'll go call Carl and get a week off for a family emergency."

Dawson had to fight really hard not to break down in sobs. "I'll call my dad and ask for money." Because he had no pride. Not about this.

"'Kay," Benji said and hugged him again. "Ready?"

"Break on three. One, two, three...."

"Break!" they both said in tandem, and Benji pulled his arms from around Dawson's shoulders to throw his hand over his head. God love Benji, Dawson didn't even have to look him in the eyes and show how totally wrecked he was.

Because that was the face Darian and Amber got to see when they came into his room to help him pack.

"Dawson, for God's sake, pack better underwear," Darian said sharply, rifling through his duffel. She pulled out a pair with little trains on it that had fit when he was twelve and he couldn't bear to give up. They were thin and holey and he thought of them as lucky even though he only wore them when he was doing laundry, when all his other underwear were dirty.

"Those are nonnegotiable," he said, his voice thick, and Darian shook her head in mock pity and put them back.

Amber rooted around his room for things and came back with the T-shirt Jared had bought him in Tahoe—fortunately clean—and two hooded sweatshirts with school logos on them.

"Can't forget where you're from," she growled, and he offered his hand for a down-low.

"Word," he said when she smacked his palm soundly.

Darian said, "Hold on just a minute. We've got clothes in the washer. I'll be back with jeans," and Dawson realized that *her* voice was wobbling.

"Hey, Darian—"

She shook her head, and he did something un-Dawson-like and grabbed her shoulder. She came back into his arms and buried her head in his shoulder. "I want him back here," she said. "He never let us mother him, and he needed it, and you just can't... can't *have* someone in your home who needs you so badly and not want to take care of him. God, Dawson, you need to bring him home."

Dawson kissed the top of her head. "Yeah. That's the idea."

And Amber was pressed up against his back, and he wished Jared could *see* this, see that quiet or not, he'd become a part of them, and he was missed.

IN AN hour, they were on their way. They stopped in Roseville to visit Dawson's dad at his brick office building in old town. There, in the glass enclosure that separated his office from the reception room, Stan Barnes wrote them a check for four thousand dollars.

Dawson looked at all the zeroes and tried to give it back. "Dad—"

"That's car repair, three plane tickets, a trip to Disneyland, a decent hotel for two weeks, food if you need it, a lawyer retainer or a bribe for a Mexican prison—"

Dawson clutched the check so tight it started to crumple in his fingers, and Benji very gently rescued it. "Thanks, Mr. Barnes."

"Benji, call me Stan. Your mother would kill me if you two went down there without backup."

Benji frowned at him. "Stan, have you ever thought that you and my mother would make an excellent couple, and that perhaps you should see her sometime other than at our house?"

Dawson looked up from his panic and his misery to see his father's ginger complexion actually *deepen* to a skin-defying maroon. "Benji, you can keep calling me Mr. Barnes or Dawson's dad any day now. In fact, I think I'll insist upon it."

Benji shook his head. "God. You and Dawson. It's like I was put into this *world* to make sure you two don't spend your lives celibate and alone."

Dawson glared at him, and Benji shook his head. "One of you at a time." He grabbed Dawson's shoulder, and Dawson followed blindly. But when Benji stopped at the door and said, "Don't knock up my mother while we're out of town, *Stan!*" Dawson had to fight not to swallow his tongue.

They talked about it during the next five hours, which was great, because it kept Dawson's mind from doing the panic gallop until his brain cells foamed at the mouth and collapsed like beaten horses.

"It's not like your mom's not already my mom," Dawson said, looking out at the barren expanse of I-5 like somehow all that staring would make it suddenly green and growing again.

"Yeah, it's not about us, Dawson. It's about your dad. He's lonely."

Dawson looked at him, knitting his brows. "My dad? He's over at our apartment two nights a week—"

"And we're over at his on Sundays. I mean, I know he has other friends, because *we're* not going to basketball games with him, but, you know... *lonely.* Jared thinks so too."

Dawson's wandering attention suddenly focused. "Jared thinks so?"

"Yeah—remember when you fell asleep on his lap during Thanksgiving? We talked about it then."

Really? "Okay, I remember our parents talking, but—"

"Yeah, after that. You were *totally* drooling on his jeans. He looked at me and said, 'Have they...?' and I was like, 'No, but they totally should.'"

Dawson made a little "humph" sound. "Really? You guys are fixing their love life while I'm drooling? God, you think you can trust people—"

"Gets better," Benji said. "And I've got to pee in ten. Think you can drive without going 140 and killing us both?"

It was a valid question—Dawson's hands had been shaking too hard for him to take the wheel when they'd gotten in at first. But now in wherever the hell they were, he could take a stretch of straight driving and maybe give the helm back to Benji at the Grapevine so Dawson could navigate them through the rest.

"Yeah. I'll be sane, I promise. 'Gets better,' Benji—you can't just fucking bail on a convo like that when—"

"Hold your horses." Then, to the truck on his left, which was totally trying to cut him off: "And *you*, motherfucker, eat my *shorts!*" Benji dove in front of the guy and floored it. For a moment they heard the pitched whine of Dawson's POS going, *What in the* fuck?, and then they were around the truck and the SUV with the attitude passed them going at least 120. Dawson wished secretly that the guy would go off the road and commune with the rattlesnakes or the cow shit or what*ever* was on the side of this stretch of road, but since he didn't see any dust plumes in the next ten minutes, he figured the asshole got off scot-free.

"So, our parents," Benji said when the car stopped making that noise and they were back on track. "So Jared waited until they went back into the kitchen and said, 'Dawson's dad needs someone. He's lonely.'"

Dawson took a short breath and then another. And then another, but it didn't work, because his eyes were burning. He remembered that conversation about Xander Karcek, and it suddenly deepened, became the core of who Jared was.

"Well, if anyone would know, it would be Jared."

"We'll get him back," Benji said quietly, but he must have been able to see that Dawson needed a little time to get himself together. They pulled off for the bathroom break at Carl's Jr. and for two chocolate-banana milkshakes, which they drank in the store.

Dawson inhaled the first one while Benji sipped his in silence, and then Benji went and got him another one for the road.

"We ready?" he asked courteously, and Dawson nodded, patting the inhaler in his pocket in case the driving excitement and the latent Jared panic got to be too much.

"Yeah. Let's go get 'em."

ONE THING to be said for the smartphone revolution—you spent a lot less time wandering around shitty areas of places you knew nothing about. They got to Jared's apartment off of Sunset West, and Benji suddenly turned into Dawson's father.

"You stay here. I'll go find out where he is."

Dawson squinted at him. "What in the he—"

"You're half-crazy, Dawson. You are. I clocked you at 110 before we hit the Grapevine. I almost shit my pants half a dozen times. You haven't said a *word* besides giving me directions since we stopped to pee before I started to drive. Right now, *I* wouldn't tell you where he lives—your eyes aren't tracking and you look like a stalker. Stay here, brush your hair, and try to remember how to focus your eyes."

Dawson glared at him—*both* of him—and realized Benji was right. His entire *body* hurt to the point of breaking. "Okay," he said quietly, leaning back into the seat and closing his eyes. "I'll stay here." He sat up suddenly and called out the window, "Hey, Benji—get the damned teddy bear, okay?"

Benji nodded like it was the most natural thing in the world and kept striding inside. Jeans, a hooded sweatshirt, and shoes from Payless ShoeSource, and Dawson's brother *still* classed up West Hollywood. Benji did men everywhere a service just by being him.

Dawson might actually have napped—something that *hadn't* happened during the trip down. He would never admit it to Benji, but the Grapevine *terrified* him. All those trucks, all that ozone from the burning brakes. He spent the entire time imagining what would happen if a truck just cut loose and ate his car at 110 mph going downhill. After a few moments of sitting in a daze, he gave a start and looked around him, trying to figure out what the place looked like.

He decided it wasn't too bad. It was an apartment complex, really—not the worst part of town, not the best. It wasn't *Rocklin*, because it was surrounded by masses of city just *everywhere*, and it felt like Benji had driven through one big strip mall to get here, but it didn't have shining lights or holy grail music or anything either.

Mostly it was just another place.

For a moment Dawson was so angry at Jared he almost couldn't breathe. He floundered for his inhaler before he realized it was all emotion. Dawson could have *been here*. He got out of the car and started to stretch out, trying to work some of the pain out of his muscles, and he was in the middle of doing neck stretches when Benji *finally* came out.

He looked like he was going to kill someone.

"He wasn't kidding about his fucking roommates," he muttered. "Jesus."

Dawson actually forgot to be angry and panicked. "What do you mean?"

"I mean five guys, all of them wandering around in their underwear, and *one* guy knew where Jared was. The other four didn't even realize he'd been hurt. The one guy? Only knew because he has that Dolph guy for an agent. If we go in there again, I swear it's gonna be to move Jared out."

Dawson squinted at him. "I thought West Hollywood was supposed to be all liberal and nice and shit," he said, thinking about stuff Jared had said.

"Yeah, well, they probably are—just *not* in that apartment. Now stop generalizing based on progay voting and let's go find your guy!"

Dawson's heart sort of plopped in little red puddly pieces around his feet. "Do we have an address?" he asked.

Benji held up a piece of paper. "Punch this into your phone and let's roll."

It wasn't hard to find Cedar-Sinai—West Hollywood *was* nicely laid out, and the hospital looked clean and orderly. They parked and made their way inside, and Benji took the lead again, finding a nurse behind an information desk and asking for Jared Emory.

She countered with a very specific stare. "Who is asking? Mr. Emory isn't taking reporters or interviews at this time."

"His boyfriend is asking," Benji said without blinking. "Dawson Barnes—he signed papers—" Dawson elbowed him, because Benji was aware of his and Jared's last disagreement. "*Jared* signed papers and stuff. Jared's agent should have cleared him."

The charge nurse blinked and looked around her furtively. "Dolph?" she asked with thinly veiled contempt. "He told us Jared had nobody."

"That's *bullshit!*" Dawson burst out, closing the distance to the counter. He knocked off a bit of tinsel that was taped there to mark the holidays and ignored it. "That's *bullshit*," he hissed, mindful of Benji's assertion that he looked crazy. "Look, I don't know what *Dolph* told you, but Jared was sick in May, and he flew to see me when he could barely *walk*. He spent Thanksgiving at my house—he tried to set my father up with the love of his life, he brings my roommates birthday gifts, he... he cannot *have* anyone more than he has us!" Dawson closed his eyes and tried not to lose it, and clutched Little Dawson to his chest. "See?" he said, knowing it sounded pathetic but not able to be anyone but himself. "We got him this when he was sick that one time. It lives in his apartment with his five shitty roommates whose names he won't tell me, and it's *his*. It's supposed to be telling Jared to take care of himself, and to get enough sleep, and to not push his body too hard when it hurts, and *Dolph* didn't know that, and Jared doesn't even have the stupid fucking teddy bear." God, Dawson. Grown-up. Way to be a fucking grown-up. "You've gotta let me see him," he whispered. "Dolph says he doesn't have anybody. He's gotta know he has me."

She was going to say no—Dawson could see it. Suddenly he remembered what grown-ups *would* know. "Zero-three-two-five-oh-four-four-seven-six-three-eight-six."

The nurse blinked. In her fifties, with a round face, red cheeks, and stunning white hair, she looked like she wouldn't fall for sentiment anyway. But this? This was proof. "What's that?" she asked suspiciously.

"That's his Kaiser number," Dawson said, pride in his voice. "I filled out his paperwork like six thousand times when he was in the hospital in Roseville. That's not public record. It's not a stupid teddy bear that you can't take seriously. That's real shit. That's his medical insurance number, and it should be in your paperwork. I'm his person. I know Dolph has the suit, probably, and the money, and the paperwork thing down, but I can tell you his driver's license number and his Social Security number too. I'm the real deal. Please."

The woman blinked, and then confirmed the numbers in her computer, and then directed them down the hall.

"I can't promise the big guy in the suit will let you in," she said seriously. "He's got all the paperwork, boys. He's got official hospital policy on his side. But if you just want him to know you were here and worried, there's your chance."

Dawson wiped his cheek with the palm of his hand. "Thanks," he said gruffly, and Benji went one better and kissed her cheek, because, well, Benji could do those things. Then Benji turned and grabbed Dawson's shoulder and walked him down the hall.

They slowed when they got near Jared's room number, and both of them pulled back and listened.

"Yeah, I think he'll be back up onstage in a month. No—I know the doc said he should do the arthroscopic thing, but I got a guy who can shove some steroids under his kneecap and pack it with pain meds. He'll be back up again in no time. He can finish out this show, *then* take the time for the surgery, and he'll be back up by May."

Dawson's jaw dropped for a minute, and he almost went charging in there to tell this guy that *no*, Jared was not going to be dancing in May, because he was going to be *recovering* in May, and because he'd *promised* he'd be done by June. That was what he'd said. That had been their promise.

Then he heard Jared's voice, gruff and loopy. "No," he slurred. "Done. Promised—June last dance."

"Yeah, babe," said Dolph—or at least the man Dawson *assumed* was Dolph. "Hold on a second, Marcy—I need to up his morphine. Look, if they didn't want me to do it myself, they wouldn't have made the button red." And then, *not* into the phone, obviously: "Okay, Jar. Let me just up the pain meds and you can forget all about quitting, okay?"

"I put it in writinnnng...," Jared slurred, and then, from the sound of it, went to sleep.

"Yeah," Dolph muttered, apparently to himself, "too bad I never got that letter." His voice picked up and he spoke into the phone again. "Okay, Marcy—put that out in the press release. He'll finish out the show, it looked worse than it really is, and then we'll get his head right and send him back for surgery. Okay—you got that? Good. Yeah—I'll be in shortly, why? You got another crisis? Omigod! Another bulimic dancer? Say it isn't so!" His voice pitched sarcastically, and Dawson felt physically ill for anyone else this guy was managing.

Benji's fingers tightened on Dawson's shoulder, and Dawson took a deep breath. Okay. Plan. They needed a plan.

Turned out Benji *was* the plan. He stood up, took a deep breath, and walked in. "Jared, man, how you doin'? God, have we ever been worried about you! I mean, we see you go down on the television and don't hear from you? Man, I'm telling you, we're getting *worried*!"

"Benji?" And oh God. Dawson thumped back against the wall and closed his eyes. Jared sounded so happy to see him. Oh man. He must have felt so alone.

"Who in the hell are you?" Ooh—Dolph did *not* sound happy. Dawson looked around quickly and saw the empty room right behind him. He stayed to listen for a minute, just to see what would happen, but he had an exit strategy.

"I'm Jared's friend," Benji said, keeping that I'm-Benji-and-I-can-charm-anyone note in his voice. "I mean, Jared gets friends, right?"

"I'm his friend. I'm the only one he needs."

"Benji? You're here. You didn't forget me?"

"Yeah, buddy—I mean, we're not going to forget you! You made pies for Thanksgiving!" Oh, smart Benji. Not mentioning Dawson's name.

"Look, kid, it's sweet that you came and all, but Jared needs his sleep."

"Well, yeah—if he's going in for knee surgery, he'll have to have it, won't he?" Dawson heard a clatter, and he figured Benji was picking up the chart. "Now see, I don't know what these numbers mean, but I *do* know that says surgery recommended." Benji's voice dropped for a second. "Jared, you need to tell the doctor you need surgery. *Every* doctor who comes in here, okay? You need surgery. Can you repeat that?"

"Need surgery," Jared mumbled. "Surgery, go home to Dawson."

"That's my boy," Benji said, and Dawson risked another look into the room and at Benji— who was so unafraid of touch that he didn't mind when Dawson laid on him, even when they'd been in high school—smoothed his hair back and kissed his forehead and whispered something Dawson couldn't hear.

And then Dolph got in behind him and hoisted his arm behind him.

"Ah-ah-ah—this is pretty illegal!"

Dawson ducked into the empty room, but he heard Dolph's response. "Kid, I don't know who you are or why you're here, but you don't know what you're talking about. He doesn't need surgery, and he doesn't need smart-assed kids coming from nowhere, and he sure as shit doesn't need you."

"Help!" Benji hollered. "Help, I'm being repressed!" and he was loud enough that nobody heard Dawson slipping from his room to Jared's as the tall, broad-faced man with the graying hair and the mustache thrust Benji down the hall, calling for security at the top of his lungs.

And Dawson finally got a look at Jared and almost ruined his chance to talk by blubbering like a two-year-old.

"God, Jared—could you *be* any whiter?"

"Dawson?" Jared had two days of stubble, which was almost a full beard on him, but there was something very young about the way he squeezed his eyes closed and tears leaked out the corners.

"Jared. Man, I gotta tell you, you've looked better."

Jared turned toward him and his lower lip quivered. "Dolph said you wouldn't come. He said I was all alone."

Dawson lowered his forehead so they were touching. "Dolph is a douche bag. Baby, no matter what happens, remember that guy lies and he is not your friend. He didn't call me. I know you signed the paperwork, but he didn't call me. He wants to delay your surgery and throw you back up onstage to finish out your term."

Jared squeezed his eyes shut and shook his head. "It hurts, Dawson. It hurts. It hurts and I don't want to do it anymore. Please, can I come home?"

"Baby, you got to get the surgery first, okay? Now Dolph, he's going to try to tell you that you don't need it. Whenever you see a guy in a white coat, you've got to tell him you need surgery. You don't dance without surgery. Now, I know you—you can't dance stoned. Not the way you want to. He can't keep you high and put you out there unless you think you're okay. You need to go in and get it fixed. If you don't get that surgery thing, you don't dance. You tell Dolph that, tell *everyone*. Nurses, doctors, orderlies—*someone* has to listen to you, okay?"

God. Dolph was going to be here any minute.

"Miss you," Jared said gruffly, and Dawson pulled out the teddy bear.

"Yeah, well, remember this?"

That smile, underneath the stubble and the pain, gave Dawson hope. That shy Jared smile—Dawson lived for it. "Yeah. It's Little Dawson," Jared slurred. "Little you. He's supposed to take care of me."

"Yeah," Dawson said, and then tucked it under Jared's arm and under the sheets so no one could tell it was there. "Look. Dolph will come back, and he'll try to fuck with your head again. I think he's got power of attorney—I didn't sign those papers, and he's ignoring your signature, so we're sort of screwed. I can't come in and fight for you, baby. You've got to hold on to Little Dawson here and remember to fight for yourself, okay?"

Jared nodded. "I want to come home," he said.

Fear reared its ugly head. "Not the stage?" Dawson asked gently, needing to hear this, even when he was so out of it.

Jared shook his head. "No. You. I'll do anything to come home."

Dawson kissed him, knowing his breath would be rank with lactic acid and not caring. "Remember I was here, baby. Remember I was here. Hide this guy from Dolph, okay? When he tries to tell you I don't give a shit, or to make you listen to him, you hold him tight and you remember I was here, and he's full of crap. Got it?"

Jared seemed to wake up a little more with each passing minute, and he nodded and lifted a hand to touch Dawson's face. His palm scrunched on Dawson's stubble, and Dawson closed his eyes and captured the hand right there.

"Yeah," he said. "I promise—I won't sign anything unless I'm awake."

Dawson nodded. "And that's another thing—he's pressing your morphine button. You understand that? You need to be really good and pretend to be asleep, and then when the doc comes in, tell him the guy's pushing your morphine button. The doc needs to know or he's going to have you stoned here forever, okay?"

Jared grimaced, and Dawson realized what he was asking.

"I'm sorry," he said, closing his eyes tight. "I'm sorry. I know it hurts—"

"Which is why you shouldn't be here!"

Dawson didn't flinch from Dolph's voice, but he did bend down and kiss Jared's forehead. "Be strong," he whispered and captured Jared's hand. Contact, as long as possible. Contact so Jared could know what was real and what was not.

"Did you hear me?" A rough hand seized his shoulder, and Dawson stayed careful to keep Jared's hand in his, even as Dolph yanked him around.

"No," Dawson said, scowling. "I didn't hear you. Bend over and I might be able to smell your breath, though. That always helps if you're talking out your ass."

"Nice," Dolph said. He really did look like a skeezy lawyer—except his suit cost about twice as much as Dawson's dad's, so he must have been making *bank*. "I can't imagine why Jared wants to spend time with you."

"'Cause Jared knows I love him," Dawson said as loud as he possibly could. "He knows I love him and you want to exploit him and—"

"Exploit?" Dolph had these really thick white eyebrows, and they waggled when he was making a point. Dawson wanted to rip them off like Velcro, and he figured if this guy got too handsy and too rough, that was exactly what he'd do. "*Exploit*? This kid was *begging* for my help when I came along. His last manager took him for *everything*, kid—and he'll tell you in his sleep that I'm square with the money."

"But not with the boyfriend," Dawson snapped. "I'm his *person*. I should be here making sure he gets surgery and not just shoved back onstage so he can fuck himself up for life!"

Dolph curled a thick pink lip. "You think that would be a bad thing for this guy? I've been his manager for four years, kid, and he's got one thing going for him and one thing only, and *that* is the dance. He's *never* given a shit what it's going to do to him or what's going to be left of him when it's over. Bad breakup with a boyfriend? He dances. Family problems? He dances. Gets the flu—"

"A bump of coke and vitamin C and he dances." He could taste the bitterness, even as he spit it out. God. Jared *had* been this person. He *had* lived for the dance. But Dawson had faith. He had to. "Yeah,

Dolph. I'm aware. But that was before me. Now he's got me, and he's got something else, and he signed the paperwork—"

Dolph sneered. "Paperwork? I don't have any paperwork. That shit must have gotten lost—you know these dancers. Flaky as hell—"

"That's bullshit and you know it!" Dawson had never hit another human being before, not and meant it. Benji had fought all his battles in grade school, and Dawson had been geeky and let him. But his fist was clenched at his side, and all he could think of was that if they hauled him out of here fighting, he'd never get to come back. He needed to be able to come back.

Dolph shook his head and spoke patiently, like Dawson was a child. Well, maybe he was, but that had never stopped him before. "Look, I know you think you mean well. True love and all that shit. But if you really cared about him, you'd let him get back up on that stage. It's the thing that keeps him breathing."

It hurts. Don't make me go back.

"You're wrong," Dawson said with as much dignity as he'd ever had. "He's got so much more—*we've* got so much more to do. If you manage to keep him doped up and shove him on the stage and he fucks himself up permanently, he'll *still* have me to fall back on. Don't you get it? You think you have him until he's used up, and then you can throw him away. I'm the one who knows you'll be throwing away the best parts, and those are who I want. But he's too strong for that—too strong for *you*. You won't be able to throw him away, because he won't let you. I've got faith in my boy. He's going to make me proud."

"That's sweet. Totally unnecessary, but sweet. He'll go out like a rock star, and we'll be fending off movie scripts for the rest of his life. Go back to Podunk, kid, and tell your next boyfriend you used to date a dancer."

"I *did* used to date a dancer. But now I'm going to date a teacher. He's lying right here." Dawson felt it, Jared's fingers squeezing his, and he squeezed back. It was hard listening to this grown-up in a suit, older, successful, sort-of-like-his-father evil guy, tell him that he was too young, too small-town, too insignificant, to mean anything to the guy he loved. He needed the tightness of those fingers, the reassurance, the flesh memories of all those pockets of time, and how they meant something more than the breaths that they were built upon.

Dolph sneered and rolled his eyes and then did what he probably should have at the very beginning if he'd wanted to win: grabbed Dawson by the shoulders and ripped him away from Jared's bedside, talking all the way.

"Jared, man, don't forget what we talked about. Remember I was here, and Jesus, Dolph, my fuckin' arm, I'm gonna use that. *Help, help, I'm being repressed! Come see the violence inherent in the system!*" And so what if it was Benji's line? It was a good one, and it gave him a way to protest without resorting to profanity. His shoulder creaked behind him. "Everybody see this? I'll *sue*, asshole! My dad's a lawyer and a fucking good one!" The pressure behind him eased up and he muttered, "Pansy little bitch. He *is* a lawyer, and we're gonna fuckin' take you!" before going back to "Help, I'm being repressed!"

He must have done something, pissed Dolph off somehow, because he didn't just get hustled to the end of the hall, oh no. He got hustled down the escalators, *past* Benji at the help desk, and out to the front, where Dolph shoved him up against the marble side of the building hard enough for his tooth to split his lip.

"Were you just bullshitting about the daddy?" Dolph hissed, and Dawson suddenly knew what *he* wanted to be when he grew up. Apparently the word "lawyer" was an automatic shit-yer-shorts threat.

"Nope, asshole. You'll know him when he hits you with the fucking paperwork."

Dolph stepped back and straightened his lapels. "What's his name?" he asked coldly.

Dawson smiled, feeling wolfish. "What's yours?"

Dolph glared at him. "None of your fucking business, little man. You try to get a suit going. Let's see how far that goes when you can't even find your guy. The next time you see him, he'll be on TV with a rent boy backstage to blow him when he's feeling down, so I hope you got your fill."

Dolph strode back into the hospital and Dawson slid down the wall, stopping himself with his elbows on his knees. By the time Benji got out there, he was squatting, trying to come up with a plan of action. God, what time was it? It was late—past eight o'clock at night. Had it really been at breakfast that morning when he'd put his fist through a wall? Jesus, wasn't it weird what a day could do.

"Are we done being repressed?" Benji asked, rolling his shoulder.

Dawson grimaced. "For the moment, yeah. I say food, hotel, and game plan. I need to call my dad and have him Google the holy fucking shit out of that asshole."

Benji offered a hand out and Dawson took it, pulling himself up and back into the fight for Jared's soul.

"WHAT DO you want me to say?" His dad's voice cracked. "I've got his name, and yeah, I already sent the restraining order—he lays hands on you again and we can do something about it. But you both want to occupy the same space with Jared, so it's got to be hands-on, not distance. And right now the legal tie-up is that space with Jared. You *swear* Jared filled out that paperwork?"

"Dad, am I your son? Do I swear something happened when I don't know for sure?"

Dad sighed. "No. No. But Dolph is saying Jared didn't give them to him—"

"That's *bullshit*—"

"I know it is! But until Jared is awake enough to tell us that's the truth, Dolph is going to be able to keep him too drugged to open his mouth."

Dawson let out a frustrated growl. He wasn't going to pound a hole in the hotel wall, but damn, he needed to break something. And he couldn't. Benji's mom used to take them to Disneyland every year—she loved the place. Benji knew his hotels, and the Westin was a nice one.

"What *is* his last name, anyway?" Dawson asked in an attempt to distract himself.

"He doesn't have one," Dad said. "He had it legally changed twenty years ago."

"To *Dolph*?"

His dad's sigh was eloquent. "I don't know what to tell you, son. If I understood how things worked down there, I would have moved there with your mother and we never would have gotten divorced."

"That's not true," Dawson said, thinking about his mom for the first time in months. "I would have come out in high school, she would have crapped her pants, and you would have moved us to Vermont just because she hurt your baby boy."

"Yeah, well, it's a course of action. And I'll do my best against 'Dolph,' but...."

Dawson wanted to cry at that sound. It was the same sound his dad made when Dawson came home from his mom's that last time. *She'd rather I not talk about being gay, so I said I'd rather not talk at all.*

"Dad, it's not your fault. The world's a shitty place—you only have a limited jurisdiction."

"Yeah, well, I wanted to do better for you and Jared. I had no idea...."

Yeah, well... who did? "It's why he wanted out," Dawson said quietly. "How bad it could get. He knew. He's seen the worst of it, Dad. I didn't tell you because... well, because it was private. But he wants a home and a life with me because he's seen the worst of how bad it can get here, and he's done."

His father took a deep breath. Dawson could hear it over the phone. "I'll do what I can, okay? But in the end, it's going to have to be him."

Dawson closed his eyes and thought of Jared as he'd first seen him: cool, self-contained, able. He was still that man. The strength that had made him the prince in the fable—that was still there. Dawson had given him the gift, the talisman, the thing to help him remember who he was. Dawson and Jared—they spent their lives making the dream true for other people. Could they do that for themselves?

"Faith," Dawson said, tapping out a rhythm on the desk in front of him. "We both believe in stories. We'll have faith that they come true."

His dad grunted. "As long as this isn't the one with the goat crapping onstage, I think that's a plan."

WELL, *SOMETHING* crapped on the stage.

Benji and Dawson managed to see him three more times, Benji going in as the distraction, Dawson going in afterward. Dolph had other clients to destroy—he couldn't be there the whole time. Dawson managed a five-minute conversation, a quick whisper in Jared's ear, a held hand, a kiss on the cheek, and a check to make sure Little Dawson was still tucked under the blankets keeping him company. Each time he went in, Jared had his eyes closed, but he opened them as soon as he heard Dawson's voice.

"You're faking it, baby?" Dawson asked the third time, and Jared looked at him from eyes unclouded by drugs and a face lined in pain.

"Yeah. I was awake the last time the doctor came in to assess the swelling. Dolph wasn't here and I told him I wanted the surgery and to bring me the papers when my agent wasn't here. I don't know if Dolph knows yet."

Dawson smiled. "You're *good*. You should *act*."

Jared's ironic eyebrows were fully functioning. Dawson took it as a sign of hope. "Cute," he said. "Really cute. But I think someone said I was a teacher now. I think I'll stick with that."

Dawson almost couldn't talk through his grin. But he had to. "Look, I don't know how many more times they're going to fall for the Benji-and-Dawson show. My dad's working on the legal end, but the whole *system* is built on shit taking time, and you need your knee worked on *now*." He'd looked into it—once the swelling from the initial injury was down, the ACL should be repaired. He wasn't sure what stage they were at—most patients would get sent home in the interim, but Dolph must have been insisting on Jared staying in the hospital. For a moment Dawson was passingly curious as to how much money Dolph was making for the both of them, but in the end, it didn't matter. What mattered was Jared was fighting for himself, and that was what they were going to have to have faith in.

"Jare—you know I'm not going to be able to stay here forever, right?" God. Even if Jared got the surgery and everything, there would be recovery and moving and....

"Dolph has my phone," Jared confessed, blinking hard like he was trying to think. "I won't have your contact info until I get home."

"But...." Dawson's throat grew tight. "We've got, like, two more days. You've got to have a place to come back to, you know? I could stay down here and quit my job and—"

Jared swallowed like he was shoring himself up and shook his head. "I'm planning to come to you," he said, and Dawson wondered if he understood how unlikely that looked while he lay there flat on his back, sweating for lack of pain meds. He squeezed Dawson's hand and nodded, because a smile just wouldn't have been Jared-like.

"Your subtext is not encouraging," Jared said with a haughty lift of his eyebrows.

Dawson lost against a grin. "Oh, so there's a law of subtext now? Because I thought that was an equal-opportunity form of communication. Oh shit!"

Because here came security, two orderlies with the bored expression of guys who really didn't want to do what they were doing but did it for the paycheck.

"Jared—man, I love you. But if you don't see us again, just...."

Don't worry about me, Dawson. I've got it covered. "I'll come to you," Jared said again.

Dawson, who had a security guard on either side of him, turned back around and grinned. "Now *that's* what I call subtext!" he crowed.

Jared waved weakly.

They came back the next day, and there was a security man in front of Jared's door, one who glared at the both of them and shut the door behind him.

"Did Dolph hire you?" Dawson asked, just to not appear too chickenshit. The guy had muscles larger than Dawson's head.

"No one is allowed to visit Mr. Emory," the middle-aged white gorilla with a crew cut intoned, and Dawson and Benji met eyes. It was time to give Jared some faith. It was time to go home.

"Hope you like being one of the bad guys, asshole," Dawson said, because God forbid he leave without saying *something*. "How's it feel to guard a guy from the only family he's ever had?"

Well, he had sunglasses on. Dawson didn't know if he flinched or not. But it was time to work another plan. It was a good thing Dawson had one ready.

"ARE YOU sure you want to go in there?" Benji asked, gazing at Jared's apartment building again.

Dawson looked at him irritably, shifting the load of cardboard in his arms. "Are you sure we got enough boxes? This is his entire life we're talking about here!"

Benji's warm brown eyes crinkled with pity. "Well, I don't know what to tell you. Wasn't much of a life."

"Time to change that shit."

"Yeah, don't forget your inhaler—I needed mine last time. The dust sucks."

Benji led the way up the stairs to the apartment, and Dawson looked around. Not a bad place. Painted white, with a functioning pool and concrete stairs and porch. It wasn't a luxury suite, but it was the sort of place Dawson and Benji might have ended up in if Dawson had stayed down in SoCal and Benji had followed him for college. (They'd thought of it, yeah. Nobody broke them up without their consent, not even parents who'd made noises about Dawson moving down for keeps. Like Dawson would have agreed to that anyway.)

So Dawson was thinking that the roommate situation must have been exaggerated. And then Benji knocked and a very pretty blond guy opened the door.

And frowned at both of them.

"What are you doing here again?"

"We're packing up some of Jared's stuff," Benji said. "So when he's out of the hospital, he can move out."

A full lip lifted up over perfect teeth. "He's still going to have to pay the rest of the month. I hope he knows that."

"I'm sure he does!" Dawson snapped. "Now get out of our way."

Benji's pursed lips and raised eyebrows said Dawson hadn't seen anything yet.

Or felt it.

Three of the roommates were there, and they must have been the gay ones, because Dawson and Benji had their asses groped and their clothes assessed more times in the next hour than they'd had in their entire lives previous. The guys were... well, white and pretty, with capped teeth. Perfect. Waiters or actors or bartenders or, well, Dawson was pretty sure one of them was a professional porn star, because he'd seen his picture on the web, but whatever they were, they were perfect. And beautiful. And annoying as hell.

"Jesus! Dylan or Sean or Steve or whatever, could you keep your hand away from my crotch long enough to let me maybe move this fucking box?"

Sean or Steve or whatever rolled his eyes. "God, no wonder Jared kept you in a hole upstate. You're as much fun as a root canal!"

Benji dropped the box he was carrying and stepped in front of Dawson. "I'm a lot more fun than a root canal. Wanna see?" he growled, and Dawson grinned from around his shoulder. He'd realized this week that he didn't really need the protection, but God, Benji wasn't ever going to let him walk without it.

"No, no, that's fine." Sean or Steve or whatever held his hands up and backed away, a smirk on his face like this was a big joke. Dawson ignored him and let Benji do the body block until he was out of the apartment with the first load of what the guys had told them was Jared's stuff.

Benji was right. There was depressingly little—not even any holiday decorations, which didn't hit Dawson until later. The setup was apparently two guys per room, with one guy in the walk-in closet. If anyone had a date, they got the walk-in closet with the twin bed and the guy in the closet got the couch.

Jared didn't have the closet, thank God, but his *clothes* did, and Dawson needed a shower and a change of clothes after kneeling on the mattress in order to pass Jared's clothes back to Benji. There was a tuxedo there—something nice that maybe Jared would wear to a fundraiser or out and about town. It had a big white flaky stain across the arm. Dawson refused to touch it.

"Really?" Benji asked doubtfully. "Dawson, those things run in the thousands of dollars. I mean, a trip to the dry cleaner's—"

"Spooge, Benji. It's got spooge." Dawson looked at it again and then down at his mattress. He wondered for the millionth time, was it the money? This was a prime piece of real estate here—Jared probably could not afford it alone. Was it the guys? Were they less obnoxious with someone they knew? Or maybe—and this was the hardest idea of all—maybe it was just that anybody, even a setup like this, was better than nobody at all.

"Yeah," Benji grunted. "Leave that. C'mon. None of the guys will confess which hygiene products are his. I think we should just let them keep it."

"The ballet shoes," Dawson said distractedly, taking the three pairs of black leather jazz flats. Each pair had to be fitted and broken in. Each shoe had bloodstains from skinned toes and memories and performances seeped into the sole. Those, Dawson would keep.

"His duffel is where the good shit is anyway," Benji said, and Dawson had to agree.

Benji clambered off the bed and looked wildly around for hand sanitizer or something. Oh, look. There was a big pump bottle of it on the window ledge above the roommate's bed, complete with tissues and a trashcan shaped like a bottle of lube. Awesome.

He got the hand sanitizer and looked around. The roommate's side of the room was pretty generic—blue sheets, a framed print of a naked guy with a giant penis, and a white IKEA dresser to match the bed. The dresser was full of hair products and skin products and sex toys (ugh!), and Dawson kept his eyes on Jared's side of the room after that.

Jared's bed was IKEA too, which was good, because Dawson and Benji were going to have to break it down and load it into the little U-Haul trailer they'd rented. God, please let Dawson's car be able to handle that thing over the Grapevine—Benji would be driving for fucking sure.

But besides the IKEA bed, they saw a few things there that suggested Jared and Jared alone. The prints over his bed of Baryshnikov, for example. Stylized modern black-and-whites of the dancer in his fifties, the lines in his face heavily etched but the lines of his body still graceful. The selfie Jared and Dawson had taken in Tahoe sat on the dresser, blown up and framed, both their smiles surprisingly shy with the promises they made that week. Behind the picture was a little framed picture of a dark-haired girl, eyes and shoulders sloped with Down syndrome, her heavy body in a pink leotard with a tutu, her arms in open position, her feet in first. Behind the bed was an Abercrombie & Fitch poster with a big red circle and slash through it in sharpie. Jared had written *Shallow misogynistic bastards!* across the bodies of the models, and Dawson bit his lip just looking at it.

"We'll leave the poster here," he said, his voice shaky, and Benji agreed.

"And you're getting his underwear drawer."

Dawson had to nod. "Oh yeah. Nobody's looking in there but me."

It didn't matter. All that was in Jared's drawer was Jared's underwear. And another framed picture of Dawson, also taken in Tahoe, when Dawson had been asleep. He was stretched out in a sunbeam from the window with the sheets wrapped around his waist and his head pillowed on his arm. Dawson stared sightlessly at the photo, which Jared had reduced to black and white and framed, and saw his face with the impossibly turned-up nose, and the long bony hands and long bony jaw, and the rumpled brown hair. It was his face and his narrow white chest—he *knew* this—but the person in the picture was somehow lovelier than he knew himself to be.

Benji came and looked over his shoulder. "Wow, Dawson, could you get any whiter?"

"It's black and white, dumbass," Dawson said, his voice thick.

Benji took the picture from his hands, then grabbed a couple of shirts, wrapped it up, and put it in the box at Dawson's feet. "It's a nice picture," he explained when he was done. "I want to make sure it survives the move."

Dawson blinked hard. "What we're doing—this will work, right? I mean, we can't make sure he has the surgery or doesn't change his mind, but this—this works, right?"

Benji nodded. "It's a real good plan, Dawson. Even your dad thought so."

In fact, Dawson's dad had added the finishing touch.

At the end, after they'd packed the clothes and broken down the furniture, it all fit into the U-Haul with depressing ease. One person's life: three crates of clothes, one crate of sundries, a bed, a dresser, and a partridge in a pear tree.

And what did they leave? In the blank corner sat Jared's duffel bag, and taped to Jared's duffel bag was an envelope with one plane ticket in it, made out to Jared's name and Social Security number. It was open-ended, call ahead to make a reservation, but it had one destination.

Dawson had been there too many goddamned times. He was sure Jared knew the way.

Dawson and Benji stood for a minute and looked around.

"You know," Dawson said, his voice wobbly, "we may end up having to send all this shit back here with him. You know that, right?"

Benji shook his head and looped that happy, goofy, comforting Benji arm around his shoulders. "Not a chance, Dawson. It's as surefire as leaving a textbook on a catwalk."

Dawson turned and looked at him and smiled, and wiped his eyes and smiled some more, and was completely reassured when Benji took him into one of those giant, all-encompassing hugs Dawson was so used to.

"Have faith, man. I do."

Dawson nodded into his shoulder. Like he'd told his dad, sometimes that was all you could do.

CURTAIN

BENJI AND Darian moved out in February, just like they'd planned.

It hurt, in the worst way, actually, but it only made sense. Benji had enough units (more than enough, if truth be told) to transfer to Sac State, and Darian had only attended the last semester at Sierra to be with him anyway. Darian had jobs in Sacramento—teaching dance, teaching aerobics, dancing in shows—and Benji and Dawson worked at frickin' Music Circus. The only reason they'd delayed in the first place had been Dawson.

And Dawson couldn't move without Jared.

"The apartment above us opens up in June," Benji said for the millionth time.

Dawson nodded, looking at the U-Haul full of their stuff. "I know. I told you—go. It will be okay."

"He's going to show up. You know it."

Dawson nodded again, feeling like a bobblehead doll. "I know. I do. I mean, I've got his stuff. If I don't mean anything to him, I've still got his stuff."

Darian came up and snuggled under Dawson's arm, and he hugged her tight. She and Amber had pretty much sandwiched him on the couch for the past four weeks, every time they'd sat down to watch television. It was a hugging-Dawson free-for-all, and on the one hand he was grateful because it kept him from going into his room and sobbing every night, but on the other hand he was resentful because it kept him from going into his room and sobbing every night.

Jared hadn't called.

Dawson knew, logically, that Jared probably had no access to his phone or to anything else. Jared's laptop was in his duffel bag like it always was, but if Jared didn't get a chance to go *home*, then how would he even e-mail Dawson? If Dolph had his phone, how would he call?

Dawson had called the hospital and asked for the helpful nurse, who told him Jared went into surgery a week after Dawson and Benji left town. That had been three weeks ago. Dawson and Benji were going back if Jared didn't contact them in another week, but in the meantime, Dawson had Darian smelling like sweat and flowers in his arms, and wanting to be his sister in the worst way.

"I'll be fine," Dawson said, his voice thick. "We still have a date for Thursday, right?"

Benji nodded. "I swear. And I'll see you at work all week, because God forbid we not see each other. And your dad is still feeding us Sunday breakfast, my mom included." Because they hadn't said anything, but the last three Sunday breakfasts since Dawson and Benji had gotten back had seemed awfully cozy. But Benji wasn't done with the reassurances, and the last one was the most important. "And our two days off next week, Dawson. I swear, we'll go down there and drag him back by the hair."

Dawson hadn't wanted to say anything. It would suck having to move all your stuff and then immediately leaving your girlfriend to go get your best friend's boyfriend out of whatever hell Dolph could imagine for him.

Dawson could imagine ones plenty bad enough as it was.

"Thanks," he whispered, and he, Benji, Darian, and Amber all succumbed to a group hug that seemed totally out of proportion for a move that was, at most, going to make battling for space in the refrigerator just a teeny bit easier.

It didn't matter. It was his brother, and the past two and a half years had been amazing, and Dawson didn't want to set him free yet, or Darian, who didn't feel new anymore. Amber was the one still clinging to him in the end, and Dawson realized she'd gotten his shirt wet in the final hug, so he just kept holding her and rocking her as Darian and Benji pulled away, waving, and probably sniffling too.

"The apartment above them has two bedrooms," he reminded her.

Amber nodded into his neck. "I know."

"June—right after finals. We'll move there."

"I know."

"My dad's coming over to help us put together the bed."

Amber looked up, and Dawson smiled because Amber loved his dad and he'd done something to make her happy. "Yeah? Will he bring pizza?"

"And beer," Dawson said, kissing her on the top of the head. Yeah, his dad only had one kid, but Dawson had done his best to rectify that. Amber hadn't heard from her family over Christmas, but Dawson's dad and Benji's mom had spoiled her rotten. Gift certificates to Spencer's, Oscar the Grouch hats—the works. Before Jared's life had fallen apart, Amber confessed to Dawson that her last Christmas gift had been a Bible and a televangelist's DVD. Dawson had felt bad enough to offer her *his* gift certificate to Spencer's, and she'd burst into tears and said no, he was the best gift ever.

Dawson sort of loved Amber the most when she *wasn't* crying on him.

But he couldn't tell her that. Not now when she was.

"C'mon," he said, pulling on her. "Let's go get the bed out from under the boxes."

They had to. All of Jared's boxes sat on top of it, leaning against the wall behind the couch. Dawson, in his infinite wisdom, said they could set Jared's bed up in Benji's old room, and Amber could sleep there. Yeah, they could buy one from IKEA, but that would make it easier for Jared to escape should he ever return to Dawson, who loved him.

Dawson's body *ached* with all of that pent up, frustrated, worried love.

Ached enough to explode in Sharpie drawings all over the boxes he and Benji had packed that horrid gray day in West Hollywood.

Dawson started it. The morning after he and Benji had arrived home, disheartened and exhausted, Darian and Amber cooked breakfast. It was January 2. In the middle of a biteful of scrambled eggs, Dawson looked over to the pile of stuff, and two things occurred to him. One was that Jared had missed Christmas and New Year's Eve completely. *Completely.* There had been no Christmas decorations in his apartment, and he was still pretending to be drugged when Dawson and Benji left on New Year's Day.

The other thing he realized was that he and Benji had forgotten to label the last box, the one with Jared's underwear and pictures in it.

Without finishing his eggs, he grabbed a giant poster-size Sharpie from the pen drawer and walked over to the box to label it.

A half an hour later, Benji came over with some regular sharpies in different colors. Dawson had doodled an entire Christmas tree on the front corner of the box. The girls had taken down the one they'd had in the apartment and put Jared and Dawson's gift in Dawson's closet, but Dawson drew it, the big comforter package with the bright striped packaging, and a stick figure with absurdly long hands and bony knees and pitcher ears sitting under the tree. Without speaking, Benji sat down next to him and started coloring in the ornaments, and he added his own stick figure with triangular gorilla shoulders, patting Dawson's pitcher-eared stick figure on the back. For a moment, the only sounds in the apartment were the scritchy-scratchy hisses of the permanent-ink pens on the brown cardboard.

They finished, closed the Sharpies, and left them on top of the boxes. Then they got up to clear off the dishes. Before he went to bed that night, Dawson saw that Amber had added a short stick figure with a black-haired ponytail sitting under the tree, and Darian had added one with brown curls.

Above the Christmas tree, someone had added a thought bubble with a stick figure in toe-shoes.

That had been the beginning.

The boxes were now graffitied from top to bottom. Benji and Darian dancing because they got their apartment. Stick figures packing. A stick figure with a tie sitting on their couch to watch a Kings game. (Over the television, Dawson's dad had written *Kings lost again.*) Benji's mom had drawn a stick figure in an A-line dress bringing a casserole, because that was what she'd done after the first week had passed.

After two weeks of silence, all Dawson could do when he got home from work was draw long, slow drops of blood from a dripping heart. Obvious and maudlin—oh hell yes. But Dawson couldn't even summon the optimism for stick figures that day.

The next week school started, and Professor Weber had asked him if he had time to help set up for the spring show. Dawson's first instinct was to say yes, of course, he could arrange his work schedule to do that.

And then he stopped. "Uhm, I don't... I mean, I may have to... I mean I don't know because...."

The professor had always loved him. "Come sit in my office, Dawson. Eat my chocolates. You have a story to tell."

Dawson had never been good at holding things back.

He finished with the story and the professor steepled his fingers. Dawson looked at him, liver spots on the back of his hands, rheumy eyes, very little hair.

"Dawson, what are you going to do with yourself, even if he does come back?"

Dawson blinked. "Go to Sac State. Get my degree in theater. Work as much as I can. Get a house"—his voice hitched—"with a duck pond."

The professor nodded. "These are good goals. They are. And you plan to do these things even if he *never* comes back?"

Dawson swallowed. "Everything except the duck pond. I'll have to, you know, be happy with a cat."

Prof Weber smiled, his dentures an incongruous sparkling white. "It's a smaller dream, yes. But don't give up hope. A month feels like forever when you are young. Sometimes a month is what it takes to close down a life."

"We packed his stuff and took his bed," Dawson said, swallowing. He thought of Jared getting to his apartment without a backup plan, and felt bad. Maybe he should have left more than a duffel bag.

There was a high, thin laugh—the results of too much mirth and not enough oxygen in old lungs. "You are precious, Dawson. You *could* live without your Benji and your young man, but you won't have to. Don't worry. You earn a charmed life."

Dawson didn't know what to think about that, but today, as he and Amber walked into the apartment, he remembered Professor Weber's kindness, and he remembered what Jared had said during that delirious week in Tahoe. *If I'm the worst thing to happen to you, Dawson, I can live with that.*

If Jared Emory was the worst thing to happen to Dawson, Dawson's life was really, truly charmed.

But that didn't stop the apartment from being really empty when they got in. Amber squeezed his waist and looked up at him. "You bought new Sharpies," she said tentatively. "Do you want to break those open?"

There were only a couple of surfaces left, so they picked the biggest one. Stick figures of Benji and Darian appeared, Benji driving the U-Haul, Darian driving Benji's car, as they took off for Sacramento.

"Almost done?" Amber asked critically, and Dawson smiled. Tears sucked. He was tired of them.

He took purple and blue, because you never could have enough purple and blue, and wrote very carefully, *Have fun without us, douche bags. We'll be the worst neighbors EVER in June.*

Amber looked at his handiwork and chuckled, then grabbed the black and circled *EVER* about six times. Then she took the pink and red and wrote, *Have noisy sex. They need to know what's coming. Heh.*

And then she drew their universal stick figure for Jared, with the little toe shoes, and Dawson, with the pitcher ears. Holding hands.

Dawson smiled at her as she worried the ring on her lower lip and pushed her dyed hair back from her forehead like a second grader. *This* was the Amber he loved best. She smiled back, and he thought maybe she loved the nonbroody Dawson best too.

He figured he could try to be optimistic Dawson. At least until he was told to ship the boxes back.

HE LEFT school early the day he and Benji were supposed to leave to go back to Los Angeles—Prof Weber waved him off with his blessing, because Dawson was blowing off his History of Theater class and had asked permission beforehand.

He checked his messages on the way to the car and his eyes widened. Fifteen? *Fifteen*? And not just from one phone, either. Benji, Amber, Darian, his dad, and some mystery number had all called, all in the past half hour.

Dawson felt horrible a lightning-strike surge of hope and anxiety so acute he almost threw up. Oh God. He couldn't do this. Not here in the parking lot of Sierra.

He had to get home to the apartment, where he could have the adrenaline shakes in peace.

The apartment door was open when he pulled up, and Amber's backpack was resting on the outside wall. He slammed his car door shut and ran inside, shouting, "Amber, what in the hell is all of the fu—"

Jared was sitting at the kitchen table, one leg propped out in front of him, his crutches resting against the side.

Amber ran out of her bedroom, wiping mascara smudges off her cheeks and smiling. She bent over and kissed Jared's cheek and hugged his shoulders, and he leaned into her, and then she came over to Dawson and hugged him hard.

He returned the hug distractedly, still taking Jared in.

"I'm spending the next two nights at Benji and Darian's," Amber said.

Dawson looked down at her. "Yeah?"

She smiled past the mascara smudges. "Promise. Don't scream too loud—we can't move out until June."

And then she was gone, the door was closed on the cold-bright February day, and Dawson was alone in the house with the man of his dreams.

"You look like shit," Dawson said distractedly, and Jared returned with a tired smile. He was thinner, if possible, and his hair had grown over his collar. Pain shadowed the mercury-blue eyes, and his rectangular eyebrows had sort of overgrown and were threatening to become one. He'd shaved recently, because he only had a little stubble, but his jeans and sweatshirt were rumpled. Amber had poured him coffee in the tacky mug they'd made his forever, and it shook in both hands as he lifted it to his lips.

Jared put the mug down and nodded to the seat next to him. Dawson sat, because his knees weren't working, and Jared took his hand.

"Some asshole moved my bed. I got home from the hospital and had to go to the airport. Yeah, I've looked better."

Dawson cried-kissed-slobbered over his knuckles. "We had to make sure you knew where home was," he apologized.

"Yeah," Jared said, leaning forward and kissing their laced fingers too. He was very close, close enough for Dawson to feel his breath against Dawson's cheek. "It's where all the artwork is." He nodded toward the boxes with their awkward storytelling in Sharpie, and Dawson swallowed.

"We wanted you to know we were thinking of you."

"Dolph found the teddy bear and threw it away. And I still remembered you'd been there."

"I hope you fired him," Dawson said seriously.

Jared smiled without humor. "I may even let your dad's friend sue him—I'll have to think about it."

"We could afford the house with the duck pond."

Jared nodded and leaned his head against their hands. "Good. Because it's nonnegotiable."

"Just never go away again, okay?" Dawson lost it then. Pain, fear, anxiety, joy—it all burst out of his chest, out of his throat, and into the air. He exploded into a sobbing, snotty, slobbering mess, too distraught even for words. He sank to his knees and buried his head on Jared's lap, and Jared made soothing, suspiciously tearful noises and stroked his hair until he could breathe without shaking.

PLANS. THEY had so many plans. They lay side-by-side on Dawson's little queen-size mattress and made plans. Jared would open the studio. Darian would help because she'd always wanted to. Dawson would get his degree. They'd find a house with a duck pond.

First they'd move to Sacramento and be roommates for a little while longer, and Dawson could grow up with the people he loved and whom Jared had come to love through him.

First they'd lie and look at each other, touch each other's skin in random patterns, and trace the new lines at the corners of their eyes.

"My professor says I live a charmed life," Dawson murmured, kissing Jared's fingertips.

"You do," Jared told him. Would he ever be able to smile like Dawson? Without the quiet reserve? Probably not. But Dawson loved the smile he had, the one that said yes, he'd been hurt, but he could live through that. He could live through anything. Dawson needed him to be able to live through anything.

"I must," Dawson said, smiling. "Because I met you."

Jared shook his head. "No, it's bigger than that. You're so charmed, you charmed my life too."

"Yeah—that whole captured-and-pumped-full-of-morphine month was really fucking charmed," Dawson said darkly. He wanted to take it back, take back the whole six weeks of Jared helpless, alone in a hospital bed. It was something he would have to live with, that he hadn't been able to throw Jared over his shoulder and take his prince to safety.

"You did enough," Jared said, pushing Dawson's hair back from his forehead. "You reminded me I wasn't alone."

Dawson swallowed. "You were so alone," he rasped.

"My parents showed up," Jared said, surprising him badly. "The day after you left, they showed up. Dolph was there yelling at the doctor and I about how I was going to ruin my career for some kid who'd never been near a dance studio. The doctor let them in and said, 'I thought he didn't have anybody. His young man said he was Jared's only family.'"

"What did you say?" Dawson asked, his voice hushed.

"Well, my mother said, 'If you want to come home, you need to forget any young men,' and Dolph said something ugly and snide that I've forgotten, and I looked at the doctor and told him to get everybody the fuck out of my hospital room, and he did."

Dawson's throat was tight and his chest was tight, and Jared's face was so taut it looked drawn in ink. "They didn't come back?"

"They tried. I told them that unless you were there, I didn't want to go. I didn't care where it was—their house, my room. I miss my sister, but Dawson...." He took a deep breath. "I've been alone, and I've been with people for really shitty reasons. I'd rather be alone than with the wrong person. Don't ever underestimate what you and your sidekick did coming into my hospital room. You reminded me. All the visits, the texts, the e-mails—they were all us getting tangled together. I'd never had a family before—not a real one—and you showed me what that was. When the doctor told Dolph that I'd signed the paper for surgery...." Jared shook his head and let out a low whistle. "It was ugly. And the things he *said*—I'd never realized I was a piece of meat until he tried to stop me from being carved up. No. You did the rescuing." Jared's smile grew a little, and his eyes crinkled warmly. "Although, you know, I could have moved my own stuff."

Dawson didn't even blush. "No. Because then I would have heard from you and there would have been time, or a week, or a day, or an hour before I saw you, and I would have died. My whole body would have frozen over with absolute panic that somehow, right at the end, you wouldn't have made it home."

Jared's eyes grew shiny, and he shifted on the bed so his cheek was resting on his hand. "Is that why you didn't move with Benji?"

Dawson's eyes, still red and burning from his outburst before, spilled over. "I needed you to be able to find me," he rasped.

"I'd always find you. I could have found you if you moved to the moon. You're my home."

Dawson nodded and smiled, because he didn't want to cry anymore. He just didn't. "They don't have duck ponds on the moon."

Jared laughed, low and warm, and he moved in for the kiss, the presex kiss that Dawson didn't think he'd even get that night but that shorted out his body like a circuit breaker in a lightning storm. Dawson opened his mouth, opened his legs and his belly and his soul, and wrapped himself carefully around Jared, because if he was Jared's home, he wanted Jared to wear home on his skin.

Jared apparently wanted his home to scare imaginary ducks—so Dawson did that too.

AMY LANE is a mother of four and a compulsive knitter who writes because she can't silence the voices in her head. She adores cats, Chi-who-whats, knitting socks, and hawt menz, and she dislikes moths, cat boxes, and knuckle-headed macspazzmatrons. She is rarely found cooking, cleaning, or doing domestic chores, but she has been known to knit up an emergency hat/blanket/pair of socks for any occasion whatsoever, or sometimes for no reason at all. She writes in the shower, while at the gym, while taxiing children to soccer/dance/gymnastics/band oh my! and has learned from necessity to type like the wind. She lives in a spider-infested, crumbling house in a shoddy suburb and counts on her beloved Mate to keep her tethered to reality—which he does, while keeping her cell phone charged as a bonus. She's been married for twenty-plus years and still believes in Twu Wuv, with a capital Twu and a capital Wuv, and she doesn't see any reason at all for that to change.

Website: www.greenshill.com
Blog: www.writerslane.blogspot.com
E-mail: amylane@greenshill.com
Facebook: www.facebook.com/amy.lane.167
Twitter: @amymaclane

The Johnnies Series from AMY LANE

http://www.dreamspinnerpress.com

Keeping Promise Rock Series from AMY LANE

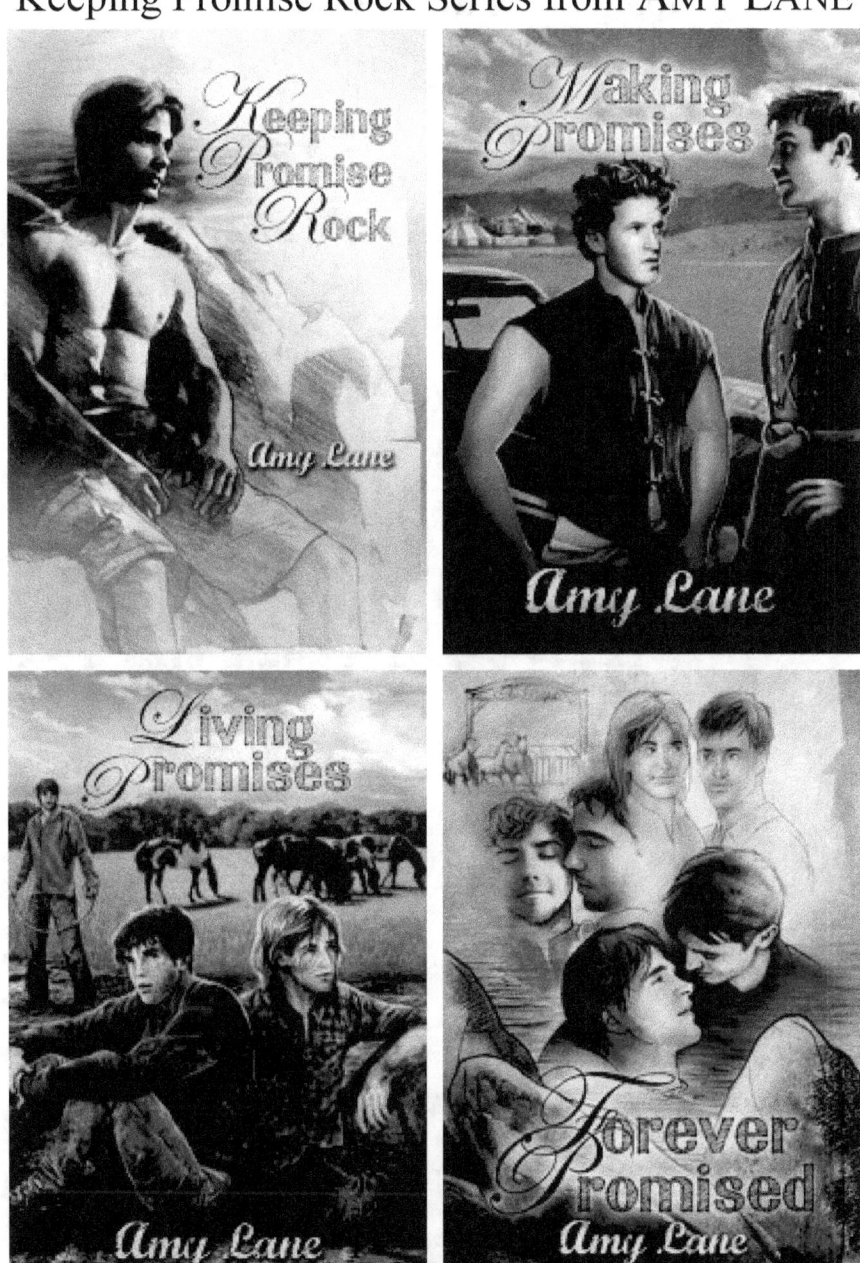

http://www.dreamspinnerpress.com

More novels from AMY LANE

http://www.dreamspinnerpress.com

More novels from AMY LANE

The Talker Series from AMY LANE

http://www.dreamspinnerpress.com

Green's Hill Stories from AMY LANE

http://www.dreamspinnerpress.com

The Knitting Series from AMY LANE

More novellas from AMY LANE

More novellas from AMY LANE

http://www.dreamspinnerpress.com